THE SHADOW'S HEIR

E. E. HORNBURG

CITY OWL
PRESS

THE SHADOW'S HEIR
The Cursed Queens, Book 2

CITY OWL PRESS
www.cityowlpress.com

Cover Design by MiblArt. All stock photos licensed appropriately. Map Design by Cartographybird.

Edited by Tee Tate.

For information on subsidiary rights, please contact the publisher at info@cityowlpress.com.

Print Edition ISBN: 978-1-64898-204-0

Digital Edition ISBN: 978-1-64898-180-7

Printed in the United States of America

Praise for E. E. Hornburg

"*The Night's Chosen* is a fairytale-like fantasy romance about the burden of duty and following your heart. From the characters to the prose, the fairytale vibes are strong in this book. The world building pulls you in immediately. I look forward to reading the rest of the series!" – *Gabrielle Ash, author of The Family Cross and For the Murder*

"This stunning fantasy debut swept me away. *The Night's Chosen* offers up a delectable blend of intrigue, magic, and romance all wrapped up in fresh takes on fantasy tropes and themes. The author's vivid, lyrical writing is perfect for the story and brings to life a world of wonder in the most divine of ways to create an immersive experience sure to completely transport the reader. Hornburg's story is a total page turner that will keep you guessing through twists and surprises." – *Kat Turner, author of Hex, Love, and Rock and Roll*

"E. E. Hornburg has invented a world with several charming aspects. Her vision of a free-thinking society with fewer sexual hang ups is refreshing. Her pantheon of deities offers cultural variation, and her main character's devout nature is an admirable trait… The value in Ms. Hornburg's story-telling lies in the smaller touches which are sprinkled like stardust throughout the pages." – *InD'tale*

For my mom and dad, who have always been there and embraced all the twists and turns of my life with grace and understanding and stood by me no matter what.

THE KNOWN KINGDOMS

TO UNCHARTED WESTERN SEAS

TOWN OF
SLANIA

KINGDOM OF
CRESIN

CITY OF
MARALIS

ILLIA
LAKE

TEMPLE
LAKE

GALLIS
HIGH TEMPLE

KINGDOM OF
IMARE

BELOVIAN
ISLANDS

DIAR
HIGH
TEMPLE

Chapter One

MYRA

MYRA WASN'T SURE IF SHE WAS NAUSEATED FROM EXCITEMENT OR DREAD. The shore of Cyre had grown larger and more distinct each day during their trip down the Lotus River. At her side, Alvis, the crowned prince of Oxare, stood tall and proud as he surveyed his home city. He rested his hands on the rail of the riverboat, tapping his fingers against the wood as though they were keys on a musical instrument.

It was a habit Myra noticed he employed when excitement swam over him. When in such close proximity to people for a week, it was easy to pick up on little things like that. Alvis had been more than generous and hospitable when Myra invited herself along with his entourage to return to her home kingdom. She assumed the boat would be large enough for her to squeeze in.

It was large, and Myra only had to share a room with one other woman, who was friendly enough. But she was surprised at how often she still ran into the prince. He liked to spend as much time on the deck under the sun as possible, and the farther south they came, the more often he was there lounging on his cushions, a small bowl of nuts at his side, and tunic loosened at the collar. Usually reading a book. He finished at least two during the trip.

Myra rocked when the boat docked at the shore, and it was only a matter of minutes before the workers tied the riverboat so it wouldn't float away, and they unloaded all the travelers' luggage.

Everyone called the beautiful structure in the distance the Golden Palace, though its proper name was Cyre Palace, after the capital city.

"It's beautiful, isn't it?" Alvis gazed in the direction of the Golden Palace.

The roof was white with gold engravings of the sun, moon, and stars etched in. The palace reflected the light from the god Ray's sunbeams, making the whole building appear to be made of gold. It had been years since Myra had been to the capital city of Oxare, but she remembered clearly the way it looked like a miniature sun when night turned into day, and how if one looked directly at it, 'they'd think 'they'd gone blind.

Now, as the sun set, there was merely a warm pink glow around the rounded tops of the palace, and if she focused enough, she could almost see the intricate engravings and paintings around the pillars. The Golden Palace was a grand mountain among the small hills of buildings surrounding it. Some of them mansions, others shacks, and everything in between.

"It is impressive," Myra admitted. She'd worked in Farren Castle in the northern kingdoms of Cresin for years, and it was stunning with its tall towers and spires. Maybe it was the Oxarian blood and pride in her, but there was something about the Golden Palace that stirred awe. The shining metals and luxurious engravings surpassed most—if not all—other buildings Myra had seen or worked in.

"They built it several centuries ago to honor Ray and his love for Luana. The roof was designed to show his majesty and glory during the day, but also so Luana could see it during the night and remember their love was still there, even if they were apart." Alvis inhaled deeply, and the remaining sunbeams of the day shone on his brown hair and dark skin. It was good he was dedicated to the sun god, as he looked as though he was born to lie out in the sand for days on end and never grow tired of its warmth.

Only a couple of months ago, he'd been painted in gold and performed the ceremony to welcome the changing of the seasons with his then betrothed, Princess Eira. Myra had sneaked into the ballroom to watch and could have sworn he was the god himself. Alvis's left wrist twitched where his betrothal band used to be.

Myra's heart sank. Princess Eira had chosen instead to be with someone else and broken off their betrothal. With his brother no less. Myra had been betrayed by family in her past as well and could imagine the hurt he must have felt. He never mentioned it or acted as though he was angry or brokenhearted. But Myra knew about hiding feelings and locking them deep inside to put on a brave face. She knew about keeping secrets and needing to get away.

It was how she'd survived her whole life. Now she needed to be away more than ever after the events of this past autumn season in Cresin.

"That's a lovely story," Myra told him with a smile. Even if she'd heard it before, he was so proud of his god and kingdom, she couldn't help but indulge him. Over the past week, she'd often sat with him on the deck of the riverboat and listened to him read passages of books or tell his favorite tales of the deities. In those moments, he didn't seem like the next king of Oxare, but a normal man who was passionate about knowledge and heritage. Sometimes, she would think of a tale and tell him one, which he always listened to with interest.

Alvis nodded, and his gaze darted toward her and then to the shore. "The Golden Palace is large, and we're always in need of extra help. We have more space than we know what to do with. I don't know what your plans are now that we have returned to Oxare, but if you need employment or a place to stay while you decide what to do next, you'd be more than welcome to stay. And I know Nell will miss you."

Myra's breath caught, and she blinked. She hadn't expected Alvis to make such an offer. Least of all, minutes before they were to depart the boat and go their separate ways. It would be easy to go with him. She'd been a servant in Farren Castle, and she was sure working in the Golden Palace wasn't much different. She could do well there, and it was an opportunity many people would jump for, and it was being handed to her on a silver platter. Besides, Myra had grown close to Nell, Amelia's daughter, who she'd helped free from the enchanted mirror. Alvis was taking the young girl in as his ward.

Myra's shoulders sank. But what happened when the generosity ran out? What if he found out the truth of how those events came to be and her involvement in it? Too many times she'd had to rely on the whims of others for her future, and in the end, either she or someone else paid the price. No. She needed to leave everything of Farren Castle behind her.

She faced the kind prince and leaned against the boat rail. "I'm going to miss Nell, and your offer is generous, but one I must decline. I have other business to attend to upon my return. Thank you though."

Something that reminded Myra of disappointment and regret flashed in Alvis's desert-gold eyes, but it was gone in a moment after it appeared. "Of course. I understand. But please remember, the invitation is always open. If you are ever in need of something, do not hesitate to come to me."

The flush of her cheeks had Myra looking away from the prince. "You are far too generous. I'm only a servant."

Alvis held her chin between soft fingers and raised her gaze to meet his. A chill ran through Myra, and she knew it wasn't from the breeze. "You are a wonderful and strong woman, and it is the least I can do after all your help in Cresin. I, and the kingdoms, am indebted to you."

The heat warming Myra's cheeks surely turned them deep red by then, and she tried to find words. She'd hardly done anything in comparison to the rest of them. If it weren't for her, none of it would have happened in the first place. He was being far too kind. And if he knew who she was, who she really was, he wouldn't be saying these things. She took a step back out of his reach, and his arm fell to his side. There were too many people around, and as innocent as his gesture was, to spying eyes, it could be taken the wrong way. Myra wouldn't let her be attached to his name, especially now when he needed to be home after being gone for so long. And without the princess of Cresin at his side.

"My small effort was for the sake of the kingdoms."

Alvis clasped his hands behind his back and smiled. "Myra, please, let me give you a compliment."

She chuckled. "Very well. Thank you, your highness."

On land, a herd of white horses with red-and-gold caparisons along with richly ornamented carts with all the luggage arrived, ready for the prince and his entourage to return to the palace. A servant attempted to assist Nell onto one of the horses, but the girl seemed like she was afraid to go on. She shook her head, her brown-and-blond curls bouncing around her shoulders. Her chin quivered, and Myra knew tears were to come next. The poor girl had lived inside a mirror her whole life and was still adjusting to the outside world.

Alvis's jaw stiffened as he watched the scene. "I should go help Nell. Maybe if she sees I'm on a horse too, she'll get on, or I can get them to let her ride on a cart instead. A palanquin could do well…"

"Good idea."

They stood facing each other for a moment, and Myra knew it was time to say good-bye. It would be best to get it done and move on. She had other places to be, and before long, Alvis would only remember in faint memories the servant girl who helped him a bit. Taking care of Nell certainly would keep him busy.

She grasped the edges of her plain skirt and knelt in a small curtsy. "Thank you for everything, your highness."

Alvis bowed to her. "It was my pleasure, Myra." The sound of Nell yelling at the servants echoed up to the deck of the boat, and his focus shifted to his ward and the scene on land. The servants struggled to get Nell onto the horse still, and tears ran down her cheeks in earnest now. Alvis placed a hand on Myra's shoulder. "I must go. Take care of yourself, and please remember my offer."

Myra could only nod as he rushed past her and raced down the plank to land. She would remember his offer, but it didn't change anything. He was a prince with a job to do, and Myra was a servant girl who needed to make her way in the world. Against her chest, the necklace kept hidden beneath her tunic, and the memories and history it held hovered on her like a dense fog. An ever-present reminder of who she was and who she never could be.

A warm breeze embraced Myra and blew a strand of hair across her face. After living in Cresin for so long, it was hard to believe it was almost the winter solstice and she didn't need to wear any furs or wool scarfs. The kingdom of Oxare did turn cool in the winter, but it wasn't anything close to the harsh and snowy winters Myra had grown used to.

Some new clothes, Myra decided, was the first thing she would need to purchase. She had money saved, and tucked away in her bag were a few pieces of clothes and jewelry she'd made and intended to sell. The other servants in Farren Castle loved her wares, and she hoped she would have the same luck in Oxare. She only had enough to fill the couple bags she carried, and it might not be enough to pay for a cart or donkey, so she would need to make her travels on foot, but she didn't mind.

On land, Alvis was at Nell's side. He knelt to her and held her hands. Myra couldn't hear what he was saying, but whatever it was had Nell wiping her tears away. He stood again and showed the young girl how to get on top of the horse. When she saw he was safe, the servants helped her climb on too, so she was sitting in front of Alvis. Her brown eyes grew big as she looked around beneath them as though the ground was a few hundred and not a few feet below them. Myra smiled. They would be just fine. Both Alvis and Nell needed a fresh start, and Myra had a feeling they'd be good for one another.

"Hey!"

Myra's attention was pulled from the scene toward the sailor who'd called to her. He pointed to the plank, and his brows were pinched together in anger. "'Get a move on, girl! We can't have you on this boat forever!"

Myra waved him off and picked up the two bags she'd brought with her few belongings. She needed to have a fresh start too. When she got to the dock, Alvis and his entourage were already on their way to the palace. Alvis's white horse faced away like a cloud blowing across the sky.

It was time to move on.

Chapter Two

ALVIS

A Few Weeks Later

ALVIS LOWERED HIMSELF ONTO THE CUSHIONS AND BRACED HIMSELF for another tea with his parents. The time to relax and enjoy being home had been short. He'd naïvely hoped he would be able to return to life as normal, reading and assisting Father with the business of ruling their kingdom. But each whenever he spoke with his mother the last few weeks, she only pestered him with questions about when he planned to find another bride.

He always had a handle on his fire magic and learned how to keep his cool when upset or angry. But each time Mother brought up the subject, a flame rolled around in the pit of his stomach. It burned and boiled, wanting to bubble out of him. He doubled his morning meditations and stretches to maintain control.

He should have been married years ago, and it had been the plan. But Eira kept putting off the wedding to go to university and to travel, and Alvis was happy to postpone their plans for her to do so. He'd been given the opportunity to attend whatever school he wished and travel the kingdoms, and there was no reason she couldn't do the same.

Apparently, those weren't her only reasons for putting off their marriage.

Mother sat on her cushion, her shoulders straight and dainty hands wrapped around a teacup. The delicate image of the sun and its rays stretched across the white porcelain like an embrace, reaching to the crescent moon on the other side. Ray always extending out to his love Luana, but never able to meet. Forever on opposite sides of the day.

If Alvis didn't know any better, he would have imagined his mother to be a quiet and demure queen who busied herself with tea parties and attending to her husband's every wish and desire. But he did know better. Behind those light-brown eyes, a storm brewed, and he had a hunch he was about to collide with it.

"*The Mystic* and the pirate queen raided the southern shore while you were in Cresin," Father said and passed the report over the low table to Alvis. With his other hand, he muffled a cough. He kept his gaze averted from Alvis, catching glimpses of his golden eyes, but then hurrying away. "Then the ship vanished. Again. It's as though it was never there."

Alvis took the parchment to read it. Mother leaned forward to watch and then bolted upright again when he looked over at her.

Over the last several years, *The Mystic* and its unnamed captain steadily rose to power, traveling from the northern Dravian Islands, and recently it seemed to favor Oxare and the southern Belovian Islands. They commanded countless fleets now, and instead of a name, people called the captain the "pirate queen." More than once, Alvis heard people singing songs about her exploits in the streets with the same jovial tone as they would when singing of the deity Diar's affairs.

"At least there were glimpses of this queen this time," Alvis observed. "Perhaps we'll catch her one of these days. Although, I'm sure the bards would be sad to be rid of such inspiration for their songs."

He looked over at Mother, who kept the same straight posture, her mouth in a closed-lipped smile, and blindly searched for something to eat as her gaze never left Alvis's face. A spark played in the corners of her eyes.

Father cleared his throat again and took a sip of tea. "We have fleets searching, but each time they think they have a lead on the ship, it vanishes again. One man captured and killed two of the crew members. We're on the lookout for him as well, because we would have rather questioned them ourselves."

Mother reached for a berry, the sleeves of her red gown sliding to show the circle of flame tattoos etched around her wrist. Her hand hit a bowl of berries, and it clattered, spilling its contents over the table.

Alvis watched as a servant rushed over to tidy the mess then set his cup on its saucer with a frustrated clink. "This is ridiculous. Mother, you hate the pirate queen, and whenever she's mentioned, you complain about how she raided your delivery of Pulmerias from the Belovian Islands once. I know you have something you want to discuss. Why don't you tell us, so we can all share in your excitement?"

Mother's mouth made a small O shape, and she batted her lashes. "I have no idea what you're talking about."

"Oh really?" Alvis laced his hands around his propped knee. "So you haven't been smiling to yourself and staring at me through this whole tea?"

Mother placed her hands in her lap and straightened her red skirt. "Maybe I wanted to listen to you and your father speak. I'm just so glad to have you home. Can you blame a mother for wanting to listen to the sound of her son's voice?"

No matter how far away he'd been or for how long, never had Queen Shideh wanted to sit back and let Alvis and his father speak and stay silent so she could listen to the sound of his voice.

Father lay reclined on his side and munched on a bowl of mixed nuts. "Darling, please tell him your outrageous plan. You're going to soon anyway, might as well get it over with."

Already, Alvis didn't like the sound of this. Mother's plans usually ended up being painful and embarrassing. He rolled his shoulders and braced himself for the worst.

Mother set her cup down when Alvis picked his up and took a deep sip. Her mouth twisted into a smile as though whatever she was about to announce was to burst out of her at any moment.

"We're going to hold a pageant to pick out your new bride!"

The heat and fire magic flowing through his veins roared, searing through his hands and the cup, scalding the tea and burning the roof of his mouth. He coughed and sputtered while he tried to compose himself. "A pageant?"

Mother was already pulling papers out from behind her and leaned forward to show him as though they were prize jewels she'd discovered herself. "It's a long-held tradition in Oxare for the royal family to hold pageants to find a bride or groom. They used to do it all the time between Chosens."

"That was centuries ago." He stared at the pile of papers now in front of him, afraid to see what they revealed.

"Which means we are going back to our roots and traditions. Something this kingdom needs to see right now. Taking pride in our heritage and traditions while also finding a new future queen." She sat back on her heels and took another sip of tea as though she'd already won the argument before it started.

"I'm not picking out a bride the way one would pick out a new horse. These are real women, Mother. Not prizes." He pushed the papers away, refusing to look at them.

"Very real women who will arrive in a couple of months. I'd like for it to be sooner, but some are coming from quite a distance and need the time to travel. You'll see everything about them right there." She waved a finger toward the papers she'd given him, and Alvis's heart dropped.

"What do you mean, they'll be here in a couple of months?" His voice was hoarse, and he could barely get the words out. Mother liked to scheme and did whatever she could to get her plans in motion. But to start a grand pageant to pick out a bride without telling him was extreme even for her.

"I've already sent news out to the other kingdoms that all their eligible women of noble birth are welcome to attend. They'll be here for six weeks, and you'll announce your decision at the spring solstice ball. It's perfect timing. I perused the stack myself before coming to tea for you to be sure there weren't any women who weren't appropriate, but I think we have a good group coming. You'll like them." She sat at looked at him as innocent as a flower.

A Venus flytrap, perhaps.

Alvis finally reached for the stack and glanced through them.

Women from all the kingdoms were coming. The Dravian Islands, Cresin, Imare, The Belovian Islands, and Mariali—all were to be represented. These were women with the world at their feet and surely countless opportunities for other matches and paths. They were duchesses and ladies and countesses and heiresses. Why in the world would they come all this way to be judged like they were pieces of jewelry instead of the powerful women they were? This was ridiculous.

"Like, but not love," Alvis argued.

Mother smirked. "The way you loved Eira?"

Alvis's cheeks burned, and he took a few deep breaths to calm the flames rolling inside. He couldn't argue with her on that point. He loved Eira, but not in the way a husband should love his wife, he'd realized. It didn't make this right though.

Father yawned and stretched. "Don't fret about it, Alvis. She didn't tell me about it either until after the messages were sent. I looked through the selection myself. The choices aren't terrible, my son. You could do far worse. They all want to be queen and have a chance—is that so awful?"

Alvis slapped the pages onto the cloth where their food sat. "If they want to pursue a match with me, why don't they do so themselves or have their families attempt to make an alliance with us?"

"They've tried!" Mother's voice was sharp, and she threw her hands in the air. "Ever since you've gotten home, we've presented woman after woman to you, but you barely give them a second glance. This way, you won't have a choice but to do something. For weeks, you've been sitting around doing nothing about your situation and trying to recover from the Eira incident. You need to show the kingdom you are strong and resilient. They need a king who can come back strong even after a loss."

"I don't understand the rush. It just happened." His mother's glare moved through him, expectation and demand hanging heavy on his shoulders. "Barely a month." No betrothal looming in the distance had freed him from the pressure he felt choking him. Glancing at his mother and the tight curve of her mouth, that small freedom slipped further from him. "Why are you pushing this? Why now?"

"Because your father is ill!"

The quiet in the room stilled further until Alvis only heard the faint gurgle of the wheeze coming from across the room, and he glanced at his father, seeing the question he hadn't asked already answered.

"It's something with my lungs."

Heat boiled inside Alvis. Not this again. Not after King Brennan was poisoned. He opened his mouth to speak, but Father stopped him.

"No curses or poisons, if that's what you're thinking. We've had the best Attendants come to my aid and see what they can do. I could have years left, or months. There isn't a way to tell. All they know is I need rest. We didn't plan for you to find out this way."

"We need to be sure we are prepared for anything." Mother's voice was low and quiet now, any hint of pride or humor wiped from her face.

Alvis closed his eyes, slowing his breath. When he opened them again, the room wasn't quite so blurry anymore. "Does Cadeyrn know?"

Father nodded. "We sent word to him a few days ago, along with an invitation to the spring equinox ball when you'll pick your bride. We also said he was welcome to return home at any time."

A heavy silenced filled the space between the three of them. The flames threatened to burn again, but Alvis tapped his fingers against the table to keep his calm and focus elsewhere. "And Eira? Is she also welcome?"

Mother and Father exchanged looks. Father cleared his throat. "From the impression we've been given of the situation, where Cadeyrn goes, Eira will also, and he will follow her. If we want to see your brother, we understand she would join him, and we will make every effort to be sure she feels welcome despite the circumstances."

Mother scowled, but Alvis breathed a sigh of relief. At least there was that. A small mercy, but Alvis was glad for it. Despite everything, Cadeyrn should know and be welcome to return whenever he wanted. Seeing the two of them together would be unpleasant, but through everything, Alvis didn't want to cut ties with them.

He sank into the cushions while the rest of him calmed. Instead of the burning anger of a bonfire, he let the heat comfort and soothe his emotions like it would if he lay out on a beach with the sun on his face.

"We need an heir to ensure the throne to our family line." Alvis's statement wasn't anything they didn't know, but a reminder to himself.

He had a responsibility to his family and kingdom. It was always there, and he never denied it but rather embraced the tasks before him. He liked the tradition and purpose behind them. But they were more important now than they'd ever been.

Alvis didn't have the privilege of running off with whoever he chose at whatever time he wanted. He didn't get to go off and find himself, for it was always laid before him. Alvis was to be the king of Oxare, and it was his responsibility to be sure their people were kept happy and safe. Never had Alvis begrudged this and was happy to take on the mantle. He hadn't thought it would come like this, though.

Resigned, he looked at his parents. "I'll do the pageant and find a suitable queen for Oxare. Our people, and our family, have waited long enough."

Mother breathed a loud sigh at his words and leaned her head back. With hands pressed together, she lifted them to her forehead in thanks to the god Ray. When she looked at Alvis again, a wide smile spread over her face, and Alvis didn't feel a hint of the dread he did at the beginning of tea. A cool calm had washed over him, which he hadn't felt in a long time. At least he knew once again what was before him and what he was supposed to do. It was good to have a strong footing.

A servant approached the table and bowed. "I hate to disturb, your majesties, your highness, but there has been an incident. The lady Nell has run away…again."

Panic ran through Alvis, and he came to his feet. Yet another fire he needed to maintain.

The servant quickly cleared his throat and stood even straighter than before. "She has been found, your highness, don't fret. One of the guards saw her sneaking a horse out of the stables. She is now in her room."

Alvis raised a brow.

"With two guards at the door and her governess is with her."

At least she was being watched. But for a child who'd been trapped inside a mirror her whole life, she was good at escaping even when eyes were always on her. Nell was terrified of horses at first, but it didn't take long for her to warm to them.

"I should still go speak with her," Alvis told the servant. "Thank you for telling me."

"Very good, your highness." With another bow, the man left the room.

Alvis crossed to the other side of the table and knelt before his father. They embraced, and Alvis tried to remain calm. "Thank you for telling me, Father. I'll do whatever I can to assist. Call on me for anything."

Father patted his shoulder. "I know."

Alvis then went to Mother and kissed her cheek. She chuckled. "You can barely manage one young girl even with her tutors and governess. It will be interesting to see how you fare with a whole group of them soon."

Alvis groaned when he stood. It was going to be interesting indeed.

Alvis knocked on Nell's door and it was opened for him by Daya, the governess. Her pale-pink robes, the outward symbol of her dedication to Yla, the deity of childhood and fertility, fluttered around her feet as she curtsied and ushered him inside. "I'm sorry, your highness. We were watching her, I promise. She's just so quick—"

Alvis raised a hand, and she quieted. "It is all right. I do not blame you."

Daya curtsied again. "It will never happen again. But if you wish to replace me, I understand."

Alvis motioned for her to rise, and she obeyed. "No one will be replacing you, Daya." He looked over at the young girl sitting on the bed, hugging her knees to her chest. "I place the blame on someone else entirely."

Nell's face flushed, and she buried it in her knees.

"Will you please go to the library and gather her books while I speak to her for a moment?"

"Of course, your highness. As you wish." With another curtsy, she hurried out of the room, her long black braid swaying behind her.

When they were alone, Alvis approached the bed. All that could be seen of Nell was the pile of blond-and-brown curls covering her curled-up body like a fuzzy blanket and a bit of her pants sticking out underneath. They'd cut her hair during the escape from the castle, but it already had grown significantly. Daya tried to help her tame it, but Nell wouldn't sit still long enough.

"Where did you want to go this time?"

"The desert," Nell mumbled into her arms. Even when embarrassed and hiding her face, Nell's voice sounded like a soft song that danced in the air.

Alvis stroked his short beard and nodded. "Interesting place to go. Why the desert?"

Nell lifted her head and pushed her hair back. "I can see horses riding through it from my window, and it's so pretty and open. I want a horse so I can go fast like them."

"I see." Alvis looked around the room for a place to sit. Mother used to sit on the edge of his bed when he was a child, but he wasn't sure if that was appropriate. There was a wooden chair by the fire, and he pulled it over. He sat and placed his hands on his knees. "I've noticed you visit the stables often. Do you like them?"

Nell tugged on a strand of her hair. "Yes, very much."

"It wasn't long ago you were afraid of horses. In fact, it wasn't long ago when you were afraid to even leave your room. You've become very brave."

She flopped against the pillows with a quiet *thunk* and let out a heavy sigh. "There's just so much to see."

"Indeed, there is. But you still need to mind Daya and listen to what she says, and not run away from her. The world is a large place, and you don't know what is out there. It can be dangerous for a young girl to go out alone."

Especially when her mother was a murderous former queen and who knew what sort of people would want to go after her. Especially when she'd been hidden her whole life and had no idea what the world was really like. Especially when she was the ward of a crowned prince. Even beyond those facts, there were vicious creatures and common thieves and pirates… This was the third time Nell had run away, and each time, the horrors of everything that could have happened to her chilled Alvis to the bone.

Nell turned on her side to face the window where she could see out into the open air. Beyond the window, the tops of buildings filled the view like rolling hills, but past the city gate lay the desert with its grand dunes and miles of sand. "But there's always so many guards around, and you're always busy."

"Ah. I see." He tapped his finger on his knee. She wanted him to go with her. Again, the realization she wished for him to be around and do these things was amazing, if not a little terrifying. "No, the guards don't make it very fun, do they?"

"No." Her voice was small and tight.

"There are many times I'm going to be busy. I have responsibilities here, unlike when we were in Cresin and I could come visit your mirror. In the coming weeks, even more of my time will be taken up."

Nell cocked her head to the side and scooted herself toward the edge of the bed and sat on her knees. "Why will you be so busy?"

He tried his best to explain the pageant to her and, in a way, explain it to himself. The whole situation still felt ridiculous. Nell sat upright and listened, scrunching her eyebrows together in concentration.

"You're going to be married?"

"That's the idea, yes."

She pressed her lips together as she contemplated the situation. "Well, that could be good. May I help?"

He hadn't thought about if Nell would participate at all in the pageant. Then again, he hadn't been able to think the situation through hardly at all yet, as he'd just found out about it only a few minutes ago. "I don't see why not. I could use another opinion, and there surely will be a way to include you."

Nell smiled. "I would like that. It would be nice to meet women from different kingdoms."

Alvis smiled back at her. "Yes, I think that would be good for you. I'll be sure to tell Daya we'll include it as part of your education. And I will be sure to make time in my schedule to go out exploring with you. We can't eliminate the guards, but I will be sure there are as few as possible. But you need to mind Daya, pay attention in your studies, and not run away. Do you promise?"

Her smile faded a bit, but she nodded. "Yes, I promise."

"Good."

A knock came at the door. "Your highness, it's Daya."

"Yes, come in. Let me help you with the door," Alvis said. He stood and opened it, and was glad he did. His guess that Daya's arms were full of Nell's books for her lessons and that she didn't have a spare hand for door handles was correct. He stepped to the side and gestured to Nell's desk for her to put the books down. Then he returned to Nell.

"Now, you need to stay in your rooms for the rest of the day. If you need to go to the library, have someone let me know. We'll come fetch you when it's time for supper. Is that understood?"

"Yes."

"Good. And I'll make arrangements for you to help with the pageant. I'll see you this evening."

Alvis was nearly to the door when Nell spoke up again.

"Will you pick someone who makes you happy?"

The notion hadn't come up in his conversation with Mother and Father. Only his duty to marry and produce an heir and show his strength to the kingdom. "I hope so."

"I hope so too."

Chapter Three

MYRA

Myra wished she could plug her ears sometimes. Especially when the tavern was such a ruckus. It had only been a few weeks since Myra arrived in Cyre and gained employment at a tavern in the slums of the city. Already she was tired of it. At least they let her stay in one of the upstairs rooms.

It was cozy enough for a single bed and small trunk, and it had enough space for three whole steps that provided a hint of privacy from the tavern. There was even a lovely view of the dark alley where the fragrance of urine and tobacco wafted through the window each day. She woke up each morning to the loud yelling of her neighbors across the way. All this luxury, and all it cost was significantly lower pay than she should have gotten and an extra hour at the end of each shift to wash dishes.

The lodgings were as different from Farren Castle or her childhood home as Ray's bleak desert was from Kutlaous' lush forest but at least it was her own space. A place to lay her head where she worked for it by herself and could keep her head down. Best of all, there was no evil queen or cruel masters who wanted to manipulate and harm her.

If only she didn't have to actually work downstairs in the tavern to in order to have said spare room, Myra couldn't help but think as yet another drunken man attempted to grab her ass when she walked by collecting empty beer mugs. She swiped a notice for hire off one of the tables while she did so and tucked it away in the pocket of her apron for later. At least there was that. If there was something else out there with offered lodging or at least a larger pay so she could get even a cheap flat to rent, she would leave the tavern faster than a mouse chasing a piece of cheese dropped on these filthy floors.

She brought the tray of empty glasses and mugs to the bar and rolled her head back and forth, letting the tension fall from her neck. Only a few more hours and she could hide away in her room and get some rest.

A roar of laughter rose from one of the tables where a group sat. A mix of men, women, fae, and even a pixie and dwarfess sat among them. They were all draped over one another and laughed and flirted in a way where Myra couldn't tell who belonged to or was interested in whom. They were so free and relaxed with themselves, laughing and kissing and holding each other, not caring who watched or saw.

It wasn't only their flirtation, but the way they could let their magic run free. A young woman with wavy blond hair and a wide-brimmed brown hat with a purple feather sticking out of it swirled the rum in her glass without even touching it, and another played with the flame of the candle on the table with casual waves of their hand. There was another woman with chin-length black hair and pale skin—even paler than the blonde's—who sat off to the side, her dark-brown eyes that met together in the corners in a kiss watched each one of the beings in their party, and when Myra observed closely enough, she saw how when the woman looked at one person and then another, the two would instantly start flirting with each other.

Myra chuckled to herself. The dark-haired woman must be a follower of Diar, deity of love, desire, and beauty. It was rumored followers of Diar made people fall in love, or at least guided hearts and attraction in certain directions. This woman must have been experimenting with the others at the table. All except for the blonde, on whom she never let her gaze fall. She seemed to be the leader of the group, for they all looked to her for approval when they told a joke or made a remark. She reclined in her seat and watched the antics of the others, an amused smile on her lips and a laugh in her ocean-blue eyes.

"A pageant! Looks like our prince can't get a woman on his own. Not even his Luana's Chosen would stay with him, and now he needs a contest to get them to pay attention," one of the men at the table announced over the commotion of the tavern. "What archaic foolishness."

Everything in Myra halted, and a fire burned within her chest. She wasn't sure what to be more upset about, the pageant or those openly mocking Alvis.

The woman in the hat leaned forward, resting her elbows on the table, and placed her chin on her folded hands like a war master plotting an attack. "And what is so foolish about it?"

The man waved his hand in the air. "Women being forced to go to the palace and be paraded around like they are pieces of food for the prince to eat for dinner."

The blonde raised her brow. "Who says they're being forced? Even beyond the potential to be queen, I'm sure living at the Golden Palace for a couple of months could open many doors and opportunities. Besides, I've heard the prince is handsome enough. Who wouldn't want the chance at him and the crown?"

"Not handsome enough to keep his betrothed away from his more handsome brother," one of the others murmured.

Myra glared at them and slapped a dishrag on the counter. She shouldn't be listening in on their conversation. How foolish and arrogant of them, though, to be speaking of their prince in such a manner. She grasped the edges of a clean tray like it was the man's words and she could crush them in her palm and moved to the other side of the tavern to get away from their conversation. Alvis would never hear this conversation and was probably used to people talking about him and criticizing his life. It was the way of the life of royalty. But still.

After a few minutes, she'd almost gotten the whole thing out of her head when there was a large crash along with yelling and thudding. Myra whipped her head around to find the blonde in the hat deep in a brawl with the man who'd initiated the conversation about Alvis. Myra threw the towel she'd been holding to the side and rushed to the scene of the fight as she was closer to the commotion than the owner was to break it up.

But it was too late. Already blades were drawn, and the flash of the blonde's sword swept through the air and sliced across the man's chest. He fell with a harsh *thunk* that, for a moment, silenced the tavern. Then the room erupted in commotion, and the group broke up.

"Finley! Not again! What have I told you?" the dark-haired woman yelled and grabbed her arm. The pair dashed and darted around the other patrons toward the door.

"Hey! Get back here!" Myra called out to them and broke into a sprint. She had no idea what she was going to do if she caught up to them, as she had no weapons to defend herself against a killer, but she couldn't let them get away with what happened either.

A sharp cold breeze blew over Myra, and she froze, the dark magic inside her stirring at the sensation. There was only one sort of air that felt so cold on a relatively mild winter day. A spirit was leaving someone's body and needing to pass on to the afterlife. The two women were already far down the road, and Myra would never catch them, but she'd gotten a good enough look to describe them to the authorities.

She turned back to the scene of the crime, and the man's spirit hovered over the body, stuck and unable to pick a direction to go.

She shouldn't help the soul. She couldn't. Stulan magic only brought on trouble, and Myra'd had enough of that.

But no one else noticed the spirit hovering in the room, meaning she was the only follower of Stula, the goddess of death, present. No one else was there to assist the spirit and perform the rite. He was one of the ones who'd tried to grope Myra through the day, and he'd said cruder things to people than she ever cared to hear again. From what she could tell, he wasn't a good man.

Mama would have helped him anyway. It wasn't up to them to judge the eternal fate of a person, but the deities. If a Stulan follower knew how to do the rite, it was their responsibility to assist the spirit in passing on. At least that's what Mama always said.

Myra balled her hands into fists and marched over to the spirit. There was enough chaos going on, and no one would notice. She could do it quickly and move on with her day. Under her breath, Myra whispered the words she knew so well, and the necklace hidden under her dress warmed. Small dark shadows grew out of her hands and drifted toward the spirit, and it lifted into the air toward the ceiling. As the words ended, the spirit faded away along with Myra's shadows. It was done, and now the deities could decide what to do with him.

She breathed a sigh of relief that it was done, but someone grabbed her by the elbow and jerked her around. The owner of the tavern snarled at her through his bushy black beard. His light-brown, almost yellow eyes were so wide she thought they'd pop out of his head.

"What is this dark magic you bring here? You told me you were not dedicated to any deity."

Myra tried to pull herself away from him, but his grip only grew tighter. "I'm not."

It wasn't a lie. She was a direct descendant of the goddess Stula on her mother's side and never went through a dedication ceremony to receive magic. Stula's magic ran through her veins and was as much a part of her as the brown hair on her head. Myra didn't even have a tattoo, leaving it easy to keep her heritage a secret. As long as she didn't do anything stupid…such as escorting a spirit to the afterlife in the middle of a tavern.

The man gripped her by both arms and shook her. "Then what is this evil you brought here? I saw the shadows come out of your hands and heard the words you were saying. You belong to Stula! You brought this upon us!"

It was happening all over again. Blamed for another death when all she'd done was help. She tightened her jaw to keep it from trembling and held back the tears that wanted to spill out. "The killer got away, no thanks to you. A murder just happened in your tavern, but your ignorance is clouding your judgment to what really is going on."

"How dare you bring this evil into my business! Get out!"

He pulled her through the panicked customers and shoved her out the door. Already, her few belongings were being thrown out the window from the spare room and fell onto the street, landing in the puddles and dirt.

"I did nothing wrong!"

"Leave before I call the authorities. I don't need you cursing me and bringing more death here." He slammed the door shut on her, and Myra was left alone on the street.

She stood there, stunned for a moment. He cared more about her not placing a curse on him and the gods-forsaken business than finding out what really happened and seeking justice. It was almost laughable, and a cold chuckle escaped her lips. This was what she got for not minding her own business and attempting to help. Now someone was dead, the murderer had gotten away, and she was homeless. Again.

She inhaled, and the sound of hooves echoed through the streets. The authorities were coming to collect the body. She needed to leave before they arrived. With the two real killers gone, Myra would get the blame, and it was her word against the tavern owner's. She swallowed her tears and knelt to the ground to gather her things. They were dirty, but salvageable.

Once everything was stuffed away in a large satchel, Myra rushed away until she made it to another street out of the gaze of people near the tavern. Once she felt it was safe, she slowed her pace and wandered, unsure of where to go next. If the tavern owner had loose lips, rumors of her could spread to other local businesses. Maybe she would have better luck on the other side of town.

She stuffed her hands in her pockets as she walked, and a paper crinkled in her palm. The hiring notice she'd swiped earlier. She pulled it out and smoothed the notice to read what it said.

Ladies' maids are needed as soon as possible at the Golden Palace. Must have experience and have vast knowledge of fashion and hair. Patient temperament. Will need to be on call at all times of day and night. Housing at the palace, meals, and a handsome salary with one day off a week. Please contact Vikas about employment. Must be available for two months.

A lady's maid at the palace. It must have been to assist with the women coming to the pageant. Myra bit her lip. She had the experience and knowledge needed. After all she'd been through, patience was not in short supply. She was used to needing to be available at any time. The whole thing was exactly what she needed. But she'd turned Alvis down when he offered her employment before. What would he think if she appeared now at his door out of nowhere looking like she did?

She folded the paper again and put it in her pocket. The Golden Palace loomed over the slum, a bright light in the cold shadows of the neighborhood she'd found herself in. Lording over them it's wealth and comfort.

It would be comfortable, and Alvis did say she was welcome if she ever needed anything. But going to the Golden Palace, even if it was only temporary until she decided her next plan, was a terrible idea. Worse than terrible, and the last place she should go to keep a low profile. She might have been trapped in a mirror, but Amelia was at the Golden Palace, and the idea of being in the same place as the former queen sent a shiver down Myra's spine.

No. The Golden Palace would be a terrible idea.

Myra peered over her shoulder to the opposite end of the road. The one that led out of the city and toward a small estate not far out of the city limits. Her father's house.

Another terrible idea.

But she didn't have any others.

Chapter Four

MYRA

Myra grasped the golden rope hanging in front of the dark wooden door, a stark contrast to the pale stucco walls of the manor. The walls were the same as she remembered, if a little worse for wear over the years. The door was the same. The rope was new though. When Myra had lived there, it had been plain brown and fraying. The loud clanging from the bell it was attached to was new too. Instead of the melodic tones Myra remembered so fondly, it was a deafening toll, alerting anyone in the manor someone had come to visit.

She tugged her shawl around her shoulders, tucked her stray strands of hair behind her ears in a poor attempt to appear presentable, and waited for someone to answer. It might have been winter, but being so far south, even with Ray's sun setting on the horizon, Myra needed little else to stay warm. She smoothed her skirt and straightened her shoulders. She didn't think she appeared haggard and worn, having been able to mend her clothing and even made herself a new shirt and skirt between shifts. Even so, she hardly looked like a lord's daughter.

Seventeen years. It had been seventeen years since Myra had stepped foot in her childhood home. It had been the night Mama died. She'd been sick for a long time, and one night she summoned Myra to her bed as she knew it was time for her spirit to go on to the next world.

Myra was only a child and tried to perform the rite as best as she could. But then Uncle Waazier caught her, and he had the same reaction the tavern owner did. The next thing Myra knew, she was sold off to be a servant and was taken away on a carriage to a stranger's home, never to see her family again or know if her weak performance of the rite had sent Mama's spirit to Stula's arms as it was supposed to.

Her stomach churned as she waited. Maybe this hadn't been such a good idea. It was a large house and could still be a few minutes before anyone arrived at the door to greet her. Plenty of time to turn around and figure out a new plan. She wasn't sure what that new plan would be or where she would go as she figured it out…

She crossed her arms across her chest and rocked back and forth on her heels. Uncle Waazir wouldn't want her there at all. He was the one who sold her in the first place. Then Papa hadn't done a single thing about it. Who knew if he wanted her back either? And here she was, coming home, the dust of the road dirtying her hem, and taking advantage of Prince Alvis's generosity by joining his caravan back to Oxare.

The offer he'd extended of working the palace flashed through her mind. Myra knelt to take her single bag of belongings. Stupid, stupid girl. Relying on the prince to take care of her wouldn't get her anywhere either. She should have stayed in Cresin. Maybe not in the castle depending on Cal for every little thing as she had been for so many years, and carrying the burden of her secrets had become too much to bear. But she could have found a flat in a town and set up a shop or worked as a housekeeper in a small household.

Yes. That would have been much smarter.

As she straightened and went to turn back to the road, the door opened. "Hello?" a light woman's voice greeted Myra. One she thought she'd never hear again.

Myra turned to face the entrance again and gasped at the same time as the woman. She was shorter and had more gray hair than Myra remembered, but with the same gentle brown eyes. The woman's eyes grew wide, and her wrinkled brown hands—the shade like her own—covered her mouth as though she'd seen a ghost.

"It can't be," the woman whispered.

Myra nodded. "Odalis, it's me. It's Myra."

Odalis tilted her head to the side as the realization came over her. "Myra. You're the spitting image of your mother. I thought you were a ghost."

Myra's shoulders sank, and her chest tightened. "I am?"

Odalis nodded. "But you might as well be one. You were just..." She lowered her hand to the height of her chest, about how tall Myra would have been at the age of seven when she'd left this house so long ago. She blinked a few times and, with shaking hands, grasped the edge of her simple white tunic and delivered a small curtsy. "My lady. You must want to see your father."

Myra stared in disbelief. She couldn't remember the last time someone had called her by a title, let alone curtsied for her. It made her want to squirm and leave. But it was too late now. Odalis would tell Papa she was here. Maybe even her uncle, and then she'd be in trouble. She cleared her throat.

"Yes, I would like to see him, if he's home."

"Of course, of course! Come, come. This way." Odalis beckoned Myra in, leading her inside and through the courtyard to get to the house as if Myra didn't know the way.

The steps and the path were familiar ones, bringing back memories of running around the courtyard, chasing after butterflies and splashing the water in the fountain. She could almost hear herself laughing as a child with Mama as they played games. But when Myra turned to look at the fountain, no one was there. Not even a single butterfly. Just a cold, dark courtyard.

After removing their shoes and leaving them in the foyer, Odalis led her through the house. As a child, Myra used to hover outside Papa's drawing room in hopes he would greet her or let her come in, or perhaps even leave the cloud of smoke and cards to join her and Mama in whatever adventure they were hatching that day. He never did though, and in time, Myra had learned to stop trying. She felt like the same silly young girl now as Odalis approached the door and knocked.

"Not now, Odalis."

Myra almost jumped at the sound of Papa's voice as though she didn't believe he was actually there, and it was a surprise he answered at all. She smoothed her tunic and held her shawl tighter around her shoulders. When arriving in Oxare, she'd taken the opportunity to stop at a shop as soon as she could to buy clothing appropriate for the southern kingdom instead of her warmer wools and furs from Cresin. She'd had some money saved and tucked aside, but she'd kept a tight budget and opted for simpler tunics and pants, and then a scarf to wrap around her head and shoulders to combat the cool breezes in town and the sand in the desert. Now she was wondering if she should have splurged a on something a bit more luxurious with beading and embroidery to make a good first impression.

Odalis offered Myra a tight-lipped smile. She knocked again. "I'm sorry to disturb you, my lord, but there is someone here to see you. It's quite important."

There was some grumbling and the sound of a chair sliding across the floor before the doorknob turned and clicked open. Myra held her breath as Papa's face appeared from behind the door. She almost wanted to take a step back at the sight. In her memories, Papa was large and imposing. Someone whose presence filled a room no matter how big it was and made everyone around him feel small.

That was not this man.

He was still tall, and Myra had to look up to see his face, but he'd faded away like an old painting whose colors weren't as vibrant as they once were. His long dark hair and beard had gray streaks, and his once stunning golden eyes were sunken in and shallow. Myra had to hold back a cough as he reeked of liquor and smoke.

He attempted to focus on Odalis, but his gaze wandered in a way where it seemed he didn't know what to look at. "Who is so important that it can't wait and calls for me to be disturbed?"

Odalis gestured toward Myra. "Your daughter."

Papa blinked and shook his head. "I don't have a daughter. Not anymore."

Myra raised her hand in a minuscule wave. "It's me, Papa. It's Myra."

Only then did Papa give her any mind, like she'd appeared in the moment she spoke. His distant gaze looked her over, and a sliver of recognition filled it. His brows pinched together as though he still couldn't place her face.

"You're not Myra…" He said the words slowly, as if he were trying to convince himself.

She should have been prepared for this, but the blow still hit her like a hit to the stomach. Myra swallowed away any hurt feelings of how at one look Odalis knew exactly who she was, and her own father wasn't sure. "I know it's been a long time, but it is me, Papa. I'm home."

Papa's face tightened, and he narrowed his eyes. She could almost see the wheels in his mind turning as he looked at her, trying to place her face. "Come inside."

Myra tried to take encouragement from the bright smile Odalis offered and stepped into the room behind Papa. The smell of smoke was even stronger now, and Myra couldn't stifle her cough this time. The study reflected the same faded image of Papa. It was the same as Myra remembered with the large windows to let in the sun and that could open wide to let a breeze in during the hot summer days. Low-set chairs with plush cushions were scattered through the space, and piles of papers, empty glasses, and decks of cards on the tables. But it was all faded, like a fog had settled into the room, dulling all the color after not properly being taken care of after all this time.

Papa lit a thin cigarette from one of the candles and took a long drag before speaking to Myra again. He peered at her through the smoke, and she stood straighter, as though she were on display to be sold.

Again.

"My daughter left long ago. You…resemble her. But how can I know for sure? It's been many years."

She searched for words. The idea of having to defend who she was to him hadn't occurred to her. Being told to leave or be thrown out, yes. But not needing to prove her relation to him. She shifted her weight back and forth. "It has been many years, but surely you must recognize me a little?"

He paced across the room and shuffled some papers on the table. He glanced in her direction but didn't meet her eyes. "You bear a strong resemblance, yes. But how can I be sure you truly are my daughter? You could be an imposter wanting to conspire against me. My daughter left me on the day her mother died and didn't even day good-bye. You must understand my hesitation."

Myra clenched her fists at her sides and tried to control her breath. That wasn't how it happened. She was only a child and was taken away while Papa hid away in this very study they were standing in now. He knew what had happened and didn't do a thing to stop it. "I didn't want to go."

"And now all of the sudden you've returned? No word. Not even a letter. After all these years, my daughter, now a grown woman, woke up one day and decided she wanted to come home?"

Dropping her bag, Myra tugged at her shawl and reached underneath her tunic. Hardly anyone had seen this object, but Papa would know what it was and what it meant. He would have no choice but to believe her and let her stay. She grasped the chain and pulled it over her head. With an extended arm out to Papa, the pendant dangled between them, swinging back and forth like a pendulum. The amethyst caught the candlelight, and the purple danced over Papa's face. For the first time, his eyes focused and became clear. He blinked a few times.

"Where did you get that?"

"Mama gave it to me so I could remember her and everything she taught me. It was the day she died. This is the first I've taken it off since then."

He reached out to touch the pendant but jerked his arm back as though it were about to burn him. "Do you still practice? Have your powers grown?"

Myra couldn't help but chuckle to herself. Superstitions still rang strong in this home, it seemed. Some things never changed. She brought the pendant back and returned it to its rightful home around her neck. "I avoid using them as often as I can. I only want to be a regular person and a good daughter. I'll worship whichever deity pleases you."

Papa raised his cigarette to his mouth with a shaking hand. Full recognition finally appeared on his face as he focused on her more, but his gaze kept darting to the pendant. "And you won't bring any of that darkness here?"

That's really what all of this was about. He knew exactly who she was but was more concerned with her magic than anything else. She should have known. His fear of her magic wasn't surprising, but it hurt nonetheless. A lump came to her throat, and she swallowed it down. Not here, not now. Once she was alone, she could let herself feel the pain, and even then, only for a short while. Feeling sorry for herself wasn't going to get her anywhere.

"No, I won't practice in this house."

He sighed as though she'd taken a weight off his shoulders, and a puff of smoke surrounded his head. He waved his hand toward the door. "You may have your old room if you like. If you don't remember the way, Odalis can show you."

Dismissed already. Not that she expected much of a reunion. She wasn't sure if she wanted one either. Any hope she'd held of him coming to her aid or showing warmth was dashed as a young girl. Never had he tried to reach her or look for her over the years. Even as a child in his home, they hadn't been particularly close. There was no reason for him to act like the doting father at this point.

At least she had a place to stay. She could work out the rest as she went, one day at a time. It was how she'd been living her entire life; she could continue to for a while longer.

Myra leaned to fetch her bag once again and took a steadying breath. The biggest challenge had been completed. Soon, she would be back in her old room, allow herself to feel whatever it was she needed to, and determine what to do next. "Thank you. I'm sure I'll be able to manage."

She made her way to the door but paused when Papa cleared his throat. So close. She turned to face him with a tight-lipped smile. "Yes, Papa?" She had to force herself to not let him see how uneasy she felt.

He raised the cigarette to his mouth and then lowered it again. "Why did you come back, after all this time?"

Her jaw clenched, and she gripped her bag until her knuckles turned white. She'd been asking herself the same question ever since ringing the bell. Each moment she was in his house, she doubted why she decided to come back at all. Out of all the places in the world she could go to, she chose the home that didn't want her. Who had thrown her out and sold her on the day she needed it's refuge the most.

With every ounce of will she had, Myra relaxed her face and softened her smile. "It's time for me to start over."

It was as honest of an answer she could give him. He didn't need to know the details, and he didn't deserve them either.

Papa didn't return her smile and only offered a single nod of his head before pouring himself a glass of something a cloudy white color.

Dismissed again. Myra knew when she was no longer welcome.

Odalis waited outside the study with her hands folded in front of her. She came to life at the sight of Myra, and together they took the walk to Myra's old room. Myra tried her hardest to listen to Odalis's friendly chatter and wanted to hear all of what life in this house was like now. As much as she pushed aside any hurt from Papa, having someone who seemed genuinely happy to see her was welcome. But as they walked, Myra was flooded with memories of her childhood. Around each corner were the ghosts of her past threatening to haunt her.

It was ironic, really. All Myra wanted was to push her past aside and start anew. She wanted to put those ghosts to sleep for good, stand on her own two feet, and live a quiet life away from politics and magic. Coming home was the first step. No one paid their miniscule portion of Oxare much mind. The title was large enough to live independently, but small enough to stay under the radar. If Myra could get back into her father's good graces, she could have her inheritance someday. Whether she ultimately resided here or elsewhere, it would be enough to live her own life.

"Here we are!" Odalis opened the door with a flourish and spread her arms wide. "Home sweet home."

It was like walking into a dream where everything felt familiar, but deep down, she knew there was something off about it. The last time she had been in this room, it was the night Mama died, and she'd been preparing to help guide Mama's soul to Stula.

"They didn't change much in here." Odalis prattled on as she busied herself around the room, tidying things up. She laughed to herself. "Well, not many things have changed in this house at all, actually. Needs updating in my opinion. Which is why it's so good you're here. You can bring some life to this place."

Myra set her bag on the floor and pulled off her shawl. An interesting choice of words.

"I'm sorry, Odalis. I'm not very talkative this evening. It's been a long day."

Odalis patted Myra on the shoulder. "I know it has. Take all the time you need and be as quiet as you like. Just know that you are a welcome sight for sore eyes."

Myra covered Odalis's hand with hers. "It's good to see you too."

It was the most genuine thing Myra had said since she stepped inside the house.

Odalis took in a deep breath and tucked stray gray strands of hair back in place. "Supper will be served soon. I'll make sure something for you to wear is brought in. Tomorrow we can discuss what you want to do with your wardrobe. Unless you want to eat in your room?"

A tempting offer, but Myra couldn't lock herself away in here forever. She might as well face this new life now. Even if the idea made her sick to her stomach. "No, I'll eat with Papa. That's fine. I don't need something else to wear though. This is fine."

Odalis raised her brows and glanced at Myra's outfit up and down. "I'll bring you something to wear. You're the lady of the house now, you know."

The words echoed in Myra's mind long after Odalis left. Lady of the house. A title she'd never pictured associated with herself. She sank onto the bed, which still had the same golden-yellow blanket from so long ago but was now faded with age like her memories. But they still weighed on her like a thick fog. Nothing seemed clear anymore.

Myra pressed her hand to her chest. She missed her adoptive brother, Cal. For so long, it had been just the two of them looking out for each other. Him for her most often. She could have stayed in Cresin with him. Princess Rose would have gladly let Myra stay in Farren Castle, but it was time for Myra to stop relying on Cal to save her at every turn. Besides, Myra would never be able to be rid of the guilt of causing the king to be poisoned a few months ago if she faced them every day. Even if she didn't know the potion was for the king, and she'd done it to protect herself and Cal, it had still been her fault.

She could have gone to The Golden Palace with Prince Alvis.

During their journey from Cresin to Oxare, Alvis had done everything in his power to make her feel welcome and comfortable. His offer still echoed in the air as though he'd said it only moments ago.

It was a generous offer. Too generous. But if she'd accepted, once again she would have been relying on someone else to save her. As kind as Prince Alvis was, she couldn't depend on his hospitality and charity for forever. Besides, she knew that even if Alvis was kind, it didn't mean the other royals were. Myra needed to make her own way in the world.

Alone.

Chapter Five

MYRA

Myra battled with Odalis when it was time to get ready for supper. Odalis insisted as lady of the house she needed assistance in getting dressed, which was ridiculous. Myra had been dressing herself for years. But seeing the dejected look on the woman's face, Myra relented. They would need to have this discussion in time though, as Myra had no intention of being waited on hand and foot.

She fidgeted with the embroidered edge on the long sleeve of the tunic Odalis had provided for her. A little too big, but it would have to do for now. It was much more ornate than the simple garments Myra wore when she arrived—bright orange with beading and embroidery all along the hem, and necklines with matching tight-fitting pants underneath, and a thin veil of a scarf that floated behind her in waves. At least it hadn't been one of the fancy dresses Mama used to wear sometimes. Myra felt like she was wearing a costume enough as it was, especially once Odalis had brought in jewelry and lined Myra's eyes with kohl.

The bracelet around Myra's bare ankle caught the lamplight, and little dots of red scattered across the floor like blood droplets as Myra made her way to the dining room. It would have been much too cold in Cresin this time of year to walk around the home barefooted, but it was customary here in Oxare out of respect for the people of the house—especially the large ones, which often held shrines and temples for the deities. It was for cleanliness too. Shoes were filthy things, and Myra never understood why in the northern kingdoms they didn't change into slippers once inside. The floors of Farren Castle would get so dirty with everyone traipsing in with their dirt-ridden boots. Slippers were one thing Myra wouldn't mind having though. It was warm enough now for bare feet, but there were nights where the temperature got a little cold, and her toes would need the warmth.

Portraits of their family still lined the halls with drapes of solstice garland between them as she remembered, ending with one of Papa and Mama on their wedding day. She paused to look at it, having not seen a portrait of Mama in so long. Mama was beautiful in her red bridal gown, but there was a sadness behind her warm golden eyes. It had been an arranged marriage, and while they hadn't loved one another, any animosity between the two, if there was any, had been well hidden from Myra's eyes. Papa let Mama and Myra live their lives as they wanted and didn't get in the way. Yet in the portrait, maybe there was more to it than that. Did Mama know what was going to happen in the end? Myra bit her lip and swallowed away tears.

Another reason she had to come home. She'd been running away from it for too long and needed to find out what happened the night Mama died. She needed to know once and for all if Mama's spirit was at peace in the arms of Stula.

"Come to finish your work and be rid of the rest of us?"

Myra jumped at the sound of her uncle's slithery voice, like a snake coming out from the brush to bite at her heels. He stepped toward her, surely to go into the dining room, but all Myra saw behind his dark-brown eyes was a sinister glimmer from the coins he'd collected all those years ago when he sold her.

She cleared her throat and resisted the urge to back away. "I didn't kill her."

A small smile that was anything but happy formed on his thin lips between his narrow mustache and beard. He knew Myra didn't kill her mother. After years of replaying the night over in her mind and growing into her adult logic of the events leading up to it, she'd finally come to realize this. Placing blame on her magic and heritage was the easiest way for him to find a way for Myra to be removed from the house and out of the memories of everyone else. What stories he must have come up with to explain her absence, she could only imagine.

"Still not admitting it?" Uncle Waazir brushed past her, and a chill ran over Myra when his shoulder bumped hers. "I shouldn't expect any less, I suppose, from one of Stula's daughters. But you're here now, aren't you? You should be grateful I found a way for you to be out of the house before anyone suspected. Who knows where you would be now if the authorities had found a child killer loose."

He led the way into the dining room, and Myra took a few deep breaths before following him. He was even worse than she'd remembered. There had been moments she'd convinced herself he might not be as terrible and unfeeling as she'd thought he was. A scared young girl not understanding the ways of adults. No. People thought the young didn't know anything, when in fact they knew more than everyone else. Her child instinct had been correct in her assessment of her uncle. She straightened her shoulders and hid the fury against him burning within her chest.

Myra sat in the chair across from Uncle Waazir and tossed her orange scarf over her shoulder. "Yes, I'm eternally grateful for being thrown out of my home and illegally sold as a slave on the night of my mother's death."

"I found you a place where you would be hidden and avoided a scandal, gave someone the help they needed, and was given minor compensation for my trouble. I don't see the wrong in that." He reclined in his seat as though this were a normal day, a king relaxing in his small kingdom. He rolled his neck, giving Myra the perfect view of his tattoo of a snake twisted around a sword, showing his dedication to Aros, the war god. He snapped his fingers, and two servants in plain white robes came into the room and placed large bowls of rice and beef on the table.

Myra furrowed her brows and turned to face the door leading out to the hall. "Where's Papa? We should wait for him to join us. I can go fetch him."

She moved to leave her seat and go to the study—any excuse to be away from Uncle Waazir was welcome—but he cleared his throat, making her pause.

"Your father likes to take his supper alone these days. You wouldn't know that, of course."

With a sinking feeling in her chest, Myra turned back to the table while one of the servants dished a scoop of rice onto her plate. She squirmed. This was all getting to be too much, and she'd only been home for a couple of hours. Being waited on for simple tasks she could do on her own when only weeks ago she'd been doing the same thing, Papa being wary of letting her stay, and now Uncle Waazir's hostility. This had been a terrible idea. There were other ways she could start over and make her own life.

A fire roared behind Uncle Waazir, casting light and shadows over him as he wolfed down his supper. He wanted her to doubt herself so she would leave again, make it abundantly clear she wasn't wanted and not get his hands dirty with finding a way to get rid of her a second time. She'd come into his domain without his permission and would fight her every step of the way. His intimidation and scare tactics might have worked when she was a child, but not anymore. What he didn't know was Myra was used to not being wanted. Almost every home, except for Cal's, she'd faced adversity and people putting her down. They underestimated her, but through it all, she persisted.

The only person who hadn't treated her so was Cal, but even he underestimated her at times. He always defended her and sacrificed himself for her own safety as though she couldn't do so herself. But she'd let him, and now it was her turn to save herself.

Prince Alvis hadn't underestimated her. She'd helped him in Cal's escape and defeating Queen Amelia. He didn't question her magic or act as though he needed to protect her. Oddly enough, the crown prince of Oxare treated her as a partner in their endeavors while Amelia had taken over Cresin.

With newfound courage, Myra smiled across the table and scooped a bite of rice and beef onto her fork. "Well, that's something we'll have to change now, isn't it? As lady of the house, I might have to insist he dines with us after today. He and I have years to catch up on." She put the food in her mouth and raised her brows at her uncle, daring him to disagree with her.

He chuckled, a cold and chilling sound. "And you know how to be a lady of a household? A servant girl?"

Myra swallowed. "This manor is my inheritance. My right. I'll learn."

Uncle Waazir smirked. "We'll see about that. I'm sure the people will be overjoyed to hear one of death's daughters will be leading this manor. You know how much they loved your mother."

Myra stiffened and had to force herself to maintain her smile. They hadn't loved Mama, no matter how kind she was. Despite it, they still came to her when their loved ones were on their deathbeds to bring them peace and guide their spirits to Stula's arms. Or when they had questions about changes in their lives and none of the other deities provided answers. It did lead her to trouble though. People yelled and mocked her on the streets of town, and the society women shunned her. Being part fae, Mama could trace her line back to the goddess of death, so people didn't treat her well. Mama was the embodiment of everything they didn't understand, and therefore they feared her.

They would fear Myra was well when they found out she'd returned.

One of the reasons she didn't practice her magic when it could be avoided. It only caused problems.

"You won't need to worry about any of that, I can assure you," she said, ashamed of the response. Despite all the hardship, Mama was proud of where she came from and the gifts it gave her. Myra could feel the pendant burning against her skin under her tunic but ignored it. This was for the best.

"I'm glad to hear it. Especially since your dark ways almost killed the King of Cresin."

It was as though the world stopped and tilted around Myra as he spoke. There was no way he knew of her involvement with the events in Cresin. He couldn't know. No one knew outside of her, Cal, and Amelia. It was why she needed to be as far away from all involved as possible. If anyone knew it had been Myra who'd given the potion to Amelia…

Myra had no idea Amelia was going to use it on the king. The whole time Myra and Cal had been in Amelia's employment, she'd used and abused Cal's skills as a hunter and Myra's magic. They'd done unspeakable things for the former queen, but it had all been for survival. Besides, Myra never imagined Amelia's dislike for her husband would have led to her poisoning him into a sleep of living death. If she had known… Well, Myra had no idea what she would have done, but she knew she would have tried everything in her power to protect the rest of the royal family.

Uncle Waazir couldn't have known about Myra's involvement. It was impossible.

"It was an ancient potion of Stula, wasn't it?" Uncle Waazir asked. "It's a lesson to us all that those who dabble in Stula's magic are never up to anything good. Is it not?"

The world returned to its axis. It was just his old suspicions and prejudices showing through again. Nothing more.

"I promise, you'll see none of it here," Myra told him.

Uncle Waazir raised a glass toward her, and Myra returned the gesture, even though the drink burned as it went down her throat.

MUCH TO MYRA'S DELIGHT, THE REMAINDER OF THE MEAL WAS SPENT IN silence, and as soon as her plate was empty, she returned to her room. Lying on the bed was a single envelope with a note attached, along with a simple white night dress. After shutting and locking the door, Myra threw herself onto the bed and flopped onto her back. Returning home had been significantly more difficult than she'd anticipated. The events of the day weighed on her like bricks, to the point where she could hardly breathe.

She sat and examined the letter and note attached to it.

This was delivered for you a few days ago. I would have thrown it away, but I've always held on to hope you would return, so I kept it for you.

- Odalis

Tears prickled at Myra's eyes. At least there was one person who was glad she was home. She should pick out one of her nicer jewelry items she'd made and give it to Odalis as a solstice gift as she was the jewel of the manor. She put the note aside and opened the envelope. It was from whom she'd expected: Cal. Once she'd found out Papa hadn't moved away, she'd sent a message to her brother to let him know where she would be staying.

She reclined against the pile of pillows and read the letter over and over again until her eyes couldn't focus anymore. Cal was worried about her and missed her but had every confidence she would be able to take care of herself and start a new life. Everyone there was preparing for the winter solstice, even though it would be different without Eira there. Rose was having a difficult time adjusting to her new role as heiress to the throne, but Cal had confidence in her as well. Myra clutched the letter to her chest.

What was she doing?

Without bothering to change into the nightdress Odalis had laid out for her, Myra curled onto her side and crushed a pillow against her chest, burying her face into it. She was alone now and didn't need to put on a strong face. She couldn't remember the last time she'd had such a luxury. Everything had always been about figuring out her next step and the next way to survive. No time to wallow.

A cool breeze wafted through the room, and Myra shivered. A blanket lay at her feet, and she pulled it around her body to shield herself from it as tears ran down her cheeks. There she was in her own bed, in her own room and house that was rightfully hers, and she'd never felt more homesick.

If only she knew what she was homesick for.

Chapter Six

ALVIS

THERE WAS NOTHING BETTER THAN THE WINTER SOLSTICE IN OXARE, and Alvis couldn't be more thrilled to be home in time. The bright sun shone on him and Nell as they strolled through the gardens to make their way to back to the palace from the stables. If they were still in Cresin, they would have still been sleeping in preparation for the overnight celebrations—and recovering from the night before. Cresin had the largest celebrations for the winter solstice out of all the kingdoms, but Alvis was glad to spend it back home in the Golden Palace where he could enjoy the sun and remember they were halfway through the long dark nights, and light would be there soon.

Especially this year.

He needed the sun and the comfort of home more than ever now.

Besides, he wouldn't be able to give this fantastic gift if they were still in Cresin.

Nell skipped at his side, pausing now and then to smell and look at the flowers of the garden. She asked what types they were, and Alvis answered as well as he could. Most of the plants he could recognize, but there were still some rare ones he wasn't familiar with. Maybe he should add agriculture to the list of the subjects she should study.

He was in the middle of interviewing tutors for Nell and planned to have her start lessons after things settled down from the solstice celebrations. It pained him that he couldn't tutor her himself, but he had other tasks to attend to. There'd been some debate of if she should go to school, but as they didn't know what sort of education Amelia had given her daughter, it was decided a tutor would be best to work with her one on one. She also then could acclimate to Oxare and palace life. Then there were plenty of nobles and visitors who came in and out of the Golden Palace through the year who had children, which would give Nell the opportunity to learn how to socialize with people her age.

Maybe next year they would consider sending her to a proper school.

At least Nell was growing accustomed to the Golden Palace and her newfound freedom. She'd only been there a week, but her curiosity about her surroundings showed more every day. Even now, as they went to the stables, Nell walked a couple of steps in front of him, her curls bouncing along behind her as she skipped. She paused and turned to face him.

"Is the horse really mine?"

Alvis chuckled and caught up to her. She'd asked the question several times ever since he presented the gift. "Yes, she's really yours."

The space between Nell's eyes wrinkled, and she looked at the ground. "But I haven't ridden by myself before."

"You'll learn. I have a teacher prepared to come tomorrow so you can begin your lessons. You'll be riding alongside me before you know it."

Nell lifted her face, and the sunlight caught in her blue eyes. "And then we can explore!"

They continued to walk back to the palace, and Nell wandered about picking flowers but always stayed close enough where she could see him. The girl moved through the world as though she were floating through a dream. She sniffed one of the flowers in her hand and brushed the petals with the tips of her fingers. "Will you be there when they teach me?"

One of her many constant questions. Never had someone wanted Alvis around so often. Meals, outings, or something as simple as reading in the library. It was flattering, but something he wasn't used to. He enjoyed the company of others, and they him, but outside his royal duties, he'd ever been asked if he would be there so often.

Alvis coughed and cleared his throat. "I'll be there to introduce you and be sure things start off well of course. If I have the time, I can stay if you like."

"That would be nice." She knelt and picked a few more flowers to add to her growing bouquet. "I can't wait to tell Mother about my gift."

The comment Nell almost said to herself, and Alvis had to resist from recoiling. Their next, and most unpleasant, task for the day.

When they returned to the palace, the pair was joined by three guards, and they all trooped through twisted corridors and stairwells down to the hidden room where the former queen was kept. Two more guards stood at the stone door in their red-and-gold tunics and turbans, the colors of Oxare, and they both bowed their heads to Alvis. They pounded their spears on the ground in a complicated rhythm, and the door opened. Two more guards greeted them, and in the back of the dark room, under one of the only small windows to let in light, stood a tall mirror, but instead of glass, it was made of ice.

Everything about the room was the opposite of the rest of the Golden Palace, which was open and bright and full of light. Here, it was dark and damp and surrounded by stone enchanted with a light frost on the ground surrounding the mirror. They all knew the ice covering the mirror was a temporary solution, for if Amelia were to strengthen her magic, she could melt it and escape. So there were precautions everywhere. Stone walls strong enough to withhold waves of water. All the guards who watched over the mirror had powers from Ray, Luana, or Colma so their magic could combat the former queen's if needed.

Nell smiled at and greeted each of the guards with a cheerful hello, and even though they never changed their stance or expression, they bowed their heads to her with a new softness in their eyes. She might have only been there a short time, but she had already charmed most everyone in the palace.

They approached the mirror, and a shiver ran through Alvis. Bumps appeared on Nell's arms when she sat on the ground and laid the bouquet of flowers in front of it, but she didn't pay them any mind. This was the worst part of their routine, and Alvis prayed to whatever deity would listen to make it go as fast and peacefully as possible so they could go on with the rest of their day and enjoy the solstice. A guard stood at Nell's side, and together they raised their arms and placed her delicate light-brown hand on the ice-coated mirror. The constellation of stars tattooed on the guard's hand glowed, and Alvis had to take a breath to soothe himself.

Nell had gone through enough changes and transitions these last few weeks. If she chose to continue to visit her mother, she would be allowed to if she was accompanied by Alvis and there were guards present. Secretly, Alvis prayed Nell would change her mind one of these days and decide to not visit any more, but it hadn't happened. The sorceress didn't deserve for this young girl to be so faithful to her. But he understood. Amelia was Nell's mother, and the only companion Nell had her entire life. To cut off communication entirely could be devastating to the poor girl's already fragile psyche.

The ice wavered at the touch of the Nell and the guard, and as if she had been waiting for them, Amelia's sharp blue eyes peered out from behind the frosted glass.

"Mother?" Nell's voice was soft like the sheer curtains of the palace brushing against the floor when a summer breeze wafted in. "I brought you some flowers from the garden."

Amelia's lips pursed in a thin smile, and she glanced at the bouquet laid before her and then looked at Alvis. "They're lovely, darling. Although I can hardly enjoy them when they're out there and I'm in here."

Hands still neatly placed in her lap, Nell turned to Alvis. Her blue eyes were a replica of her mother's, but there was a brightness to them lacking in the former queen. "May I hand them to her?"

The attention of all present was now on Alvis, and he swallowed. It was risky, but there were enough people and magic there to prevent anything from happening. He gave her a single nod.

A hush fell over the room, and it was as though everyone's hearts stopped beating all at once as Nell took the bouquet. The guard at her side placed his hand on the ice, and Nell put her free hand next to his. Together they melted the ice just enough for Nell to pass the flowers from their world to Amelia's, their fingers brushing against one another.

Alvis held his breath and only released it once Nell's hand was out of the mirror again and the ice was sealed.

Amelia ran a finger over the top of the bouquet and chuckled. As delicate as a bell but held the same chill as the ice covering her mirror. "Here I am, trapped, alone, and heavy with child, and still you all tremble at the smallest gesture of my daughter giving me flowers." She looked at Alvis again. "Do you think I'll be able to escape here?"

Alvis took a deep breath to keep his face from turning red. The fire of Ray burned within him with anger and embarrassment at letting himself show any indication of being afraid of her. She wished to get a rise out of him, to show that she still made him nervous and could get awaken the fire within him, and it was his own fault for letting her know she succeeded. He needed to block her out.

He crossed his arms and nodded to the guards. "We won't let that happen."

Amelia raised a brow and shrugged. "If you say so."

Nell straightened her back and put her hands in her lap. "Prince Alvis gave me a horse as a solstice gift!"

Amelia returned her attention to her daughter, and while there was a smile on her face, her eyes were dark. "How generous of the prince. But horses can be dangerous, you know. You'll fall. After all my years protecting you, I'd hate for you to fall and hurt yourself."

She was trying to get a rise out of him again. Amelia hadn't protected Nell; she'd trapped her. But Alvis willed himself to keep his face calm and relaxed.

If Nell noticed the tension, she didn't show it and only twisted one of her brown curls around her finger. Her hair wasn't as long as it was when she was trapped in the mirror where it dragged along the floor and all the way behind her. But it still was unruly and tangled most of the time. "I like horses now, Mother. I used to be afraid, but I've ridden one a few times. Prince Alvis is going to have someone teach me so I can ride on my own. I can't wait to go out and explore."

Amelia sniffed the flowers and put them aside, out of sight. Not so much as a thank-you. "Is he now? He'll let you wander about a kingdom you've never seen before. Sounds reckless to me."

"She will be supervised and protected at all times," Alvis clarified.

"Your daughter will have the best instructors and guards in all the kingdoms. I made sure of it."

Amelia sighed and placed her hands on her swollen belly. She would be entering her third trimester soon. "Very well. Nell, I'm growing tired and my back aches. Can we resume this tomorrow?"

For the first time that day, the brightness in Nell's eyes faded, and she looked at her lap. "Yes, of course, Mother. Whatever you like."

As much as he hated these visits, something in Alvis ached. Amelia didn't deserve a daughter like Nell. She looked forward to this every day, and so many times Amelia cut them short. But as long as Nell requested it, Alvis would bring her.

But if she didn't request a visit, Alvis wouldn't question it and silently rejoiced.

"Happy solstice, Mother." Nell's voice was so quiet one had to strain to hear her.

"Yes, happy solstice, Nell. Now go on. I'm sure the royal family has something *glorious* planned for the day." The hatred poured out of the words like a flood.

Nell stood and went to Alvis's side. At least she wasn't hesitant to join him. And Amelia was right about one thing—they did have glorious plans for the evening. They always had a grand feast filled with music and dancing. It was the first big event Nell would be attending since her arrival, and Alvis hoped she would enjoy it.

"And please send a new Attendant for my next checkup. The last one was rude," Amelia called after Alvis before they left. To keep an eye on her and the progress of the child growing in her belly, they'd sent an Attendant every few days to be sure she was still healthy, and nothing was wrong with the child. This was already the second time she requested a new Attendant. Alvis had a feeling this was going to become a routine.

Alvis nodded to her. "Of course."

It was late by the time Alvis returned to his chamber that night after the solstice festivities. Not nearly as late as it would have been in Cresin, whose residents were surely still up celebrating until dawn, but

Alvis was exhausted. He'd been looking forward to the feast, and it had been as grand and luxurious as he'd expected. The decadent and spicy food and the wine that poured freely filled his belly, and the bells and cymbals from the dancers' costumes echoed in his mind.

But it wasn't the same as it was before. In previous years, he and Cadeyrn spent the holy day in Cresin with Eira and her family. Or they would be here, and Cadeyrn would be sure to come to the palace for a few weeks. Alvis didn't particularly enjoy and wasn't very good at these big celebrations, but with his brother at his side, he'd been able to bear them better. When he faltered for something clever to say, Cadeyrn was there with a witty antidote. Alvis was hurt by the secrets Cadeyrn and Eira had kept from him, but he still missed his brother.

Alvis dismissed the servant who was there to help him undress and decided to prepare for bed on his own. He'd been around people enough, and if he was near one more person, he was going to go mad. It took him longer on his own, with all the buttons and ties for his formal wear. But it gave him something to distract himself from his own thoughts.

What had made the evening even worse was all the attention spent on his being available to marry. No one spoke of it outright. But almost every person he spoke with either was a woman—in one case, a man—bringing up the fact they were eligible, or they were telling him about their daughter or niece who happened to be the loveliest in the kingdom.

He sighed as he pulled on a pair of loose-fitting pants and shrugged into a robe. Returning home was more draining than he'd anticipated. During the journey on the riverboat, Alvis had been grateful for the open air and time to clear his mind. For hours, he sat on the deck reading, many times accompanied by Myra, who would let him read passages out loud and discuss them.

Alvis summoned his magic, and the sun tattoo on his chest glowed as he extinguished the torches around the room, except for one lantern by his bed. He wondered what Myra might be doing for the solstice and who she spent it with. Her family, he hoped. Maybe this feast would have been more bearable if he'd seen her friendly face in the crowd. He shook his head. Myra made her choice and didn't want to come to the

Golden Palace. She had her own life and goals she wanted to accomplish, and he was glad for it. But she had been a good reprieve for him. Wherever she was, he hoped she was happy.

He climbed into bed and picked up the book on the nightstand. As tired as he was, his mind raced and needed to calm before he had any sort of chance of sleeping. Books, fictional or not, had always been his escape. The place where he could grow in knowledge and make sense of the world around him. So he read until sleep took him, in the hope that with the morning sun he would see the world in a different light.

Chapter Seven

MYRA

THE NEXT MORNING, MYRA WOKE WITH THE SUN STREAMING IN through the east-facing windows as she'd forgotten to close the curtains. It was customary in Oxare to have the bedrooms facing east so people could greet Ray each morning as he began the day. Bells from the nearest temple rang, and the faint sounds of trumpets played, making Myra want to cover her head with the pillows to block out the sun and trumpets. Myra lived in Cresin so long, she was used to sleeping in. While the servants always woke long before everyone else, they still slept in later than people in Oxare. Their focus had been on Luana, goddess of the moon, and late nights under the stars were common. Especially the week of the winter solstice, when festivals and balls went until sunrise.

Her journey to Oxare with Prince Alvis and his entourage had included early mornings, but they'd been respectful of those who wanted to sleep in. Even if it usually was only Myra who wished to do so.

Myra groaned and tried to cover herself up more. A second blanket was on top of her now, and she didn't remember putting it there. She must have gotten cold in the middle of the night and gathered it around her.

A knock came at the door, and Myra hoped whoever was on the other side would give up trying to wake her if she stayed silent enough. If she was the lady of the house now, she should be able to decide for herself when to wake in the mornings.

The knocking continued, and in time, the door cracked open. Odalis's cheerful voice sang through the room like a bird. "Happy solstice, my lady. Are you awake?"

Myra only groaned for a reply.

Odalis tsked as she pushed the door open with her elbow and carried a tray over to the table and chairs set near the fireplace. She then lit the fireplace, and it roared into action to warm the chilly room. Despite her being tired, the smell of the coffee Odalis poured from a metal carafe and the sight of the flatbread with dips and jams on the side drew Myra out of bed. With a blanket wrapped around her shoulders, she padded over to the table and took a whiff of the food.

"Are those spiced potatoes too?"

Odalis raised her brows. "They were always your favorite. Every day you would have this for breakfast and wouldn't accept anything else. Although I took a gamble on you drinking coffee now."

The steaming clay mug was the first thing Myra reached for, and she breathed in the rich aroma before taking a sip. This alone was enough to perk her senses into the waking world. Amelia made sure Myra was busy from the moment she awoke, and she'd always gotten the last of whatever batch the kitchen staff had made, which was usually cold by the time she got to it. Having something warm and fresh for her, with a meal to go along with it, was a luxury she wasn't used to.

"The coffee is perfect," Myra said once she'd had a sip. "Thank you."

"Of course, my lady."

Myra grimaced as she dipped the flatbread in one of the jams. "Please, call me Myra. I'm not a lady."

Technically, she was. But Myra wasn't above or any better than Odalis. They were the same. Myra had done the same work, if not even more grueling and disgusting work depending on who she'd been serving at the time. No matter what her heritage proclaimed or what clothes she wore, Myra would always be a servant.

"If you insist."

While Myra ate, Odalis busied herself with making the bed and putting away the night dress Myra hadn't worn that night. "I hope you don't mind that I didn't wake you for the sunrise service at the temple. It's been many years since your father or uncle have gone, and you were so tired last night."

The potatoes were soft and spicy and practically melted in Myra's mouth. She almost moaned in joy. How had she gone so long without having these? She finished chewing and swallowed before answering Odalis. "You guessed right. Thank you for the sleep."

"We'll have food and treats available all day though, and a feast tonight."

"Will Papa be there?"

"Usually we can tear him away from his study for the holy days."

Myra breathed a sigh of relief. At least she wouldn't have to endure the meal alone. She also wouldn't have to put up with her uncle until then if she could help it. But what would she do all day? She was so used to having to help prepare for the day's festivities in Cresin, she'd never had the day to spend by herself to celebrate and honor the day. She took another sip of coffee and strummed her fingers on the table. Usually there were gifts at the solstice, and Myra had been so focused on getting home, bringing gifts hadn't crossed her mind. Not that there would be any for her, but it could be a good way to get Papa to open himself up to accepting her.

Odalis's light voice interrupted her silent plans. "There are still some candles and cloths in the trunk."

Myra paused mid-sip, and her heart stopped. She set the mug on the table and cleared her throat in an attempt to sound as neutral as possible. "Are there? Why would you keep them?"

"I couldn't find it in myself to throw them away." Over the bed, the older woman lay a deep-green and black dress, which had a large shawl draped over one shoulder and gold beading along the neckline, making it appear there was a heavy necklace on the garment. Myra's heart stopped again. It was Mama's solstice dress.

Odalis gave Myra a knowing look. "She's under the tree behind the house."

Myra's chin quivered, and the magic flowing inside her chilled. She'd never been to Mama's burial spot. Didn't even know where it was until now. It was a relief to hear she was buried under the tree. Mama had planted it herself when she first married Papa, and Myra had spent countless afternoons playing and having picnics there. She nodded. "Thank you, Odalis."

After she finished breakfast, Myra let Odalis help her into the dress. It was easier than doing it on her own for this outfit with all the buttons going down the back. The dress didn't fit her perfectly. Myra was a little too short and her breasts too small, but those minor details didn't bother her. She fit in it well enough for it to work for the day. She ran the fabric of the shawl between her fingers the way Mama used to stroke Myra's hair. She would stay warm in this dress while outside, and it was casual enough to wear through the day while still formal for the feast in the evening. Mama had worn this dress the last solstice they spent together, and it looked as though it was still brand-new instead of being stored away.

Odalis squeezed Myra's shoulders. "Lovely."

The remainder of the day was spent wandering the manor and gardens, getting to know it all again, and gathering items to make gifts. All of it was like what Myra remembered with very few changes. Lamps and rugs or minor pieces of furniture had been updated here and there, but overall, the house was the same as it always was. In the courtyard and garden, there were some new plants, but most of it was the same as when Mama tended it. While walking through the petunias, Myra could almost see Mama kneeling in the flower beds pruning the plants. She always insisted on tending her own garden instead of letting a servant do it.

"It never hurts to get your hands dirty," Myra could almost hear her saying.

Myra gathered different flowers and pieces of greenery in a basket she'd found and took them inside. After letting herself indulge and grab the various treats and goodies set out for the solstice, she took her wares into her room. She was better with clothes and jewelry, but still managed to make chains, bookmarks, and a couple of miniature wreaths. They were small gifts, but better than nothing.

When those were done, she wrote a letter to Cal and made sure it was with the rest of the correspondence to go out the following day. There had been no sight of Papa or Uncle Waazir the whole day. The door to Papa's study was closed when Myra walked past it, and she heard his footsteps as he paced back and forth. She'd seen and heard less from Uncle Waazir, which was perfectly fine. The more she could avoid him, the better.

Before long, it was time for the sun to set, and Myra knelt in front of the mahogany chest at the foot of her bed. Quiet trumpets from the town's temple sounded through the air, preparing the people for Ray's departure for the day. The deep, spiced scent of the wood filled her nostrils, and one by one, she lifted the items out. Dried paints. Old brushes. Empty bottles. Then the thin black cloths with round candles wrapped inside them.

The candles knocked together as they were lifted out of the trunk, and she placed them in a satchel. Myra promised Papa she didn't practice her magic anymore, but being here on the longest night of the year, it didn't feel right to not perform the rites Mama always had. Papa and Uncle Waazir weren't around spying on her. It would be fine.

Besides, she had to know where Mama's spirit was.

Myra tiptoed through the manor and went out to the back where Mama's tree stood tall and proud. Its thick brown trunk placed in the ground like a mountain, and the big green leaves formed a canopy over the lawn. At its foot lay a long gray stone slab with another stone standing upright in front of it. Myra's chest tightened when she approached the grave.

Loving Wife.
Beloved Mother.

A SIMPLE ENGRAVING WITH NO SIGN OF MAMA'S HERITAGE AS A descendent of the goddess Stula. Not even a hint of how it meant she was part fae. Myra's face burned, and she gripped the items in her bag so tight the candles could have broken. She might have decided to follow a different path and not practice their magic, but it meant everything to Mama. Their magic was a gift, Mama used to always say. Other people had to go through a dedication ceremony to receive power from the deities and have tattoos etched into their skin, but not them. They were descendants of the goddess herself, with magic running through their veins. Magic to guide spirits into Stula's arms when they passed, to manipulate shadows, see and speak with spirits, and to bring peace and comfort in times of change and distress.

With a cleansing breath, Myra removed the items from her satchel and spread the thin black cloth over the ground. It was ridiculous how superstitious people were over followers of Stula. The goddess was known for her role in death, and therefore people feared her. They thought all her followers were killers, which wasn't true. There was a select few who were handpicked to be her servants and do her bidding in the world to take those who had been running from death or to be the hand of justice. But they were few and far between.

There were times Stula seemed cruel and unfair—and maybe she was sometimes. But she was also peaceful and comforting. She was the goddess accepting of change and those who were different and didn't fit in.

It didn't help that there were people who took advantage of these gifts though. Found ways to exploit them and those who possessed such powers. Myra closed her eyes and tried to wipe away the memories of her past. The owners who made her do such terrible things with her magic. The moments she'd lost control. Or when Amelia would force Myra to uncover old magic and spells that went against the teachings of Stula.

Maybe people should be afraid of her after all.

The candles were next, and she set them on the cloth in a large circle so she could stand and kneel in the center in prayer and song. What most people forgot was Stula was the goddess of many other things too. Change, chronic and terminal illness, disability, and maturity. Over the years, Myra had seen countless people as they grew older embrace the goddess and recognize the gift of a long life. When people went through a transition in their life, Stula brought them strength and comfort. Mama sat at the side of many people who were ill or with permanent injuries and gave them peace.

Myra lit the candles, each flame like a floating star of hope in the fading daylight. For so long, Myra had wanted to encourage Princess Rose to reach out to Stula as she'd been born with a twisted leg. But she didn't know how without revealing her heritage. Mama would have been ashamed of Myra behaving in such a way. The truth was any time she had revealed her heritage, it had only brought trouble. Better to practice in secret and keep a low profile. Myra prayed for the princess daily though, even now being away from Cresin, so she could find strength and peace.

She knelt in the center of the circle and lowered a gossamer black veil over her face. She bit her bottom lip, remembering all the good Mama had done. Then, when it was Myra's turn to help her, she might have failed. The one important task of escorting Mama's spirit into Stula's arms when she died, and Myra had been interrupted at the very end when Uncle Waazir caught her. The rite might have been finished and Mama could very well be at peace in the afterlife now. But since she'd been interrupted, Myra didn't know for sure.

Myra lowered her body to the ground, so her chest and forehead lay flat and her arms stretched forward. She sang with her mouth pointed to the ground and then rose so she sat on her feet with hands lifted to the sky.

For those who worshiped Stula, the winter solstice was a time to welcome the new season. Any time there was a significant change, whether it was seasons turning, lives being celebrated, births, deaths, or weddings, Stula was there to help people welcome it with open arms. Winter solstice was particularly special, it being the longest night of the year, and during the night, spirits who hadn't gone into the afterlife were the most active. They came out often during the solstice and other holy days, for they wanted to relive their own joyous memories. It was a time for Stulan followers to connect with them and help them to be welcomed into Stula's realm if possible.

It was appropriate for Myra to arrive home during the solstice, as she, too, was entering a new season of her life.

She sang as quietly as possible. Not because she was embarrassed of her voice, she could hold a tune just fine. Despite wanting to honor Mama and Stula, being caught by Papa or Uncle Waazir would only make matters worse, and she would be back out on the street where she started. The song was hopeful and somber at the same time—the way the start of winter was. There was death, darkness, and cold all around, but through it all, in the season there was an elegant beauty and hope of warmth and light to come again.

The flames danced and swayed along with the melody, and shadows as black as night swirled from Myra's fingers and formed images of roses with their thorns, skulls, and stars that hovered over her head. It was as though the shadows carried the notes of the song out of her mouth and into the sky, wafting through the branches of the trees, for they started to dance with the song too. The leaves and branches rustling against each other were the instruments accompanying Myra's voice.

She'd listened to Mama sing this song every year. Spirits would come and dance and sing along, and Myra felt at one with all people, the living and the dead. Mama's sweet and tender voice echoed through her mind, almost as though she was there at her side singing along. The memory was so potent she could smell Mama's jasmine perfume. Myra rose to her feet and turned in a circle with arms outstretched to welcome Stula and any spirits who cared to listen and join in her winter solstice rite.

The wind swelled and blew Myra's veil and hair across her face. The shawl of her dress ruffled behind her and a chill ran through her, but Myra continued with the song. Now she included arm and foot movements. Her performance wasn't perfect. In fact, it was rusty, and her arms and legs moved more like a stumbling toddler learning to walk than a skilled dancer as it had been so long since she'd practiced. But it came from her soul, which was what mattered more than how precise and perfect it was.

Everything stopped the moment Myra completed the song. The wind, the shadows, the music of the tree, and even the candle flames blew out, all of it stilled as though a spell had been cast on the world to pause everything. Myra blinked and realized her cheeks were wet with tears she hadn't noticed. She wiped them away with the back of her sleeve and shivered from the cold. The sun had set now, and any warmth from the day had left with it.

Myra's shoulders sagged. No sign of Mama, or any spirits. She'd never been good at calling them the way Mama had. Maybe it meant she had passed and no longer haunted the living world. The thought should have comforted Myra, but she would be lying if part of her hadn't hoped to see Mama one last time, even if it was only in spirit.

It would be time for supper soon, and she scooped up the candles, put them in her satchel, and hurried inside.

Chapter Eight

MYRA

Myra heaved a sigh and sipped her coffee while she looked out of her bedroom window. It had been raining for days now, thwarting any plans she had of going into town to get to know the people and see what opportunities lay there. She'd gone a handful of times since arriving home a few weeks ago, and while she'd intended to remain anonymous, word spread quickly about how the long-lost daughter of the manor had returned.

For some, she was a source of curiosity, and they were eager to help her learn her way around and to sell their goods to the lord's daughter. For many, they looked at her with wary eyes and scurried far away as they remembered who her mother was. As though they would be cursed by breathing the same air as a daughter of Stula. At least those people left her alone.

Besides, going into town was a way for her to get away from Uncle Waazir.

She strummed her fingers on the clay mug while the rain fell. It was an unusual amount for this time of year, which would normally be pleasant and sunny, with only a need for long sleeves and a scarf to stay warm. The manor was large enough where she and Waazir could avoid one another, but after they both spent the last few days cooped up inside, their interactions increased. Myra took another sip. The rain was lighter than was the day before, so maybe a short walk wouldn't be too terrible.

A cool and gentle breeze wafted through the room, and Myra tugged her shawl closer around her. This was room was draftier than she'd remembered, and she could never pinpoint where it came from. With another sigh, she stepped away from the window and sat at the table in front of the fire to finish reading a letter someone delivered the day before from a villager.

...WE'VE TRIED TO GET HER OUT OF BED, FOR THE ATTENDANTS SAY IT would be good for her to get up and move about the house and it will strengthen her leg. Yet she refuses. I remember your mother possessed certain...skills...to assist in matters such as these. Even if you don't have the same skills, I'm sure a visit from the manor would lift her spirits immensely—

MYRA'D READ THE LETTER A DOZEN TIMES SINCE IT ARRIVED MUCH TO her surprise. Any correspondence from the village went to Uncle Waazir as he handled all the affairs. The messenger specifically said this letter was for Myra's eyes only. Upon reading the contents, it was no surprise for they wanted to utilize Myra's gifts from Stula.

The cool breeze caressed Myra's cheek, sending a shiver through her, and she pulled her shawl even closer. Mama would have gone. Even if it had been at night so fewer people would see her, she would have gone.

"But I can't! I don't do those things. Not anymore." With a huff, she leaned back in the chair, crossed one leg over the other, and continued to sip her coffee. She hadn't touched her magic since the winter solstice and had no intentions of trying again.

A knock came at the door, followed by Odalis's cheerful voice. "My lady, your father wishes to see you."

Myra straightened at the announcement. While he'd finally begun to join them for meals on occasion, Papa hadn't asked for her specifically a single time since she'd arrived home. "I'll be right out."

She made her way to Papa's study and knocked on the door. At his greeting, she opened it to find Uncle Waazir was in the room with him. Her heart sank. Whatever this was about, it couldn't be good.

Leather cases and boxes were stacked all along the room, and a servant busied himself with filling them with various books and papers. Father stood over his desk and examined a map, the smoke from his cigarette swirling around his head.

His eyes, which had a clarity Myra hadn't seen the whole time she'd been home, glanced at her and then back down to the map. "Ah, good, you're here. I'm to leave for the Belovian Islands this afternoon on some business. I'll be back in a couple of months. Waazir will still be here to handle all my affairs, so you won't have to worry about anything. I thought you would want to know."

Myra opened and closed her mouth, unsure of how to respond. He was leaving? But she'd only just arrived! If she was left on her own at the manor, that would be one thing, but with Uncle Waazir there... She rushed to his side.

"Why don't I go with you? I don't have many things, so it won't take me long to pack. I'll fetch Odalis."

Papa waved her off and almost hit Myra in the face in the process. "No, no. This will be no trip for a young lady. You'll be bored to tears. Besides, Waazir can show you how things are done around here. Since it seems as though you aren't going anywhere for a while, it's time you learned."

As if Waazir would allow Myra anywhere near the affairs of the manor and the lands they ran. Her uncle pointedly turned his back away from them and busied himself with filling another box.

Myra pursed her lips. "But it's raining. This is no time for travel. Surely you want to wait until the weather gets better."

Papa looked out the window as though it was the first time he'd noticed the outdoors existed. "It looks it is calming down. Besides, I need to be sure I reach the riverboat in time."

No. This couldn't be happening. It was bad enough for Papa to be holed up in his study all the time, but at least he was joining them for the occasional meal now. With him being gone, there was no telling what Waazir might do to her.

She gripped his arm, forcing him to turn to look at her. "Please, Papa. Let me come with you. I've never been to the Belovian Islands. I'd love to see them."

Papa froze, in shock at her touch. They stood there for a moment, for Myra was as equally shocked she'd had the audacity to grab him in such a way. Even as a child, she couldn't recall a moment when she'd done so. Myra let her hands drop to her sides, and Papa cleared his throat.

"You'll be fine here, Myra. I want you to learn about the lands and how we handle things, and I'll be back before you know it."

Sure enough, by the time Papa was packed and ready to leave, the rain stopped completely, and he was well on his way. Myra waved good-bye as his cart traveled along the path and farther away from the house.

Uncle Waazir turned to her, his brown eyes dancing, and a slick smile was plastered across his face. "Well, it looks like it's just us now, doesn't it?"

MYRA OPENED MAMA'S TRUNK AND DUG THROUGH IT. ONE THING WAS for certain: she needed to spend as much time as possible away from Uncle Waazir until Papa came home. Cloths and candles were tossed aside until the bottom of the trunk was reached. From there, Myra pulled out the carefully placed black bowl with silver engravings of words of a long-lost language etched into it. Inside the bowl, wrapped in cloths and tiny satchels, were oils and herbs. They still smelled fresh. Myra put them to the side next to her bag and continued to dig. Among all the supplies lay the most valuable of all—which part of Myra was shocked was still there—*The Book of Souls*. Stula's book.

The ancient book's spine groaned upon opening, and Myra turned each page with gentle fingers to search for the correct recipe. She couldn't remember what it was called. But there was a picture of a bowl with black swirls rising from it in the corner somewhere.

A chill ran through Myra when that damned draft wafted through the room. So much so she stood to grab her shawl. The draft picked up into a wind and blew around the room, and she gasped from the cold when the fire went out. Her breath puffed out in front of her in small clouds, but before she could marvel at how quickly the temperature changed, the pages of *The Book of Souls* flipped on their own. They fluttered in the breeze, and all Myra could do was stare and clutch her shawl around her shuddering body.

The wind stopped, and one final puff of breath disintegrated in the air as the pages fell flat once again. There was a caress across Myra's cheek as though it were a soft but cold hand encouraging her. Only one person ever touched her that way.

"Mama?"

But there was no response. The cold wind was gone, and the room returned to the normal comfortable temperature and the fire blazed once again.

Had the rite Myra'd performed at the solstice worked? Was Mama's soul still there haunting the manor? If she was…it must have meant she was there the whole time and the final rite at her death hadn't succeeded. Myra clutched her necklace, unsure if she was heartbroken Mama wasn't in Stula's arms or grateful she was still there to comfort and guide her.

But why couldn't she see Mama's spirit? She should have been able to.

Myra fell to her knees in front of the book and examined the page Mama had turned it to: the soothing and comforting concoction she'd been searching for. Of course. Mama wanted her to go to the family who'd written the letter asking for help. Nothing about putting her spirit to rest, but to help others.

Her instinct to leave the house had been correct, and a knot tied in her stomach. There was no escaping her heritage and magic, no matter how hard she tried. If she was stealthy enough and avoided Uncle Waazir, she could still go out and assist the people of the town. She could practice her magic again and maybe even help Mama's spirit. The two of them had been able to stay away from one another enough.

He wouldn't notice what she was doing. Especially if it wasn't inside the house.

With a deep cleansing breath, Myra read the pages and committed the words to memory. She mouthed the magical words to herself until she didn't need to read them anymore and collected the proper ingredients. The book was too large to carry around, so she would need to leave it behind. Especially to be sure Waazir didn't notice anything.

"I'll be gone for the rest of the day," Myra told Odalis when she was ready to go. "I may not be back in time for dinner, so please do not wait for me."

Odalis eyed the satchel at Myra's side and smiled to herself. "Of course, my lady. Please be careful."

Myra nodded. "I will."

She fetched one of the horses from the stables and set off into town. The family lived in one of the poorer sections of the town, and as she rode through the streets, memories of similar visits flooded through her mind. Deathbeds Mama sat next to, celebrating new changes in the residents' lives, or the simple act of enjoying the company of the elderly and listening to their stories.

The small buildings were crowded together in this portion of the town, and barefooted children ran through the dirt road. They trotted next to Myra's horse and asked for food or money or whatever she could offer. She didn't have much but gave each one a silver coin, at which they smiled and bowed and thanked her as though it were a whole trunk of gold.

Maybe she could make some clothes to bring with her next time to give out, so they didn't have those threadbare tunics and pants. But she had a task to attend to today, and she slowed her pace to find the correct house. Recognition hit her when she arrived at the home described in the letter. She and Mama had gone to this residence a few times when she was a child. They weren't dedicated to Stula or descended from her, but were devout followers, nevertheless.

Myra tied the horse to a wooden post hammered into the ground and approached the orange-colored wooden door. The home was built with clay but painted a bright-teal color with simple images of the deities—including Stula—drawn around the doorframe. A sun and moon crowned the top to symbolize Ray and Luana looking over everyone while the other deities' symbols danced along the sides.

She rapped on the door three times, and after a minute or so, it opened to reveal a plump woman around Myra's height with dark-brown skin. At the sight of Myra, her eyes lit up, and she clutched the flower-pattered shawl around her head.

"Fatima?"

"Praise the deities! You have come!" She raised her hands in thanksgiving and then grasped Myra's wrist to lead her into their humble home. The woman had recognized Myra in an instant. She put a hand on Myra's cheek the way Mama used to, and something in Myra ached at the touch. "The image of your mother. It is as though she has returned to us after so many years. We have missed your presence here."

Myra swallowed the lump forming in her throat. "I'm sorry I didn't come sooner."

Not only for the time from when they sent her the letter until now, but for all the years when she was gone.

Fatima patted Myra's hand. "You are here now, and that is what matters. Come, come. I'll show you where my wife is."

She led Myra through the small house to the second room in back—a luxury for this part of town. Dirt from the floor gathered on the bottom of Myra's pants and shoes, and she had to step around various pots and trunks. There was evidence of attempts to keep the home clean and tidy, but with the size—or lack of size rather—of the building, it was difficult.

A few starlit lanterns were scattered through the back room, and a bed hardly large enough for two people sat in the corner. A fire blazed on the other side of the room, and another woman sat in a tattered armchair with her leg propped on a stool. A simple wooden crutch and a set of sticks and straps Myra assumed were used for a brace leaned against the hearth. The reflection of the flames danced across the woman's face, but there was a vacant stare in her brown eyes. Despite the lanterns and the fire, there was a darkness in the room, which sent a chill over Myra.

Still, Myra straightened her shoulders and approached the woman. "Hello, are you Pari?"

The woman broke her gaze from the fire to glance at Myra as though she only just then noticed other people had entered the room. Her eyes narrowed as she examined Myra, winkles forming in the creases and across her forehead. "Yes, my lady."

Myra bit her lip. Mama had been so good at these visits, but Myra wasn't sure what she should do. "No need to call me my lady. Myra is fine. May I sit?"

Pari observed Myra for a moment as though she was trying to place her face and deciding if she was to be trusted or not. Although she extended her arm to a stool across from her and nodded toward it.

Myra offered a smile and sat.

"You're not Qila."

"No, I'm her daughter."

Pari nodded again, a small movement. "I thought you both died."

"My mother did many years ago, yes. I..." She searched for the words. It wasn't surprising people thought Myra had died along with her mother. "I was gone for a long time. But I'm back now."

Pari pursed her lips and leaned back in her seat. "And I'm sure Fatima here thought you could get me to leave this room." While her face was tight with tension and pain, there was still a gentleness about her tone of voice when she spoke about her wife.

"Something like that. She thought if I visited, you would appreciate it." Myra lifted her bowl out of the satchel and showed it to Pari. "Do you mind if I use this?"

Pari shrugged. "If that's what pleases you. But you think some herbs and magic words will make everything better or change my mood?"

Myra knelt in front of the fire and raised her black shawl over her head. One by one, she placed the various herbs and spices into the bowl and crushed them with a stone. "Not exactly. The mixture is to help calm the atmosphere of the space. Make it more peaceful and drive away any energy that may not be serving for the good. Clear the mind and help to focus on what's needed. Sometimes it's needed to make room for happiness or peace. Other times, it helps to lower guards to embrace sadness or anger, which can also be needed. It mostly is here to welcome Stula and any energy she may find useful."

Fatima pulled over another stool and sat next to Pari. She patted the armrest. "Do you remember how Qila did the same when one of the children died so many years ago?"

Pari wordlessly mumbled something to herself and sank even farther into the chair. "Yes, I remember that a little."

Once the ingredients were mixed, Myra closed her eyes and hovered her hands over the concoction. She let her mind clear and focused on the mood of the room. At first, it was all darkness and heaviness as though a deep fog had settled in the room. As she focused more, she let in the crackle of the fire, the racketing of a cart going by outside, and the patter of feet running across the road. There was warmth, too, and love. Deep love. Myra hummed and recalled the words from *The Book of Souls*, letting them pour from her mind, out her mouth, and into the dark swirls rising from the bowl. When she opened her eyes, the words etched into the bowl glowed.

She breathed a sigh of relief. She did it correctly. Praise Stula.

Myra lifted herself back onto the stool, and Fatima had a glowing smile. Pari wasn't smiling, but there was an alertness to her to eyes that hadn't been there before. For the first time, Myra dared to look at Pari's injury. Her leg was bruised and swollen, a little crooked and scarred, but it wasn't twisted in the way Princess Rose's was. Myra cleared her throat.

"Can you tell me about the injury?"

"It was an accident a few months ago," Fatima said. "We were walking—"

"Oh, I can tell it myself," Pari snapped.

Fatima raised her brows and lifted her hands in mock surrender. "You barely speak of it to me. How was I to know you would tell her?"

Pari adjusted her position so she sat a little straighter. "We were coming back home after going to market, and someone lost control of their cart. It turned sideways and landed on my leg. The bone broke in three places."

Myra tried not to wince, picturing the scene and imagining the pain Pari must have been in. "Were you able to access an Attendant?"

Pari nodded and fidgeted with her blanket. "I did, and they did what they could to set the bone again and aid in my healing. I can walk some, but not the way I did before. I limp a lot. Can't run or be on it very long. I can't help around the home the way I used to."

For people in their position, that would be difficult, and an extra set of hands was good. If they were wealthier, they'd be able to hire people to help them around the house. Myra hated having other people do things for her all the time that she could do on her own, and it was an adjustment living back in the manor. It wasn't the same as Pari's situation, but she knew loss of ability would be a challenge.

"It's a large transition, and a different way of living your life," Myra agreed. She folded her hands in her lap and rubbed one thumb over the other as she thought. Her time in Cresin didn't particularly need to be a secret, but it didn't mean she wanted to outright admit she'd been a servant. "But it's not impossible. While I was gone, I spent some time in Cresin and had the pleasure of meeting Princess Rose. She has a permanent ankle injury she's had since birth."

Pari sneered. "Yes, I've heard of her. But she was gifted with enchanted straps from the fae descended from Gallis. She wears it, and it is as though there's no injury at all. Do you have access to such things?"

"No," Myra said carefully. "But the straps don't work all the time, only for a few hours. Then they need to rest so the magic can grow strong again. Most of the time, Rose uses a crutch to get from place to place, and it doesn't stop her. Now, she's had it since birth, so it's all she knows and learned to adapt from an early age, so it is different from your situation. But it is comparable." Myra gestured to the crutch and brace by the fireplace. "Your Attendant seems to have provided you with some aids. They may not contain magic, but I'm sure they're still helpful."

"We have tried to use them," Fatima piped up. "I encourage her to try at least once a day. But..."

Pari groaned. "The brace can be uncomfortable, and the crutch cumbersome. Besides, I hardly wish to be the cripple of the town where people will point and whisper, and children laugh."

Myra raised a brow. Afraid of mockery and rejection, was she? "There is no shame is getting help and having to deal with such a condition. Besides, I'd rather be the cripple of town than the miserable crone who never leaves home and children will be afraid of. Either way, people will talk, so you might as well show them you aren't afraid. If a crutch is good enough for a princess, surely it is good enough for you."

Pari stared at Myra for a moment as though she was in shock at what she'd said. Myra's cheeks started to grow warm. Mama would never be so harsh with someone, but Myra couldn't help herself. Stula was the goddess of the disabled and critically ill along with all the other things she reigned over, and there was no reason to be ashamed of it. Then, a burst of laughter came out of Pari's mouth. It was loud and rang through the house. Now it was Fatima and Myra's turn to stare.

When she was able to catch her breath, Pari spoke again with a wide smile across her face, making her look positively lovely. "Well then, she has magic and a backbone. Fatima and the Attendants have been tiptoeing around me as though I'm a fragile doll. It's time someone put me in my place."

Over the next few weeks, Myra settled into an easy rhythm. After her visit with Fatima and Pari, other villagers sent her messages or would stop her in the street to ask for assistance. Many still found their way on the other side of the road when she approached or gave her a wary glance and a quiet mutter under their breath when she passed by, but they left her alone. She made clothing for the children, and Fatima and Pari helped to make sure they were distributed where they were most needed, which proved to be a good task for Pari to get out of her room and transition into this new phase of her life.

Meanwhile, when Myra was home, she did everything she could to connect with Mama's spirit. Or at least what she assumed was Mama's spirit since she couldn't see it. Mama had always been gifted at seeing the spirits, and Myra hadn't learned enough to get the hang of it at such a young age. As she got older, Myra tried to learn on her own, but without *The Book of Souls* in her possession, it proved itself to be difficult.

Despite her efforts, Myra never saw the face or shape of the spirit haunting the manor and only felt the cold yet gentle breeze wafting by. Sometimes she would wake in the morning with an extra blanket draped over her, or the breeze would turn the pages in *The Book of Souls* to whatever spell or potion was needed. Even though Myra had to wrap herself in shawls and blankets when the spirit was there, it was a comforting presence, and she was grateful for it being there. So much so, in time, her efforts to find out how to send it to the afterlife for Stula faded away. She was almost convinced it was Mama, and she didn't want to let go of this last piece of her.

To make the challenges even worse was keeping her attempts a secret from Uncle Waazir. Any scent from the herbs and spells in the manor he would be able to detect. At least they both were able to keep to themselves. The only time Myra saw him most days was at meals. It was tempting to take all her meals on her own, but she didn't want to give him any reason to suspect her of practicing her magic again and give him a sense of security. Let him see her from time to time, show him she wasn't afraid and not going anywhere anytime soon. Meals were tense times and often ended in bickering and arguments, but usually were done quickly.

Praise the deities for small blessings.

Myra lowered the shawl from covering her head to her shoulders and strolled into the house as she read Cal's latest letter. Things in Cresin seemed to be as it always was, with Princess Rose adjusting to her new role as heiress. There was a lightness to the tone of the letter, and Myra could tell he was enjoying his new position as second in command to captain of the guard. It warmed her heart to know he was no longer under Amelia's thumb and was able to protect his kingdom and princess in an honorable and noble way.

She smiled to herself. Even though she had to keep her magic a secret from Uncle Waazir, it was good for her too. Amelia and every other owner or employer Myra had had over the years wanted to abuse and exploit her magic and heritage. They wanted to twist it in ways it was never meant to be used, and now she was able to lean into the way it was intended.

When she reached her room, the door was already open, and her heart sank into her stomach. Her door was never open unless she left it that way. Her hands shook, and she swallowed in a poor attempt to remain calm. It all had been too good to be true. She'd promised herself she would keep a low profile and not practice magic, but she had been swept away by it once again. This was bound to happen one of these days, but why did it have to be so soon?

Uncle Waazir stood at the table next to the fire, a letter clutched in his hand, and the others were scattered through the room. All the correspondence the villagers had sent her over the last weeks. Mama's trunk was open, the herbs and ingredients smashed.

With a steadying breath, Myra straightened her shoulders. She wasn't going to back down from him this time. She was a grieving child before, but now she was a grown woman who made her own choices. "What are you doing in my room?"

Uncle Waazir sneered and crumpled the letter in his hand before tossing it into the blazing fire. "I'll be asking the questions. What is all of this? I should have known you were still practicing your evil magic."

"It's not evil. And who told you?"

He crossed his arms in front of him and looked down at her over his pointed nose. "A villager came to the door while you were gone and said he saw you take someone's soul away yesterday."

Myra clenched her jaw. "I did nothing of the sort. A family had a loved one who was passing on and wanted me to perform Stula's rights. I don't kill people."

He took a handful of letters and shoved them in her face, his eyes blazing like the fire warming the room. "Then what is all this? That is all your kind does! You take lives! I will not have it in this house, and you swore to your father you no longer did these things!"

His voice rose with each sentence, and he stood before her nose to nose, lording over her to make her afraid. His yells echoed through the room, but Myra continued to breathe in and out, unwilling to let him think he shook her. She was exhausted of letting other people control her and her magic.

"It is who I am, and the villagers asked for my help, so I did my duty. Which is more than what I can say for you. I have seen the state of some portions of the town, which is supposed to be in the car of my father and when he is gone, in yours. If the people are dying, it is hardly my fault."

Waazir's mustache trembled, and he crumpled another letter. They stared at one another for what felt like an eternity until he finally spoke, quiet and lethal. "Get out. We will not have this in this home again. I told your father at the solstice he shouldn't have permitted you to stay, but he swore you no longer used your magic. You tricked him, and I knew you would. I've already written to him of your treachery."

A cold breeze blew through the room, blowing all the letters in circles like a snowstorm. Waazir's eyes grew wide. "What is this? What have you summoned?"

Mama—or whoever the spirit was—wasn't happy with the situation. She could make Waazir's life a living nightmare. Myra smiled up at him as though this was all her doing. "Wouldn't you love to know?"

But then, his face calmed. The way a storm calms right when you're in the middle of it and you know the worst is yet to come. "Well, I won't have to worry about it any longer."

From his pocket, Uncle Waazir pulled another piece of paper. He unfolded it and held it out to Myra. "I found this in one of your pockets, and I think it is the perfect solution to our little predicament." It was the advertisement for the Golden Palace needing ladies' maids for the pageant. But the pageant was to begin in only a few days. "I've already inquired, and they need one more person. They're aware you'll be arriving soon."

Myra's heart sank. No. Not the same palace where Amelia was. Not again. She shook her head. "You can't make me."

"Out!" he shouted over the cold wind blowing through the room, and guards appeared in an instant.

They grasped Myra by the arms, and she tried to rip herself away from them, but their grip was so strong it would leave bruises later. "You can't do this."

"Take her away!"

No. This wasn't happening. Not again. It was exactly as it was seventeen years ago when Mama died. But she would fight it. Even if they kicked her out, she would fight. With every step, she screamed and yelled and pulled and twisted and kicked. She called on Stula, and the spirit followed them through the manor to the door where her travel bag was already waiting and packed for her.

Odalis ran toward the scene and grabbed one of the guard's tunics. "Let her go! She is the lady of the house. This isn't right!"

"Off me, woman!" The guard pushed her aside, and she fell back, hitting her head on the wall.

"Odalis!" Myra yelled, but no matter how hard she tried, she couldn't escape. They all must have been followers of Aros, for their arms felt like steel, and they pushed her out of the manor and into a carriage, taking her away.

Chapter Nine

ALVIS

THE DESERTS SET BEFORE ALVIS MOCKED HIM. WHY MOTHER INSISTED he was at her side for every step of planning the pageant, he didn't know. He should be assisting in plans for the new school in the city, or how to find the still missing *Mystic*, or ways to strengthen the irrigation system in the drier areas of the kingdom. He was good at those things. He enjoyed those tasks. Not deciding between pudding or dumplings for the dessert they'd be having in only a few days when the women for the pageant arrived.

He leaned forward in his seat and pointed at one of the treats laid out on the table. "The dumplings look pleasant." It wouldn't matter which one he picked anyway. While his choice would be delicious, the queen would find another one even more so to put the entire crowd in awe.

Mother tapped her thin finger on the table, the long talon of a nail clicking against the wood. "Those are lovely. But what about the pudding?"

Alvis held back a grin and took a spoon to taste the swirl of chocolate cream. She was correct. As usual. "That is exceptional."

"Of course it is." Mother waved to the servants to take the remaining dishes away. "Now for the wine selection."

It needed to stop at some point. Alvis rubbed the back of his neck. He couldn't look at another array of food or drink for another minute. "Mother, I'm not sure if I'm needed here."

Trays of wine and glasses were already being brought out, and Alvis could feel a headache coming on. Mother's face fell at his words and then hardened with her brows furrowed and mouth tight.

"Alvis, I wish you would take this more seriously. It's your wife we're trying to please. You'd think this would be important to you, but instead you're behaving like a petulant adolescent. They don't have to only impress you, you know. We need to convince them as well. Any one of these women could decide she doesn't want to be your queen. We need to show them the best Oxare, meaning you, has to offer."

Or the queen, rather. Celebrations and desserts and wines were a fabulous way to get to know Queen Shideh. If they wanted to get to know Alvis, they would have much better luck joining him in the library or visiting the city. But his mother did have a point—he could have cooperated more.

"I am taking this seriously. But we all know you're much better at this than I am."

This must have appeased her, at least for the moment, as she patted his arm and reached for a glass to begin the tasting. As she did, a servant walked into the room and bowed before Alvis.

"Your highness, there is a girl here to see you."

Mother laughed after she swallowed the red wine she'd been tasting. "Already? They aren't supposed to be here for another few days!"

The servant stammered, "Not for the pageant. It's a girl in need of employment as a lady's maid."

Lady's maid? Another thing he shouldn't have anything to do with when it came to this ridiculous pageant. "I thought Vikas was taking care of all of that."

He shifted back and forth between his feet and clasped his hands behind him. "He is, your highness. But this particular young woman asked for you specifically. She insists she knows you and you had told her to seek him out if she ever had need. Mary is her name?"

Something sparked inside Alvis, like a candle on a cold day. It was small and could be snuffed out at any moment, but it still flickered deep in his chest. He straightened in his seat. She'd changed her mind? It couldn't be. She'd been so determined when they parted all those weeks ago on the boat. "Myra?"

The servant's eyes brightened in recognition of the name and nodded. "Yes. That was it. Her story is correct? You know this young lady?"

Mother paused her wine tasting. She placed her fingertips to her chest as she swallowed, but a mischievous smile crept across her red lips. "Alvis, you know a servant girl? What have you been up to?"

Alvis felt his face warm, and he cleared his throat. "She was of assistance in Cresin. I told her if she needed anything to let me know as a way to thank her."

"How kind of you." The smile vanished from her face, and a light dimmed from her eyes.

"What? Are you disappointed that's all it is? Do you want me to marry a servant girl? I didn't realize that was all it took to make you satisfied."

"Oh, don't be ridiculous." The queen waved one tray of wine away and gestured for another to be brought over. "Of course I don't want you to marry a servant girl. But it would have been nice to know you've done something other than wallow all this time."

He shouldn't have expected any other sort of answer. He hadn't been wallowing either. He preferred to think he was being contemplative lately. Determining what—or perhaps who in this situation—he wanted. He got to his feet and went toward the door, equally excited to leave this conversation and tasting as he was to see if it really was Myra who was there to see him. "I'll see her immediately. Lead the way."

His heart pounded as they made their way to the grand hall where they met with visitors. As much as he'd tried to push Myra from his mind, he couldn't help but worry and wonder about where she was and if they'd ever cross paths again. When they entered the hall, Myra stood in the center, her petite but strong body leaning back with jaw dropped almost to the floor as she stared at the painted ceiling depicting Ray and Luna at sunrise. The light streaming into the room caught in her brown hair, giving it a shining bronze-and-gold glimmer. A smile overtook him at the sight, even if she was in a simple dress. It was a step up from the servant garments Amelia had her wear.

The light inside him warmed at the sight of his friend. At least he hoped she was his friend. He could use one these days. But something else stirred inside him. Deep in his stomach, a roiling heat that, if he wasn't careful, could become a raging fire and needed to be squelched as soon as possible.

With as quiet of steps as he could, he walked across the floor and stood at her side to look at the ceiling along with her. "It's remarkable, isn't it? It took the artist a year to paint."

Myra jumped at the sound of his voice, and her soft brown eyes grew large when she looked at him. Dropping her satchel, she grasped the edges of her dress and curtsied. "Your highness."

Alvis waved away the servant who'd escorted him and, once he was gone, focused on Myra again. "So you changed your mind?"

A blush appeared on her cheeks, making her warm brown skin a lovely dusty rose color. From her pocket, she pulled out a notice for hire and showed it to him. "Only for a couple of months, if the position is still available."

Alvis didn't need to look at the notice. The last he heard, they were in fact still looking for one more, but even if they weren't, he would have been sure to find a place for her. "It is, and it's yours."

Myra narrowed her eyes, her brows furrowed over them, and she folded the paper and put it in her pocket again. "Don't you want to interview me? Run it by the man who is hiring? I know there are many important women coming, and they should have the best service—"

Alvis raised a hand, and she stopped talking. "I can't imagine anyone better suited. And if you need to stay longer than the pageant, you know you are more than welcome. We can find a place for you."

Myra's back was as straight as a pole, and her voice as strong. "I only need the two months. My situation has recently changed, and I only need the employment while I decide what to do next. I would hate to overstep and take advantage of your hospitality."

He hoped his disappointment didn't show on his face. It would be for the best anyway. All Myra had ever expressed was the want to be independent and on her own. If he could help her at least for these next several weeks, then that was what he would do. It was what a friend would do. He offered a smile. "However I can be of service. I'll speak to Vikas and sort out the details to be sure you receive your pay and make arrangements for the lucky young woman you'll be assisting."

With an outstretched arm, Alvis guided Myra out of the grand hall and toward the servants' wing where Vikas handled all the hiring and coordinating. They walked in silence, and Alvis struggled to find what to speak to her about and to not stare. Now that he was able to look at her more closely, while her dark-blue dress was simple, it was finely made. It wasn't the garment of a servant by any means. But there was a tired hollowness behind her gentle eyes.

What happened between when they'd parted on the boat and now?

Through the whole walk, Myra's jaw was dropped as she took in the Golden Palace. Farren Castle in Cresin was beautiful and nothing to scoff at. But it didn't have the same awe factor the Golden Palace did with all the paintings and engraved walls and pillars. The entire place was filled with marble and glass, with wide-open windows and rooms to let the breeze waft through the building. Especially on the hot summer days.

So many questions ran through his mind as to where she'd been, how she was, and why she looked as tired as she did. But in the short time he'd known her, she never shared many details about herself or her life, and the last thing he wanted was to pry and make her uncomfortable. If she wanted to tell him about what led her there, she would in her own time.

"So you're already wanting to find a new bride?" Myra asked, her light voice breaking the silence and echoing off the walls.

Ah. Yes. The subject he didn't want to face. But even if she never brought it up, it would be there in front of them each day. It wasn't as though he wanted to talk about the pageant to her, but maybe if he shared a little, it would encourage her to trust him too. "I have a duty to my family and kingdom," he explained. "My family needs an heir to the throne, and there are many noble families I can align myself with now. It would be foolish to let them all find other matches before I had the chance to find my own queen."

Without the information about Father's sickness, the words felt hallow and silly. He knew Myra would be less than impressed by the explanation, but they didn't want people knowing about Father yet. Even though he didn't owe her, or anyone else, an explanation.

Myra only raised her brows. "Oh. I see."

She didn't see at all, and he wished she could. But he kept his mouth shut. Everyone would know the real reason in time, and he didn't need to defend himself to anyone. But there was something about Myra that made him want her to understand.

They arrived at the room, and Alvis introduced her to Vikas, who was happy and eager to have someone with so much experience and such a high recommendation from Alvis himself. They arranged her pay and her day off and determined she would serve Lady Charis from the kingdom of Marali. The women would all arrive in a few days, which gave Myra time to settle into her quarters and prepare for Lady Charis. Some of the women's belongings were already arriving at the palace, and any of the lady's maids who had been hired to assist, and other servants available, were busy preparing the rooms for them. It was going to be a full and busy two months.

On top of all that, Myra had her own fittings and preparations to have done for herself. In the Golden Palace, they always made sure the servants had simple and comfortable, but fine and well-made clothing and quarters. They were a representation of the royal family, and if they were to serve royalty, they needed to feel like it.

Not wanting to go back to Mother just yet, Alvis escorted Myra to her room. In silence, again. "I hope you find this acceptable."

For a moment, it looked as though Myra's eyes were misty. But any hint of emotion was gone in an instant. "Yes, this looks fine. Thank you."

"Someone will be here shortly to take your measurements. In the meantime, you can unpack and rest for a bit."

Myra lifted her satchel off her back slightly and shrugged. "Won't take me long."

Alvis's cheeks heated. She owned less than she had when they'd gotten off the riverboat. What a foolish thing for him to say. Each time he was with her, he saw more and more how much he had in comparison. It wasn't as though he wasn't aware of his privilege or the differences in class before. He wasn't that naïve and sheltered. When he was around Myra though, ever since he met her, the differences in their lives glared out to him like blinding light. He didn't know what to do about it.

"Nevertheless, I'll let you rest. It's good to see you though. I'll be glad to have you here these next few weeks."

At least he could stop worrying about her for a little while and learn about where she came from and where she was off to next. It would also be good to have someone he trusted here during this whole ridiculous circus.

For the first time since she'd arrived, a genuine smile appeared over her face. "It's good to see you too."

Chapter Ten

MYRA

HER OWN ROOM. WHEN ALVIS SHOWED IT TO HER, RELIEF AND COMFORT settled over her like a warm blanket. Even in comparison to Papa's manor, the room might not have been as ornate or spacious but was still lovely. She was in the Golden Palace and with her own room, and a seamstress was there taking her measurements. When not under the control of Amelia, Myra was well treated at Farren Castle. They had good clothing, delicious food, and fine accommodations. But even there she shared her room with another girl. Her clothes were simple and durable. She always looked put together and sharp, but easy to blend into the background unnoticed.

That wasn't the case in the Golden Palace. Here, the servants were as much of the ornamentation and decoration as everything and everyone else. They were there to be shown off and displayed like trophies. The clothes she was provided with while she waited for her custom-made ones were comfortable and flexible for a long day of work. But they still made Myra feel elegant and refined.

She could only imagine what sort of accommodations would be given to the women participating in the pageant.

When Myra arrived at the Golden Palace, she'd stood in front of the gate as though a spell had her glued to the spot, unable to move forward. For a moment, she considered turning around and finding another place to go. But one of Waazier's men nudged her forward, and she couldn't make an escape without word getting to her uncle. After she went inside and they left her alone, she again thought about escaping and making it on her own somewhere else. Then, she saw portraits of the royal family and the image of Alvis's golden eyes looking out at her. Her chest warmed, and she thought it wouldn't be so terrible to see him again. If anything, he could help her make connections for where to go after this job was done. So she'd gone in.

As embarrassing as the situation was, Myra was glad she did.

She sat at the simple wooden table to write to Cal and let him know of yet another change of address. Where to even begin? She couldn't wrap her mind around the events of the day. It would be a lie to say part of her near tears were from relief of being out from under Uncle Waazier's eye. She might have settled into a routine there but was far from happy. Why did he send her here, though, of all places? Knowing Uncle Waazier, it couldn't be a simple, convenient way to get her out of the house. There must have been more to it.

Ever since she'd arrived at the palace, she couldn't calm her pounding heart and had to breathe deep to keep her hands from shaking. When Alvis stood next to her, it was like her heart had stopped. His golden eyes danced when he spoke to her, and his smile made her warm all the way from her head to her toes.

Myra grasped the pen together in her hand as though the silly crush she'd developed could be squashed while she wrote. She'd hoped her time away from him would make her forget the way his gentle voice caressed her like an embrace, or how his eyes made her knees weak. Even if there had been moments during their travels she swore he looked at her in a way she knew she looked at him, it was ridiculous to consider. Alvis was the crown prince of Oxare, and to him, she was only a servant he felt he owed a favor.

Alvis didn't know her past and where she came from. She could tell him, and technically she would be eligible to be part of the pageant if it was what she wanted. Uncle Waazir would have a good laugh at that. A daughter of Stula vying for the favor of a prince. That aside, her father's title and wealth was likely miniscule compared to those women who were really coming to the pageant. The match wouldn't make sense.

She took in a deep breath to focus on her letter once again. It was a silly infatuation, like the one she'd had years ago when she first came to Farren Castle. He'd been much older than her and worked in the stables, 'and had shown Myra kindness. Nothing ever came of it, and the crush went away when he started courting one of the kitchen maids, and that was that. This was the same. It had been so long since a kind man paid any attention to her, and it was natural she'd been drawn to Alvis. Once the pageant started and he courted the other women, any feelings lingering would float away in the wind.

Then she would leave and never think of the prince ever again.

THE NEXT DAY, BEFORE MYRA EVEN HAD THE CHANCE TO SIP HER coffee, a letter was delivered to her room by a boy, maybe around eleven or twelve, in plain white clothes. Servants to help the servants? The Golden Palace certainly was different from working for Amelia. Myra took the letter from him, and he hurried off to his next destination.

Myra scowled at the handwriting. It was from Uncle Waazier. He might have sent her there, but if he thought she was going to keep any connections with him, he was mistaken. Whatever warped games he was playing, she wasn't going to have any of it and hoped to never see him or speak to him again.

"Um…boy? Can you come back here please?"

The boy returned with a quizzical look on his face. "Did I do something wrong, ma'am?"

Myra bristled at being called "ma'am." It was worse than when Odalis referred to her as "my lady."

She shook her head. "No, you did nothing wrong." She held the letter out to him and pointed out the handwriting. "You see this? If you ever see a letter with this handwriting here for me again, throw it to the fire."

The boy blinked a few times and nodded. "Yes, ma'am."

Good. At least that was settled. Myra went back into her room and threw it into the fire, the flames offering a satisfying crackle as they burned Waazier's words.

As Myra finished her coffee, Lady Charis's belongings began to arrive. She had more boxes and packages sent to the palace than any of the other contestants, and Myra spent most of the next few days unpacking her trunks and bags leading up to the arrival of the other women. It was as though Lady Charis thought she'd already won Alvis's heart and was planning to stay for forever instead of only a couple of months. Along with the luggage, there were strict instructions on how to arrange the room and how to care for each belonging.

She slung a bag from the latest arrival over her shoulder and picked up one of the boxes. What could one woman possibly need all of this for? Myra took a deep breath and made her way to what would be Lady Charis's room. It didn't matter, and it wasn't her business. Myra was being paid handsomely for this, and she would do it to the best of her ability.

Another lady's maid had arrived that morning, later than any of the others as the pageant contestants would arrive the next day. There weren't nearly as many trunks and boxes on her cart, but the containers were large and looked heavy. The maid swung her luxurious blond locks to the side and with surprising strength pushed the cart into the room. Her sharp blue eyes met Myra's, and she raised her brows.

"Are you going to help me or just stare? Not that I blame you." She winked.

Myra froze and felt the blood drain from her face. The girl from the tavern with the feather in her hat. A murderer was going to be one of the ladies' maids. Without thinking, Myra dropped everything she held and stomped up to the young woman. "What are you doing here?"

The blonde stood upright and rested a hand on her cocked hip. She smirked. "The tavern girl. Fancy seeing you here."

Myra clenched her jaw and hissed at her through her teeth. "You shouldn't be here. I'll call the authorities." She lowered her voice. "You're a murderer."

The other woman rolled her eyes and leaned forward like they were fellow conspirators. "What if I were to tell you he had killed several of my friends not long ago? Besides, I saw how he treated you. I doubt you're missing him much."

While her voice was light and teasing, there was a darkness filling her eyes that Myra couldn't deny. She was no stranger to thieves and killers, especially since technically she and Cal were those things as well, and Myra learned to tell when people were lying, and this woman wasn't. She took in a deep breath and took a small step back. "I'm sorry for your loss. But you should have let the law deal with him then, instead of taking matters into your own hands. You shouldn't be bringing your trouble into the palace."

The woman chuckled and crossed her arms over her chest. "Life and death are complicated. Besides, I doubt they'd believe me, and I doubt they'd believe you if you were to turn me in. I heard the serving girl there is thought of as an accomplice. She was seen performing Stulan magic in the moments he died."

Myra gulped. Rumors traveled quickly. "That's different. I didn't kill him."

The woman raised her brows. "Maybe you didn't kill *him*, but with your gifts, there haven't been any casualties? Perhaps when you were younger with less control?"

Myra gulped. The woman wasn't wrong. As a child, Myra had a difficult time controlling her magic. Usually, it was only leaving a trail of dead grass and flowers in her path, but there had been other incidents... some of them even intentional. Her first master had made sure of that with his odd experiments. He had been fascinated by death and those who followed Stula, and he loved to push the boundaries between this world and the afterlife. She didn't want to go along with the experiments, but she'd only been a child and found out the hard way what happened when she didn't obey orders.

After Cal's family won Myra in a bet, she didn't practice her magic except for one time. It was how Amelia had found Cal and Myra in the first place. Their parents had been killed, and Cal went out to seek revenge. He thought Myra stayed behind, but she'd followed. Her anger and grief at the loss of the only family she'd had since Mama died rose to the surface, and she doled out vengeance along with her brother. It might not have been as violent as his, but did the job just the same. To the very few people who knew the story, Cal only told them about his part and left Myra out of it. The only ones who knew the truth were him, Myra, and Amelia.

That day still haunted Myra, and it took years for her to sleep well again. She'd never killed outright since then, but it didn't mean Amelia didn't find other ways to abuse and misuse her magic.

The woman winked, bringing Myra back to the present. She must have seen on Myra's face all the answers she needed. "That's what I thought. But don't worry. Your secret is safe with me, daughter of Stula. How about we keep each other's secrets, hm?" She outstretched her hand. "I'm Finley."

Myra eyed her cautiously. Part of her wanted to go to Alvis and report there was a killer in their midst. This was a woman who knew exactly what she was doing, not a child grieving over her parents who didn't understand the extent of her powers. But as Myra remembered the scene of the murder, she couldn't help but wonder if there was more to it than met the eye. Finley and her companion who had run away together didn't look like they'd been servants or working class. As casual as their tight pants, tunics, and boots had been, they were well made. Expensive fabric and shining shoes, and the hat Finley wore was far from inconspicuous. Also, Myra couldn't afford the rumors of her involvement spreading.

But a man was dead because of Finley. And her friends were dead because of him.

Although in the grand scheme of things, there were times in Myra's past she'd dealt with worse. As Finley had said—life and death were complicated.

She extended her hand out to Finley and shook it. "Myra."

Finley's smirk spread into a wide grin, and her blue eyes brightened. "Good to meet you, Myra. Now, let's help each other with these things. I don't know about you, but I'm beat."

Myra had to admit, the help would be nice, as well as having an ally. It wasn't as though she and Alvis could spend time together the way they had on the riverboat anyway. She needed someone else in her corner, and in an odd way, someone like Finley could be useful.

Together they pushed the cart Finley was using into the room and unloaded the trunks and boxes, and then took it back out to retrieve the rest of Lady Charis's belongings. Which took significantly longer. By the time they were done, Finley was yawning and stretching her arms over her head, and a glazed look fell over her eyes.

"I should get some rest before tomorrow," Finley announced. "Think you can handle the rest of it on your own?"

Myra nodded. "Trust me, this is the least of it. You should have seen the trunks of gowns I had to unpack yesterday."

Finley chuckled. "Yes, I've heard rumors about Lady Charis. Watch out for that one."

Myra pinched her brows together as Finley made her way to the doorway. "What sort of rumors?"

Finley waved her away and yawned again. "Another time. See you later."

With that, her new…friend?…was gone. Myra watched the space where Finley had stood as though she was still there and would reveal her secrets at any moment. As strong and quick with a sword as Finley was, she grew tired easily. She must not have been used to physical labor. Myra wondered if Finley had ever worked as a servant before. There was a finesse about her Myra usually didn't see in servants, but her hands were calloused and her arms and legs strong, unlike most noblewomen.

Life was complicated.

Myra worked through the rest of the afternoon and into the evening and took dinner alone in Lady Charis's room as she finished unpacking. Finley's warning made her nervous, and she wanted everything to be perfect in time for the morning when the women would arrive. It wouldn't do to start off on the wrong foot. Otherwise, it would be a long six weeks.

It was late by the time Myra went to bed in the servants' quarters, which wasn't far from the hall where the contestants would be so the maids could be there to assist at a moment's notice. There were a couple of other maids still milling about, but Myra didn't see or hear a word from Finley since they had parted ways.

Not that it was any of Myra's business. She yawned and stretched after changing into a nightdress and lay down on the bed. Her stomach turned at the thought of the pageant starting the next day. The idea of watching Alvis attempting to woo all these women was nauseating, and Finley's words didn't bring Myra much comfort either.

She reached across the bed to the notebook she'd kept there and worked on writing a letter to Cal. She'd already finished and sent the letter she'd started the other night to inform him of her new temporary residence. Usually, she waited for a response before writing again, but her mind and heart were too full to keep it all to herself. Cal always had a way of putting her at ease. Even if they couldn't be in the same room talking, it helped to still be able to share what was on her mind with him. For so long, he'd been the one person in the world she could count on, but now they were apart.

Yes, it was by her own choice, and deep down, Myra knew it was the right one. It didn't mean she couldn't miss her brother from time to time though.

But through her exhaustion, her head fell back against the pillows, and she was asleep before she was halfway through the letter.

Myra woke with a start when the bell on the wall of her room clanged like a gong. She bolted upright and looked around the room. It was still pitch dark without a hint of sunlight. What time was it? The bell rang again, and she stared at it in disbelief.

The bell was only for the use of the lady she was serving or for emergencies. She crawled out of bed and found her robe discarded on an armchair off to the side of the room. With a yawn, she pulled it on and went out into the hallway.

No other bells were ringing, and she was the only one out of their room. No emergency then. She wrapped the robe around her good and tight and wandered to the hall where the women for the pageant were to be staying. They weren't supposed to arrive for several hours though.

The door to Lady Charis's room was propped open, and light from the sun lanterns poured into the hallway. There was a sinking feeling in Myra's stomach when she approached. It couldn't be.

A woman with long wavy light-blond hair and pale skin popped her head out the door and glared at Myra with an intense gaze only made greater by the dark kohl around her eyes. Her pink lip curled in a sneer. "It's about time you got here. I have to get ready."

Myra blinked a few times as she processed what was happening in her sleepy haze. How much sleep had she gotten? A couple of hours, maybe?

The woman stepped out of the room and snapped her fingers in front of Myra's face. She was pale, with her cheeks turning bright red with frustration. It looked as though she'd never seen the sun a day in her life, she was so pale. Not quite the same porcelain as Princess Eira was, but close.

"Hello? Can you understand me?" The woman enunciated each word loud enough to wake the rest of the palace in a slow pace as though Myra were a child.

"Lady Charis?"

The woman threw her head back and her hands in the air. The long drapery of her red sleeves waved about like wings. "Of course! Didn't they tell you anything?"

Myra dipped into a small curtsy. "My apologizes, my lady. You weren't supposed to come for a few hours after the sunrise service was over."

Lady Charis's eyes went wide, and she placed her hands on her hips. "Exactly. It's the perfect way to get a leg up in the competition. Prince Alvis is wholly devoted to Ray, and what better way to impress him than to be there for the sunrise service?"

Myra opened and closed her mouth in search of what to say. She needed coffee. Badly. Maybe someone from the kitchen staff was already awake and would have some prepared. "There are no words as to what a surprise that would be."

"I know. I'm brilliant like that." Lady Charis ran her fingers through her long silky hair and tossed it off to the side. "Now come on and help me dress. Whoever set up my room did everything wrong, and it's going to take forever to find the perfect ensemble. We only have two hours until the service begins." She turned on her heel and went inside the room, her dress fluttering behind her like a river of blood.

Myra's heart dropped. But she'd followed the instructions exactly.

How was the room not set up properly? And there was still two *hours* until the service? This was going to be a long day.

Charis' popped her head back out again. "Well? What are you waiting for? Come on!"

Myra dipped in another curtsy. "Yes, of course, my lady. I'm coming."

Chapter Eleven

MYRA

AFTER SEARCHING THROUGH ALL THE TRUNKS WHAT FELT LIKE A MILLION times, and pairing together different pieces of outfits, Charis finally decided on an understated but elegant mustard-yellow—almost gold—dress with wide long sleeves and flowing skirt with a belt around her narrow waist. Nothing like Oxarian fashions, and she was going to stand out among the small crowd. Especially since there was a lot of physical movement during the service, which Myra had tried to explain to Charis, but she wouldn't hear of it.

Maybe they could use her as the sun if it was a cloudy morning, her dress shone so brightly.

There wasn't time to do anything different with her hair other than place a gold chain around her head that had a small jewel resting on her forehead. Charis said she didn't want to appear as though she were trying too hard anyway.

Even if she had arrived hours early so she could attend a service no one else would be going to.

Charis permitted Myra a few minutes to get changed herself, and she chose plain loose dark-blue pants and a blue top with big sleeves that capped at the wrists and landed just above the waistline of her pants. Simple, easy, comfortable. But no time for coffee.

Myra had to remind Charis to remove her shoes when they arrived at the temple, at which she rolled her eyes but complied. The temple was a majestic stone building with pillars as tall as mountains and an imposing staircase at the front, which gave the appearance that Ray himself would come down to earth from the sky. Myra had only been there a few days, and even though she'd gone to a sunset service or two, the grandness of it all still put her in awe. She paused at the head of the still rectangle pool to take it all in.

Charis, on the other hand, only groaned in frustration and waved her hands to the sides, not noticing any of the beauty around her. "Where are we supposed to sit?" Her voice echoed through the room, and the few people around them stopped in their path to look.

Myra wanted to shush her but had a feeling that wouldn't be a welcome gesture, so she lowered her voice and hoped Charis would follow suit. "We don't sit in chairs. You go wherever you like, except at the very front. That's where the royal family sits."

One of the temple priests in golden robes greeted them with a bow of his head and offered them cushions to sit on. Myra accepted them with a smile and then showed the cushion to Charis.

"We use these. You can pick a spot."

Charis eyed the place where the priests laid cushions on the floor for the royal family in front of the pool. She tugged on Myra's sleeve. "Which spot will be Prince Alvis?"

"The one on the left."

With a resolute nod of her head, Charis made her way toward the front and pointed to a spot on the left side of the pool. It was behind where the royal family would sit, but off to the side enough where Alvis could see her in his peripheral vision. Once the cushion was in place, Charis sat on it prim as a flower and spread her skirt out around her in a delicate circle.

Myra stifled a yawn as she sat next to her and dreamed of coffee and food. She hoped the service would go fast.

Charis ran her fingers through her hair and kept adjusting her locks, so they fell in perfect waves over her shoulders. "I'm dedicated to the goddess Efarae. You know, inspiration."

"Yes, I know who Efarae is."

Charis raised a brow. "Well, I don't know how well-educated servants are, and there are many deities to keep track of. Anyway. We have chairs and stools and benches everywhere in our temples. Then we arrange them in different ways depending on what sort of service or performance is being given. None of this sitting on the floor. Is it dirty? Who knows who's been walking around here."

She was going to have to get used to sitting on the floor if she planned on being queen of Oxare. Some households used dining room tables, but many had cushions and blankets on the floor. And since they rarely wore shoes inside, the floors were able to be kept clean easily. But Myra decided now wasn't the best time to bring this up.

"What art do you practice?" she asked instead. She hadn't known many people dedicated to Efarae who weren't priests or priestesses or part of a traveling group. But those people had to go through intense training, and Myra had a hunch Charis wasn't interested in that.

"Oh, this and that. I've tinkered with painting, which didn't last long, performance art for a while, a few instruments here and there, but right now I'm working on my voice. I'll work on something for a few months until I see that's not the gift the goddess has wanted me to have and then move on. I've noticed the goddess wants me to experiment, and my inspiration likes to play with different mediums."

Trumpets sounded from the balconies, and Myra was grateful because it meant their service was to start and she didn't have to respond. It seemed to her Charis didn't want to stick with something long enough to perfect it, rather than it not being her gift. From what she understood, Efarae's magic did more to enhance and build up on what someone practiced and learned—not automatically give them the talent. But that wasn't for Myra to comment on anyway.

The royal family processed in, the King Rahim with Queen Shideh and Prince Alvis behind him. Alvis nodded to those he passed, and Lady Charis preened when he came by her. While he gave no indication of recognizing her and smiled the way he did to everyone else, Charis's chest puffed out like a proud bird.

Priests stood all throughout the temple, so everyone present had a view of someone leading and guided the group various chants, with one priest in the front to lead them all. They read from sacred texts and followed the priests in a series of movements where they stretched, focused on their breathing and prayer to focus their minds for a new day. Some of the positions Myra still hadn't gotten the hang of, and she found herself losing balance through the routine, but thought it was relaxing, nevertheless.

At her side, Lady Charis grunted and moaned. "My body can't move this way."

A small cry disrupted the peace, and Myra's attention went to the source of the sound. Finley was there only a couple of rows behind Myra and to the right. She'd lost her balance, and as she returned to her standing position, she wiggled her shoulders and waved to Myra. When noticing Charis, she grimaced. Myra offered a small wave back, and from the look on Finley's face, she had a feeling the loss of balance was only a way to get Myra's attention. At her side, Charis scoffed.

"How rude to interrupt the service in such a way."

It was no more of an interruption than Charis's moaning and groaning and complaining.

As the sun rose higher in the sky, the congregation was on their feet, and the priest in the front of the room made his way up the steep staircase. By the time he reached the top, the sun had risen, and it looked as though he held it in his hands. The glow was almost blinding, but the room turned shades of pink and gold with the arrival of the morning.

When the service was complete, Charis wiped the dust she was sure on her dress—which there wasn't any as the mats and floor were immaculate—and fluffed her curls. "I had no idea the sunrise service was so...active. Why didn't you tell me? I would have worn something more practical."

Myra tried not to sigh and knelt to gather the mats and cushions to return to the priests for cleaning. She had tried to tell her, but the woman wouldn't listen. "My apologies, my lady."

She'd learned quickly with Amelia that most times, simple matters such as these weren't worth arguing about unless she wanted to deal with a severe punishment. Charis didn't seem to be as cruel as Amelia, and she wasn't worried about the same type of abuse. But considering they'd only known each other for a few hours, it was best to play it safe.

Although she had a hunch it was going to be a long couple of months no matter what she did.

Charis squealed and returned to primping herself. "He's coming this way! No! Don't look, don't look!"

Which was difficult to do, considering Myra was facing Alvis. There was a question in his eyes as he approached, which Myra couldn't answer even silently without Charis noticing. He cleared his throat, and Charis turned to see him. She placed her hand over her chest, and her eyes widened in feigned surprise. She knelt into a deep curtsy, and Myra followed suit.

"Your highness."

Alvis bowed and gestured for them to rise again. Any hint of his confusion was wiped away, and all that could be seen on his face was a gentle and welcoming smile. "I'm afraid we haven't met yet. I wanted to be sure to welcome you to the Golden Palace."

Charis extended her hand for her him to grasp, which he did with only a slight hesitation and kissed it softly. "The pleasure is all mine, your highness. I'm Lady Charis of Cloishire in Marali."

Alvis's face brightened, but Myra noticed his throat bobbing as he gulped. "Wonderful, you're here for the pageant. Although, I thought everyone wasn't supposed to arrive for another few hours."

There was only a hint of the edge of panic in his voice from being caught off guard, and Myra's heart went out to him. He wasn't quite prepared to have to entertain and impress any ladies yet. But if Charis noticed, she didn't give any sign. She only smiled and batted her lashes at him.

"I know. I'd overestimated how long it would take to get here and arrived late last night. I thought about getting a room at an inn, but I was so close to the palace I thought I would give it a try. Thankfully, I was let in and was able to get a few hours of sleep. But then I was so excited for everything, I woke up early!" She laughed at herself and her slick lie. "So I thought, why not come to the sunrise service? It's good to start the day off well by greeting Ray. Don't you agree?"

Alvis clasped his hands behind his back and nodded. "Yes, wise choice. I'm glad you arrived safely, and we were able to accommodate you. I know Myra here has been hard at work the last few days preparing things for you."

Charis glanced at Myra as though she'd forgotten she was standing there. "Oh, yes. Of course. Myra has been a big help. Although, there are a few things we'll need to work on to make everything just right."

Myra's jaw clenched. She'd done everything exactly the way she'd been instructed. It was Charis who decided the instructions she'd been given were wrong. But she kept a placid smile on her face.

"I hope all this commotion didn't disturb your sleep, Myra?"

She paused and gripped the cushions and mats tighter. She was used to standing silently to the side and making herself as invisible as possible during conversations such as this. Yes, she and Alvis had always been friendly to each other. But those had been much different circumstances. "I…I'm fine. I'm just glad to be of service, your highness."

Even if she was only on a couple hours of sleep, and Charis had arrived this morning—not the night before—it was fine. She would get some food and coffee in her, and she'd be ready to face the day.

A glimmer of amusement danced behind Alvis's golden eyes. From their travels, he knew how she detested waking up early. "I'm sure you're doing a wonderful job. Well, I'll be having breakfast in my room so I can prepare myself for the big day. I'll be seeing you this evening."

He bowed, and the two women curtsied again. Charis practically swooned as he walked away. "I've always heard his younger brother was the handsome one, but he's quite good-looking, don't you agree? That dark wavy hair and golden eyes."

A priest came their way and took the cushions and mats from Myra's arms, for which she was grateful. They were getting a little heavy after standing there for so long. "Yes, he's nice to look at."

Charis rolled her eyes. "I can't wait for the other women to arrive so I can have some real woman-to-woman talk."

AFTER GETTING CHARIS SETTLED—AT LEAST FOR THE TIME BEING— with breakfast and a change of clothes, Myra finally made her way back to her own room to relax for a little while before she was sure Charis would come calling again. She opened the door, only to gasp and step back when she saw Finley was already in there, sitting in the armchair and nibbling at a pastry. On the side table were two steaming cups of coffee and a plate of food for breakfast.

"I see you met Lady Charis," Finley said as she licked her fingers.

"How…why…what are you doing in my room?"

"When I saw Lady Charis had already arrived, I had the hunch you were going to need food soon." She gestured to the bed. "Sit, sit, relax."

Myra sat on the bed with one leg tucked under her and grasped a mug of coffee. It was still warm. "But you just barged in here."

Finley only shrugged. "It wasn't hard."

Myra sighed. While it was unconventional, she was grateful there was someone looking out for her and had brought breakfast. She was starving. "Well…thank you for the food. It's definitely needed."

"If I'd been able to spike your coffee, I'm sure you'd be even more grateful. But I haven't found the kitchen's booze stash yet."

Myra couldn't help but chuckle. She was sure that would be tempting after a few days of serving Lady Charis.

Finley grabbed a piece of mango and bit into it. "So what do you think of Lady Charis?"

Myra thought of how to answer as she sipped at the coffee, taking in its rich scent. "She's…enthusiastic about being here."

Her companion threw her head back and laughed loudly. "You're too nice. That's going to have to change if you're going to deal with her."

"What do you know about it?" Myra tore off a piece of pastry and stuck it in her mouth. It practically melted on her tongue.

Finley leaned forward as though they were coconspirators in a devilish scheme. "I met her a few years ago in the Dravian Islands. She was at an event at a baron's castle. All the servants hated her because of her mistreatment, and you know they see *everything*. From what I've heard, she's been trying to nab a crown for years and will turn on anyone to get what she wants."

Myra knew this information should frighten her, or at least make her nervous. But after working with Amelia for so long, anyone—no matter how mean or unfair—would be easy to deal with. No terrible beatings for seemingly no reason unless her brother went out and killed someone? Sounded like paradise. In response, she merely shrugged.

"I can take care of myself. But thanks for the tip."

Finley leaned back in her chair again and propped her feet on the table. "Suit yourself. Just don't say I didn't warn you. She has her eyes on being queen and will stop at nothing to get it."

Myra made herself comfortable as well and scooted farther back on the bed so her back rested against the wall. "I'm sure Alvis will see right through her. He's very smart."

"If he's smart, he might take her seriously."

A gold-digging, self-serving woman who mistreated her servants? It was unlikely. Amelia had made advances on Alvis when he was in Cresin while Eira was missing, and he'd turned her down at every opportunity. Granted, he had no idea his betrothed was about to leave him for his brother and thought she was coming back…but for all he knew, she could also have been dead. But still. He was above those petty details.

"I doubt it, but why do you say that?"

Finley had taken a coin out of her pocket and tossed it up in the air, catching it in her palm as she spoke. "Because her family is richer than a god and has control over half her kingdom. As a future king who's on the rebound and needs a new alliance? He'd be a fool to push her aside. This isn't some cute little romantic contest to win his heart. These women are here to win a crown and a kingdom. If he happens to be kind to them and good in bed, it's a nice bonus."

Myra rested her hands in her lap, still grasping her mug. "Why are you telling me all this?"

Finley caught the coin one more time. "Because I felt bad for how things went at the tavern, and I want to show you that I'm not a completely terrible person. Besides, we'll both need a friend here, and I thought I'd extend an olive branch."

"Who is the lady you'll be serving?" Myra strummed her fingers against the side of the mug.

This brought a smile on Finley's face dazzling enough to make the stars fall out of the sky. "Lady Ai of the Dravian Islands. She's the future Countess of Hont in the Dravian Islands. She's my best friend. You met her at the tavern."

This almost made Myra spit out her drink. She gulped and sputtered. "What? The other woman who was there with you and ran away? The follower of Diar?"

Finley cocked her head to the side. "You noticed that?"

Myra felt heat rush to her cheeks. "I saw the way everyone was flirting with one another, and it coincided with who she made eye contact with."

"Interesting." She looked at Myra thoughtfully, as though she were tucking the information away in her mind for later use. "But yes, Lady Ai is my best friend."

"Why is a future countess best friends with a servant girl? Not that it's impossible, but highly unlikely."

Finley winked. "Let's just say there's more to her than meets the eye."

As terrible as Myra felt about gaining an alliance—if not a potential friendship—with a murderess, she had to admit she was terribly intriguing. She wondered what sort of stories and tricks Finley had up her sleeve. Myra took another sip of her coffee as she contemplated the woman in front of her.

"If your best friend is here, then why do you need my friendship?"

"Ai is going to be a bit preoccupied with the pageant. Who else am I supposed to spend time with while she's snagging a crown? Besides, I think there's more to you than you're letting on."

If she only knew.

Finley extended her mug out to Myra, making her sleeve fall to reveal a tattoo around her wrist, which made it appear she had a bracelet made of waves. The sign of her dedication to the water god, Colma. She had a hopeful, almost childlike look in her blue eyes. "Friends?"

It would be nice to have someone on her side for a change. Outside of Odalis and Alvis giving her this job, Myra hadn't had much luck in that area since arriving back in Oxare. She extended her mug out as well. "Friends."

Chapter Twelve

ALVIS

ALVIS TOOK HIS PLACE IN THE CENTER OF THE BALLROOM AND FACED THE staircase. Supposedly, his future wife was to walk down those stairs within a matter of minutes. He wiped his palms on the sides of his pants. All day, the women for the pageant had been arriving, and Alvis did everything in his power to avoid them. He'd done at least five prayer and stretching sessions to calm himself before the opening ceremony. When Lady Charis appeared at the sunrise service, it was like someone was strangling him. She'd been too early and caught him off guard when he wasn't prepared. It had made the event all too real, and he hoped neither Charis nor Myra noticed his nervousness.

How in the world was he supposed to woo all these women? He'd rarely attempted to woo anyone, and the few times he had out of curiosity, despite his betrothal to Eira, it hadn't gone well. He tripped over words and made a fool out of himself. The women would only smile and laugh politely out of kindness and because he was a crowned prince. Even the times when he and Eira had been intimate, it was from at first mutual curiosity and then as an outlet for their own desires. Over the last couple months, he'd been able to examine their relationship more closely and seen how there was no wooing or romance there.

It was a strong friendship, to be sure. There was mutual respect, admiration, and trust. But not the sort of love to sweep a woman off her feet. It was an arrangement.

Alvis swallowed and fixed the blood orange sash across his shoulder that was falling off. Maybe that was all these women wanted. An arrangement so they could have a crown of their own. Oddly, it made him relax a little more. He was used to arrangements and deals and transactions. Those he could do.

At his side, Nell shifted her weight from foot to foot and swung her deep-blue sari back and forth, making the beads rustle around her legs. Outside of the winter solstice, this was her first public event. For a little while, he'd considered letting Nell stay in her room and not bother with the opening feast and dance when he was to greet all the women. She was still nervous around crowds sometimes, and she was his ward—not a princess—so it wasn't necessary for her to attend every palace event. But he'd told her she could help, and as one of these women was supposedly to become his future wife and queen, he thought it would be good for her to meet them along with him. His choice would affect her too.

"How long is this going to be?" Nell looked up at him. One of her stray curls that hadn't made it into the fancy style that her governess piled on top of her head fell in her eye, and she tried to blow it away.

"It might be a while," Alvis admitted. "Each woman will come down the stairs and present herself and her kingdom, and we'll greet them and then have supper. If you're tired after that, you may return to your room if that is what you wish. But I would like for you to stay as long as you can. I could use the help."

Nell's lip curled. "How will I be able to help you?"

"Having someone I know and trust here with me is always helpful. You're the most honest person I know, and if there's something amiss with one of the women, I know you'll tell me." It was one of the gifts of Nell being so sheltered her whole life. She hadn't learned how to lie or hide her emotions well yet, and it made her refreshingly honest and frank. "Just…be polite to them, even if they aren't your favorite. Can you do that?"

Nell looked at the floor and wiggled her toes. She'd been barefoot most of the time when she lived in the enchanted mirror, so the custom of not wearing shoes while indoors was one she enjoyed. "I'll try. But... what if they don't like me? I know a lot of people don't like Mother; I hear how they talk about her. If they know who I am, maybe they won't like me either."

Now where had she gotten that idea? Alvis clasped his hands behind his back. While he knew he couldn't—and shouldn't—shelter her from everything, she was already being exposed to so much more than she was used to. Adding the burden of what her mother had done wouldn't be fair. He was going to have to have a talk with Daya and be sure no one was speaking poorly of Amelia or Nell in front of her.

Alvis crouched lower so he could meet her eyes. When he did this, she was taller than him, being eleven and already seeming to have grown since they first met. But he didn't like to tower over her. "They're going to love you. But if any of them treat you poorly, be sure to tell me immediately, and I promise I will send her home."

Nell tucked her stray strand of hair behind her ear. "You promise?"

"Absolutely."

She nodded, and Alvis straightened himself. At least that was settled. If only it was that simple to calm his own nerves and worries.

Vikas walked through the doors and stood at the top of the stairs, and all the ladies' maids walked in and took their own places along the front wall. For a moment, his gaze met Myra's, and she gave him a small smile. Well, there was no turning back now. Vikas gave Alvis a single nod, and trumpets sounded around the room, making all who were there fall into a hush.

Alvis didn't even register the words Vikas spoke to the crowd, for all he could focus on was the set of closed doors blocking him and the women he was about to meet. Before he realized what was happening, the door opened and the first woman stepped through, and he stopped breathing for a moment.

"Presenting Lady Ai of the Dravian Islands."

A woman with pale skin and straight, short black hair walked through the doors. Her red gown swept over the stairs, and the gold embroidery fell in waves as she lifted delicate hands to the sky, causing her long sleeves to fall to her elbows. Light-pink swirls escaped her fingers and wafted through the room, letting out the scent of fresh blooming roses. Alvis breathed it in when she approached and felt his shoulders soften and relax.

Lady Ai curtsied with a flourish of her skirt and pressed her hand against the fur-trimmed collar of her dress. "It is an honor to meet you, your highness."

Alvis bowed and took her hand to help her stand. "The pleasure is mine, Lady Ai. May I present my ward, Nell."

Nell bopped a small curtsy and offered a shy smile, to which Ai nodded in return. "I'd heard you'd taken in a ward. She's lovely." Her deep-brown eyes studied the two of them for a long moment, making Alvis feel as though he were being tested for something. The corner of her mouth twitched like she held a secret there. "There is a strong bond between the two of you that will not be easily broken."

Understanding washed over Alvis. "You are dedicated to Diar."

Ai opened her hands making it seem she was revealing her secrets. "Indeed, your highness."

"Should I worry of your influencing the pageant?" Alvis attempted to keep his tone light so she would know he was teasing. Diar didn't cause people to fall in love, despite some of the rumors people liked to spread.

Ai chuckled. "I would never dream of it."

She winked at him as she walked away, revealing the back of her gown, which cut all the way down to her waist and showed off the glowing red rose vine tattoo sprawled over her spine. When she reached her spot, a servant was there to slide a golden anklet around her foot, a gift that was to be given to each of the contestants of the pageant.

One by one, the women descended the staircase in clothing depicting their kingdoms and territories and showed off their magic.

Next came Lady Adeena of the western kingdom of Imare, dressed in a thin silver gown adorned in beads and jewels that shimmered against her dark as night skin and descended the steps while playing the flute. The purple streams of Efarae's magic flowed through the room and danced to the melody around them. While the song from her flute was gentle and sweet, her stance and eyes were sharp, and Nell tensed next to Alvis when she introduced herself to them.

Countess Salome of Cresin came after and looked as though at the slightest wind she might topple over. Her white skin turned paler when she approached Alvis and Nell, a shimmer of stars haloed around her dark-brown hair.

"She reminds me of Princess Eira a little," Nell whispered when she left.

Alvis nodded and pursed his lips. "I expect that's the idea."

Salome took her place next to Adeena, who only raised a silent brow at the woman, and she quickly lowered her eyes. A part of Alvis softened toward her. She might not have wanted to be there as much as Alvis, to be used as a pawn in her kingdom's politics.

There wasn't time to ponder Salome's situation though as Lady Nazneen of Oxare approached, a young woman Alvis was familiar with and knew would be present. Her name came from the lips of several other nobles ever since he came home in hints of them making a match. She lived even farther south in the kingdom. Flames floated over her dark hands, so close to her that if he didn't know better Alvis would have been afraid they would ignite her long dark wavy hair or her linen dress. Her bare feet glided across the floor as she made the flames dance and tossed them back and forth between her hands. She danced around the room with the fire as though it was her second nature. The flame tattoos circling around her bare arms glowed as she danced, and with an outstretched hand, she beckoned to Alvis.

A pleased murmur spread through the room. They wanted a display of Alvis's magic, which matched hers. He took in a deep breath to calm his nerves. As much as he loved his magic and using it for his kingdom, he'd never been comfortable with public displays. When he had to dance with Eira at the Moon festival, he almost threw up beforehand. But this was the way of his life.

Nazneen knelt to the ground in a curtsy when Alvis joined her in the middle of the room, her flames still in complete control. Summoning his own magic, the sun tattoo over his chest warmed, and flames came from his hands, and he pushed them to join hers. She stood, and together they made their fire dance together.

When the dance was over, they bowed to each other and then to the crowd, who applauded. Nazneen smiled at Alvis, a lovely and warm sight. "It is good to see you again, your highness."

"You as well, Lady Nazneen."

It was true. She was younger than him, but not so much so that they didn't run in the same circles all through their lives, and she was always pleasant to be around. The match would make sense.

At Alvis's side, Nell cried out in delight. A small red bird soared through the ballroom entrance, leaving a shimmering trail behind it. It swept and flew through the room, dipping over the heads of those present. The crowd gasped, and the bird flew and twirled in front of Alvis and Nell so they could clearly see the varying shades of red and orange in its feathers and the necklace-like black ring around its neck. Nell giggled in delight when it tapped its tiny beak on her nose as though it were a kiss.

The bird hovered for a moment before turning around to join the woman entering the room. Her strapless, bright-red dress tied in front at her chest and flowed out around her. She stretched out her toned brown arm, beckoning the bird to her, and it perched on her shoulder where her dark-brown hair fell in waves with only a large shimmering red flower behind her ear as an ornament. The colors of the flowers all around the room deepened as she walked past. Her pink lips held a bright smile as she patted her bird's head, and it chirped in reply. She laughed as though they shared a joke only the two of them knew.

Brylee, daughter of the southern Belovian Islands' chief.

She knelt in front of Alvis and Nell, the slit in her dress revealing a shapely leg with a tattoo of a flock of birds flying. They bowed and curtsied in return.

"Welcome to the continent, Brylee," Alvis said when she stood upright. "I trust your journey was safe and uneventful."

She raised a brow. "While it may have been safe, I was bored to tears. I couldn't wait to get off the ship and be here to have some excitement, your highness."

Alvis swallowed and smiled. Cadeyrn would have been much more suited to this situation of meeting all the women and have a quick-witted response to charm her. "I'll be sure we have plans that don't disappoint then."

Her lips quirked in a brighter smile. "I hope so, your highness."

He had a feeling Brylee would be fun though. They needed that around here.

At the sight of the next, and final, woman joining the pageant, Alvis's stomach dropped. Lady Charis of Marali stepped into the room in a billowing white gown with sleeves reaching all the way to the floor and an equally low-cut neckline. Out of the corner of his eye, Mother sat straighter in her seat and beamed. Thanks to Charis's family's wealth and military connections, 'his mother had dropped more than one hint at her approval of this match when going over who would be participating'.

Lady Charis pressed her pale hands to her diaphragm, and after an introduction from Adeena's flute, she sang. Alvis tried not to flinch at the first few out-of-tune notes of the song about love, beauty, and flowers. In time, they evened out enough but were feeble and shaky. When she released her hands, thin purple streams of magic swirled around the room, and when Alvis looked closely enough, they had the vague image of the flowers mentioned in her song.

When the song ended, the crowd applauded politely as Lady Charis beamed and bowed as though she'd performed the world greatest opera. She bowed again in front of Alvis and Nell, giving him a clear view of her chest.

"Thank you for that…gift, Lady Charis," Alvis said and averted his eyes to her golden hair.

Charis's blue eyes shone at him through her long lashes. "Thank you, your highness. I had the song commissioned specifically for this occasion."

"The gesture is greatly appreciated."

Nell gave him a wary side glance when Charis joined the rest of the women. "That was the worst song I've ever heard in my life."

"Be polite," Alvis murmured to her before addressing the crowd. "Thank you all for coming. I know many of you have traveled long and far to be here, and your efforts have not gone unnoticed by myself and my family." A servant came by with two glasses, one for Alvis and one for Nell. They each took one, and Alvis raised his glass over his head. "May we all welcome the coming weeks with open arms and the blessings of the deities. Now, let's feast and enjoy each other's company before the real events begin."

The crowd all raised their own glasses and drank. When the professional musicians took up their instruments, Alvis and Nell made their way to the head table for the feast. At least for a little while, he could relax before making the rounds to the other tables to greet the women again. They all ate and watched the dancers in the center of the room for entertainment, and Alvis let the cymbals and beads from their costumes fill his ears, so he didn't have to think about what came next. Having conversations with all the women.

Thankfully, when the meal was over, Nell came with Alvis from woman to woman to meet them, which helped to relieve any awkward interactions. He shook his head at himself for needing to rely on an eleven-year-old girl for these matters. But having a third person present gave him the ease of fooling himself to think it was a normal conversation, instead of courting.

Until it came time to dance, of course.

They all had their turn with him, and he couldn't help but have a sense of whiplash, jumping from interaction to interaction. He started with Nazneen, for he'd danced with her in the past and knew she would help him ease into the night. Salome danced well enough, but hardly said a word. Adeena and Charis, who seemed to already be good friends, were well on their way to drunkenness. But at least Adeena was able to keep in step with the dance. Charis kept tripping over her skirt, tearing the hem and yelling for Myra to get it fixed.

Any sign of exhaustion or annoyance was kept hidden on Myra's face as she examined the dress after they excused themselves to the side of the room.

"It is utterly ruined!" Charis threw one arm over her head and moaned.

"It's hardly ruined. I can have this patched up. It will only take a few moments." Myra let all Charis's moaning and groaning and demands slide off her delicate shoulders as though it were a mere passing breeze.

"Thank you, Myra," Alvis told her. He wanted to put his hand on her shoulder but resisted the urge. "It is greatly appreciated. And I know

Lady Charis will be back here to enjoy the rest of the evening's festivities."

"You're too kind, your highness." Charis attempted to bow but only tripped over herself again, landing on Alvis's arm, and he struggled to hold her upright. Instead of assisting him in the endeavor, she only pressed herself closer to him. He averted his gaze to the ceiling, away from her bosom attempting to shove its way out of her low-cut gown.

Myra grasped Charis's arm and assisted in getting the drunken lady on her own two feet, leaving Alvis a bit shaken. "We'll go get her straightened out, your highness. My apologies."

Together they managed to drape Charis's arm over Myra's shoulder. He had an excuse to touch Myra after all. He blinked at the thought. No, that's not why she was here. She was here to help Lady Charis and to determine her next steps for her own life. Not to indulge in Alvis's own daydreams about her.

Which happened more often than he cared to admit. He'd thought about Myra often since their travels, but his mind wandered to her even more so ever since she came to the palace to ask for the position. It was silly though. She was lovely, kind, and intelligent of course. But it could never be more than admiration from afar.

"It seems as though I am grateful to you once again," Alvis said once Charis was properly ready to walk on two feet.

A slight blush came to Myra's soft cheeks. "It is my pleasure, your highness."

The awkward pair dipped in a curtsy and turned to go fix the gown.

"I'll be back soon, your highness! Don't you worry!" Charis yelled over her shoulder.

To Alvis's relief, Charis did not return to the ballroom over the course of the night. She was so intoxicated at that point; a good night's rest and some water was more needed than a night of dancing. He would stop by the ladies' quarters later to check on her though. It was the polite thing to do.

Alvis chuckled at a joke Brylee told while her bird flew in circles overhead and took a sip of wine, pausing when one of the guards approached. The guard bowed and then leaned forward to speak to

Alvis in hushed tones. "We are in need of you, your highness. It is urgent."

There was a harsh intensity to the guard's voice that Alvis didn't like, and he knew he needed to excuse himself. They didn't come to him often when there was a problem unless they needed the opinion of both him and Father. Only one thing came to mind as to why they would come to him and not someone else, especially during this event.

After a whole day of anxiety, Alvis finally had been able to calm himself enough to attempt conversations with these women. He took in a deep breath, placed his glass on a tray, and bowed to Brylee. "My apologies, it appears as though I am needed. I will be back momentarily."

He hated to have to bow out on the women so soon. But if one of them was to become queen, they needed to understand the well-being of the palace and kingdom was a priority. Being royalty wasn't just parties and grand feasts.

Brylee curtsied. "Don't worry, your highness. We'll all be here waiting for you."

At least it happened in front of one of the women who seemed to be more relaxed. If he'd had to walk out on someone like Adeena or Charis if she wasn't already indisposed, he was certain he would get an earful about it.

With hasty steps, he followed the guard out into the hall where two more guards waited. "What's so important it had to take me away so soon?"

The guards looked at one another warily before one answered. "Someone attempted to break into the mirror's cell."

It was as he feared. With so many people from various kingdoms in the palace, it was logical someone who sympathized with the former queen might want to sneak in and free her. Or even someone who was an extremist who hated Amelia and felt they were too lenient on her could want to come and take justice into their own hands.

He put his hands on his hips and took in a deep breath. "Has the mirror been compromised?"

"No," another guard answered. "Whoever it was was unable to get in thanks to the protections around the mirror."

At least there was that. But still, Alvis didn't like the idea of someone trying to get into that room. "Do we know who it was? Were they caught? When did this happen?"

The guard who had gotten Alvis sighed. "They got away before we'd gotten a good look. Their face was shadowed, and they were quick. Whoever it was, though, was a follower of Colma. There was water everywhere. It was just moments ago."

This piece of information didn't sit well with Alvis either, as Amelia was a sorceress with water magic. The water could have come from her or a sympathizer, and neither option brought much comfort. He was sure several of her sympathizers were also followers of Colma but knew not all of them were. The Marquess of Marallis in Cresin was a follower of Colma and had been a great help to Alvis in going against Amelia. Besides, this information, while helpful, didn't narrow things down much. With all the people who were visiting from various kingdoms, there was a good chance many of them were dedicated to Colma.

"I want extra guards on the mirror at all times. The palace is going to be full the next several weeks, and we can't be too careful."

They'd already placed extra precautions around the mirror leading up to the pageant, and it still hadn't been enough to ward off an attempt. At least whoever the culprit was hadn't succeeded. But they couldn't risk anything.

"Keep me informed, but I should get back. Thank you for telling me."

They all bowed to him, and he returned to the ballroom. Shaken, but grateful to have guards who knew how important it was to interrupt the festivities to keep him in the loop for these events. He would keep a close eye on the visitors also, not wanting to miss any hints of who this culprit could be. Just because they were thwarted once didn't mean they wouldn't try again.

He came back in time for the festivities to end for the night and he could address the ladies before they all retired for the night. With a deep breath, Alvis cleared the stress from his mind, prayed to Ray for clarity and strength, and descended to the bottom of the staircase. He stopped when he was about midway so he could be seen by all the women while also not lording over them.

They all gathered at the bottom of the staircase and smiled up at him. Alvis wasn't sure if he'd ever had the attention of so many women all at once. "It has been a pleasure to meet every single one of you. I can't imagine a better way to begin. I know you all have traveled far to be here, and the kingdom of Oxare and I welcome you with open arms. Now, I suggest you get a good night's rest, and we have big plans for tomorrow. Thank you all again and have a wonderful night."

He extended his hand out to Nell, who joined him on the stairs, and arm in arm, they went back up. Nell paused for a moment, then turned, and gave them all one final wave good night, and they went on their way. A swell of pride rose in him at her small gesture. Nell had done what he'd asked and stayed the whole time. She even seemed to have a bit of fun.

Perhaps this venture wouldn't be a disaster after all.

Chapter Thirteen

ALVIS

Alvis still couldn't sleep well that night. Meeting the women had gone more smoothly than he anticipated, but the idea of someone trying to get to the mirror was disturbing. He climbed out of bed and put on a robe and a pair of house slippers. Sometimes a stroll through the quiet palace did wonders to calm his mind.

Other than a few guards on night patrol, the Golden Palace was quiet at this time, and Alvis enjoyed the peace. But on this night, he wasn't alone.

Hurrying through the hall came Myra with a basket of clothes in her arms. Her brown hair was piled on top of her head in a tangled nest with a few runaway strands in her face. Alvis paused. The warmth and fire that ran through his veins from his magic from Ray flickered and simmered while he watched as she tried to not drop the basket while rushing to wherever she was headed next.

"Myra? Where are you off to in such a hurry?"

Myra stopped in her tracks, and her eyes went wide. Apparently, she hadn't noticed him. "Your—your highness. I didn't see you there." She tried to dip into a curtsy but almost dropped her basket.

Alvis grabbed the edges of the basket to help her balance it again, his fingers brushing hers, making the heat roil in the pit of his stomach. "It's all right. It's just us. You can remain upright."

Myra's soft brown cheeks turned pink. He didn't mean to embarrass her so often but couldn't help but find the shade on her quite lovely. "Thank you. I was trying to get these clothes pressed and prepared for tomorrow. Lady Charis picked an outfit that wasn't ready yet and needs it first thing in the morning…"

"Well, you're not going to do much good if you drop everything and if you don't get enough sleep. Especially after the early morning you had." He took the basket out of her hands and went down the hall to a guard with instructions to take it to the overnight laundress to have them prepared and then brought back to Myra's room.

Alvis nodded in the direction of where the other ladies' maids were staying. "Come, I'll walk you back to your room. I intended to check on Lady Charis after the festivities anyway as I didn't see her return. Is she all right?"

"Thank you. That wasn't necessary though," Myra said as they walked side by side. "I'm sure Lady Charis appreciates the gesture, but she is sound asleep now and has been for hours."

It was a relief to hear. Alvis raised a palm. "It's my pleasure. I know Lady Charis didn't arrive as scheduled, and you've been working hard to prepare for her. I'm sure you need the rest also. How are things going with her thus far? Are you getting along?"

Myra paused before answering and glanced around the hall. "I've been busy. Lady Charis knows what she wants and makes sure it happens."

Interesting. He tucked this piece of information in the back of his mind.

"Well, regardless. I'm sure you can't help her with that unless you have sleep."

"I appreciate your concern, but I've handled worse on less sleep."

Right. Of course she had.

"And what about you? I doubt you'll be able to win over the hearts of any of these women if you're prowling the halls at night and yawning tomorrow." She raised her brows and smirked. "Unless you planned on surprising them in the middle of the night? Did one catch your eye already?"

Now it was Alvis's turn to blush, and he looked at the floor. "Hardly. Not that they aren't all lovely, they are. I have a lot on my mind is all."

"I'm sorry to hear that."

"Thank you."

He nodded to another guard who walked past.

"Is there any way I can help? Even to just hear what's on your mind. I'm sure it's filled with thoughts of all the beautiful woman you'll be surrounded by in the coming weeks." Myra looked at him through her lashes. "I've been told I'm a good listener."

Out of anyone in the palace, Myra would be the one person who would understand the severity of the threat of Amelia's mirror being infiltrated. She, out of everyone, would want Amelia trapped in that mirror as long as possible.

"You'd think that was it, but I'm sad to admit it's not. In fact, a part of me is anxious for this nonsense to be over so we can return to a semblance of normalcy." Myra's face looked shocked at this confession, so he clamped his mouth shut. He shouldn't say such things in front of one of the ladies' maids.

Alvis reached his arms over his head and cradled his neck in his hands. He was feeling stiff and should do some stretches before he returned to bed. He lowered his voice. While most everyone was sleeping, they still never knew who could overhear. "Someone tried to get to the mirror tonight during the feast."

Myra stopped in her tracks, her jaw dropped. "They what? But it's so heavily guarded."

Alvis lowered his hands and stood next to her. "They didn't succeed, but whoever it was got away before they could be caught. We're putting more protections in. I plan to do more research on ways to protect it and be sure Amelia can't escape. She's powerful, and I worry that while the spells we placed on it in Cresin are good, they may not be good enough. I'm not sure when I'll have the time to do such things."

"I see."

He hated to ask this next part, but he needed to cover all the possibilities. "Lady Charis hasn't left her room at all this evening, has she?"

Myra gave a dark chuckled. "She's been inebriated since we last saw you and hasn't left her bed."

Alvis breathed a sigh of relief. While it didn't mean Charis or any of the other women weren't involved just because they weren't there when it happened, it did put his mind at ease, even if only a little. "I thought so. I don't want to accuse anyone, and there is no reason to suspect her, but I have to be sure."

"I completely understand."

They returned to their walking in silence, but Myra bowed her head with a furrowed brow as though she were deep in thought. Curtains covering the wall-length windows flapped as a soft breeze went past, the rustling of fabric like whispered secrets shared in the night, only interrupted by the pattering of their slippered feet across the floor.

"What if I were to help?" she asked.

He tilted his head so he could see her better. The dim light of the lanterns reflected in her brown hair. "You wish to help?"

"I know what Amelia can do better than anyone here in the palace. I worked for her for years." As if she knew he noticed her hair, she tucked it behind her ear and pushed it to one side. "Besides, you know the servants know everything. I'll be around all these women from other kingdoms and their servants, so I can easily gather information for you."

Indeed, she could. It wasn't as though Alvis could go questioning all the women and servants about breaking in to capture the mirror. He could do some digging on his own as he got to know the women, but they wouldn't be forthright with him on this matter. While Alvis tried to see the best in people, even he wasn't naïve enough to think they would confess to any treachery to him.

"Will you have time? I'm sure Lady Charis will be needing you often."

If this past day had been any indication, between the early-morning arrival and then needing to be taken care of during the dance, Alvis had a feeling Myra was going to have her hands full.

Myra only shrugged. "I can't imagine I'll need to be present through every event she'll be attending while here. I'll use those times to research other types of magic and investigate. If I'd be allowed to use the library—"

"Anyone is allowed to use the library."

Myra blinked at his abrupt interruption, and he cleared his throat.

"At least to all those who are here in the palace. I wish we could extend it to anyone in the city. Was it not that way in Cresin? I can't imagine King Brennan or Princess Eira denying people access to it."

"The servants usually needed permission to go. They always questioned us when we went inside. I'm sure King Brennan and Princess Eira didn't mind us being there, but if we didn't have a specific reason, those who worked in the library questioned us. I think they were afraid of any damage being done to the books."

Alvis shook his head. "Books should be a bit battered. It means they've been used. Well, you are welcome to use our library whenever you wish. To research for our task or your own pleasure. We encourage all those who live and work here to read as much as they wish. Or at least I do. Many are too busy with their own work, but you'll find nobles and servants alike in there. In fact, we can use it as a place to rendezvous and share information we've learned. No one would find it suspicious if we are in there at the same time."

"As I'm sure you are in the library almost daily." There was a gentle tease to her voice, and it made something in Alvis's chest feel light and tight at the same time.

He chuckled. "Indeed." They arrived at the hall where Myra would turn to go to her room, and they paused. "I suppose this is where we must part ways. Shall we meet there in two days? There should be a break in the activities after the midday meal where we can both manage to escape for a few moments."

Myra nodded and fingered the edge of her shawl. "It sounds perfect. I'll see you then."

Alvis couldn't erase the smile spread over his face. He rarely invited people to join him at the library. It was the one sanctuary where he could be around people but not be obligated to put on a show or speak to everyone. They left him alone there. But he would be lying to himself if he wasn't glad to have the excuse to spend time with her, and to have something to think and focus on other than the pageant. Not that he wanted this sort of trouble with Amelia, but having this task would help him to focus. "Wonderful. Have a good night, Myra. Sleep well."

Myra bobbed in a curtsy. "Good night, your highness."

Chapter Fourteen

MYRA

Myra took her place next to Finley along with the other ladies' maids against the wall behind the contestants who gathered in one of the halls. It was the first day of the pageant, and they'd been instructed to meet there after breakfast. Finley inspected her nails with one leg bent and propped against the wall, while the other maids stood upright with prim hands clasped together in front of them.

"You could attempt to pretend you're a servant," Myra said with a side glance. Finley hadn't told her outright she wasn't truly a maid, but Myra wasn't stupid. She could figure out on her own there was more to Finley than she was sharing.

"Ai doesn't care what I do as long as I don't cause trouble."

"So no sword fights."

Finley smiled as though she were remembering a secret joke. "Only if no one is threatening Ai or anyone else."

Finley wore a simple outfit of black leggings and a blue tunic with a white belt wrapped around her waist. There were some pockets in the ensemble, but Myra couldn't tell if anything significant could be hidden in them. "What? Are you her bodyguard? Are you hiding weapons?"

Finley wagged her brows. "Wouldn't you like to know?"

Myra had a hunch there must have been at least one blade hidden somewhere on her person. She wasn't sure if it made her feel more secure or in danger.

The chatter in the hall came to a hush when Alvis and Vikas approached and stood in front of the double doors they were all gathered around. Everyone present curtsied and bowed to the prince.

"I trust you all had an enjoyable and restful night. It was a pleasure to meet you all and welcome you to the Golden Palace." Alvis wore a warm smile, but there was a slight hesitancy behind his eyes as though he searched for the next thing to say. Even though Myra was sure he had a plan and thought through his morning speech.

"We have a special treat for you all this morning. You all come from different places and cultures, and we welcome your traditions and skills. But you may not be used to the kingdom of Oxare, or our capital, or the palace. If you are to be the future queen of Oxare, we want to know we can blend our worlds together and appreciate all you bring, while also embracing our kingdom. Besides, we want you to be comfortable in our courts and in our climate. Therefore, we have gathered the kingdom's greatest seamstresses and cosmeticians to the Golden Palace. They are here to help you build your Oxarian wardrobe and cosmetic regime."

There was a collective, excited gasp from the women, and their eyes lit up. Lady Charis particularly had a devilish gleam in her blue eyes as she looked past Alvis and to the doors behind him.

"Have fun and show us who you are while also blending your own styles and cultures with ours." Alvis and Vikas extended their arms, and then pulled the doors open to reveal a large room with dozens of beauticians surrounded by colorful cloth, jewels, gowns, and cosmetics.

Jasmine and incense wafted through the room while the fluttering of silk and light laughter made the music of the morning. It was a woman's dream world where they could look and be anyone they imagined or wanted. There were plenty of already-made pieces, but with the merest glance, a bolt of fabric could be rushed over to be created into something beautiful and new.

Before long, there were piles of clothing and beauty supplies at

Charis's station. Each woman had one with three full-length mirrors, their own personal stylists, seamstresses, and rolling carts to gather beauty items. Along with the other ladies' maids, Myra ran back and forth through the morning across the room to help collect things and take notes on their preferences and styles chosen. It was tiring work, but Myra appreciated the opportunity and excuse to listen in on other conversations and observe the choices of the other women. Any opportunity to glean information and clues as to who might have tried to compromise Amelia's mirror.

The thought of Amelia being freed sent a chill through Myra when Alvis told her of the situation the night before. She'd been so consumed with thinking about her attempts to find her mother's spirit and gaining her father's favor, then what to do next when she left the manor, Myra hadn't put much thought into not being in Amelia's clutches any longer. Once the possibility Amelia could escape and be out in the world again was presented, it was as though the breath was sucked out of Myra. The idea she could be back under Amelia's control put a weight back on Myra's chest that she hadn't realized before had been lifted.

She and Cal wouldn't go back to working for the sorceress ever again, even if she escaped. They would find a way to be away from her. But it didn't mean other people wouldn't be in danger, and the only way to guarantee they or anyone else wouldn't be put into that situation again was to be sure Amelia didn't escape the mirror.

A burst of laughter came from Ai's station as Myra walked past, a box of jewelry in one hand and scarves draped over the other arm. Finley had taken a hat with feathers from one of the stands, perched it on her golden hair like an exotic bird, and held a deep-blue silk against her body.

"What do you think of this one?" Finley asked Myra.

Myra paused. "It's beautiful, but aren't you supposed to be making clothes for Lady Ai, not yourself?"

Ai stood tall on top of a flat pedestal as a seamstress pinned a pink sari around her, which reminded Myra of roses. She pointed to a silver shawl off to the side and gestured for Finley to take it. "There's going to be a ball at the end of the pageant, and everyone, including the maids, is invited. I want to be sure Finley has something fine to wear too."

Myra didn't know she could go to the ball too. She'd never attended one of the formal events at Farren Castle unless it was to help serve. But Amelia always made sure Myra was hidden away and unable to enjoy it. Although that didn't mean Myra didn't find ways to escape and spy on whatever was happening. She'd become good at getting back to wherever she was supposed to be before Amelia noticed.

Over her shoulder, Myra saw Charis snap her fingers at one of the seamstresses before noticing Myra lingering. She glared at her and put her hands on her hips. Myra pressed her lips together. It was difficult to spy when Charis kept demanding her attention even though there were four other people there to assist.

Of course, Charis hadn't said a word to Myra about attending the ball, let alone helping her find a gown.

"I'm sure I'll find something." Myra had never made herself a gown before—it could be a fun challenge.

Ai's thin brows pinched together, and her gaze darted between Myra and Charis as though she were following an invisible line between them. A faint pink glow came from Ai's back as she considered the two of them before it faded again and offered Myra a warm smile. "I'm sure you'll be lovely."

The shrill yell of Charis echoed through the room, and Myra flinched. "Myra! Stop chitchatting and help me like you're supposed to!"

Myra turned and gave her a nod. She turned to face Ai and Finley before moving on. "I should be going."

Ai waved her off. "She'll be fine." She winked and then leaned forward as though they were fellow conspirators. "I know Charis, and she's not always the most pleasant person to be around. If she gives you any trouble, tell me, and I'll be sure to have the situation rectified."

There was a sudden coldness in Ai's eyes that Myra hadn't seen before, and it caused her to pause. It was an unusual look for a follower of Diar. Who were these women she'd found herself allied to?

"And come to my room this evening when you have the chance. I wish for us to be friends."

Myra swallowed the lump in her throat and nodded. "Thank you. I will."

She took in a deep breath as she returned to Charis's station and tried to look as unnerved as possible. As she'd suspected from the moment she laid eyes on them, Finley and Ai were not who they appeared to be. To her disappointment, it meant she would have to keep an eye on them and see them not as allies, but suspects.

Chapter Fifteen

MYRA

The following night, admittance to the library was exactly as Alvis promised. No one questioned Myra when she entered; the woman at the desk only smiled and nodded to her and then pushed her glasses back up her nose to return to her work. Myra had never been able to explore and enjoy a library as vast as this one before, and she had to be conscious to keep her jaw from dropping to the floor at all the tall shelves of books and scrolls as she passed through the stacks.

With a note Alvis sent of where to meet him—between the sections on Colma and Diar—clutched in her hand, Myra wandered through the vast room. Its arched windows offered views of the city and the river, and left streams of light across the floor, making the mosaics adorning the tops and edges of the shelves glimmer with their purple images of Efarae blessing those pursuing their own inspiration.

As she searched for the correct location, no one paid her any mind, and the only sounds were those of the soft rustling of pages, the sweep of robes across the ground, or the patter of bare feet. Here and there a gentle whisper would float through the air, so quiet one couldn't understand what the person was saying.

Myra let her fingers graze the worn edges of the leather-bound books while she waited and almost thought if she touched them, they would vanish like a mirage. This room alone was a treasure trove of knowledge and worlds to be discovered, ready for anyone who wished to have it. She'd never been much of a reader as she didn't have the time or energy for it. But no one bothered to give her the opportunity to explore literature either. She could take one of these volumes and bring it back to her room without anyone batting an eyelash or questioning why she wanted it, and the realization made something in her chest tighten.

"I'm sorry I'm late."

Myra jumped at the sound of Alvis's voice, a bell ringing in the silence despite his attempt to remain as quiet as possible. He gave an apologetic smile, and Myra's stomach flipped.

"I—I— No apology needed, your highness." She swallowed and tried to get ahold of herself. "Your library is beautiful. It's almost like a temple."

Alvis put his hands in the pockets of his loose-fitting orange pants and looked around. "It is, isn't it? In a way, libraries could be considered temples for Efarae. We always think of her for art and music, but we often forget writing and knowledge are forms of inspiration as well. It's amazing to think of all the people the goddess has influenced through the ages. The words they found to share their thoughts and ideas. This place practically sings with silent praises to her."

The awe and reverence in his voice as he whispered his thoughts made Myra's chest tighten again.

"You would have made a wonderful follower for Efarae if you hadn't been Chosen." Myra snapped her mouth shut and lowered her head. "I'm sorry, your highness. I know your place with Ray and your magic—"

"There is no need to apologize, Myra. It is a thought that has come to my mind on occasion." He looked away from her as though he'd confessed a dark secret and cleared his throat. "I thought this section would be a good place to start. We could learn about the different spells and magic of Colma, and it would give us more ideas on how to protect the mirror and seal Amelia in more securely."

"Excellent, your highness."

In silence, they scanned through the volumes of books and gathered their findings. Myra was keenly aware of Alvis's presence, even when he ventured farther down a row or went across the aisle. He navigated the library as easily as a ship's captain across the sea, knowing where each topic and book belonged, and jotted a note when a book was already in use so he would go back to it later. Myra kept getting distracted from her own task as she watched him out of the corner of her eye. There was a lightness about him she hadn't seen elsewhere and a spark in his eye when he found something he'd been searching for.

Myra almost didn't notice the chill that blew past as they searched the books. She froze.

Oh no, not here.

The last thing she needed was for a spirit to be hovering over them in hopes Myra would guide them to the afterlife.

Alvis shivered and shook his head. "Amazing how drafty this room can get sometimes."

"Yes, it is surprising." Myra glanced at the small stack of books in her arms and the ones Alvis had gathered. "I think we have enough for us to get started. Should we find a place to sit?"

As though taken out of a trance, Alvis followed Myra's gaze at all their findings and smiled to himself. "Good idea. I doubt we'll be able to carry much more. Follow me. I know of a place where no one will bother us."

Alvis led her through the library to a secluded corner with pillows and blankets along with a few sun lanterns flickering overhead. He set his pile on the ground and beckoned for Myra to sit with him. "Hardly anyone comes back here, and they know it is my favorite spot to read. We will not be bothered."

Myra was not only keenly aware of Alvis's presence now, but also of being alone with him. They'd spent time together before, but always in open spaces where others would pass by. This setting was oddly intimate and private. She swallowed the lump in her throat and knelt at his side. Alvis seemed perfectly oblivious to the oddity of the situation and settled into the pillows, already buried deep into his stack of tomes. It was as though there was nothing else in the world except for him and the books. She did her best to follow suit and make herself comfortable.

The truth was, she wasn't sure where to start. Did she read the whole book from front to back? Alvis seemed to be able to skip around from chapter to chapter and book to book with ease. But how did he know where to search? If this had been *The Book of Souls*, perhaps she could research as easily as he did. But she didn't know anything about Colma's magic.

Besides, the chill in the air lingered and wisps of a spirit floated around the corners of the room. It was distracting. If this spirit lived here in the library, certainly it could recognize when someone was attempting to get work done. Why didn't it leave them alone?

Alvis visibly shivered at her side, a line forming between his eyes. With a wave of a hand, a small ball of flames ignited in his palm, and the sun tattoo carved onto his chest flashed through his shirt. After a moment, he released his hand, and the flames floated in the air between them, radiating a gentle heat.

"That should help," Alvis said with a decisive nod and returned to his studying.

Myra could only nod and tried not to acknowledge the spirit whooshing past and around the corners of the shelves. "Yes, thank you."

While the flames did help to take the edge off the spirit's chill, it was still difficult to focus. Outside *The Book of Souls,* she'd never had long study sessions before. Each page took what felt like an eternity to get through as she had to reread it several times before moving on. She rubbed her temple and slumped into one of the pillows. Between the reading and the spirit, she was getting a headache.

Alvis tore himself away from his book and observed Myra as though she were part of the text. "Is everything all right?"

"Of course, your highness. Why wouldn't it be?"

"You keep looking at those shelves." He pointed to the area where the spirit had been hovering. "Is someone bothering you?"

She tried to protest, but he'd already stood to go investigate the area. "It's nothing, your highness. Please, don't worry yourself."

Alvis walked with the determination of a lion prepared to defend his pride but stopped cold as he intersected with the spirit. He shook his head and stepped back, rubbing his arms. "What is that? Do you see something?"

Myra swallowed a lump in her throat. She shouldn't tell him anything about her magic or heritage. It would only bring doubt and suspicion. But how could she lie when he stood right before it? Alvis was an intelligent man. If she didn't tell him at least part of the truth, he'd figure it out on his own.

She nodded. "Yes. There's a spirit there."

His face turned from confusion to recognition, as though a light had turned on and he couldn't be more delighted by its presence. "You're a follower of Stula. I'd wondered which deity you were dedicated to. I should have known. You can see spirits? How long have you been dedicated?"

Myra blinked, stunned at his acceptance of her magic, even if he didn't know the whole truth of it—especially her involvement with the events in Cresin. If he did, his reaction wouldn't be as pleasant. This small acceptance, though, warmed her. Maybe he wouldn't mind her heritage as much as she'd anticipated.

"I was very young," she answered. It was close enough to the truth. He didn't need to know everything.

The prince stepped back, away from the spirit, and looked around as though if he peered closely enough, he'd be able to see it too. "What do they want?"

Myra shrugged. "I haven't asked. Sometimes they want assistance in being guided to the afterlife, and sometimes they have a message they want to share. Many times they're just grateful someone can see them."

He continued to look in the general area of where the spirit had been, even though they'd already moved aside. It was a man in common clothes of a tunic and loose pants. While he was pale and took on a gray tone, she could tell he would have had dark skin and hair in life. He gave her a look expressing his annoyance at her not acknowledging him before now.

"He's not very happy with me, I don't think," Myra said and pursed her lips.

"Why not?"

"Because I've been ignoring him."

"Well, that is rather rude."

Was the usually so formal and reserved prince teasing her? It was a refreshing change.

"Would you like to see him too?"

The gold in his eyes gleamed as though the fire magic running through his veins lit up behind them with the idea of being able to see a spirit. He leaned toward her. "You can do that? I've heard of it, but never seen it done. But if it's possible...I would hate to also be rude and not see and speak with them if I'm able."

His calm tone did nothing to hide his excitement.

Myra gathered herself and rose to her feet, so she stood side by side with Alvis. It was something to focus on other than being insecure about the task. "I haven't often, and not many have the ability to be able to share their sight with others. But yes, I can show you."

The spirit sighed and threw his head back in exasperation. Myra gave him a look that she hoped told him to be patient.

She outstretched her arm and grasped Alvis's hand in hers. It was softer and smoother than hers. The hand of a man who never had to do a day of hard labor in his life. But still strong and sturdy. Safe. She swallowed. "Close your eyes and relax."

He followed her directions, and she closed her eyes with him. It wasn't a necessary action, but it helped for people to relax, and this way he wouldn't notice there was no tattoo to make glow when summoning magic. The darkness and inner cold swirled around inside her. It wasn't the darkness of night or the cold of winter, but as though she were reaching into the depths of the afterlife, where not even a glimmering star could shine its light. Not even Alvis's sun and fire magic could gather enough energy to warm it. Myra drew it up and out of her and willed it toward the prince.

She'd only done this a small handful of times. The first time with Mama guiding her and showing her how with Odalis. Then, with her first master, who'd used the magic to perform unthinkable experiments. He was fascinated with the afterlife and never assisted the spirits who wanted to move on from this world. He only wanted to learn more about the ways of death and ways to cause it.

This wasn't the time to go back through dark memories. With a deep breath, Myra returned her focus to the present and spreading the magic to Alvis. It was as though a piece of her was leaving her body and making residence in his. He shuddered as the cold and darkness entered him but didn't balk or shy away.

"You can open your eyes now."

His hand remained in hers, and he went still as he took in the sight of the spirit. "Incredible."

The spirit offered a deep bow to the prince. "My apologies for interrupting, your highness." His voice was soft and distant, as though it were a flickering flame ready to go out at any moment.

"No apology needed. It's my honor to have you here with us."

"And I should be the one apologizing for not acknowledging you sooner," Myra interrupted. Even though it still would have been nice to have a moment when her magic didn't interrupt life or get in the way. The life—or afterlife rather—of a spirit must be lonely. "What is your name, and how can we help you?"

"My name is Ramin, and I have a message for his highness. I know about the mirror and the danger it is in. Or rather, the danger we all could be in."

The air itself stood still at his announcement.

"What do you know?" Alvis asked.

"I know someone is trying to steal the mirror, and it's one of the women of the pageant."

Alvis's hand tensed in Myra's, but he didn't pull it away. Whether it was because he knew the magic would stop working if they didn't stop touching, or if he merely felt like holding it, Myra didn't know. It was probably the first. "How do you know? Do you know who it is?"

Ramin shook his head. "I didn't see her face. She was dressed in all black with a hood covering her head. But she wore the anklet you gave each of the women, and she had someone with her. I believe it was another woman."

It was evident the weight of this news was heavy on Alvis's shoulders. The excited light in his eyes dimmed. "It was my worst fear."

It was Myra's worst fear too, and she couldn't help but think of Finley and Ai. They were so mysterious, and given their sordid history, it was almost inevitable Myra would suspect them first.

The spirit bowed his head. "I'm sorry to disappoint your highness, but I thought you would want to know."

Alvis nodded. "You're right, I did. The truth might not be beautiful, but it is necessary. I thank you for telling me."

"If you wish, I can continue to help to keep an eye out for you," the spirit offered. "I see so much in the palace but so rarely have the opportunity or means to do anything about it, and I know more than one of the women has secrets."

"Your assistance would be most appreciated. When did you see them?"

"Last night, your highness. It was after dinner."

Myra breathed a sigh of relief. She'd been with Finley and Ai at that time. As selfish as it made her feel, she didn't want to have to suspect the first people in years she could picture as being friends. But it did leave all the others.

"Is there anything we can do for you, Ramin, in exchange?" Myra asked. "I'm happy to help."

Ramin's smile was gentle and understanding. "Thank you, but I am content where I am at this time. Someday, though, I may take you up on your offer."

With bows and curtsies, they parted, leaving Myra and Alvis alone once again. Myra let her magic fade, and Alvis sighed from what must have been relief for the coldness to depart from him and to be warm again. She tugged her hand away from his, though it still burned from his touch. Some of his magic must have spread to her as well.

"I suppose it's even more important now we keep an eye on my guests and find a way to ensure the mirror's safety," Alvis said. He already went back to their study area and crouched to gather the books with barely a glance toward her. "I have a couple of ideas, but I need to ruminate on them for a bit. Besides, it's getting late. We should both get rest."

Myra followed his lead and went to gather her books. It was awkward to be standing over him. "I'm sorry, your highness. About the women. They're people you should be able to trust if you are to pick one to be your wife."

There was no pause in his movements or falter in his voice. "Yes, well, I've become accustomed to betrayal these days. It comes along with the territory of my station, I suppose." The last book hit the top of the stack with a thud. "We'll both keep an eye on the women tomorrow and can report in the evening with our observations and ideas. Agreed?"

Only then did he look at Myra again, his golden eyes clear and focused.

She nodded. "Agreed. Have a good night, your highness."

"Good night, Myra." With that, he took the books and made his exit, leaving Myra to wonder if the chill she felt was from the presence of the spirit or the absence of the prince.

Chapter Sixteen

ALVIS

THE SUN GLIMMERED OVER BUCKETS OF PAINT AND WARMED ALVIS'S FACE as he and Daya helped Nell set up her painting station. Today's activity for the pageant was painting led by a priest and priestess of Efarae, and they could depict whatever subject they chose. When Nell heard about it, she insisted on doing a painting of her own. At least this one was outside as opposed to the previous day when they'd been indoors and focused on their clothing and makeup. Over where Mother sat next to Father, the queen glared at him and gestured for him to pay more attention to the women.

He wasn't cooperating, but after the declaration Ramin made that it was one of the pageant contestants who was attempting to steal the mirror, how could he? Any one of them could be the betrayer.

"Myra!" Charis's voice rang out, causing more than one person to pause their work to glance in her direction. She perched on a stool in front of an easel with a palette of paint in one hand. With the other, she pointed a long and graceful finger toward the table of supplies. "Not that brush, the other one. The delicate one. No. That one is too small. Next to it. Yes, of course that's the one. I was pointing to it! Now come back so I can finish this painting."

If Myra was flustered or frustrated at Lady Charis's demands, she didn't show it. Her gentle and soft face remained neutral with raised interested brows and the smallest of quirks to a smile. Alvis flexed the hand she'd held in the library. Sometimes he still felt a faint chill through his veins from her magic. He'd never felt anything like it before. The depth and cold of Stula's magic was nothing like the fire and heat that coursed through Alvis's veins. It was dark and mysterious with no end, as though he'd fallen into a never-ending tunnel. But there was something calming about it. It had soothed the fire he carried with him all the time, and he almost hated to let go of her hand.

Except she could be one of the betrayers, a fact Alvis couldn't ignore. She and Charis could be working together as Ramin said he saw two women there. It was probably one of the contestants and her maid. Myra had worked for Amelia for years, and while she had helped Alvis when they were in Cresin and gave no indication she worked with Amelia, it would be naïve of him to not consider the possibility. For too long he'd blindly been trusting those around him, and look where it had gotten him. He couldn't let his guard down again when there was so much at stake.

Even if it was someone who made him feel more at ease than he had been in months with big soft brown eyes he could drown in.

Alvis shook his head. He was being ridiculous. Even without the threat of Amelia looming over them, developing this fanciful infatuation with Myra was ridiculous. Plenty of royals and nobles had affairs with the servants, but they never ended well, with the one in a higher station walking away with perhaps a small mark on their reputation, while the other either lost their position or tarnished their good name, or both. Even if Myra was the betrayer, Alvis refused to abuse his position in such a way.

Nell bounced on the balls of her feet as Daya tied an apron around her. "I think I'm going to do a painting of my horse!"

"That sounds like a wonderful idea. Have you painted before? A horse could be tricky."

Nell nodded and, once Daya was done tying the strings of her apron, crouched by her supply bucket to search for a paintbrush. "A little when I was in the mirror. But not like this."

Interesting. It appeared as though Amelia didn't completely neglect

Nell's education, and it was evident in her studies. She might not have been at the same level as other children her age, but she was catching on according to what her tutors reported. She had an "unusual view of the world," they'd told him.

He had no doubt.

Mother caught his eye again and raised her brows. He should play along. As much as the idea pained him, it was the best way to find out who wanted to steal the mirror.

"Prince Alvis, let me know your thoughts on my painting so far." Lady Ai beckoned him toward her. At her side, her maid yawned and stretched. Ai's brows pinched in concern, but her maid waved her off. "If you're tired, Finley, you can go take a rest for a bit. I'll be fine."

The maid—Finley—sighed and said something Alvis couldn't hear, but eventually nodded and made her departure.

Alvis pushed aside one of the sun lanterns floating around to keep off the hint of a chill and made his way to Ai's easel. It was full of blues, greens, and whites, with waves crashing against rocks. The incomplete painting didn't have the technique or artistry as one done by a person dedicated to Efarae, but still had the free and open feeling of the ocean.

"It looks lovely," Alvis commented. "What gave you the inspiration? Do you live near the ocean in the Dravian Islands?"

Ai continued with her painting but glanced at him out of the corner of her dark eyes with a soft curiosity the way someone did when were deciding an opinion on something. She'd given him the same look at the opening ceremony of the pageant, like he were something to be inspected. Which…wasn't that what he was supposed to be doing to her? It was oddly comforting to know at least one of them needed to make her mind up about him as much as he did about them.

"Nearly everyone living on the islands lives near the ocean or has easy access to it. I'd say I'm in the water or on a ship more often than I am on land. The ocean is my home."

An extra wooden stool was next to her easel, and Alvis perched on it so they were more at eye level and she didn't have to continually look up. "It's a wonder then that you've dedicated yourself to Diar and not Colma."

She pursed her lips, and they quirked up as though it was a joke

Alvis wasn't privy to. "Not everyone from the islands is dedicated Colma, even if we do love the ocean." She dabbed dots of white along a crashing wave on the canvas. "And not everyone who follows Colma or is from the Dravian Islands are in alliance with Amelia."

Her implied accusation took Alvis by surprise. He opened and closed his mouth a few times and tried to find a way to salvage the conversation so it wouldn't seem like he'd been suspicious of her. This was the sort of situation Cadeyrn would have been a master in. He thought at thirty years old and as the future king, he would have figured out how to navigate these conversations, but it was another moment proving how sheltered his life had been until now. There hadn't been a reason to spy and interrogate people. "I—I didn't mean—I wasn't accusing you…"

Ai chuckled and softened her gaze. "It's all right. If I were in your position, I would suspect every single person who walked through the door. From what I've heard of the events in Cresin, Amelia may be trapped, but she isn't dead, which leaves the potential for her to try to retaliate. I'm sure she has plenty of people loyal to her. Otherwise, she wouldn't have been able to hold on to her power even if it had been for a short time. In fact, if you weren't suspicious and investigating people, I'd be disappointed."

A strand of hair fluttered over her eyes, and she brushed it away, but it left a dash of white paint on her forehead. "My family does know Amelia's. The islands are a small community, but we never trusted them. They are a power-hungry and cruel family. My parents told me they were shocked when they were told King Brennan had decided to marry her and were organizing our own people to come help relieve those suffering from her raids this autumn. If you are still in contact with King Brennan and he needs assistance, please let him know they are still willing to help with recovery efforts."

Well, this was a surprise. Alvis was certain the petite and charming woman would have been offended if she thought he was accusing her of anything. Most of the women likely would be. Or at least a few who came to mind. Lady Ai was a pleasant surprise, and the insight into her family was another comfort. While Alvis no longer had any direct connection to the kingdom of Cresin, as he was no longer it's future king, he still felt protective over it and its people. He'd been preparing to help lead them his whole life and was fond of the northern kingdom. It wasn't a feeling that vanished overnight.

While he might not have been able to eliminate any suspicion of Lady Ai until there was evidence of someone else more likely, or evidence that she was innocent, Alvis still felt more at ease around her. She was a welcome surprise, and regardless of how things turned out, if she was not to the betrayer, he hoped they could at least come out of this with a friendship.

"Prince Alvis! Come look at my painting too!" Lady Charis's high-pitched voice rang out through the air, causing Alvis and Ai to flinch.

He peered over his shoulder to see Charis waving at him, paint splattering off her brush and onto Myra's dress. The only indication Myra gave of annoyance of the paint was a barely audible sigh. Her gaze met Alvis's, and she offered a small but tired smile.

"She's going to look lovely at the ball, don't you think?" Ai asked.

Alvis furrowed his brows. Why would she comment on how one of the other contestants would look at the ball? "Yes…I'm sure Lady Charis will look lovely."

Ai rolled her eyes. "Not Lady Charis. Her maid, Myra. I'm assuming she's coming. I'm considering helping her with a dress."

Alvis's shoulders relaxed, and he glanced in Myra's direction again. They'd invited all the ladies' maids to the ball, so of course Myra would be among them. He pictured her in a long and ornate dress, his hand around her waist and whisking her around the dance floor. Myra was already beautiful on her own, but picturing her dressed as a princess stirred something else in him.

"That's very kind of you," he said once he'd cleared his mind.

"Prince Alvis! It's my turn now!" Lady Charis shrieked, but she had a smile plastered to her face. Maybe she thought she was being playful?

He said good-bye to Ai and made his departure for Lady Charis's easel. It was only fair for him to spend time with each woman after all, both for the pageant and for his investigation. Besides, now he could be closer to Myra without being suspicious. He just hoped he wouldn't be distracted by her too much.

Lady Charis was the picture of an Efarae painter with her golden hair gleaming in the sun and bright-purple apron covering her gown. Although he couldn't help but notice how it didn't cover her décolletage. It might not have been practical, but she was lovely and curvaceous, even he had to admit while he attempted to keep his eyes on her face. Which was also nothing to complain about.

She stood from her stool and met him halfway, looping her arm through his to lead him to the painting. A small enough gesture, but it sent a jolt through his body, and a jab a guilt stabbed at his gut. Although, he was allowed to admire and even desire her. In fact, she was welcoming it. For so long, he of course was allowed to acknowledge other women's beauty, but he'd always felt guilty when he thought it was a betrayal to Eira and the tradition of the Chosens. Now, there was no need for the guilt.

His shoulders relaxed, and he placed his hand over hers. It was all right to enjoy the attention.

"I do hope you like it, your highness. I've been working so hard," Charis said and looked up at him through her eyelashes.

More like working her vocals to order Myra about all day. A woman who knew what she wanted and how to get it was to be admired, but he hoped Charis wasn't being unfair to Myra either. She'd already dealt with a cruel mistress and didn't need another one.

Charis pressed herself against Alvis's arm and gestured to her painting. It was the image of a person; he could tell that much.

"It's a self-portrait," Charis explained. "Something for you to remember me by."

Ah, yes, he could see it now. The long blond hair and bright-blue eyes. Maybe she'd been aiming for a more abstract piece of art. "Yes, I see. The use of color is astonishing," he told her. "And you're hardly forgettable, Lady Charis."

Charis preened as she sat back on her stool. "You're too kind, your highness."

"You are dedicated to Efarae, correct? Did you choose painting as your focus?"

"Of course not, singing is my focus. That's why I performed at the opening ceremony." She tossed her hair over her shoulder and admired her painting. "I did dabble in painting and drawing for a little while though. But the goddess showed me it wasn't where she wanted me to spend my time."

From what he heard that first night, Alvis wasn't sure if singing was where the goddess wished for her to spend her time either, but maybe she'd had an off day or was still new to the art.

A squeal rang through the air and over at their stations. Brylee stood with wide eyes and jaw dropped at the red paint as bright as her bird spilled all over her. Salome at her side was in shock, a bucket of paint fallen on the ground next to her.

"Brylee...I...I'm so sorry. I didn't mean..."

But Brylee only burst into laughter and dabbed Salome on the nose with her paintbrush, painting it blue. Within moments, utter chaos ensued with paint and brushes flying everywhere. Charis and Adeena screeched and screamed as they gathered their skirts and ran for safety, while the others, perhaps shocked at first, joined in on the paint fight. Before long, they were all covered in paint, a rainbow of living color.

Mother stood from her seat and looked out at the scene in horror while Father laughed at her side. "What is the meaning of all of this? You're supposed to be future queens!"

But the laughter of the group overpowered her words, and Alvis couldn't help but laugh with them. He knew Brylee would bring some much-needed fun to the palace. Something hit him square in the back, and when he turned to look, Myra and Nell stood side by side, unable to contain their giggles, their hands soaked in yellow paint. The flames inside him danced and flickered.

Three could play at that game.

"You better watch yourselves."

With a mischievous grin, he picked up a cup and dipped it into a paint bucket. Myra and Nell dashed off, but with his long legs, Alvis was able to catch up to them and dumped yellow paint down Myra's back. She screeched, but there was a smile on her face so bright it rivaled Ray's sun, igniting the heat inside Alvis.

He'd never seen anything so beautiful.

Chapter Seventeen

MYRA

MYRA NESTLED INTO THE CUSHIONS AND PILLOWS LAID OUT IN HER AND Alvis's usual spot in the library as she delved further into a book about Ray's magic. She'd come up with a theory that if Alvis could make the room holding the mirror warm and dry enough, it could dry up any water magic Amelia could summon. Already they'd frozen the area directly surrounding the mirror, so it encased the mirror even more. Still, they both were concerned that if Amelia and whoever she was partnered with were patient enough, they could melt the ice. They could surround the area with fire, but Amelia's water could put that out. If there was a way the air was so dry it would evaporate and quench Amelia's water, it was a possibility. Amelia put so much reliance on her magic, it would greatly debilitate her and slow her down if she ever were to escape. They'd already attempted to put a ring of fire around the area, but it melted the ice.

To her side, Alvis had also made himself comfortable as he studied his own book, but she couldn't tell what it was about. He reclined against the pillows with one leg extended out in front of him, the other bent and propping up the book. Their evenings in the library were the most relaxed and content Myra had ever seen him—far more than he ever was during the events for the pageant.

Any of the stiff awkwardness present the first time she'd met him in the library had faded away over the last couple of weeks, and this now was Myra's favorite time of day. No one bothered them there. Not even Ramin, unless they had something to discuss with him. While here and there the air would chill when he was present, for the most part he left them alone.

A sigh—maybe of contentment—escaped from Alvis's lips as he sank deeper into the pillows. His wavy brown locks fell into his eyes, and with a casual hand, he brushed it away. Myra couldn't help but grin. The prince rarely ever had a moment where he wasn't completely put together, including his hair. He was always the picture of refinement and excellency.

Except for that day early on when a paint fight broke out during an activity. She'd never seen him laugh and have fun like that before, and how he ran and chased and played with Nell warmed her heart. Then when he chased her down, the paint making his clothes stick to his body like a second skin... She couldn't help but admit she'd wished no one else was around because there were a few things she'd like to do with him when he caught her.

His golden gaze darted away from his book to hers. "What?"

Myra blinked and flipped through the pages of his book. He'd caught her staring. She didn't mean to be. She was sure her face was turning pink as though he could read her thoughts. "I was wondering if you'd found anything new we could use. Maybe something more with heat."

Alvis pushed himself upright. "It's a possibility, but I'm concerned water will still overtake it. I was actually researching more about your magic." He scooted closer toward her so he could show her the book. Close enough that his legs almost touched hers.

Her heart stopped for a moment. The book didn't have any words on the spine, only the rough image of a rose with its petals falling off in a dark-purple ink. It was a thin book, one which could easily be slid between two others without being noticed unless someone was specifically looking for it.

"What book is this?"

Alvis shook his head. "I'm not sure. Not even the librarians know.

I'd asked them about books about Stulan magic because we don't have much about it. Your goddess likes to keep her secrets. But one said she'd seen a few and directed me to a shelf. I'd been by that shelf a million times but never noticed the Stulan books. When I saw the inscription on the spine and how it was like the one on your necklace, I thought maybe there was something to it."

"May I?"

"Of course."

Alvis passed the book to her, and they sat shoulder to shoulder as she paged through it. Myra wasn't even sure what she was looking for in the book, only wanted to touch it to know it was real. The only book she'd known of was *The Book of Shadows*.

"I didn't know there were any books about my magic," she confessed and carefully turned the soft, thin pages. "Everything I know was passed down from my mother and a grimoire we once had. Other things I've only picked up bits and pieces from the few other followers I've encountered or experiments."

Alvis's brows raised. "Experiments?"

"One of my former masters. My first one when I was a young girl. It was why he took me on. He enjoyed pushing the boundaries and wanted to see what I could do. Who and what I could kill and bring back to life." She looked away from Alvis and back at the book when she told him this, not even sure why she said anything. If she wasn't careful, she could let more details of her past slip, and any fascination or intrigue he had in her or her magic would vanish. "He wasn't a kind man."

Alvis nodded as though he understood. "I imagine you didn't have many choices in the matter back then with the experiments he wanted you to do. Or with any of your other masters or mistresses."

Myra swallowed a lump in her throat. He had no business being so kind and understanding. "Not particularly."

"How many have you worked for?"

Alvis was entering dangerous territory, one where he could find out the truth about everything. Her heritage, how she came to be in Amelia's household, and the potion she'd used for King Brennan. There was something about the way Alvis looked at her though. Those golden eyes soft and understanding and curious. A whole world lingered behind those eyes of his. Over the time she'd spent getting to know him, Myra'd been given glimpses into. As crown prince, Alvis was required to make conversation with anyone and everyone and be willing to engage. But when left to his own devices, he preferred the comfortable and quiet company of his books and a choice few people. He was terribly curious, though, and willing to dive into the deep waters of a topic he was interested in to sort out and think through in the depths of his mind.

Myra wanted to see more into his world. How he saw it and the way it worked.

And he wanted to know more about hers, too, as though there was a place among all his other curiosities for her. She was just as fascinating and interesting. Out of all the people he wanted to spend evenings with and know more about, it was her.

They were working together to protect the mirror. He wanted to be sure he could trust her. That must have been all it was. But Myra couldn't help but wonder and hope if it was more. That kernel of ridiculous hope led her to open her mouth.

"Two for the most part. The one with the experiments, and we traveled around a lot. Sometimes he would hire me out to other people. Then, when we were in the Dravian Islands, he lost a bet, and I was sent to Cal's family. They adopted me. But when our parents died... Well, that's when Amelia found us." At least she could leave out the details of how she helped Cal kill those who killed their parents.

Alvis nodded solemnly, as though it was the most important and serious thing he'd ever heard. "I knew you and Cal weren't blood related, but never knew how you came to be family. Although, what of your own family? Those who raised you. Where were you before your first master?"

"Cal practically raised me. 'He's always been the one person I can rely on," Myra explained. "But I was sold to my first master as a young girl by my family. My uncle, actually. My mother was gone then. I learned most of what I know about Stula from her."

"Oh. I see. And your father? He had no say in the matter?"

"If he objected, I never heard."

Alvis brought in a tiny intake of breath. Not quite a gasp, but as though he wanted to be careful with even his breathing so he would say the right thing. "I'm sorry."

It wasn't pity, and he didn't have that glazed-over, uncomfortable look in his eyes so many others had when they'd heard pieces of her history, knowing fully well how far below them she probably was but 'not wanting to be rude. He seemed genuinely sorry.

Myra shifted in her seat and shrugged. "It's fine. Well, it's not fine. But I've determined if he didn't object to my leaving, then he shouldn't be someone I should waste my time on."

Alvis reached out and touched her wrist. His skin was so warm but sent a jolt through her anyway. "He doesn't know what he's missing."

Myra dared to meet his gaze. He was much closer than she'd originally realized, his hand still resting on her wrist. So close she could feel his breath on her skin. She turned her head away and went back to focus on her book. "That's kind of you to say."

Alvis removed his hand from her wrist but didn't distance himself. As much as she should have wanted him to, Myra didn't mind the closeness. It was like when they were in the middle of the paint fight. For a moment, she thought he'd wanted to kiss her, and desperately hoped he would. Which of course was ridiculous. It didn't stop her from daydreaming about it and imagining if he had though. At night, when she finally could escape from her duties and rest, she imagined that day. What could have happened if the other women hadn't been there, if they' had been able to be so close in other circumstances. How he would have held her and what his lips would have felt like.

A situation such as this when they were alone.

Myra bit her lip and kept her gaze on the book. If she looked back at him, surely he would be able to see what was going through her mind, written clear as day across her face. How mortifying.

Alvis shifted in his seat and paged through the book in his lap. "I've been thinking about your magic lately and how it might be of some use to us."

"How would my magic help?"

He propped one knee up and rested his arm on top of it. "I know typically when we think of Stula, we think of death to living things.

People, animal, plants…but what if it could mean death to other things as well?"

Myra blinked a few times and set her book aside. She should be hesitant to do any sort of experimentation, especially after what she'd just confessed to him. But Alvis wasn't the sort of man who would want to bring death to anyone. "What other types of things do you mean?"

"Magic."

She'd never thought of that before and hadn't heard of anyone else thinking of it either. It was an interesting thought. "I'm not sure I know what you're getting at."

He scooted forward and leaned on his knee, an excited gleam in his eyes. "Nothing permanent or which would be harmful to someone. I wouldn't want to do that. But what if we could create a space where magic was neutralized? Or there was a spell you could cast on someone where their magic wouldn't work anymore for a short amount of time? In a sense, kill the magic temporarily."

Myra pulled her knees up to her chest and rested her chin on top of them. How would she be able to do that though? In theory, it could work.

"Maybe it's possible," she said after a few moments of consideration. Alvis hadn't rushed her answer and let her ponder on it for a time. He didn't mind those quiet moments. "It wouldn't prevent Amelia from escaping though."

"No. Maybe it would bring certain barriers though. Make the space more neutral so she couldn't use her magic against anyone else."

"No one else would be able to use their magic against her."

"No, it would be neutral ground, and if we have skilled guards who can fight even without magic, they could more easily detain her as she wouldn't be able to rely on water the way she usually does. It also would prevent other people from using their own magic to help free her."

This was a good point. She was so used to people being able to use their powers whenever they wanted, a place where it wasn't possible to use those powers was difficult to imagine. There were some who decided to not dedicate themselves to a deity of course and didn't have magic at all, but it was rare.

"We need magic around the mirror though, so the Attendants can have their weekly checkups and for Nell to be able to see her during their visits," Myra pointed out.

Alvis sighed. She must have stumped him there. "You're right. It's one of the many factors we need to consider."

"I would need to think about it though. Many times, I need to connect to the energy or spirit of someone or something to manipulate and guide it, so I would need to determine a way where my magic could do that on its own without my being there. And I've never manipulated someone else's magic before."

Only their spirits. Although, for so many, their magic was such a deep part of them they would claim they were one and the same. It wasn't, but taking someone's magic away from them, even temporarily, seemed to be risky. For their intents and purposes, it could be useful and helpful.

"And people could abuse it, if we were able to figure out a way to achieve this," Alvis added after another moment of thought. "Which is the way of most things, I suppose. If it's something you aren't comfortable with, I'll understand. Considering everything."

The sentiment warmed her. As he'd said, she'd never had much of a choice in these matters. If she did, it was "Do what I say, or you or someone you care about will be harmed." What other option did she have but to obey? Knowing Alvis wouldn't demand this of her made something inside Myra relax and breathe as though it had never done so before.

"I would need to practice."

"Naturally. If it can't be done well and correctly, then it shouldn't be done at all. We need to be prompt of course, but if I can help, I'd be more than happy." He babbled on like a nervous young boy and ran his fingers through his hair. Was something bothering him? Myra couldn't imagine what it could possibly be, but she also couldn't help but think it was rather adorable. "I can help you if you like. Use my magic as a test. You can experiment with it."

Myra closed the book and set it on the pile next to her. "I suppose there's no time like the present." It was late, and she should be going to get some sleep as Charis would no doubt wake her up early as she had been every morning. But each evening Myra spent with Alvis in the library, they'd been staying later and later. She sat on her feet and faced Alvis, and he followed her lead, his knees almost brushing against her black pants. "Light a flame and see if I can manipulate it."

Alvis took in a deep breath, and the sun tattoo on his chest lightly glowed through his yellow tunic, almost making him look like the sun itself. Not bright and blinding on a hot summer day, but gentle and soft as though it was peeking through the clouds after a rainstorm. In his outstretched palm, a swirl of light twisted and turned in circles until it developed into a ball of flames hovering in the small space between them. The heat warmed Myra's face, and it was close enough that with the slightest breeze, it could burn her. The flames reflected in Alvis's golden eyes, and she knew he would never allow that to happen.

Myra let her shoulders relax and summoned her magic. The cold and dark stirred within, and black streams poured from her hands, swirling around the flames. The darkness and light danced independently but still blended as though they wanted to combine and dance with one another but didn't know how.

"Beautiful," Alvis breathed.

It was beautiful. Myra almost hated to do anything else to it so they could sit and be mesmerized by the sight. She wet her drying lips and tried to sense the magic coming from the flames. It was so much warmer than her magic. What must it be like for Alvis to have this pulsing through him all the time and always be radiating heat and light ready to escape and burst out into the world?

Myra imagined her magic smothering the flame like a heavy blanket. The dark swirls flickered in and out of the fire as though it wanted to touch it but was too afraid to be burned. Each time she did, she felt a bit of heat flash through her. Alvis flinched.

"Did you feel that?" she asked.

Alvis nodded. "It's cold. But don't stop. I think it's working, whatever you're doing."

She raised her hands and positioned them around the shadows and flames as though she were holding a large sphere between her palms. The shadows pressed in on the flames, and little by little, they shrank but still fought back. His magic was much stronger and more practiced

than hers. A bead of sweat dripped from Myra's forehead, but she
continued to concentrate.

Her arms grew tired and shook, but even so, the flames shrank and
the heat within her softened as the shadows grew stronger. The familiar
chill slowly took control. But it was still too much, the magic of the fire
too strong. It was smaller and the light dimmed, but she couldn't
completely smother it. All the while, Alvis continued to watch her
through the mix of darkness and light. Sometimes he flinched or
shivered, but his intense gaze never left hers.

Finally, her arms collapsed at her sides, and the shadows
disappeared, the flames overtaking the small space between them.
They'd come even closer together as it almost singed her hair, but with a
wave of his hand, the flames vanished, and she knelt face-to-face with
Alvis, his chest heaving as much as hers.

"Myra…"

She couldn't tell who moved first, but his lips were on hers. They
were soft and warm, and Myra felt herself melt as he cupped her face
with his hands, his fingers tangled in her hair. It was as though the
whole world stopped and there was only the two of them. She wrapped
her arms around him, and they pulled in closer, letting their mouths
explore one another the way Myra had imagined so many times.

When their lips parted, they didn't break their embrace, and Alvis
smiled. "I've been wanting to do that for a long time."

Myra pressed her forehead against his. His skin was hot to the
touch, and now that her eyes were open, she could have sworn steam
was floating off him. "I have too."

"I'm glad the feeling is mutual."

Cupping the back of her head with his palm, Alvis pulled Myra in
once again. His kisses were everything she'd imagined and more, and
she couldn't help but wonder if she were back in one of her fantasies.
But the feel of his chest pressed against hers was real. How his tongue
mingled with hers was real. The softness of his lips was real. The way
the magic running through him warmed her was real.

It went against everything Myra had been telling herself to stay
away. To tame those thoughts and push them deep down until they were
smothered the way she should have with those flames. But like those real

flames, she wasn't strong enough to extinguish them. Instead, she let them overtake her.

A cold breeze blew through the space, and someone cleared their throat. Alvis froze, and Myra reluctantly broke away from him. Ramin hovered in the space before them, and her cheeks heated. A sudden return to reality. She pulled herself away as quickly as possible but grasped Alvis's hand to share her magic so he could see the spirit along with her, and his face turned as red as she was sure hers was.

"I'm sorry to interrupt...but someone is here," Ramin said. He didn't seem sorry at all, a small smirk plastered on his transparent face. "I heard them inquire about you at the desk, and they are coming this way."

Myra's heart sank into her stomach as the cold reality of the world returned. She'd just kissed Prince Alvis. Multiple times. And someone saw. It might have been a spirit, but they'd still been seen. Who knew who else could have seen them? How could she be so stupid?

"Thank you for telling us, Ramin," Alvis said with a slight shake to his voice.

Ramin bowed his head and floated away, leaving Myra and Alvis there to catch their breath. She looked over at him and swallowed a lump in her throat.

"Myra...I..."

"Alvis?"

A light voice came through from the stacks. Before them, a shimmer of stardust floated through the dark library, and through it appeared Princess Eira, Prince Cadeyrn, and the shape-shifting dragon Aytigin. Her blue dress swished along the floor, and her own inner star glow radiated around the trio.

The princess blinked a few times when she saw Myra there and then smiled. "Myra, we didn't expect you here as well. But that's wonderful. And we're sorry to surprise you, but we're in need of your help."

Chapter Eighteen

ALVIS

EIRA AND CADEYRN WERE HERE, BUT ALL ALVIS COULD THINK ABOUT was how he wished he were kissing Myra again. Eira and Cadeyrn—and that dragon man—were here. But they weren't supposed to arrive until the ball next week. What were they doing here early? He hadn't had the chance to prepare himself.

Myra looked as shocked as he was, her chest heaving and a blush at her light-brown cheeks. That beautiful, perfect chest he'd had more dreams about than he should admit. No. He had to focus. He blinked a few times and forced himself to look at his brother and Eira and smother the flames that erupted inside him when he and Myra had kissed.

"I'm sorry to surprise you," Eira said. "But it is an important matter, and we weren't sure where else to go."

His former betrothed had the same ethereal glow around her he remembered from when she first returned from her quest. Eira had always been beautiful. But now, she was stunning. Almost too much to even look at, with her black as night hair that still shone with stardust, skin pale as the moon, and bright-red rose lips. Touched by Luana, she had said happened. The goddess's representative in the world.

Supposedly, that was what the two of them were supposed to be.

The Chosens of Ray and Luana, to be the representatives of the deities in physical form to be vessels for them to share their love. According to Eira's story, this wasn't the case. The tradition of the Chosens was just that—a tradition. Nothing mandated or brought to the people by the deities, and created by a king and queen long ago to unite their kingdoms and bring peace.

Alvis was reminded of this each time he saw Eira and knew she told the truth. The magic inside him sang at the sight of her as though it knew a piece of the goddess dwelled in her. All the people who doubted her words and removed her from her rightful place as heiress to the Cresin throne either were blind or simply stubborn.

At Alvis's side, Myra straightened her shirt and moved to get on her feet. "I should let you all talk."

Alvis's chest tightened at the thought of her leaving, and he instinctively grabbed her hand. "Please stay."

She had no reason to be embarrassed or wish to leave. In fact, the group seemed glad Myra was there. Besides, if anyone should be embarrassed, it was Alvis. He was the one who shouldn't have put Myra in such a compromising position. He was the one who should have controlled himself. Even if Myra did say she wanted it too. He couldn't even remember who kissed whom first. Alvis took in a deep breath and attempted to calm and lower his voice.

"Please, Myra. I would like you to stay if you are able to. And if you wish. You're among friends here."

"Yes, please stay. We're the ones intruding. There's no reason for you to go," Eira added. Her smile was soft and gentle, one hardly anyone could say no to.

Myra looked at Alvis, and the tension in her face subsided. "Very well, if that is what you wish."

Alvis realized he hadn't let go of her hand yet, but he couldn't find the will to let it go and gave it a soft squeeze. "It is."

To the side, the dragon man—Aytigin—leaned against a bookcase and raised his brows. His white wings were tucked behind his back but still stuck out and almost hit the other shelves. He had a suggestive smirk on his face as though he had seen them kissing the way Ramin had. "Well, I'm glad that's settled of who's leaving and who's staying then."

Cadeyrn waved him off. "Never mind him. He's an old grouch."

Alvis and Myra made room among their cushions for the trio to sit, and Eira and Cadeyrn took seats on the ground. After an icy look from Eira, Aytigin sat as well.

Cadeyrn offered Alvis a single nod. "It's good to see you. Have you been well?"

There was something familiar yet oddly distant about seeing his brother again. Cade still had the same wild hair and playful gleam in his eyes. But there was a new maturity and confidence about the way he presented himself that took Alvis off guard.

It was odd, being the first time Alvis had seen or spoken to his brother since he'd been in Cresin. They'd gone through periods of time apart of course. Cadeyrn off on campaigns or running his estate, and Alvis traveling around the kingdom and to and from Cresin. But both knew it was different this time. Through this whole process of the pageant, Alvis had been wanting his brother there for advice and encouragement. Now, he wasn't sure what to say.

The flames inside him subsided. Almost cooled as much as they possibly could. Whenever Alvis thought about what happened in Cresin, his magic stirred and boiled in the pit of his stomach. Now that Cadeyrn and Eira were here, he felt nothing beyond shock.

"Well enough, and you?"

"I seem to enjoy mountain life," Cadeyrn admitted. "Even with all the snow. And Father? How has he been?"

"He's fine, as much as to be expected. Gets tired often." He cleared his throat. "Not that I don't want to catch up, but what is it that brings you here? We weren't expecting you until next week."

They might as well get to the point. Then maybe once he got some sleep, he could calm himself and gather his thoughts about…everything.

Eira nodded, her lips in a tight line. "Right." She arranged her skirts around her in a circle as though she needed something to occupy herself with other than looking at Alvis. "Well, I've been trying to break the curse in Luana's Castle that binds Aytigin to the castle and me. I've made progress in repairing the temple. At least until…"

Her shoulders fell, and she massaged her temple. "I'm not sure how it happened."

Cadeyrn placed his hand on her knee and rubbed it with his thumb. It was so calm and natural for him to comfort her. The gesture should have bothered Alvis. Made him jealous or angry or hurt. But there was nothing. Out of the corner of his eye, Myra looked at him, and he gave her a small nod. He was fine.

How odd. But freeing too. It was as though something in him released and breathed once again.

Aytigin harrumphed. "Our Little Luana made a mess of things."

Cadeyrn turned his head toward the dragon with a snap and glared.

"She didn't make a mess of things," he snarled.

"I did a bit."

"Well, things are a disaster in my once peaceful home." Aytigin stretched and stood once again. "I'm going out for a fly." Before any of them could say another word, he left the room. Alvis could only hope the dragon wouldn't frighten the people of Cyre.

Eira gave Alvis and Myra an apologetic look. "He's been a bit moody lately."

A dark chuckle came from Cadeyrn. "Lately?"

She grimaced. "Fine. More than usual. It's been the most difficult on him. You see, as I was repairing the temple and working at a stone table, I awoke a spirit. The spirit of Malle."

Alvis had heard the history of Malle before. How the Chosen of Ray she'd married was a cruel man and she'd taken another lover. When they'd been found out, she was banished from the kingdom and stripped of her title. Apparently, that hadn't been the entire story. Aytigin was the lover, and they escaped to Luana's Castle in the Paravian Mountains. Aytigin had a perverse obsession with finding new ways to connect with Luana and would perform dangerous experiments with Luana's priests. One of them resulted in Malle's death, thus causing Aytigin's curse and the banning of all men from being priests in Luana's temples.

Cadeyrn bent one knee, rested his arm on it, and continued the story. "At first, everything seemed fine. She was peaceful, although quiet, and Aytigin was happy to have her here. He would try to communicate with her but without much luck. But he didn't mind and was happy with her presence. He was almost pleasant to be around."

"For a while at least," Eira corrected. "After some time, Malle became more and more disturbed. She undoes any repairs I make on the temple. She has wild fits and tantrums. Aytigin tries to calm her as much as he can, but she's not who she once was."

Now it was Alvis's turn to look at Myra. He didn't want to draw much attention to her, but still wished to see her reaction. The blush from their kiss earlier had vanished, and her face turned pale. She blinked a few times, and from the crease between her soft brown eyes, he could tell thoughts were swirling around in her mind.

As far as Alvis was aware, Eira and Cadeyrn didn't know about Myra's magic, and he didn't want to reveal any of her secrets. As unfortunate as it was, those who followed Stula were looked at with suspicion, so he didn't blame her for wanting to not share it with everyone. Especially after what she'd told him this evening about her past. Even her tattoo was well hidden.

He'd been curious as to where her dedication tattoo was, though. Even for those whose tattoos were covered with clothing, it would glow through the fabric at times when they performed magic, and he never saw a hint of it, no matter how often she practiced her magic in front of him. Too many nights he'd dreamed about exploring her body to find it. And to do other things as well. He'd even thought about it as they'd kissed. His flames sparked and stirred again.

Alvis swallowed. No. This wasn't the time. He was being ridiculous. He'd never been this way about any woman before, and she was all he could think about. Damn the timing of it all.

"We've tried to put her to rest. Found some Stulan priests to assist," Eira continued and brought Alvis's thoughts back to the conversation at hand. "But we haven't had any luck. What's even more confusing is when her spirit awakened, a big cloud appeared. It was shadowy and dark, and a symbol was formed in it. We've exhausted the materials in Paravia and can't find anything. Which is why we came here in hopes your library might have something that tells us about it."

Cadeyrn dug into his pockets, pulled out a folded piece of paper, and handed it to Alvis. When opened, it revealed a purple rose with petals falling off it. Myra took in a breath. It was the same one as on her necklace and the book Alvis had been reading. The page almost ripped when she reached over and took it out of his hand. Her gaze searched the page as though she couldn't believe what was on it.

"Why? How?" she asked, almost to herself.

Eira leaned forward and scooted herself closer to Myra. "Do you know something about this symbol?"

As though it took all the effort she could muster, Myra broke her gaze from the symbol to look at Eira, then to Alvis, and then to the paper again. If there was something she could do to help break the curse, it would be wonderful for Eira and Cadeyrn. Whatever awkwardness there was between them didn't mean Alvis didn't want them to succeed. At the same time, he didn't want Myra to be forced to use her magic if she didn't want to. He had a sense there was more to her past and her magic she wasn't sharing with him, and it was up to her when was the best time to share. If ever.

Not wanting to reveal anything to the others, Alvis didn't say a word. He only gave Myra a look he hoped showed she didn't have to tell them about her magic.

From the soft smile she gave in return and a small nod of her head, it seemed to say she knew.

"It's a symbol of Stula," she said. She handed the page to Eira and pulled out the necklace from underneath her white tunic. Eira's eyes grew wide at the sight, and she gasped. "It's a family heirloom my mother gave me. We've all followed her for generations. It's on this book Alvis showed me as well."

Eira sank back on her heels, and her face lit up like the stars. "You have Stulan magic. I always wondered who you were dedicated to."

"Not many people know. Cal does, of course. But others don't like Stulan magic, so I've found it best to keep it quiet."

Cadeyrn took the paper from Eira when she handed it to him and slid it back into his pockets. "Understandable."

"Cade! No one should have to hide their magic."

He raised his hand in surrender. "I agree. But I'm sure Myra is being generous when she only says people don't like Stulan magic. We don't know much about it, and people fear what they don't know. Even you have admitted you were frightened when you encountered the priest to get the cure for your father. I have no doubt others have acted poorly around Myra when they've found out about her magic. It's understandable, the desire to keep it quiet."

"Yes, I can understand that." Eira looked at Alvis and Myra. "But if you are willing and think you may be able to assist us in any way possible, we would be forever grateful. And we promise to keep your secret."

"I'd be happy to help however I can. I trust you. All of you."

A swell of pride rose in Alvis at Myra's words. After everything she'd gone through, she was still willing to help them. And she trusted them, which couldn't have been easy. He could only hope he was included in that group. Yet they needed to share their own problem they were solving. He glanced at Myra with the question in his eyes. She nodded.

"Although Myra is helping me in a pressing matter as well," Alvis said. "It's about Amelia."

EIRA'S DRESS BILLOWED OUT BEHIND HER IN WAVES AS SHE STORMED through the palace halls and to the chamber holding the mirror. When they updated her and Cadeyrn on what had been happening, she demanded to see for herself immediately. Stardust and shadows floated around in her wake, leaving a trail behind her. The floor sparkled with its shimmer, and shadows hovered in the air in tiny thin clouds.

The rest of them followed, flecks of stardust dusting their clothes. At Alvis's side, Myra smiled while she observed the shimmer on her tunic. He couldn't help but admire her lovely glow, and his chest warmed. "The castle must be filled with stars," she mused.

The smile on Cadeyrn's face was wide and bright, and the stardust reflected in his eyes. "She hasn't learned to control it all when her emotions run high."

The guards gawked and then bowed as the princess went past, and sighs of relief came from them when they saw Alvis was with her. She paused when she arrived in the room and took in her surroundings.

Ignoring the guards on either side of the mirror, she approached it and examined the glass. Next to her, Cadeyrn walked around it and did his own investigations. Alvis and Myra followed in their wake, allowing them space. One thing Alvis knew about Eira, while she was kind and understanding, once she had her mind on something, it was best to be out of the way and let her at the task at hand. It would appear as though Cadeyrn had already learned how to keep up with her and partner in her excursions. Or maybe he always knew.

Around the edges of the glass, the ice was soft and melting. Eira pinched her brows together and pursed her lips. "It's not much, but that even someone could come in here and do that little is concerning."

The tattoo on Eira's chest glowed as she put her hands on the mirror and covered it with another layer of ice. Then she turned to the guards. "How could this have happened?"

The guards sputtered and gawked, bowing before the ethereal woman before them.

"We're not sure, your highness," one of them said, a quiver in his voice. "All I know is each time we grow tired all of the sudden, and there's music. By the time we open our eyes, they're gone, and we've only caught glimpses of them. They keep their heads and faces hidden. From what I can tell, we're only asleep for a few minutes."

"And you're certain it's two women?" Cadeyrn asked.

"It would appear so, sir," the other guard answered. "We can see snippets of hair sometimes when it falls out of place."

Eira paced around the room, her tattoo still glowing, and let a chill fall over the room. It had always been cold in there to keep the ice from melting, but there was something more solidified about the sensation now.

"It's as we told you, your highness," Myra said.

Eira turned to her, a gentle look in her blue eyes. "I know. It wasn't as though I didn't believe you. I just wanted to see for myself." She wrapped her arms around herself, not from the cold as it didn't bother her after her encounter with Luana, but perhaps for comfort. "I can't stand the idea of Amelia getting out and possibly harming people again."

"Me either," Myra said.

The two women met eyes with a shared understanding of what it was like to be manipulated and terrorized by the former queen. Alvis's chest tightened. If only there was more he could do to help and protect them. Not that either of them needed his protection. Time and time again, each in their own ways had proved they were more than capable of taking care of themselves and overcoming any obstacles they faced. Yet the feeling to protect didn't go away.

Eira, he knew, had Cadeyrn now, who was far more able to protect anyone than Alvis was anyway. But Myra... Alvis had to fight the urge to wrap her in his arms and take her as far away from Amelia and the mirror as he possibly could. To be sure she was safe and happy, never needing to work for someone so cruel ever again.

After Eira and Cadeyrn double- and triple-checked the area, they all went back upstairs to bed. It was much later than any of them anticipated to be up, and Alvis still had pageant activities to attend in the morning.

"I'll check back again tomorrow," Eira told them before she and Cadeyrn went to their room. "And every day if I need to. Do you really think you can nullify magic, Myra?"

"I can try," was Myra's response. "It's not anything I've done before. But I think with enough practice it could work."

"We're happy to offer our magic for you to practice on," Cadeyrn said.

"I appreciate that, your highness."

They agreed to meet in the library the next evening to help Myra practice and went on their way, leaving Myra and Alvis alone so they could also go to their separate rooms. Alvis knew they needed to get the rest but couldn't bring himself to leave Myra's side. The fire within him still burned and simmered, and the more he was around her, the more it threatened to burn through him. When they kissed, he could have sworn steam floated off his body. It was as though he was a young man first discovering desire and want for the first time. Even with such serious matters at hand, all he wanted was to go back and kiss Myra again. Then again, regardless of the matters at hand, he shouldn't kiss Myra—or do anything he imagined—at all. Which only made it more desirable and exciting.

"Are you all right, Alvis?" Myra asked as they walked. "I'm sure their arrival was a shock."

Her *question* was a shock, and it took Alvis a moment to process it. "Yes, I'm fine. It was surprisingly good to see them, and I'm glad they're here."

Oddly enough, the only bitterness or anger he had at their arrival was interrupting the moment he'd had with Myra. One he wanted to relive, even though he knew he shouldn't. He cleared his throat. "I didn't intend to be so forward...earlier."

A mischievous glint appeared in Myra's eyes. "I didn't intend to either. Are you sorry?"

Sorry? Perhaps he should have been, but he wasn't.

"Because I'm not."

Alvis stopped walking at her confession. She did tell him she'd wanted it too. "I confess, I'm happy to hear that."

"But there is the matter of the pageant. I'm sure the other women wouldn't be happy with you kissing someone else."

With those words, it all crashed around him. Of course. The pageant. That damn pageant. All of this with Amelia wouldn't be happening if it weren't for it. But at the same time, Myra wouldn't be there either if it wasn't for the pageant.

Alvis drew in a deep breath and rubbed the back of his neck. "If only I felt as comfortable around them as I do with you. I've found our evenings in the library to be my favorite time of day."

He was being too forward again. Saying and doing things he shouldn't be. Nothing good could come of this. But he was exhausted. Exhausted from keeping his thoughts to himself and always doing what was right. For once, he wanted to say and do as he pleased and not what was best for everyone else. And that was being honest with Myra and wrap his arms around her small body, to feel her supple, round rear in his palms, and kiss those soft lips again.

And if he didn't get his desire and magic under control, he thought he might explode.

A broad smile swept across Myra's face, and there was a sparkle in those lovely brown eyes. He could look at her all day. There was a certain gentleness and welcomeness to her that didn't make Alvis feel as though he needed to look away. Did she know how lovely she was? The entire time he'd known her, Myra easily slid herself in and out of the shadows so as not to be noticed. Maybe it was because of the job she held. But he wished she didn't hide away so often.

"It's my favorite time of day too," she said. She pointed to the book he'd been carrying around. The one about Stulan magic. "May I borrow that?"

He reached out to her and placed the book in her delicate but strong and worked hands. "Please do. Keep it as long as you wish."

"Thank you. Good night, Alvis."

Myra hugged the book to her chest and then, stretching on tiptoes, kissed Alvis on the cheek. That simple act made his heart race and desire pulse through him. She lingered there, and they breathed each other in, soaking in the moment. Surely she could not only feel the heat radiating off his body but him throbbing below his waist with how she was pressed so close to him. She swallowed and parted her lips, and her skin turned a soft pink. She looked from the book back up to his face. He could tell she was thinking about something but wasn't sure what. If only he could see into her mind to know what was going on in there.

"Myra, I'm so exhausted."

"It is late," she said, her breath soft against his skin.

He shook his head. "Not like that. Of doing what I'm supposed to and not what I want."

She gazed up at him. Was there hope and that same desire in her eyes? He prayed to Diar it was. "And what do you want?"

"For the night to not end."

"Neither do I. So what are you going to do about it?"

Alvis cupped Myra's face in his hands, and he kissed her as though he would never stop.

Chapter Nineteen

MYRA

ALVIS WAS IN HER ROOM. WHEN SHE'D ASKED HIM WHAT HE WANTED AND what he was going to do about it, Myra had only hoped this was what he meant. The entire time as he kissed her in the hall and they made their way to her room, all the while making sure no one saw them, she knew it was reckless and stupid to bring Alvis to her room.

But there he was. Once the door was closed and locked, he pulled her back into his arms and kissed her in a way that made her head spin. In these moments when they were alone and when he held her, he wasn't the prince and future king of Oxare. He was only Alvis. A man who loved knowledge and had a curiosity that knew no bounds. A man who cared for and respected the people around him. A man who made her feel excited and rebellious, while peaceful and safe at the same time.

She'd never felt like this before. She'd been attracted to other men, slept with them, and cared for them. But this was something new. It was dizzying and exciting, but it scared her to her core. She couldn't get enough of it.

He led her to the bed, and they collapsed onto it together and lay side by side in a tangle of limbs. His kisses became more urgent and desperate. She grasped his tunic and pulled him up against her body, wanting to feel every inch of him. His shaft pressed against her legs grew larger and harder with each moment, and his skin was so hot it warmed Myra all the way down to her bones. His lips traveled to her neck, and she moaned.

"I can't believe you're here," she confessed.

His kisses trailed to the round tops of her breasts begging to be freed from her shirt. "Is it all right?"

"It's perfect."

Alvis lifted his head so his gaze met hers. "You're perfect."

She was far from it, but instead of arguing, she kissed him, her hips rocking against his. Bless Diar, he felt so good. She slid her hand between them and down his torso to the bulge in his trousers. There was a spark when she touched him. His skin almost burned hers when her hand found its way underneath the waistband of it as she kissed his neck and rubbed his burning member that fit perfectly in her hand.

Alvis groaned and grasped her hair. "Gods, Myra."

The sound of her name on his lips ignited a fire in her, and she kissed his mouth, their tongues intertwining like two dancers as she continued to stroke him. "I've imagined this so many times," she confessed between kisses. Far too many nights, in fact.

"I have too."

"You have?"

He nodded and reached down to grasp her hand, and brought it to his lips, kissing each finger softly. "What do you imagine? Show me."

She ran her fingers across the bottom of his tunic. "Well, we have far less clothing than this."

What could only be called a wicked smile—if he was even capable of being wicked—came across his face. "I think that can be arranged."

She grasped the edge of his shirt and pulled it up and over his head so all that remained was his bare chest. He was smooth and soft and strong all at once beneath her hands as she ran them across his torso, almost feeling like her hands would burn from his skin. He then did the same to her shirt and undergarments until her breasts were free and exposed before him.

All Alvis did for a moment was admire her, lust filling his eyes. "Beautiful. May I…"

"Please."

Gods, please.

He cupped one of her breasts and rubbed the nipple with this thumb until he leaned forward and kissed and sucked it. A jolt went through Myra, and she gasped, grasping his dark locks in her hands and pulling him in closer. "More. Alvis. Please."

He sucked and licked her until she was certain he was going to leave a mark, a thought that thrilled her to her core. A hidden mark as evidence of their night together. How, at least for this one night, they belonged to each other.

"Was this all you imagined?"

Myra shook her head. "Yes, but there's more." Even though this already far exceeded her dreams.

"Praise Diar." He kissed her mouth again as she lowered her trousers, and when she couldn't move them down farther without bending over, Alvis helped her the rest of the way, tossing them aside with the rest of their clothing so she was fully bare.

She took his hand and guided it down her body, over her breasts, down her stomach, across her hips, until she had it land between her legs, his heat spreading to her so much that a bead of sweat already formed at her brow. "This is usually when I have to start rubbing myself."

Heat filled her face. She couldn't believe she just told him that.

He leaned forward and whispered in her ear. A shiver ran through her. "Show me."

Still grasping his hand, she guided his fingers to her folds and moved them in the way she would have done herself. Showing him the places to rub and the pressure she enjoyed. Myra moaned as he found her clit and soon let her hand slide away as she could barely even think anymore.

She gasped and cried out as he slid one of his fingers inside her while his palm still rubbed her clit. All the while, Alvis's eyes never left her face as he took in all her reactions and her pleasure. Normally she would have been self-conscious about him watching her like this, but she found she didn't care. In fact, she liked him watching her.

He kissed her neck and spoke against her skin. "May I taste you? Is that part of what you imagined?"

Myra could only nod, and he moved down and spread her legs wide open for him. He kissed the inside of her thigh. "So beautiful."

His mouth met her womanhood, and Myra sighed as she sank deeper into the bed. Each lick and kiss and stroke were full of purpose and care, making sure she enjoyed every moment of it. She gripped the sheets in her fists as his grasp on her thighs grew tighter and the orgasm built up inside her until her whole body shook from it. When she looked down, Alvis's gaze met hers, and a wave of desire pulsed through her. She clutched his hair and urged him on until she thought she would explode and cried out.

Alvis rose to meet her, his golden eyes filled with lust and desire. A dazzling, fiery red and gold flashed through them. "You taste amazing."

He lowered himself over Myra's body, covering it with his, and kissed her. She grasped the top of his trousers and tugged them down, and as they kissed, he kicked them off so they were pressed together, skin to skin, with nothing to separate them. His hot and hard cock rubbed against her, and Myra rocked against it, relishing the reaction she drew from him. He groaned into her mouth as they continued to kiss and rock against each other.

When she couldn't stand it anymore, Myra grasped his shoulders and turned to flip him over. Getting the idea, Alvis finished the job, so he was on his back and Myra splayed over him. She straddled her legs over each side of him and sat upright. Alvis dragged his hands over her thighs and stomach until they reached her small, round breasts. He cupped one in each hand and rubbed over her nipples and leaned forward to gift each one with a kiss, a lick, and a nibble. One of them indeed was already forming a mark from where he'd sucked her before. The sight brought a smile to Myra's lips.

She kissed him one more time before he lay back down, and she reached between them to find his swollen manhood that was desperate for release. She held it as though it was the most precious thing she'd ever touched, guided it inside her, and moaned as it filled her. Gods, his dick was perfect.

Alvis' leaned against the pillows, and he groaned, tiny beads of sweat forming at his brow. "Bless Diar, Myra, you feel amazing."

Myra didn't even have words as she rocked against him, savoring every moment and touch and movement. She rested her hands on his stomach for support, and he pushed his pelvis up to meet hers, bringing his cock deeper inside her. He slapped her rear with a loud smack and gripped it tight. She moved against him faster and faster until they both were gasping and crying out for more. Beads of sweat formed at their brows and threatened to fall into their eyes. Myra grew hotter each second. Then…Myra couldn't believe her eyes.

"Alvis, are you steaming?"

He grasped her by the hips and flipped them back over again in one swift movement, so Myra was on her back again. He hooked her leg around his waist and proceeded to pound his cock deeper into her body, the steam pouring off him in waves. "I burn, Myra. When you're near, I can hardly control it."

Myra's back arched, and she cried out, another orgasm taking over her. "Alvis, yes, please, don't ever stop."

Her words seemed to encourage him, and he moved even harder, faster, until Myra hit the headboard, and small flames flashed through the air. But she didn't care. All she wanted was for Alvis to continue to fuck her for the rest of time.

Alvis shook and groaned again and then pulled himself out. His seed spilled over her stomach, and he collapsed onto the bed next to Myra, breathless.

"You have quite an imagination, Myra," Alvis said.

Myra laughed. "It was one of the tamer ones."

"I can't wait to find out about one of the wild ones." He rolled over and kissed her. "I'll remember to bring the tonic next time."

The tonic that men took to prevent pregnancy. Myra's heart warmed at the thought of him wanting a next time. "That would be a good idea."

They kissed again, and when they broke apart, Myra got up and grabbed a couple of washing cloths so they could clean themselves up. Once those were tossed aside, Myra curled up back in bed with him, his arms wrapped tight around her, and after some time, they fell into a peaceful asleep as tiny flames flickered around them like stars in the night.

• • •

Myra woke at the sound of Alvis rustling against the sheets. It was still dark out, and Myra turned over to see Alvis sitting on the edge of the bed, putting his clothes back on. All the flames were gone now, and his skin returned to its usual brown instead of the burning red and pink it was the night before, cooled off after their exploits.

"Is everything all right?" she asked, her voice groggy from sleep.

Alvis twisted to see her and smiled. "Yes. Sorry, I didn't mean to wake you. I was going to leave a note."

Myra shook her head and sat up, letting the sheets fall around her waist. "It's all right. Are you going?"

His shoulders slumped and brows furrowed together. "It'll be morning soon, so I probably should. I figured it probably wouldn't be good for me to be seen coming from your room when everyone awakens."

Oh. Yes. Of course. As much as the words saddened her, Myra knew he was right. It wouldn't the good for either of them. The harsh reality of their situation. "Yes, that makes sense."

He finished getting dressed and kissed her soundly, making her head spin. "But I'll see you soon. And if you wish...perhaps tonight?"

So he did want to be with her again. Even if he only wanted it for the one night, it would have been worth it. But Myra couldn't help but be glad he wanted to see her again. She nodded. "I'd love that."

He smiled and made his way to the door. Before he could exit, Myra got out of bed and rushed to his side, kissing him one last time. He wrapped his arms around her and kissed her back, squeezing her rear. "Soon," he murmured against her forehead and kissed it.

Myra nodded. "Soon."

Chapter Twenty

MYRA

"Myra! Get over here and help me with this dress!"

Charis's voice rang through the air, and Myra snapped her head up. They were with the seamstress for Charis's final fitting for her ball gown, and she'd lost her train of thought while looking at the beaded trims. The green in one of them reminded her of the gardens where Alvis made love to her against a tree.

Not that it was love of course. But any other word for it sounded too crude. The way he spoke to her and touched her, their time together had been more than just a quick fuck.

At least she thought so.

They'd been doing that often the last few days. Stealing away in the evenings after Myra practiced her magic to be together for even a few moments when they could. Sneaking into each other's rooms late at night to wake up early before everyone else to leave before anyone saw. But even beyond bedding each other, they stayed up late into the night talking and sharing pieces of their lives with each other. It was foolish and served no purpose other than their own wants and amusements. But at least they could enjoy one another before Alvis picked a bride and Myra left with Eira to assist with putting Malle's spirit to rest. She hadn't intended to return to Cresin so soon, but Eira promised Aytigin would fly Myra to wherever she wanted to go once the task was complete.

It was to be a short-lived happiness, but it was one Myra could carry with her when life became unbearable. Like the memories with Mama, or the short time she lived with Cal and his parents and she could pretend to have a family. Just because something wasn't going to last forever didn't mean it wasn't worth having in the moment.

Myra turned and presented a shimmering pink trim to Charis. "I was wanting to be sure I found the right thing for you," she said and walked over to the mirror where Charis stood.

At her side in front of a second mirror was Adeena, who smirked and placed her hands on her hips. "She's worse than my girl was. Always daydreaming and getting distracted. Almost makes me wish I hadn't thrown her out."

Myra wished Adeena hadn't fired her lady's maid the week before for not being quick enough. Then Charis had *generously* offered to share Myra with her for the remainder of the pageant. As if Myra didn't have her hands full already only serving Charis alone. On top of it, she still had to complete her own dress for the ball as well as protect the mirror.

At least the whole thing was almost over. Myra couldn't decide if she was more relieved to be rid of Charis and Adeena, or sad to be leaving Alvis and the Golden Palace.

Charis ripped the trim out of Myra's hand and held it against the fabric of her ball gown. It accented the pink of the gown perfectly and gave it a lovely sparkle when she swayed and moved her hips. Her lip curled in a sneer, and she tossed the trim aside onto a pile of all the other discarded trims she'd already tried.

"That's hideous. Find something else."

There were three sharp raps on the door, and when it opened, Ai and Finley poked their heads in, two seamstresses with them. "Is there room for a few more?" Ai asked, a bright smile on her face. "There are a few things we need adjusted on our dresses."

Adeena and Charis glanced over their shoulders at the new arrivals, causing the seamstresses to have to pause their work, and annoyance clearly etched on their faces. While the two of them were close friends, they didn't let any of the other women into their circle and resisted any companionship with them outside of when it was required with pageant activities. Even then, they kept to themselves.

"I suppose," Adeena answered slowly.

But Ai and Finley had already made themselves welcome and set up at another set of mirrors. Fabric and jewels draped in their seamstresses' arms in waves of color and sparkle.

"Lovely. It's so kind of you to let us join you," Ai said, hardly giving Adeena and Charis the opportunity to respond. "My gown is almost done, but we have some finishing touches to do for Finley's."

Charis raised a single brow. "You're having a gown made for your servant?"

Ai shrugged. "She needs something to wear to the ball. I could hardly let her wear her usual clothes."

Finley, with no regard for modesty, was already half naked and changing into a bead-filled, low-cut blue gown. The gown was in three pieces, as was the custom in Oxare: a short, cropped top to show off Finley's toned stomach, a long flowing skirt, and a shawl draped over everything. It shimmered like the ocean as the fabric flowed around her. "Ai is certainly generous. And the other maids are getting their dresses done too."

Ai stepped behind a screen and threw pieces of her clothing over the top as she changed. "It's Prince Alvis who is the generous one, allowing all the maids who've been helping to come to the ball. Not many would be so thoughtful. Myra, how is your gown coming along?"

Charis and Adeena both perked up at this, and Myra wished Ai hadn't said anything. She'd been working on a dress in secret and hoped to go to the ball and stay on the sidelines, away from Charis and out of the way. It was the first ball she'd been invited to, and she didn't want to miss out. Even if it was the moment when Alvis would be announcing his bride.

Myra knelt and gathered the discarded trims Charis had been throwing around. Anything to avoid Charis's steel gaze. "It's fine. Almost done."

"You're planning to attend?" Charis asked, each word clipped and short.

"All the other maids are, and I am invited." Myra stood, careful not to drop any of the fabric bundled in her arms. "Besides, then I'll be there to attend to you as needed."

"And I'm sure you're going to be lovely," Ai said as she came out from behind the screen wearing a deep-red gown filled with beading. The top was cropped the way Finley's was, but longer to only show a small sliver of her pale stomach, and the neckline went up around her neck in a collar like the one she'd worn at the opening ceremony. A combination of the two cultures. Modest, but still stunning. "And I know Finley and I will enjoy the company."

Adeena scoffed and laughed. "I've never heard of such a thing. Inviting the servants to a grand ball and letting them dress in fine gowns."

"Well, it's a good thing you won't be here much longer to have to endure such terrible customs," Ai countered.

Charis's and Adeena's jaws dropped at her statement. "Why would you say such a thing?" Charis asked.

Finley and Ai stood in front of a large mirror and twisted and turned to admire themselves in their finery. The beading and jewels glimmered and sparkled in the light of the sun lanterns.

"Everyone knows Prince Alvis is likely to pick Nazneen," Ai said, looking at them through the reflection of the mirror. "It makes the most sense. She's from Oxare and is from a powerful family they both are dedicated to Ray, and have known each other for years."

Myra's heart plummeted to her stomach at Ai's announcement, and she took in a few deep breaths to control her shaking hands as she worked to organize the discarded trims. Of course it was assumed he would pick Nazneen for all the reasons Ai said. Along with all of those things, she was kind and lovely, and she got along with Nell. Alvis would be fortunate to have such a wonderful woman as his queen. But the thought of it made Myra sick. Him picking a bride was always a vague notion of something that was going to happen in the future. The fact that one person in the group was already assumed by many to be his choice brought a new reality to the situation.

Charis blinked and swallowed. Her usual proud and haughty countenance jarred. "You…you don't know that. He could pick any one of us." She shook her head. "Besides, if that's the case, then why are you here if you know so certainly it won't be you?"

Ai shrugged. "I've always wanted to visit Oxare, and when else would I be able to be surrounded by such finery?" She picked up the full skirt of her gown and swished it around.

"Myra, are you all right? You look pale." Finley caught Myra's gaze in the mirror's reflection. The color in her face had indeed drained.

Myra turned her face away from Finley and back at what she was working on before it revealed more of what she was truly feeling. "I'm fine. A bit tired is all."

"Well, wake up." Charis snapped her fingers at her. "Bring me that pink trim over there."

Myra glanced through the pile she'd been organizing, and the only pink trim she saw was the one Charis had already disregarded. She picked it up and held it out to Charis. "This one, my lady?"

Charis rolled her eyes. "Yes, that one, of course. Why didn't you show it to me before? It's perfect."

It took everything in Myra to not roll her eyes along with her, but she brought the trim over and held it up next to the dress. Charis smiled, as lovely as a crocodile. "Ah, yes, that's it exactly."

A knock came at the door, and when it opened, a familiar male voice greeted them.

"Good afternoon, ladies," Alvis said.

Charis and Adeena squealed and giggled.

"Your highness! What are you doing here? We're preparing our gowns!" Adeena said.

"Don't peek, or you'll ruin the surprise of seeing how they turn out!" Charis added.

Alvis had only poked his head through the door, and he obliged their wishes by holding a hand over his face so as not to see them. "I would never dream of ruining the surprise, Lady Charis. But I was wondering if I could borrow Myra. Princess Eira would like to see her."

Myra's heart jumped up again back into her chest. Usually, they didn't see each other until the evening. Considering the conversation they were just having, there was no reason for Myra to be excited to see him, but she couldn't help herself.

"Oh." Charis's voice was light but with a small tightness to it. "Of course, your highness, if she is needed by Princess Eira. I was done with her for now anyway."

"How generous of you."

Myra could almost see Alvis smile from behind his raised hand. She put the remaining fabric in her arms down in a pile, curtsied to the ladies in the room, and slid out the door after Alvis. They walked side by side in the direction of the holding place for the mirror. "Did Princess Eira really ask for me?"

"No," Alvis answered with a mischievous glint in his eyes. "I had a rare free moment and wanted to see you. But I figured it wouldn't be difficult to twist Eira's arm to work on preparing the mirror's protection for the ball."

Alvis pulled Myra into a secluded corner and kissed her, leaving her desperate and breathless and wanting more. The wall was cool against her back as he pressed her against it, her top gathering and bunching when it rose over her stomach. The touch him against her bare skin sent shivers through her, and she softly moaned when his hand climbed up her torso and cupped her breast. With a wave of a hand, Myra made light shadows surround them. Enough to conceal them more than they already were, but not so dark as to cause someone else to take notice of something unusual.

"I wanted to see you too," Myra said between kisses, and he pressed himself even closer, his dick hardening more with each moment against her leg. His body warmed along with it, but his skin didn't turn pink and red the way it did the first time. He was learning to control the burning.

She wished they were truly alone and free to do what they wanted. The desire she had for Alvis already was stronger than anything she'd felt before for other men, but now, over the last few days, knowing what it was like to be with him made it almost unbearable. He squeezed her breast and rubbed her nipple with his thumb, and she moaned again.

Yet the conversation with the ladies clouded Myra's mind. Meeting in secret and sharing stolen kisses was oddly fun and exciting at first. But the reality of the situation hovered over them like the shadows she'd created. In a short while, it was likely Nazneen Alvis would be kissing and holding. The young noblewoman from the south had always been kind to Myra and was a lovely person. She would make a wonderful queen and wife. But Myra couldn't help but let bitterness and envy take hold.

"What will happen once the ball is over?"

Alvis paused the amazing thing his mouth was doing to her neck and looked at her. "What?"

Myra lowered her arms from around his neck and placed them on his chest. His own hand was removed from her breast and rested on her waist. Which was unfortunate. "Have you thought about it? What will happen between you and me once you announce your bride and the pageant is over?"

Alvis took in a deep breath and stroked Myra's hair. "I suppose I could be asking you the same question, as it partly depends on what you want. Are you still planning to leave after all of this is through?"

The truth of it was, Myra hardly had time to make her own plans between serving Charis and now Adeena, and then working with Alvis to protect the mirror. She should have been preparing for her own future instead of that silly dress for the ball in her few spare moments.

"I haven't decided where I am going yet," she confessed.

"You're welcome to stay here if that is what you want. You've always been welcome."

"To continue to be a servant and what? Be your secret mistress while you and your future wife bear children?"

So many times Alvis made Myra blush, but now his face turned red. She had a hunch it wasn't from flattery or her charms. "I know it's not the most ideal. But I don't see any other options."

The giddiness and delight Myra felt when he'd pulled her away faded like the sun's light when it set in the evening. Bright and beautiful and colorful one moment, and then in a matter of moments, darkness.

"I see."

Alvis's face fell, and there was genuine guilt and sadness behind his golden eyes. "I don't know what else to do. I have a duty to my family, and my kingdom."

The worst of it was one of the things Myra admired most about him was how dedicated he was to said duty. And what else did she expect? But something about it still didn't seem right.

It wasn't only the idea of being Alvis's secret mistress, which should have been enough to make her to turn away from him, but also the thought that she'd still be in the same household as Amelia. Trapped in a mirror, but still there. Myra couldn't and wouldn't live in the same home as the former queen again. While Amelia might not have any more power over her, the memories still lingered, and it would be impossible to leave the past behind her. Besides, the longer she and Amelia were under the same roof, the more likely it was Alvis would find out about Myra and her involvement in Cresin.

Myra looked away from him and to the floor. "Perhaps it will be best if we go our separate ways once the ball is over."

It was as though a fire extinguished inside Alvis as his shoulders sank and face crumpled. "Is that what you want?"

What Myra wanted? It was high time she accepted what she wanted rarely ever came into play for her life. The reality of it was she took what was handed to her, and she did her best to keep her head above water and survive. If she had a few moments of happiness to grasp onto, she enjoyed it while it lasted and then let it go.

Sets of footsteps echoed through the hall, and the two of them straightened their stance. They might have been hidden in her shadows, but they weren't invisible.

Myra pushed herself away from the wall. "We should go find Princess Eira."

It was done. When Myra returned to her room that night, the task was complete. She'd created a large ring of shadows around the mirror where any magic would be nullified. The area directly in front of the mirror magic still worked, so those approved had access to it, but for everything else in the room, Myra's magic caused anyone else's to temporarily die. Or maybe sleep was a better word for it.

She took in a deep breath and sank into one of the chairs. The work of it was exhausting, and she felt she could sleep for days. But knowing the mirror was better protected before the ball was a relief.

In the corner of the room stood the mannequin she'd been creating her dress on. It was simple and a plain light blue. There was more work that could be done on it. Additional garnishes here and there. But it would have to do. It was time Myra started to gather her things and make plans for what was to come next.

Chapter Twenty-One

MYRA

Myra walked back into the Golden Palace, for one of the last times, but now with her head held high. She patted the bag slung over her shoulder and smiled to herself as she made her way to her room. Charis surely was furious she'd been gone all day, but it was worth it. Myra got a job. A real respectable job that had nothing to do with Stulan magic or at a seedy tavern. She'd always been good at sewing and took the dress she'd been working on to every seamstress she could find in Cyre. Many were hesitant about a strange girl walking in without any seamstress experience, but there was one kind older woman whose hands and fingers were getting tired and her assistant had quit recently, so she was desperate for the help and willing to take the risk on her.

Myra would start the next day. She didn't have a place to live yet, but she would figure that out later. At least she had a job and a plan. For the first time, Myra was on the way to get what she wanted. A normal life where no one would have to know about her magic, and she could stay away from political antics and power-hungry uncles or cruel people who wanted to experiment. She couldn't wait to tell Cal of this new development and quickened her steps so she could write to him.

At least it was partially what she wanted.

But no one could ever have everything. This was enough, and she was grateful.

"Myra, there you are."

A lump formed in her throat, and her stomach tightened at the sound of the man's voice. No. It couldn't be. What was he doing here?

Myra turned on her heel to find Uncle Waazir walking toward her, and with each step he took, she saw him stomping on each of the plans she'd made.

"I've been looking all over for you, but everyone says you mysteriously left for the day," he said as he walked, voice as light as an arrow prepared to pierce her through. "You haven't responded to any of my letters."

No, she hadn't. The delivery boy who'd delivered his first message weeks ago followed her instructions, as she hadn't seen any letters from Uncle Waazier since then. The moment she'd taken the job, Myra vowed to cut off all ties with the man.

Myra straightened her shoulders and gripped the strap of her satchel in hopes it would disguise her trembling. "What are you doing here?"

"I'm here for the ball of course. All the nobles are invited, and as your father is still away, I came in his stead. I'm anxious to see who our future queen will be." His stance was casual and calm, but there was a glint in his eyes that made Myra inwardly recoil. There was more to his being here than curiosity. She was sure of it.

"I'm sure many are. Now please excuse me, I have work to do." Myra kept her chin up and attempted to walk past him, but he caught her by the elbow. A strong and pinching grip.

"I also think it's time you came home."

Myra glared at his hand holding her and then up at him. "I'm not coming home. Besides, you kicked me out."

He shrugged. "I've had a change of heart."

She tried to tear her arm away, but he only held on tighter. "I'm not coming back. Now I have work to do," she repeated. Her voice echoed through the hall, and someone walking by looked at them with raised brows.

"Myra!"

This time, Myra's heart leapt at the sound of her name and smiled as Finley strolled through the hall and came toward them. Her blond locks cascaded over her shoulders in waves over her light-blue tunic like the sun shining on a summer day. Uncle Waazir craned his neck to see over his shoulder and pinched his brows. His grip loosened on Myra's elbow and completely let go when Finley swept next to them and looped her arm through Myra's.

"I've been searching for you all day. We have so much to do before the ball tonight." Finley tossed her hair over her shoulder and then glanced Uncle Waazir up and down as though she were examining something terribly interesting. "Although I suppose I don't blame you for being distracted." She giggled, something high and girly that Myra had never heard come out of her mouth before. "But I do need to take dear Myra away. Please excuse us, sir."

Before Waazir had the chance to protest, Finley swept Myra away in the direction of their rooms. When they were far enough away, Finley leaned down and spoke in a conspiratorial whisper. "How do you know that vile Waazir man?"

Myra gaped at her. "How do *you* know him?"

Finley groaned. "Thankfully he didn't recognize me. But Ai and I met him briefly in our travels a year or two ago. He's positively awful."

Myra nodded in agreement. "You have no idea."

"So how do you know him? What did he want with you?"

Myra raised a brow and wanted to look over her shoulder to be sure he didn't follow, but kept her focus on moving forward. "Not here. Come with me to my room."

They hurried along, and Myra shut and locked the door to her room once they were inside. Finley made herself at home and flopped onto the bed as Myra carefully unfolded her dress from the satchel and worked on putting it back on the mannequin with shaking hands.

Now that Myra had a plan and the mirror was protected, all she wanted to do was enjoy this last day in the Golden Palace with Alvis and her new friends. Why did Uncle Waazir have to come and possibly ruin it all? On top of it, he wanted her to go back home. It didn't make sense. She wouldn't go. At least not willingly. He couldn't make her, could he?

"So why so mysterious about Waazir? And where were you all day? Charis is furious she hasn't been able to find you. It's been highly amusing, of course, so thank you for that. But she's not going to make your life pleasant, you can be sure of it. Especially with the ball being tonight."

Myra let out a low laugh. "Charis being angry is the least of my worries."

She hadn't meant to say anything, but it came out, nevertheless.

No, she had more reason to be concerned about Waazir. Maybe she could leave early and escape while no one was paying attention. During the ball, perhaps. But that would mean less time with Finley and Ai and Alvis. She probably shouldn't even tell them she was going or where. The fewer people who knew, the less likely Waazir could find her. She rubbed her chest and tried to take in a few deep breaths.

Her past was never going to let go of her.

"Myra? What's wrong?" The bed creaked as Finley stood and went to Myra's side. "Are you crying?"

Was she? Myra touched her damp cheeks and wiped her eyes. "It's fine. Just a long day."

Finley put her hands on her hips and raised her brows. "Liar. Out with it. Something about Waazir shook you up. Did he do something to you?"

Pressure built up in her chest, and Myra's magic pulsed through her. Myra rubbed her temple and took in a few deep breaths to calm it down. "No, it's not that. It's…" She shouldn't say anything. But she was so tired of all the secrets, and she was leaving soon anyway. Who knew if or when she'd ever see Finley again? "He's my uncle."

Finley took a step back and blinked a few times. Her hands fell to her sides. "He's what? But that would mean…" Her blue eyes darted back and forth as though the pieces of the puzzle were fitting together in front of her. "He lives with his brother, but his wife and daughter died, I was told. They were terribly ill."

Myra wiped the last of her tears away and stared at Finley until a light lit in her eyes.

"His brother's daughter isn't dead, is she?"

Myra shook her head and went to her trunk to start unloading her belongings. If she was going to escape, she needed to pack. "That's what they told people? I suppose it makes sense. Waazir sold me after my mother died. He said he wants to take me home."

"Which I'm assuming you don't want."

"No. I was planning to go to the ball tomorrow, but…I think I need to take my leave before then so he doesn't find me." She knelt by the trunk and folded a shirt she'd tossed in there. There wasn't enough room in her bags to take everything she'd collected during her time at the palace, but if she folded them neatly enough, there could be room for a fair number of things.

Finley bit her bottom lip and tapped her finger against her thigh. Then, she smiled so bright Luana's stars would be jealous. "You know what this means, don't you?"

"What?"

Finley knelt next to Myra with wide eyes. "You're a noble. You could be part of the pageant."

Myra paused her folding and stared at Finley. She wasn't sure what sort of reaction Finley was going to have to this insight into Myra's past —but that wasn't it. "Excuse me? What does that have to do with anything?"

Finley threw her head back and laughed. "Myra. I know you care for the prince, and I'm almost certain he cares for you too. I see the way you look at each other, and I know you sneak away at night. Is it to see him?"

Had they been that obvious? Myra could feel her cheeks warm and focused again on her sorting and folding. "You're being ridiculous."

"So you have been sneaking away to see him?" She laughed again and clapped her hands. "Don't you see? This is perfect. You can be with Alvis, and what better revenge on your uncle for selling you off than to become his future queen?"

Myra sank back and sat on her heels. "I wasn't aware you were such a romantic."

Finley shrugged and tossed her golden locks over her shoulder. "I'm not. But I do love showing people who've done us wrong what's what and coming out on top. There's nothing better than doing the opposite of what others expect."

Myra resumed her packing. "Well, I hate to disappoint you, but Alvis isn't going to find out anything, and I'm leaving as soon as possible. I want to leave my past behind me."

"Yes, that I can understand." Finley's mouth tightened, and her eyes went unusually dark, as though she were remembering something from her own past. But the look was gone in an instant, and she was back to her usual clever smile. "At least come to the ball for a little while. Ai and I are making our own escape at midnight, and I know she'd like to say good-bye."

Myra cocked her head to the side. "You're not staying for the whole ball? What if Alvis picks Ai?"

Finley waved a dismissive hand. "Ai never had any intention of marrying Alvis and told him so weeks ago. She said if he chose her at the ball, she'd reject him in front of the deities and everyone." She looked at Myra out of the side of her eye, a mischievous glint hidden there. "I don't know what your plans are, but you're welcome to join us. We know a thing or two about wanting to escape."

Myra had the feeling this wasn't a lie. "Where are you going?"

Finley wagged her brows, but her playful smile was interrupted with a yawn. "You'll have to join us to find out."

Myra closed the trunk and clicked it shut. There would be so many things left behind, yet again. She should have known by now that she would never get a straight answer out of Finley and Ai. They were always so mysterious, those two, but Myra had to admit she liked that about them. It kept life interesting. Besides, she didn't tell them everything either. "Thank you for the offer, but I have a position lined up already."

"Suit yourself. Anyway, I need to get a nap in before Ai and I get ready." She stood and went over to the door but paused and looked back before leaving. "But do come to the ball tonight. One last hurrah, and we promise to keep you as far away from Waazier and Charis as possible."

Myra had been looking forward to the festivities for the night. Maybe she could sneak away before Alvis made his announcement and Waazier could get a hold of her. If she stuck with Finley and Ai, it was possible. She sighed. "Very well. I'll come for a little while."

Finley yawned again, a big thing that made her arms stretch over her head. "Good. We'll see you tonight."

Once Finley left, Myra packed as many things as possible so after the ball, she could grab her belongings and leave. She had enough money stashed away where she could rent a room for a few days while she found a more permanent residence. Nowhere fancy, but a roof over her head and a few hot meals. Then, she put on the dress she'd made. That way she wouldn't have to worry about changing after helping Charis get dressed.

"It's about time you got here," Charis snapped when Myra walked into her room. Adeena was already there, a sneer on her delicate face as she looked over her shoulder at the new arrival. "We're going to be late!"

"Apologies, my lady," Myra said and contained her sigh and went to the wardrobe to fetch Charis's gown. They were hardly going to be late. And maybe if she didn't have to split her time between the two of them now, she'd be able to focus on Charis more. Only a few more hours, not even a whole day, and Myra would be done with both of them. Hopefully for good. She could get through preparations for the ball.

"I'm so glad you decided not to go to the ball, Myra. You wouldn't have had any fun anyway. Not your type of crowd," Charis said as she slid out of her robe. She'd already been to a stylist, and her hair was piled on top of her head in a tower of curls.

Myra brought the pink gown over and helped Charis step into it. "I'm still going to the ball."

Charis paused, her gaze meeting Adeena's, a hint of panic hidden in the sparkling blue. "Oh. I would have thought you would have gotten yourself ready before coming to us and that was why I couldn't find you all day."

"I am ready."

Adeena's eyes went wide, and the two of them looked Myra up and down. Adeena snickered, not even an attempt to hide it, and Charis's upper lip curled. Myra resisted the urge to cover herself up and held her chin high. It didn't matter what they thought anyway. This dress was well made and had landed her a job. It might not have been as extravagant as theirs, but it was one of the best she'd ever created.

Everything in Charis stiffened as she looked at Myra, a strange nervousness and anger in her face. "How quaint. Now stop dawdling and help me in this! If you hadn't been so busy pampering yourself, we wouldn't be in such a hurry!"

Myra went back and forth between the two ladies. A flurry of fabric and jewels and last-minute touch-ups to their hair and makeup. As much as Myra hated to admit it, Adeena and Charis were both beautiful, and at first glance, they were the ideal images of one a prince would pick to be his bride. Adeena with her dark skin and perfectly straightened hair swirled into a soft twist, in a sleek sliver gown laced with lavender beading. Then Charis with her golden locks falling gently around her face, and the pink of her dress showing off her fair complexion.

"Myra, go fetch me some tea," Charis ordered. "I'm positively parched."

A tray of food and beverages for the two of them was set out on a table that someone from the kitchen staff had already brought up before Myra's arrival. She went over and prepared the beverage the way Charis liked, with enough cream and sugar where it hardly tasted like tea anymore, and brought it over.

"Wonderful." Charis reached across to grab the cup but instead clumsily knocked it over, spilling all the contents over Myra's dress.

She gasped, the liquid hot against her skin as it soaked through the fabric. Fabric that was now wet and stained.

Charis's brows were pinched together in feigned concern, and she fluttered her lashes. "Oh dear, did I do that? Your poor dress. There's no possible way you could wear that to the ball now, is there?"

Adeena snickered in the background, not bothering to conceal her smile. Myra's gaze rose from the stain to the two beautiful and cruel women. No hint of remorse in their eyes sparkling from the makeup. Having a dress with spilled tea was hardly the worst thing someone had done to Myra. But there was something unique about the sting of this particular offense that made her have to blink tears away. There was no greater purpose or motivation for the cruelty. No other goal Adeena and Charis must have had. It was to be mean for the sake of being mean.

Enough was enough.

Myra narrowed her eyes and glared at Charis. "What have I ever done to you?"

Charis blinked, a faint hint of surprise on her face. "Excuse me?"

But Myra only shook her head. "You can finish getting ready on your own."

With that, she turned on her heel and left the room, angry shouts from Charis and Adeena following after her. But Myra didn't care anymore. Let them tell Alvis or whoever they wanted that she'd walked out on them. Her time here was done.

Myra stormed into her room and gathered her small bags. She would say good-bye to Ai and Finley, let them know where they could reach her, and then leave. There was nothing to wear to the ball now anyway, and there was no way in Stula's realm she would sit off to the side or hide in her room while the festivities went on without her. Finley and Ai would understand.

With one last look around the room to be sure she hadn't forgotten anything, she then opened the door.

"And where do you think you're going?"

Myra's heart jumped into her throat at the sight of Uncle Waazir standing before her. No. She wasn't going to let this horrid man stop her. She gripped the straps of her bags tighter. "I'm leaving, and not with you."

He shook his head, a thin and sneering smile on his lips. "I don't think so."

The snake tattoo on his neck glowed, and before Myra could do anything, he shoved her back into the room and against a wall. The shock of the force stunned Myra for a moment, and she couldn't get herself to gather her own magic to diffuse his. "You're going to stay in here, and after the ball, you're coming with me."

Myra struggled against him, but his magic formed bonds around her, keeping her in place and unable to move. When he was satisfied, the tattoo faded and he nodded, but she only continued to struggle against the invisible bonds.

"You can't keep me here! People will be asking about me."

Uncle Waazier's shoulders jostled from a silent laugh. "I doubt that. I'll see you after the ball."

He left the room, and Myra heard him lock the door behind him. *How in the world did he get a key?* After several long minutes, Myra was finally able to gather her bearings and used her magic to nullify his, and the invisible bonds released. She ran to the door and shook it as hard as she could, but it wouldn't budge.

There was no way in Stula's realm she was staying here to wait around for the ball to be carried off with Uncle Waazier again. She continued to pound and shake the door to open it, but it was no use. Instead, she went to the outside wall.

Myra opened the window and peered out. Maybe there was a way she could climb down and escape that way. But the outside wall was smooth and high up, without any trees nearby that she could climb down either. The one downside to the style of architecture here as compared to up north. There she might have at least been able to grip bricks or stones.

There was a pounding at the door, and Myra whipped her head around toward it. Now what did that man want? But maybe if he opened the door, she could get around him before he hit her again. The pounding continued, and she grabbed a poker from the fireplace, holding it over her head and ready to pounce.

Then the pounding stopped, and water leaked through the door's keyhole. Little by little, the water trickled out, and the lock disintegrated until it popped open.

What in Stula's' realm…

She gripped the poker even tighter until her knuckles were white, prepared for whoever it was that came through that door. When it opened wider, she let out a loud yell and ran toward the intruder.

"Hey!" Finley called out and caught the poker, stopping Myra from attacking her. "That's hardly a way to greet someone who's coming to rescue you."

Myra paused and blinked. Finley and Ai stood before her in their ball gowns with amused grins on their faces. Finley waved her free hand, and the water that had spilled from the door dried, and Ai shut it again.

Myra lowered the poker. "What are you doing here?"

"We saw Waazir coming from this direction, and when we didn't see you with Charis, we knew something had to be amiss," Ai answered.

She raised her brows as she examined Myra. "That can't possibly be what you're wearing to the ball."

Myra sighed and put the poker back where it belonged. "I'm not going."

Finley groaned. "We've already discussed this. Of course you're going. You need to show Prince Alvis what he's missing and have some fun with us one last time."

Myra's heart twisted, thinking about not seeing Alvis again one last time, but ignored it and let it harden. If he didn't want to be with her when she was a servant, he didn't deserve to be with her knowing about her noble blood. "If Alvis hasn't figured that out yet, he never will. He's had ample opportunity."

Ai stepped forward and took Myra's hands in hers. She closed her eyes, and a strange yet comforting warmth spread from Ai to Myra. She opened her eyes again. "It's as I thought. Your connection with the prince runs deep, and your feelings for him are stronger than you admit. I've seen it and felt it. Myra, it is such a rare thing to have a connection this powerful and Diar blessed. You must pursue it, or at least give it a chance."

So it wasn't all in her head. There was something there between them. It was what Myra had hoped but never wanted to believe. She released Ai's hands and took a step back, showing off her ruined dress. "And you expect me to go in this?"

Finley cocked her head to the side and wagged her brows. "I think we can find something else for you."

Chapter Twenty-Two

ALVIS

ALVIS WAS A BLITHERING IDIOT. HE'D REPLAYED THE SCENE WITH MYRA the day before countless times in his mind and couldn't comprehend why he didn't say more. Why he didn't do more. It was all he could think about as he wandered and greeted the ball guests when all he wanted was to see Myra. But she was nowhere to be found. He caught glimpses of his formal wear in mirrors all along the walls. The fabric was a shimmering gold with red, yellow, and orange embroidery all through it. The very image of the perfect Oxarian prince radiating Ray's light.

The embroidery should have spelled out "idiot" to show everyone who he truly was. All that talk about his duty to his family and kingdom, and the hurt in Myra's eyes. His chest tightened at the memory.

Nobles and their families from all around the kingdom gathered in the Golden Palace dressed in their finery, yet still not ashamed to express their awe at the curtains of flowers that covered the ceiling and the bright colored banners all around. The whole room was a rainbow of color in celebration of Luana's season ending and welcoming spring once again when Ray's day would be longer than the night.

He'd always loved the spring equinox celebration with all the colors.

Even though it didn't get terribly cold in Oxare, he did miss the long hours of sunlight during the winter. With sunshine returning, it was time for new beginnings and the promise of brighter days ahead.

Now the pageant put a dark cloud over the whole thing.

Alvis had hated the idea of the pageant in the first place, and now that the moment was here, he still had no idea what he was going to do. He didn't deserve any of these women. They'd wasted the last six weeks of their lives, leaving their homes and traveling far away to win his heart. What a disappointment he must have been for them.

"Alvis!" Nell's voice rang through the room like a cheerful bell, and she darted toward him, dodging guests left and right, her light-pink dress and shawl flying behind her. She was breathless by the time she got to him, but the smile on her face couldn't be denied. The beads and gems on her dress and the jewelry adorning her wrists jingled merrily as she held out the sides of her skirt and twirled. "What do you think?"

Alvis applauded. "Lovely."

And she was. Daya used all her tricks to dress Nell up for the ball. The bright-pink dress was the picture of spring and youthful innocence, but the light makeup and how Nell's curly hair was tied back with beads and flowers woven in gave hints that before long, Nell would be a young woman.

Nell grasped his hand and dragged him toward the dance floor. "Let's do the dance we've been practicing. The one you had the women learn last week. Please?"

Alvis wasn't a talented dancer, but it was one most everyone in Oxare knew. He was glad Nell learned it along with the other women and enjoyed it so much, a sign that she could learn to call this place home. And how could he say no to that face? The girl was going to be more spoiled than a princess at the rate they were going.

"All right, tell the others, and I'll be sure the musicians know which song to play."

Nell squealed in delight and hurried off to go find the other women, and Alvis spoke with the conductor about what they planned. All the while, he tried to keep an eye out for Myra but couldn't find her. The ballroom was crowded, but he knew he'd be able to find her anywhere.

But his search was interrupted when Nell and the women gathered in the center of the dance floor and the music started. It was the perfect dance for the spring equinox, as the foot and hand movements told the story of Ray and how he brought light to the world and brings new life year after year. Alvis joined when it was the men's turn, and a few others from the audience joined in as well, including Cadeyrn. Nell beamed ear to ear as she spun and clapped to the beat, and the women surrounding Alvis were beautiful. He should have felt like the luckiest man in the world, but he could help but feeling hollow.

Off to the side, he heard Eira laughing as Cadeyrn attempted to show her the steps, and she leaned into him when she tripped over her feet. Cadeyrn held her up and laughed with her. Jealousy burned within Alvis as he watched them. They were brave, letting their relationship show to all the world despite the people giving them sidelong looks.

They chose for themselves and weren't ashamed. They didn't care what others thought. He should be able to do that too.

When the dance ended, Alvis sought out Nell. "Have you seen Myra anywhere?"

Nell looked up at him and blinked a few times. "No. Why?"

Alvis squeezed her shoulder and gave one last look around the ballroom and then knelt before her. "I need to tell her something, and it's very important. If you see her, can you be sure to let me know right away?"

Nell nodded. "All right."

Someone cleared their throat, and Alvis looked up again to see Salome was there. "May I dance with you, your highness?" Her voice was small and quaked as she spoke, but there was an unusual sense of certainty in her gaze.

"Yes, of course. It would be my pleasure."

He could look for Myra as they went around the dance floor. It was a good way to keep an eye out without raising suspicion or causing too much of a stir. As much as he wanted to stop everything to find her, he knew it would only make Myra uncomfortable.

He took Salome's hand and spun her out onto the dance floor. She was a lovely woman, but so quiet. Her asking him to dance was a shock.

"I...I wanted to talk to you, your highness," Salome sputtered out.

"Whatever you wish, Salome. You have my full attention."

Maybe not *full* attention, as he still wanted to search for Myra. But he would try.

Salome took in a deep breath, but he could feel her trembling beneath his touch as they danced. "I know Ai requested you don't pick her, and I thought that was admirable of her. So I want to ask you the same thing. Please, do not pick me tonight."

Her request took Alvis by surprise, and for a moment, he forgot about searching for Myra. "You don't want me to?"

Salome gulped, and her grip on his arm tightened. "You see... I... I..." She looked over Alvis's shoulder, and whatever she saw there must have given her courage. She gulped, and what came out of her mouth next poured out like a waterfall. "I'm in love with Brylee, and she's in love with me. We didn't plan for it to happen, but it did, and I want to go live in the Belovian Islands with her. She said there was no reason to tell you, but I couldn't stand the idea of you picking one of us and not knowing. So please, don't do it."

Her already pale skin turned even whiter by the time she finished, but her voice had grown stronger with each word. Alvis could have burst out laughing. Here was Salome, the timidest person he'd ever met, and even she was going after who she loved regardless of the consequences.

"I think that's wonderful," Alvis said. "And I promise I will not pick either of you."

Salome's shoulders relaxed, and he almost thought she was about to sink to the floor and kept his grip on her firm as they danced. "Really? Oh, your highness, you have no idea how grateful I am."

"Just promise me I'm invited to the wedding."

"Of course."

At the top of the stairs, a female figure appeared as Alvis spun around the dance floor with Salome in his arms. But everyone should have already arrived. Hope fluttered in his chest. Maybe it was Myra, and she was running late. The woman was petite, in a gorgeous jewel-filled deep-purple gown. She could be the same height as Myra, but there was no way for him to tell for sure as she wore a short veil covering her eyes.

"Is everything all right, your highness?" Salome asked and turned to look as well where the mysterious woman descended the stairs. "I wonder who that is. She's stunning."

She was, and Alvis recognized the brown hair twirled and pinned on top of her head like a crown. But he needed to be sure. "I should go greet this new guest. But now you can escape me and go tell Brylee the good news."

A smile played on Salome's lips as though she knew what he was thinking. "If you insist, your highness." They broke apart, and she curtsied. "And thank you, Alvis."

He nodded to her and then made his way through the ballroom, attempting to not bump into the other dancers. They all stared as he reached the stairs and ascended them, meeting the woman halfway. Maybe it was only his wishful thinking that this new guest was Myra, but it was as though a string connected the two of them and it pulled him toward her.

"Alvis." The woman said his name in a breath, and he smiled wider than he ever thought possible. Now that he was close, he could see those beautiful brown eyes through the veil, and he knew that voice anywhere.

"Myra, you came." He took her hands and rubbed the backs of them with his thumbs. "When I didn't see you, I thought you'd decided not to come."

"I...I was detained. I'm sorry. A problem with my dress." She looked down at the gown.

He cupped her chin in his hand and raised her head so her gaze met his. "It doesn't matter. You're here now."

She gulped, but a small smile flirted on her lovely pink lips. The swell of her breasts over the top of her dress rose and fell with each of her nervous breaths. While they were usually covered by higher necked tunics and shirts...it was going to take every bit of self-control to not stare at them all night or touch them or kiss them...

Soon. If she accepted his offer and apology for being such an idiot.

"Everyone is staring," Myra whispered.

Alvis hadn't noticed before, but when he paid attention to what was happening around them, it was as though everything and everyone in the world stood still. He was used to people staring, but Myra wasn't.

"Only because you're the most beautiful woman here." He lowered his hand from her chin and, with the one grasping her hand, pulled her toward the ballroom. "Would you like to dance with me?"

She offered a small and tight nod. "I would love to."

Alvis gestured to the musicians, and they started their music again. Conversation fluttered through the ball once more as the guests all returned to their partners and danced. He could practically see the weight of their gazes leaving Myra's shoulders as he led her into the ballroom, and she relaxed into his arms to dance.

They turned and swirled across the floor with ease, with more than a few curious glances in their direction. But Alvis didn't care anymore. He was exhausted from caring. He placed one hand on the small of her back in the space between her top and skirt, reveling in the feel of her soft brown skin. The rustle of the skirt swooshed across the floor in time with the song, adding to the music. "You look amazing. When did you have time to make this dress? It must have taken hours every day."

Myra nodded over to where Ai and Finley were standing off to the side watching them. They smiled and waved back, sipping goblets of wine. Although, knowing them, they could have slipped something entirely different into their drinks. "Ai had it made for me. I normally wouldn't receive such a grand gift, but...this was a special circumstance."

"I'm glad you did."

He was more than glad. Thrilled. Over the moon. If she was willing to come and take the dress from Ai to come to the ball, maybe it meant she would accept his apology. Accept him. He just needed the courage to tell her.

Alvis cleared his throat. "Myra, I'm sorry for yesterday and our conversation. And for everything. I've been behaving like an idiot. Even hinting that you be my mistress, you deserve so much more than that. I don't blame you for a moment for wanting to leave."

Myra tightened her grip on his hand with a reassuring squeeze. While he couldn't see her well through the thin purple veil, the compassion in her eyes was still evident. "It is a difficult position we are in. There are no easy solutions."

He didn't deserve her understanding, and his heart swelled at her words. "Maybe, maybe not. The thing of it is…"

Diar bless it. Out with it, man!

The words got caught in his throat. They were right there, ready to be said. They were felt and known. But when he opened his mouth to say them, it was as though there was a wall blocking them from coming out.

What if she rejected him? She could hear what he had to say and laugh in his face and leave. Or even if she did care for him, and he thought she did, but this was too soon for her, and it frightened her away?

"The thing of it is?" Myra repeated, bringing Alvis out of his thoughts and back to the moment. "Is everything all right, Alvis?"

The thing of it was she deserved to know, regardless of her response. Everyone deserved to know they were loved, but especially Myra. After all she'd gone through, she should at least have this.

Alvis regained his courage and looked at her through the thin veil. Gods, she was beautiful. "Come with me, somewhere more private. Not here."

She deserved his apology and all he thought and felt, but not when he could be pulled away or distracted by events of the ball. Myra only nodded. He took her hand and led her out of the ballroom and to the courtyard. They sat side by side on a stone bench with sun lanterns floating overhead, the light kissing the flowers with the promise of spring and new beginnings. "The thing of it is, I don't want the other women. I know it's not intelligent or what I'm supposed to do or what's expected. But I don't. I only want you. I love you."

It was as though the world stopped around them as Myra stared back at him. Her grip on his hand tightened, and the silence felt endless.

So of course, he decided to ramble on, if only to fill the silence. Now the words were out there, he didn't want to stop. "And I want to choose you. If you'll have me after what a fool I've been. I know it's much to ask, and maybe you don't even want to. And we don't have to do anything right away. We can take as long of a time as you need."

Myra swallowed, and her chest heaved with each breath. "Alvis, you…you… But there's so much you don't know."

"Then I'll learn. There's much about me you don't know either. We'll learn together."

She looked at him through the veil, as though any response she would have could be written on his face. He only hoped she wouldn't see the sense of panic he was feeling. Panic, and freedom. Everything in his life, each choice he made, had always been the logical one. Something in a book that said the exact answer he needed to solve the problem. But everything about Myra went against his logic. And it was wonderful.

"I love you too, Alvis. Of course I'll be with you."

And just like that, everything came into place. The waves of panic calmed, and nothing else mattered. Everyone was going to have a fit, but for once, Alvis didn't care about the reactions and opinions of other people. He lifted the veil away to reveal her beautiful face and kissed her with all the love he possessed.

He wrapped his arms around her as they kissed and crushed her body against his. Each of her lovely and soft curves pressed against his, melding together as one person, as they would soon be as husband and wife. She threw her arms around his neck, and she tightened her hold on him as her kisses grew deeper and more needy.

Alvis pulled Myra onto his lap, her legs straddling over him and skirt hitched around her hips. Already, he was growing hard. With a wave of her hand, she hid them in her shadows. They were already in a secluded area, private and away from the ball. But the extra darkness, even if it did make him shiver, made him only kiss her more fiercely. He trailed his lips down her neck to her heaving breasts. He kissed and sucked the tops of them, and Myra only pushed him closer to her.

"You're so greedy," he murmured into her skin before pulling her top down to free one of her breasts. Her brown, puckered nipple popped out without hardly any encouragement, and he covered it with his mouth, sucking and licking it. He'd never desired someone so desperately before that he would risk being caught, but it only sent a thrill through him, and he gave her breast a nibble.

Myra moaned and rocked against him. "I'm only greedy when it comes to you." She kissed the top of his head and moved her hand down between them to where he thought he would burst out of his trousers. "Seems as though I'm not the only one."

He could barely focus as she rubbed him, and he thought he could come right then and there. But no, he had to control himself even for just a few moments longer. He raised his head and put his hand over her breast where his mouth had been and whispered into her ear, "Is this one of the ways you've imagined having me?"

When she'd told him she'd pictured them together the way he had, he hadn't been able to get it out of his mind and wanted to do every single scenario she'd come up with. All the ways he could please her.

"Something like this," she answered.

His hands wandered beneath her skirt, savoring the warm soft skin of her thighs until he reached her womanhood, which was already wet and willing to have him. He wished he could see that glimmering pussy, waiting for him to fill it, but there was no time for that right now. The feel of it alone was enough.

Together they lowered his trousers enough so he could break free and guided his throbbing cock inside her, and they moaned in unison as they came together. They moved hard and fast, Myra's one freed tit bouncing as she rode him. He rocked his hips in time with her and groaned at how incredible she was.

"You feel amazing," he said and gripped her rear.

"I want this every day," Myra told him as she shoved her pelvis against his, making him go even deeper inside. "Us fucking, making love, I want to make everyone in the palace sick of us and leave, so you can have me wherever and whenever you want."

He laughed and let his fingers find their way between them and rubbed her in the place he knew she liked. "Whatever you want, my darling."

They were able to take their time and savor the moment, and Myra fucked him even faster until she cried out as he rubbed her back until finally Alvis couldn't contain himself any longer. He pulled himself out and let his seed spill over her thighs.

Breathless and panting, Myra giggled and pressed her forehead against his as he lowered her back to a seat on the bench next to him. "We're getting married. I...can hardly believe it."

"I can hardly believe you said yes."

"It's just so fast."

It was fast, and he was sure Mother and Father would be furious. Cadeyrn would be shocked. The women left who hadn't said they didn't want to marry him would probably be betrayed. He wasn't going to choose Adeena or Charis anyway; they might have been beautiful and wealthy, but he couldn't see them as partners in life. They were too different. He did have a stab of guilt about Nazneen though. From the first day, everyone assumed she would be the one he picked. It made the most sense. He would need to speak to her privately about it, but he had the feeling she would understand.

"We can have as long of an engagement as you want. I know you had plans for when you returned to Oxare. Take all the time you need to do what you need to, resolve anything, whatever you want."

Myra adjusted her skirt so it lay flat and tucked herself back into her top while Alvis fixed his own clothing. Her shawl was discarded on the ground somewhere. He wished they could stay there forever, just the two of them, and not have to worry about the rest of the world. They would need to sooner rather than later, at least for tonight. Then, once the ball was over, they could take as much time as they wanted to get to know one another and ease everyone else into it.

"Let's go break the news to the king and queen."

He took her hand to lead her to the ballroom, but Myra froze. Her stillness tugged Alvis back to where she stood. "Now?" she asked in a quiet voice. "It has to be right this moment?"

Alvis looked toward the palace and then at his bride. What was wrong? He thought everything was all right now. "Isn't this what you want? I don't want to hide my love for you anymore, and I want to tell them."

"It is. And I know you do. It's just…" She picked up her shawl and twisted it in her hands. "There's something you need to know."

Did she still doubt him? It was like a punch to the stomach. "Myra, you can tell me anything. Whatever it is, I'm sure it's something we can work through together."

"It's just—"

A scream came from the ballroom, causing them to turn. There was a pit in Alvis's stomach that reminded him far too much of the night King Brennan was poisoned. He and Myra rushed into the ballroom where the music had stopped, and the guests were all in a tizzy.

In the center of it all was Daya, tears streaming down her face. "Nell! They took her!"

With her exclamation, Alvis's world fell apart.

Chapter Twenty-Three

MYRA

MYRA'S HEART STOPPED AT DAYA'S ANNOUNCEMENT. NELL. ONLY moments ago, she'd been so happy—albeit a bit nervous—but now it all vanished at the thought of Nell being kidnapped.

"It was like they were made of water," Daya said through her tears. "They weren't there, and all of the sudden there was a puddle of water beside us. Nell fell to the ground, and a figure appeared, taking her away."

Alvis and Myra looked at each other, and she knew he was thinking the same thing she was.

Water magic. Amelia.

Myra gathered her magic from within her as Alvis darted out the door. It took every bit of strength to nullify the magic to protect the mirror, and she wasn't sure if she'd be able to do so for the whole ballroom. But if whoever this was stole Nell using magic, she had to try.

Clouds of shadows surrounded Myra, and she felt for the energy of everyone else's magic around her. Little by little, a chill filled the room, and the guests shivered. Women wrapped their shawls around their bare arms. Murmurs spread across the crowd in waves.

Myra couldn't listen or worry about them right now. What mattered was being sure Nell was safe. She closed her eyes and focused on where her magic needed to go. Someone and something was moving out in the hall. She knew Alvis was there, but there was another magic mingled with it. Something stronger and darker. Myra aimed her magic toward it, hoping it would nullify whatever was out there. She heard the cry of a young girl echo in the hall, and her eyes popped open.

Nell.

Myra dropped her hands and ran out into the hall where Alvis was running back toward her, Nell wrapped in his arms, and both were soaked to the bone. But they were all right. Praise the deities, they were all right.

She rushed to their side where Nell hugged Alvis around the neck and her teeth chattered.

"You were able to stop them," Alvis said, his own usually dark skin paled from cold. "Nell must have been under a sleeping spell, but when you nullified magic, it woke her up. I was able to get Nell, but whoever it was that tried to kidnap her got away."

The king and queen made their way to the scene. The crowd parted before them, and each gave a deep bow as they passed.

"What is the meaning of all of this?" the queen demanded.

"She took our magic!" someone from the ballroom yelled out.

Myra turned to find an angry guest, a woman in a pale-blue gown, pointing at Myra, her eyes blazing with anger and fear.

"She did!" another person piped up. A man this time. "She had dark shadows surrounding her. She must be from Stula!"

An anxious murmur went through the crowd at these declarations, followed by more people claiming they'd seen what Myra had done. Myra stepped back, closer to Alvis and Nell.

"No, you don't understand…" Alvis tried to say.

"Myra saved me!" Nell piped up, but their voices were lost in the sound of all the accusations.

"I can speak for her," a dark voice boomed through the crowd. Everyone quieted as Uncle Waazir stepped forward, and not far from him stood Charis and Adeena with shocked looks on their faces, their jaws practically on the ground.

"He doesn't speak for me," Myra said and tried to keep her chin up, but her heart pounded. What was he going to say?

Alvis set Nell on the ground, and Daya wrapped a shawl around the shivering girl. "Myra, you know this man?"

Myra opened and closed her mouth and tried to think of something to say, but panic swept through her. She was going to tell Alvis everything, and why she wanted to wait until she did to tell his family anything about their engagement. It was what she wanted to do before they heard Daya's scream, and now it was too late. "Alvis, I—"

"Would someone please tell us what in Ray's name is going on here?" the king demanded.

"Your majesty, this young woman here is my niece, the daughter of Lord Gennady of Taka," Uncle Waazier answered. He stood in the center of the group and gestured toward Myra. "She is a descendant of Stula, and dark magic runs in her veins. She killed her mother as a child, and I've been trying to keep her out of sight to not create scandal for the family name." He hung his head like he was ashamed of his actions. Myra's blood boiled. The man had never shown a hint of remorse for his actions in his pitiful life. "But it appears it was wrong of me to do so, as she only has created more problems. You see, as she got older and was no longer in our household, she learned the dark ways of her magic and was responsible for the killing of several fae in the Dravian Islands and was then taken into the household of Lady Amelia, who then became queen of Cresin, as you all know."

Several people in the crowd gasped. Some even gave out cries of shock and stepped away. Myra's lip trembled. He was twisting everything around.

"It was she who gave Amelia the Stulan poison that nearly killed King Brennan. Surely she must still be in contact with the former queen and tried to steal her daughter," Waazier continued.

By now, Myra couldn't control her trembling. She blinked back tears and spoke out with a cracked voice, "No, that's not true…"

The king and queen stared at Myra in shock, their eyes wide, while the ball guests all shouted and called out.

"She must be stopped!"

"Take this dark magic away from us!"

"We can't have Amelia come back!"

Myra's heart pounded, and her chest tightened. Everything felt like it was closing in on her and there was no escape. Her worst nightmare was coming to life. No matter what she did, no matter how good her intentions, her past and people's fear of her magic always came back to haunt her.

Worst of all, was the dismay on Alvis's face. He was pale, and his golden eyes searched her face for answers. He didn't do anything to stop Waazier from saying these things or try to come to her defense. "Myra, is this true?"

Myra gulped. "I wanted to tell you, but there wasn't any time. And it's not…it's not what you think."

Alvis didn't say anything, only looked at her with shock and dismay in his eyes. His silence was all Myra needed to know, and her heart crumpled.

"I'm here to take her home. She won't bother you again, your majesties," Waazier announced and grabbed Myra's elbow.

His touch ignited a fire in her, and she ripped it away from him and then hit him across the face with all the strength she had. It didn't knock him over, the strong man he was and with his magic from Aros, but it was enough to make him stagger back a few steps and pause in shock.

Then she ran.

Cries of people yelling to go be sure she didn't get out of the palace rang out behind her, but she kept running. Out of the ballroom, through the crowds, past Charis and Adeena with their jaws dropped to the floor. Despite the demands for her capture, no one bothered to stop her from mere shock at the scene they'd witnessed. No one came after her.

But why would they? She was only a servant girl. A servant girl associated with Stula and Amelia. They would want nothing to do with her, and surely news of the ball disaster would spread like wildfire through the capital, including to her new employer.

It wasn't all of that which brought the tears to Myra's eyes as she ran and stumbled out of the Golden Palace. It was Alvis's silence. The bewilderment and betrayal on his face. It was all she needed to see to know it was over.

Myra gasped and tried to wipe away the tears streaming down her face as she made her way down the stairs. She was going to tell him everything, but there hadn't been enough time... 'They'd let their passion get away with them. If she'd been able to control herself, maybe she would have told Alvis everything.

And now it was over. It was too late.

The tears came too quickly, and Myra could barely see anything as she descended to the road below. It was cool and rough against her feet, and a stone jabbed at her. She hiked up her skirt and lifted her foot to remove her shoe and the stone wedged inside it, only to find her foot was already bare.

With a cry, she dropped her skirt back down, and it swished against her legs. "Damn it all to Stula's realm!"

Now she'd lost her shoe. She wasn't even sure at what point she lost it.

What the fuck was she supposed to do with only one shoe?

As though her legs lost the will to hold her up any longer, Myra sank to the ground and sobbed. Alvis said he loved her. Clearly not enough to speak up for her or give her the chance to explain.

"What happened to you?"

Myra' shot her head up to see Finley and Ai in front of her on two black horses, still wearing their ball gowns. She gulped. "I lost my shoe."

And destroyed her relationship with Alvis. And created a scandal in the middle of one of the largest celebrations of the year in front of the king and queen. And once they all got over the shock, surely people would be coming after her about the murder attempt on King Brennan that past autumn.

"Tragic," Finley said dryly and stretched a hand toward her. "Sounds like you need to escape."

Myra could only nod furiously. Any means of escape was a welcome one. She grasped Finley's hand and managed to pull herself to her feet and then onto the back of the horse behind her. She wrapped her arms around Finley's waist.

"Myra, wait!"

The three of them turned to find Alvis racing down the steps of the palace. *Now* he came after her. Of course.

But it was too late. *He* was too late. All of it had been a big mistake, and they both would be better off if she were to leave.

Myra's chest tightened and pursed her lips. "Go!"

With a yell and a flick of the reins, Finley and Ai set the horses off on a run toward the river. Myra held on to Finley for dear life, the wind drying any remaining tears away from her face as though they'd never been there, leaving it all behind at the palace steps.

"Do you want to know where we're going?" Finley asked.

"As long as it's far away from here."

She felt Finley laugh against her arms. "I knew I liked you!"

The three of them raced through back alleys and hidden paths through the capital until they reached a portion of the river outside the city. It was secluded and surrounded by trees and shrubs. Ai slid off her horse, and Finley did the same, holding out her arms to help Myra down. With a slap on each of the horses' rumps, they trotted away.

"You're just going to leave them to wander the streets of the capital?" Myra asked.

"I'm sure the palace guards are searching for them," Ai answered as she inspected her gown as though it was the most important thing she could be focusing on now and not being chased after by palace guards. "They'll be found and returned. I'm sure a couple of horses is going to be the least of the palace's worries. Besides, we don't have room for them on the ship."

"The ship?"

Myra looked up and down the vast river, and there wasn't a single boat or ship in sight. They were completely alone.

"There is no ship. What are you talking about? Don't you have a plan? We can't just stand here!"

An amused smile played on Finley's lips. She yawned and stretched her arms out wide. "Now she asks questions. Yes, we have a plan. And a ship. The most glorious ship on all the seas, might I add. Calm down."

She knelt beside the river and placed her palms on top of the water. Her tattoo glowed, and the light spread across the river, creating small ripples and waves that grew larger with each moment until something poked through the surface. A tall, pointed mast. Little by little, it crested up from the water, and within a few minutes, a ship floated before them. It was good the river was vast. Otherwise, the ship wouldn't have fit. Myra gasped.

"By the deities… How… What? Is this yours?"

Finley stood, still yawning, and stretched, rubbing her eyes. "It is. Glorious, isn't it? Now come on, I have to get this thing back underwater before I fall asleep."

Crew members aboard the ship lowered a gangplank to the shore, and Ai and Finley each grabbed one of Myra's hands and led her on. Too bewildered to ask questions or pull away, she followed them across the plank and onto the deck.

A ragtag group of crew members hustled around the ship, setting sails, and cleaning and preparing to sail. None of them wore uniforms, but instead they had tattered trousers and dirty shirts, revealing arms and chests covered in tattoos. Myra's mouth went dry.

"You're pirates."

Finley stretched and yawned again and almost fell over. Ai rushed to her side and led her to the railing to lean on. "Well observed," Finley drawled.

Myra followed them to the ship's rail and looked across at the shore. The Golden Palace loomed over the capital as though watching their escape. "You never told me."

Ai raised a brow. "It seems we all have secrets to share, daughter of Stula."

Myra flushed. Fair enough.

Finley grasped onto the ship's railing like it was the only thing capable of holding her upright. "Not now. We need to get this thing underwater again. You might want to hold on to something, Myra."

The pirate's tattoo glowed again, and this time, the light and magic spread to the entirety of the ship. All the crew members onboard grasped onto different parts of the ship. Railings, masts, ropes, whatever they could get their hands on. Myra held on to the railing, and with a jerk, the ship plunged under the water.

Myra wanted to cry out, but it happened so fast, and she drew in a deep breath before the water hit her. But there was no need. As the ship dived into the river, it was a bubble formed around them, keeping air onboard so no one would drown, and they could walk and breathe freely.

As the glow of magic faded and the speed of the ship slowed and floated along the bottom of the river, Myra loosened her grasp on the rail and looked around as fish swam around them. But before she could ask any questions or take in her new surroundings, Finley collapsed to the ship's deck, fast asleep.

Myra gaped. It was seemed the magic had taken all the energy out of her. "Is Finley all right?"

"She's fine," Ai answered with a sigh and waved a few crew members over. "Take Captain Finley to her quarters. I'll guide us out to sea, but first get us a change of clothes, will you?"

Captain?

The crew members did as she asked and hoisted the sleeping Finley into their arms and took her away.

Ai only smiled. "Welcome aboard *The Mystic.*"

Chapter Twenty-Four

MYRA

Myra could only stand and stare out at the scene before her. She was on a ship. A pirate ship. A pirate ship that could sail underwater, and no one would drown. All of this sounded so familiar. The name set off a signal in her mind. "If this is *The Mystic* and Finley is the captain, that would make her…"

"The pirate queen, yes," Ai answered. Crew members, a mix of men, women, fae, and even a pixie, circled around them as Ai led her through the ship and down the stairs to where Myra assumed their quarters would be. "And I'm her quartermaster."

A crew member shoved a pile of clothing into Myra's arms. "So you're not a lady from the Dravian Islands?"

Ai grabbed the clothing and inspected it, and once she was satisfied, she nodded. "I am, but Finley is not my servant. Obviously. And these clothes are for you. They'll have to do until we find something else. I doubt you'll want to wear that gown while at sea."

They reached a doorway, and Ai opened it to reveal a small but well-kept cabin with a single bed and a couple simple trunks. A miniature shrine to Diar sat on a table propped against the wall.

"This is my room," Ai explained and gestured to the side of the room while she undressed. "You'll stay in here for now, and I'll have a cot brought over. Go ahead and get changed, and we can be sure the gown is taken care of."

A million thoughts swam around in Myra's mind as she followed orders, but she was glad to get out of the gown at least. "Get rid of it. Throw it into the ocean. I'd be fine if I never saw it again. I want to forget tonight ever happened."

"You're going to throw away a small fortune of jewels? If you don't want it, we'll take it. Don't want it to go to waste."

Myra stared at the glittery skirt now in her hands and blinked. Almost everyone had sparkles and beads on their gowns. It never would have occurred to her that there were actual jewels sewn into the dress. Now that she looked closer, what she'd assumed were silver, red, and blue beads were diamonds, rubies, and sapphires. "A small fortune? Where did you get all of these?"

Ai had already taken her gown off and pulled on a pair of tight-fitting trousers. "Where do you think?"

Myra paled. As they rode away, Finley did say that a pair of horses was going to be the least of the palace's worries. "You…"

Ai shrugged. "Pirates."

"Right."

Myra folded the skirt before putting on the trousers she'd been given and debated what to do. She'd left everything behind at the Golden Palace. Clothes. Money. She sighed. "I suppose I'll keep it."

"Good choice."

Myra finished changing, glad to be in more comfortable clothes now, and took a seat at the small desk tucked away in a corner. It was neatly organized with leather-bound notebooks stacked along the edge, held up with bookends in the shape of ships, and a quill stood in its holder with an inkwell next to it. "Have you come back to the ship at all since you've been in the palace?"

Ai dug a hairbrush out from one of the trunks, sat cross-legged on the bed, and got to work on brushing her formal hairdo out. There was something more relaxed about her even in such a short time being away from the palace. As though she were home and took off a heavy load she'd been carrying. "Here and there. It was a challenge to get away, I'll tell you that."

It was a whole world and life they'd been keeping a secret this entire time. What else didn't she know? "You told Alvis that you would turn him down if he proposed. Then why did you come to the pageant at all? There must have been something else you wanted. Was it just the jewels in our gowns? Surely there must have been less complicated and time-consuming ways to get them."

"The jewels were a perk and a motivator," Ai answered. She finished brushing her hair and let it lay straight, the edges of it landing a perfect and clean line brushing her chin. "Go ahead and get some rest. It might be a while until Finley wakes up, and I'm going to check on the crew, give them some directions, and get you a bed. Although you can use mine for now. It's been a long night. When the three of us are awake, we can talk more."

Myra nodded. "Is Finley all right? I've never seen someone collapse and fall asleep like that before."

Ai paused and considered the question. "For the moment, she's all right. It's complicated, but something she'll have to tell you about herself."

More secrets and stories to share. It was a night full of that. But oddly enough, despite it all, Myra still felt safe and at ease here. Maybe it was the exhaustion from all that had happened. "Very well. Go command your crew."

It was odd saying that. Ai and Finley had a whole pirate crew to command.

Ai offered Myra one last comforting smile and left. Now that it was quiet, Myra realized how tired she was. According to the clock on the wall, it wasn't even one a.m. yet. She must have run out of the palace around midnight. She'd had much later nights than this, but after all that had happened, it came crashing down on her, and Myra was ready to rest.

She got up from the chair and made her way to the bed. She collapsed onto it, letting herself sink into the blanket and pillows. It wasn't as soft and luxurious as the one she'd had in the palace, but she didn't care and let herself drift into a dreamless sleep.

. . .

A LOUD BANG WOKE MYRA THE NEXT MORNING. THE WATER OUTSIDE the porthole was a slightly brighter shade in the morning sun, and a school of fish swam by. Standing in the doorway was Finley, wide awake and in a billowing navy-blue coat, tight white pants, and a brimmed hat with a large purple feather sticking out of it. She put her fists onto her hips and looked down at Myra. "We need to talk."

Myra groaned and turned herself over. "Did you kick the door open or something?"

"Yes."

Naturally. It was ridiculous to think otherwise. And it was far too early for such nonsense without coffee. By the deities, she hoped they had coffee on this thing. "You need to stop doing things like barging into people's rooms."

"It's my ship. I do what I want. Now let's go."

Myra groaned again. "Aye, aye, Captain," she mumbled and stumbled out of the bed. After sliding on a pair of shoes left on the floor, she followed Finley.

The Mystic was a bustle of people and creatures going about their day. Some of them looked at Myra with curious glances, but most ignored her. Probably used to unusual people coming aboard, and if she was with the captain, they must have assumed she was to be trusted.

Or that if she wasn't, the captain would handle it.

She was led farther and deeper into the belly of the ship, with only starlight and sun lanterns to light the way. Myra shivered. At least Ai was already waiting for them next to a wooden door with tin cups of coffee in each hand. She passed one to Myra, who took it gratefully. At least one of them had sympathy for her struggle with early mornings.

Finley stood in front of the door with her arms crossed and a shining sword hung at her hip. A woman in charge and on a mission. Oddly enough, it seemed natural to have her standing there in her pirate captain's garb. Like Ai, 'who'd been so much more relaxed in her cabin, it was as though Finley had shed off an old skin and was now relaxed and comfortable again. Myra knew there had been more to these two than met the eye, but she felt foolish for not realizing just how much more.

"Are you truly a descendent of Stula?" Finley asked.

Myra clenched and unclenched her hands around the tin cup. She wanted to trust them. They'd done so much for her over the past several weeks, and they did come to her aid last night when she needed an escape. But they were pirates. How much could she truly trust a pirate?

But on the other hand, who else would understand more? If anything, maybe they would find her magic useful.

Myra nodded. "Yes."

"Did you give Amelia the potion for King Brennan?"

A pause. "Yes. But I didn't know who it was for. My brother and I worked for Amelia since we were young, and she never told us the details of such things."

"Did you kill your mother?"

"No."

The relief in Ai's face was evident, but Finley didn't change her stance or hard stare at Myra. "Why did Waazier claim otherwise?"

"Waazier is a very superstitious man who has never liked the magic my mother and I possessed. The night she died, I was escorting her spirit into Stula's arms, but he caught me and thought I had killed her. He had me sold off that night."

"Have you been in touch with him?"

"Barely. I hadn't spoken to my uncle or my father for seventeen years. This autumn, Alvis granted me passage with him back to Oxare after assisting him and Princess Eira with Amelia's capture. I didn't want word of my involvement with the poison to get out in Cresin, so I thought returning here would be the most logical solution. After I lost my position at the tavern"—she gave Finley, who only grinned back proudly, a pointed glance—"I returned to my father's house as I had nowhere else to go. My father then left on business, and when Waazier caught me practicing my magic again, he kicked me out and sent me to work in the Golden Palace. He sent me a letter when I arrived, but I had it burned and made sure I didn't see any more correspondence from him after. I never had intentions of seeing or speaking to him again."

She stood there with her head high as Finley and Ai stared, probably weighing the validity of her story and if she could be trusted. If they didn't, Myra would survive. She always had. But the thought of being tossed off the ship into the river—or the ocean if they'd made it that far —wasn't an appealing one. Swimming was never one of her strong suits.

The two pirates continued to glance back and forth between each other and Myra in their own secret and silent language. Finley' strummed her fingers against the hilt of the sword on her hip and sighed while Ai smiled. "You *were* frazzled after seeing Waazier in the hall. Fine." She nodded to the door behind her. "Follow me. But you have to swear you're not going to panic or tell anyone what you see."

What a reassuring statement. The most guaranteed way to make someone panic was to tell them not to. Myra was sure that whatever they were about to show her, she'd probably seen worse. "I promise."

The door opened, and nothing would have prepared Myra for the sight before her. She gasped. "The mirror. You stole the mirror."

Her jaw dropped as she looked at the mirror she'd worked so hard to protect. Her heart dropped along with it at the knowledge of her friends being the ones to betray them all. And didn't Myra suspect them in the first place? But they couldn't have been the ones she'd been trying to stop. They'd been somewhere else when Ramin saw a pair of women sneaking in. Hadn't they?

Finley leaned against the wall and propped her foot against it. "Yes, and thank you for the distraction, by the way. All that hullabaloo about your magic and Nell's almost kidnapping made things much more difficult. Especially with our magic being nullified."

Her heart pounded as she took it in. "But...how? We had it protected."

All their work gone to waste. And all while they'd been saving Nell, another crime had been committed. A crime that could be detrimental not only to them, but all the kingdoms.

"You did that?" Ai asked, leading the way toward the mirror. "Very impressive."

Myra followed, hands clenched at her sides. "It's what Alvis and I were working on every night. I can't believe you stole Amelia! Don't you understand the danger we all could be in?"

Finley pushed herself off the wall and sauntered over to them. "We didn't steal Amelia. Just the mirror."

Myra whipped her head around to look at her. "What do you mean? Amelia is inside the mirror."

"No, she's not. She's gone. Which is perfectly fine with me."

Myra felt the blood drain from her face and suddenly felt queasy. "What are you talking about? Where is she?"

Finley shrugged. "Who knows? She was supposed to be in the mirror, but when we got it back to the ship and inspected it, she was nowhere to be found."

Between this and the rocking of the ship, Myra needed to sit, but the room was empty save for the mirror. She sank to the floor and held her head in her hands. "I can't believe this. Why... How? What are you doing with the mirror? Why did you want it?"

Finley groaned, but she and Ai joined Myra on the floor. There were no portholes or other ways to see what was happening outside the ship, so the only light came from the lantern Finley brought in. She set it on the floor in the middle of their little circle, and with the sway of the ship, their shadows rocked back and forth across the wooden boards.

"We didn't *want* it per se," Finley explained. "It was more like an offer we couldn't refuse. Amelia is my cousin."

Myra's heart might as well have stopped. The surprises never ended. "Your cousin? Are you a sorceress?"

Finley waved a dismissive hand. "Distant cousin, and I'm more human than sorceress. The way Princess Eira and Princess Rose are part fae. They have some of Kutlaous's magic from their heritage, but not enough to have any real power." She slid her sleeve up to show off the tattoo of a mermaid and treasure chest. "I still had a dedication ceremony and everything. Anyway. A few months ago, we received notice to meet with someone about a mission, but they wouldn't tell us who they were, only there was a significant reward involved."

"Very significant," Ai repeated. "Something more. The gold and the jewels on our dresses were an incredible incentive on their own, but there's more to it."

This piqued Myra's interest even more. Even outside of being pirates, she was hard-pressed to find people who were willing to turn away from significant wealth. If there was something even more valuable to them than gold or jewels, it had to be quite impressive. She leaned forward. "Who was it? What did they offer?"

Ai shrugged. "We don't know who it was. We met them at a pub, and they kept their face covered. All we know is that it sounded like a man. They knew about our background, and they'd heard about the pageant and how the mirror was in the Golden Palace. With Ai's position in society being what it was, it was an easy in for us to be in the palace and get Amelia out of there."

Myra blinked a few times and rubbed a tense spot on the back of her neck. "But you said you didn't care where Amelia was. It doesn't make sense. And what was in it for you?"

"We don't care where she is. We can't stand her or her family," Ai said, her voice full of venom and steel in her eyes. It was the most bitter Myra had ever seen her. "But they said we could have the mirror."

"Because it's worth a lot of money? For it's magic?"

They needed to get to the point. The more time they spent chatting, the longer it was that they didn't know where Amelia was located. Not that Myra was particularly eager to encounter the former queen again, but her desire to be sure Amelia was locked away to keep everyone else safe superseded that.

Finley scoffed. "Some things are more valuable than money. It would grant us access to Gallis's chalice."

For a moment, the only sound was that of the ship rocking back and forth. It was the chalice Eira had sought out to cure her father. Until then, everyone had assumed it was only a legend. According to the stories, the goddess Gallis had a chalice that could help cure any disease. But people abused its powers, toying with the lines between life and death. Some would even kill to get their hands on it. From the legends Myra had been told as a young girl, Stula despised the chalice and told Gallis to have it destroyed as it prevented Stula from doing her own work and went against the natural order of things. Whether it was the violence of people or Stula's advice, Gallis eventually had the goddess Luana hide it away in her abandoned castle, and it was never seen again.

When Eira found the castle and the chalice, it proved the legends, or at least the chalice and castle, were real. After healing her father, Eira took it back to the castle to be protected once again. But it was only natural people would soon hear about its existence and want to seek it out.

"What do you want with it?" Myra asked, afraid of what the answer would be. As much as she wanted to give her friends the benefit of the doubt, she had a hard time believing they wanted to go heal the world and use it for some noble cause.

Ai and Finley looked at each other, using that silent language only the closest of friends had, where they could have entire conversations without uttering a single word.

Ai gave Finley a gentle smile. "It's your story to tell."

Finley tapped her finger against the top of her tall black boots, looking at the ground and then back up at Myra. Her blue eyes pierced through Myra. "You must swear you won't tell a soul. Only a few people know this."

The intensity of Finley's voice took Myra off guard. "I swear."

Finley nodded and took in a deep breath. "My family is wealthy. Not like Ai's, but they are well off. When I had my dedication ceremony when I was sixteen, they wanted to throw a large party. The largest celebration the Dravian Islands had seen."

It was a common practice among the wealthy to throw such gatherings for their children's dedication ceremonies. Myra had heard of some of them being larger than weddings.

"But we didn't invite Amelia's family. While technically they are my family, we never liked or trusted them. They're cruel and power hungry, and we wanted nothing to do with them. Well, Amelia's mother didn't take that kindly. Especially since it was around the time King Brennan was going to come visit the islands. She must have been worried that if the king knew other families didn't want them in their social circles, he may not want Amelia for his bride.

"She wasn't happy with us. She invaded the celebration and put a curse on me. A sleeping curse. At first, we didn't think anything of it, and I seemed fine. But then I would fall asleep at random times, get tired easily, things of that nature. The older I get, the curse worsens, and I sleep more often and for longer periods of time. When I perform intense pieces of magic, it wipes me out."

Which explained the night before when Finley collapsed onto the ship deck and her frequent naps.

"Eventually, it'll completely overtake me, and I'll be stuck in an eternal slumber. Not unlike the one King Brennan was under."

It would seem Amelia's family was a fan of sleeping. Not that Myra blamed them, but not to curse people with.

But Finley's desire for the chalice made sense. "And you can travel through the mirror to the castle, which would lead you to the chalice, which would mean..."

"I might be able to break the curse. Exactly. In fact, having Amelia missing makes things easier for me. I never wanted to keep the mirror, only use it to get to the chalice. If we took it or it stayed at the palace, I didn't care. I still don't know who the person requesting it was, so what do I care if I fulfill my end of the bargain? But Amelia never let us go past her, and eventually stealing it just to get her out so we could use it ourselves was the best choice. Now that she's out of the picture..."

The three of them turned to look at the mirror. The glass was dark and murky with black clouds swirling around in it. Myra shivered. She still didn't like the idea of Amelia being out, but she could also see why her whereabouts were low on Finley's priority list.

"Why don't you just go to the castle yourself? Princess Eira is kind. She may let you use without having to go through all of this," Myra asked.

Finley laughed. "Yes, I'm sure the woman Amelia wanted to kill will let her relative, who's also a pirate, waltz into Luana's Castle to use an ancient, enchanted chalice."

Myra sighed. Fair enough. "Let's go get it. Then we need to track down Amelia, and we can't do that if you're falling over asleep."

She stood and faced the mirror while Ai and Finley clamored to their feet behind her. "You'll help me?"

"Obviously. But only if you help me track down Amelia."

Through the dim reflection of the glass, she could see Finley and Ai eyeing her warily.

"I couldn't care less as to her whereabouts and hope she's off hiding somewhere never to be seen again. I'd think you would feel the same way," Finley answered.

Myra spun on her heel and faced her unlikely allies. "I don't want to see her. Encountering Amelia is the last thing I want. But we all should be worried about her whereabouts. She's dangerous, powerful, and about to have a child at any moment. For all our sakes, I would be very worried."

Ai nudged Finley with her elbow. "She has a point."

"Besides, you could be infamous. The pirate queen who also took down the most dangerous sorceress of all the kingdoms."

Finley narrowed her eyes, and a clever smile crept over her lips. "That does sound appealing. And the revenge factor is also tempting."

"That's the Finley I know."

The trio turned back and faced their reflections the mirror. For years, Myra had seen this mirror. Known what it could do and who lived inside it. Not that Amelia knew Myra knew. She tried so hard to keep her secrets but didn't take into consideration Myra's own curiosity and observational skills. Despite seeing it for so long, Myra never truly looked at it. All the details of the engravings and the dark shadows and swirls on the other side of the glass. She'd never used it herself.

"I believe we need your magic, Finley," Myra said.

Finley nodded. "Right."

She stepped forward in front of the other two and placed her palm onto the glass. Her tattoo glowed, and the light spread out of her fingertips across the mirror, turning the glass wavy and water-like. Ai took Finley's free hand, and Myra took Ai's. Together they stepped through.

Chapter Twenty-Five

MYRA

THE WORLD OF THE MIRROR WAS ONE MYRA HAD NEVER EXPERIENCED before. When they first stepped through, it appeared to be a room like any other. In fact, it reminded her of Amelia's room in Farren Castle, with a plush blue bed and a stream of water running through the middle of the floor. But there was a dreamlike quality to it, and everything was fuzzy and soft around the edges. Stacks of books and bottles of tonics and medicines for pregnancy littered the tables, and a fuzzy blanket was draped over a rocking chair. If Myra hadn't known any better, it would have been the bedroom of any other pregnant woman.

Daughter of Stula.

She paused and looked around. The faintest of whispers, but it sent a shiver down Myra's spine. It wasn't a voice she recognized, but one that felt familiar all the same, beckoning her to it.

"Did you hear that?"

Finley and Ai had already walked a few steps ahead of her and glanced back at her with quizzical looks.

"Hear what?" Ai asked.

Myra continued to look back and forth, and her hair whipped

around her face. But no one was there but the three of them. She must have been imagining things. "Nothing. Let's keep going."

There were no walls to the space, at least not tangible ones, as once Myra thought they were at the edge of the room, it just kept going. The walls faded away into dark and swirling clouds with a pale light in the distance.

What must have it been like for Nell to grow up here? Did she hear the voices too? Myra would have to ask her. The idea made her heart sink. She wasn't sure when she would see the child next. If ever. Running away at the ball didn't just take her away from Alvis, but from Nell too. Her chest twisted. She couldn't think about that now.

"I think that's where the next mirror is," Finley said, gesturing toward the light.

"I hope so. This place is creeping me out," Myra admitted.

Finley and Ai nodded in agreement and kept going with their hands on the hilts of their swords, prepared to strike at any moment. Although Myra had a hunch if they encountered anything in the mirror world, it wouldn't be able to be conquered by a human weapon.

The distance between Amelia's room and the opening to the other mirror was short, but the areas side to side of them felt vast and unending. Or there could even be something beyond the second mirror if they dared to go past it.

A large rectangle hung before them, as though a piece of the air was out of place, all wavy and wobbly with a faint light shining through it. Not fazed by anything, Finley put her hand on it, and it opened to reveal another room. They stepped through onto a solid stone floor. This new room had another bed and piles and piles of knickknacks, jewels, and treasures. The glitter of them shone in Ai and Finley's eyes.

"A dragon's hoard," Ai whispered. "Can you imagine what we could do…"

This must have been Aytigin's room then. But this could only be the start of it. There must have been hundreds of legendary artifacts and treasure stores in this castle.

Finley's lip curled, and she greedily walked through the space, looking at all the treasure there. "I can. But we need the chalice."

Yes. Focus.

Careful to not disturb anything, they tiptoed through the room and out into the rest of the castle. Myra's eyes grew wider with each step as she took in the sight of Luana's legendary castle. Parts of it were old and run-down with stones crumbling the corners and stripped painting canvases. But other portions seemed brand-new and sparkled with starlight. Through the windows, both the sun and the moon shone as though night and day could exist at the same time.

Myra paused at a window ledge and observed her surroundings. When she looked carefully, there were cavern walls surrounding the castle. The walls of the mountain. Luana had built the castle inside the mountain but made the illusion of the sky and outdoors. It took Myra's breath away.

The window ledge underneath her palms shook, and a cold wind blew through the hall. Ai and Finley stopped their pursuit and wrapped their arms around themselves to stay warm, their breath coming out in small puffs.

"Of course, the dragon had to come home *now*," Finley grumbled.

Myra gulped, and her necklace warmed against her chest. "No, it's not Aytigin."

A piercing scream rang through the castle, and the trio covered their ears. "Intruders!"

It was the spirit of Malle.

Myra had almost forgotten about the spirit Eira had told her about and how she was disturbing the castle.

Malle soared toward them, and Myra ducked, while Ai and Finley continued to stand, and the spirit ran directly through them. They screeched from the cold and froze in shock. The two of them couldn't see the spirit, only feel her presence.

"What was that?" Ai asked through chattering teeth.

"A spirit," Myra explained. Malle hovered toward the end of the hall, eyes ablaze and dark hair swirling. In life, she probably looked like Princess Eira. But as a spirit, her face was sunken in and as hard as a stone. "And she's not happy."

"Leave this place. I know what you want, and you can't have it."

With those words, she charged toward them again. "Duck!" Myra ordered, and they all crouched to the ground before Malle could go through them again.

The floor shook beneath them and rattled the windows. Paintings crashed to the ground, and bits of the stone walls crumbled along with them. All the while, Malle floated in front of a door with her arms outstretched.

"Go!" the spirit screamed, and a cold wind blew past, pushing them away from the door no matter how much they tried to fight against it.

Myra closed her eyes and summoned her magic, letting it roll and swirl beneath her skin and through her veins. Under her breath, she murmured the words Mama taught her so long ago to connect to and soothe unruly spirits. Shadows circled and surrounded Myra and her friends, who stood by her, shivering from Malle's chill.

For a moment, Malle stilled and seemed to listen to Myra's incantation. The ghost's face became soft, and clarity came to her eyes. But as quickly as it came, her expression hardened again. Her body grew so large it took up the entire wall, and her eyes turned red. "How dare you try to trick me!"

A harsh wind blew through the room and knocked the three of them over, and more stones crashed around them. The floor shook, and little by little, the stone crumbled beneath them.

"Run!" Ai yelled.

They scrambled to their feet and darted away and back to where they came, the floor falling apart in their wake.

They ran through the castle halls to Aytigin's room, where the mirror stood. Finley pressed her hand against the glass, and the three of them barged through. The voices and shadows in the mirror world called out to Myra, but she ignored them until they got back onto the ship, collapsing on the other side in a heap.

Myra's heart pounded against her ribs as they tried to gather themselves again. Finley flopped on to her back and stared at the ceiling.

"Well, that will be a bit more complicated than I anticipated."

Chapter Twenty-Six

MYRA

M YRA'S TEETH CHATTERED AS MALLE'S SPIRIT RAN THROUGH HER YET again. She'd been at this for hours and made no progress. It was the second time Myra had gone back to Luana's Castle since they'd escaped the Golden Palace, and while Finley searched for the chalice, she wanted to see what she could do to put Malle's spirit to rest for Eira. Ai was back on *The Mystic* commanding the crew. They were out at sea now, but not too far out as Finley wanted to stop at a port she knew of on the Oxarian coast for supplies.

They might have been stealing from the princess, so the least Myra could do was attempt to fulfill the favor she'd promised Eira.

Myra clenched her jaw and rested her hands on the stone table in the temple Eira must have been working on to break the curse. Parts of the temple, like the stone table, were in pristine condition and glimmered and sparkled with ice and stardust. While others... Well, Eira had a long way to go.

Malle was unlike any spirit she had encountered before. Most had at least elements of their old selves in them. There was something deep down Myra could draw out to remind them of their humanity when they were alive and use it to calm them and eventually guide to Stula's arms. Malle was only full of bitterness and anger and chaos. She screamed at random times and destroyed everything and anything in her path. The place she was strongest was the temple, so Myra went there to see if there was something she could use to help.

For now, Malle was calm. At least calm in comparison to how she'd behaved before. She hovered near a window, and her vacant eyes stared out to the mountain beyond. Her dark hair was shorter than Eira's, and if hadn't been for her sunken-in eyes and cheeks, her face might have been rounder than Eira's too. But it was hard to tell what she might have looked like in life. Death and destruction had eroded her being the way water did to rocks on the shore. Some of it might have been heartbreak.

Myra's heart softened toward the spirit. There was something painfully sad about her. The human spirit could withstand so much pain and hardship, but maybe even the strongest had a breaking point, and Malle had reached hers long ago, leaving what was left a cloud of destruction.

Malle screamed, something piercing and awful that made the walls and floors tremble at the sound. Myra covered her ears, and the pity she felt a moment ago vanished as the scream rang through the temple.

Damn it all to Stula's realm.

If only she had a grimoire or access to Alvis's library and she could do more to learn on how to put Malle to rest. But she didn't have those things anymore. She'd lost them like she'd lost everything else. She slammed her fist against the stone table, leaving it aching, but Myra didn't care. This was supposed to be the one thing she was good at.

The sound of the temple doors opening and slamming shut filled the room, followed by Finley's footsteps and mumbling. "Can't you get that thing to stop screaming?"

"Don't you think I'm trying?" Myra snapped back.

Another cry came from Malle's direction, and stones flew toward them. Myra and Finley ducked, and they crashed against the walls, breaking into tiny pieces. Poor Eira was going to have more work to do by the time she came back.

"I didn't think ghosts could hold objects," Finley said.

"Most don't, but some powerful ones can," Myra explained as she and Finley ducked again when Malle threw a chair at them. "Malle seems pretty powerful."

"Clearly."

Malle paced back and forth on the other side of the temple and glared at them. But she didn't seem to be aiming toward throwing anything again, so Myra hoped she was done with her tantrum at least for the moment.

"It's not like you've been able to get to the chalice yet," Myra pointed out.

Finley snarled. "That damn dragon has the most booby traps I've ever seen." She stepped forward and showed off her jacket, which now that there weren't stones and furniture being launched at her head, Myra was able to examine the state Finley was in. Her once fine captain's coat had scorch marks across it in long streaks going all the way through her shirt and to her stomach.

"Finley! We need to get back to the ship and have that looked at!"

Finley shrugged and pulled her jacket on tighter as though nothing happened at all. "I've had worse. The chalice will be worth it. I just wanted to see if you could come help me."

"And have my skin burned off? No, thank you. We're taking you back to the ship."

Myra grabbed Finley's sleeve to lead her out the door. She was sick and tired of this ghost, and all she wanted to do was relax on the bunk Ai scrounged up for her.

"Whoa, wait a minute," Finley said and tugged her arm away from Myra. "What is happening to your necklace?"

Myra looked down at her chest where her pendant softly glowed. She sighed. "It's been doing that all day. It's never done it before, but it's strongest by the table."

She led Finley over to the table and pointed out one of the inscriptions on its surface. "It matches the one on my necklace. I think this is the piece Eira was working on when she woke Malle and said she saw the symbol appear in the air."

Finley ran her hand over the symbol. "What do you think it means?"

Myra tapped her finger on the table as though if she continued to touch it, the answer would appear, or it would all fix itself. "I'm not sure. Malle favors this area of the temple when I'm not over here, and she's the most powerful here. I think it's where she died. I've been trying to draw magic from it to see if it'll help Malle, but nothing is working."

Finley's lip curled, and she frowned. "If I were a ghost, I wouldn't want to spend my time at the place where I died."

"Many spirits have a connection to that location though. It's one of their strongest ties to the living world."

"Well, I'll be sure that when I die, you're with me so that we're certain I'm escorted to Stula correctly. Because when I'll want nothing to do with this world or having the possibility of turning into that."

Over in the corner, Malle glared at the two of them as they inspected the table, and between her hands, it was as though she twirled the air around in a circle between them. Stones and pieces of glass and ice spun around in the air.

Myra gulped. "I think it's time for us to go."

As the words came out of her mouth, Malle released the circle and pushed it toward them with a shriek, and the stones and shards came flying toward them. The pair ran to the door and bolted out into the hallway, all while being scratched and bombarded by the pieces Malle flung at them. They made it to the mirror with only a few minor scratches and barreled through, Malle's shrieks now only echoes behind them. Once back on the ship, they collapsed to their knees with heaving breaths.

Finley coughed and held her stomach where she'd been burned. "I need a drink."

"ARE YOU SURE THIS IS A GOOD IDEA? I'M SURE THERE'S PEOPLE searching for us everywhere," Myra asked as she walked to the tavern, arm in arm with Finley and Ai. The moment they'd gotten back on the ship, Ai insisted they saw the Attendant to get cleaned up and have healing salves applied to their wounds. Especially the burn across Finley's stomach. The resources they had on *The Mystic* were limited, but at least they could get some bandages. Even though she was injured, Finley still demanded they get a drink.

"I don't know what you mean. All my ideas are brilliant," Finley answered with a smile.

"Brilliantly idiotic," Ai fake whispered to Myra, which made them all laugh.

Gods, Myra needed to laugh.

Finley tossed her hair over one shoulder. "Besides, *The Mystic* is far faster than any of the Golden Palace's soldiers' horses. They won't be here at the coast yet."

Myra hoped she was right.

The tavern was loud and crowded with patrons filling each dark corner. A tall fae male flirted with a sailor on the staircase and a dwarfess sat at a table running a card game. Myra coughed from the smoke coming from the dwarfess's pipe and then grimaced as she stepped in something sticky. Other members of the crew were already there, sprinkled through the room in various states of sobriety. Finley raised three fingers in the air, and the bartender, who smiled at her in recognition, nodded as they pushed their way to a table.

Finley stopped at one already occupied by four men, but with one jerk of her chin, they looked at her with wide eyes and scurried away. Myra gaped in awe as she slid into her seat. They'd barely sat down, and a server already placed three giant pints in front of them.

"I take it they know you here?"

Ai tilted her head to the side and swished her pint around. "We're what you would call 'infamous' in these parts."

Patrons who passed by their table either nodded toward the two pirates or scampered away in fear. It made Myra's stomach twist. "Doesn't that make it even more dangerous that we're here?"

Finley was already gulping down her drink and then set it down with a loud thunk. "We'll be fine. Places like this, people don't snitch on each other. Every single being in this building has some sort of dirt on them. If one person turns someone else in, the business will go under because it won't be a safe place anymore." She gestured to Myra's pint. "Drink! It'll calm you down."

Everything in Myra screamed to run back to the ship and hide. Who knew what sort of search party the royal family had out for the three of them? But she did need to relax, and Finley and Ai must have been used to being on the run, so they must know where it would be safe to hide out. Even when Myra attempted to relax on *The Mystic*, it was restless and interrupted by dreams and swirling thoughts of Alvis.

Alvis.

No. She wasn't going to think about him. She needed to forget about him.

Myra grabbed her pint and took a large gulp. And before long, one gulp became several, and one pint became three. Finley leaned back, propping her feet on the table where a collection of empty cups now gathered. She removed her hat and ran her fingers through the feather.

"Myra, what actually happened the night of the ball between you and Alvis? Ai and I were a tad occupied you know, so we didn't get to see what went wrong. The last we knew you were all ready to declare your feelings for him, and by the time we get back, you're rescuing Nell from being kidnapped, Waazier is spreading lies about you, and then you ran away with us." She'd had as much as Myra to drink, but hardly slurred a single word.

Myra, on the other hand, felt like she was back on the swaying ship. She hadn't told them the details of what happened at the ball and wasn't sure if she wanted to. Only because it meant thinking about Alvis. She reached for her cup, but it felt too light. She looked inside, only to see it was empty.

"It's all gone."

Finley chuckled and waved to the bartender. It was funny—no one else had their drinks brought to their table but the three of them. There were perks to being friends with the Pirate Queen.

Ai rubbed Myra's back. "She doesn't have to tell us if she doesn't want to."

"No, it's *fine*," Myra slurred and rested her head against Ai's shoulder. She sighed. "He proposed, and we were going to tell his family before announcing it at the ball."

Finley sputtered. "Do you mean we're drinking with the future queen of Oxare right now?"

Myra groaned and leaned forward until her head hit the table. "No. He didn't defend me!" Myra sat up again. She couldn't figure out if she wanted to lie down or do her best to remain upright. Up for as long as possible was probably the best option. "I went and saved Nell, but was that enough? Nooooooo. When Uncle Waazier said all those awful things, I didn't have the chance to defend myself, and everyone was so mad about my magic, and he just stood there. He didn't say anything or do anything."

The server brought more beers to the table, and Myra slid one over to her and took another long swig.

"He did try to get you, though," Ai offered hopefully. "He came after you."

"He did, didn't he?" Myra frowned and took another sip. "But it was too late. I was going to tell him everything about my past, but I never had the chance. You didn't see his face when my uncle said all those things. Alvis doesn't want me for a queen. And what kind of fiancé lets other people say such horrible things anyway?"

Even if they were at least partially true.

Finley and Ai nodded in understanding, and the three of them all took another drink.

Finley patted Myra on the shoulder. "Well, I think it's good you didn't marry him. You're fabulous, Myra, and I don't say that to many people. Besides, I bet he's awful in bed."

Myra groaned again, slouched in her seat, and leaned her head back so she looked up at the dusty ceiling rafters. "No, he was wonderful. I think the best I ever had."

Ai and Finley locked eyes and raised their brows and then burst into laughter.

Finley lifted her cup. "Then here's to sleeping with the handsome prince but not getting tied down!"

They all clinked their cups together and drank.

When they had their fill, Myra felt as though the world spun around her, and Finley and Ai had to support her between them as they stumbled out into the streets. The rest of the crew had already gone back to *The Mystic*, and the streets were quiet in the dark night. Maybe it was all the years spent in Cresin, but in moments like these, Myra could understand and appreciate the followers of Luana. The full moon shone over the small oceanside town with its sparkling stars blinking around it. Even for those with dark histories—or present—Luana still watched over them and gave them these lovely moments in the night where everything was peaceful and safe.

Until a shadowed figure from one of the alleys appeared and pointed a sword right at them.

"We knew you had to come out eventually."

One by one, soldiers appeared from the shadows, their weapons drawn at the ready. Myra groaned. Of course they had to come while she was rip-roaring drunk.

"Looks like someone snitched," Myra drawled her words, all stumbling and running together.

"We said the tavern was safe, didn't say anything about everywhere else," Finley pointed out.

"If you come quietly, you won't come to any harm. We've been given instructions to bring you all to the palace alive. But if you make a scene…" The first soldier smirked and gripped his sword. "We didn't say we wouldn't leave a few scratches on you."

Ai looked over Myra's head toward Finley. "The wise thing would be to go quietly."

Finley took in a deep breath and nodded. "You're right. That would be the wise thing."

Before Myra had the chance to say or do anything, in easy swift movements, her friends removed their hold around her, pushed her behind them, and drew their swords. Myra stumbled back, her head spinning, and as she gained her balance, Finley and Ai were already clashing swords with the soldiers.

Soldiers' tattoos glowed through their clothing, making their already muscular arms bulge, hitting the pirates' swords with their own, and Myra's head pounded from the clashing sounds. Finley and Ai made sure to keep Myra protected and covered behind them, but they were outnumbered five to three. Well, more like two as Myra didn't have any weapons and did more cowering than anything.

Finley's tattoo glowed, and water from various places on the street—a fountain and some puddles—flowed toward them and gathered to form a small stream, soaking the cobblestones at their feet. Some of the soldiers slipped and tripped from the suddenly slick ground but kept fighting on.

Myra had to do something; she couldn't let them be captured. She closed her eyes tight and then opened them again, trying to pay attention as best she could through the alcohol fog. She summoned her magic and let a shadowy haze hover over the fight and tried to focus on the Aros magic from the soldiers. She didn't want to nullify Finley and Ai's magic, but if she could put her magic on just the soldiers, it could give them more of an advantage.

"Wha-What's she doing?" one soldier asked.

The first soldier shook his head and hit Ai's sword with a particularly hard blow. "She's nothing! Get them!"

Soldiers came from all sides, and Finley and Ai fought left and right as Myra concentrated her magic on other attackers. One by one, their tattoos faded, but they were still outnumbered.

"Myra, go!" Finley ordered, the commanding tone of a captain in her voice.

"I can't leave you," Myra answered.

Finley gritted her teeth, and as she spun around to fight against one soldier, with her free arm she pushed Myra away. She stumbled back again, away from the fighting. They didn't really expect her to just run away and leave them, did they? Using all the focus she had, Myra continued to step back but kept aiming her magic toward the soldiers, who shivered, and goosebumps appeared on their arms.

Her back bumped into something hard and strong. She looked up and only saw a male figure.

"Got you."

With a hard *thwack*, Myra fell to the ground, and everything went black.

Chapter Twenty-Seven

MYRA

MYRA BLINKED HER EYES OPEN. HER HEAD POUNDED, HER BACK WAS stiff, and her throat as dry as the Khadi desert. She pushed herself into a sitting position on the cold floor and tried to get her bearings. The last thing she remembered was being attacked after leaving the tavern.

Where was she?

She sat on a hard, cold wooden floor with only a couple of small windows to let in light. Old trunks and discarded furniture littered the cold room.

It wasn't a dungeon then, but where else could she be? If she was captured by royal soldiers, she must be somewhere back in the Golden Palace, and perhaps Finley and Ai were there too.

"Hello?" Her voice bounced off the walls. "Is anyone there?"

Through the dim light, she could only see more trunks and chairs and tables.

"Hello?" she called out again.

There wasn't even a guard on duty, which was odd. Even outside of stealing the mirror, Finley and Ai were notorious criminals and would be under high supervision. Unless they indeed had been separated and the two of them were in an entirely different holding place than she. Myra's heart sank at the thought. They shouldn't have left *The Mystic*.

Even if the tavern had been a supposedly safe place, clearly the area around it wasn't.

Myra groaned and leaned her head against the wall. She felt like her body was about to turn inside out, and she needed water. She couldn't remember the last time she'd drank so much, if she'd ever drank that much. Myra took in a deep breath.

Focus. There must be a way out.

"Ah, you're awake."

A chill ran down Myra's spine. "Uncle Waazier."

He strolled toward her through the darkness, only a lantern in his hand illuminating the sharp panes of his face and pointed beard. In his free hand, he extended out to her a cup of water. "You sound surprised."

She took a step back and eyed the cup he held out to her. The water was tempting, but she didn't trust him past the tip of her nose. Who knew what was in that liquid? "Where am I? What's going on?"

Uncle Waazier chuckled, a dark and chilling sound. "You mean you don't recognize it? You're home. I can't believe you don't recognize your own attic."

Myra barely went up into the attic of the estate growing up. Hardly anything was up there, and it always made strange noises. When she was younger and didn't know much about her magic, Myra was afraid of spirits and thought they lived up there and avoided it at all costs.

So no, Myra did not recognize her own home at first.

But she wasn't afraid of spirits any longer, and somewhere in this house there should still be a spirit. They came to her aid before, and Myra could only pray to Stula they would again.

It would be impossible to summon the spirit to her without the knowledge of Waazier, but if she could get it to the attic fast enough, it wouldn't matter. Myra took in a deep breath and let the magic within her swirl and dance in her veins.

"What do you want? And where's Finley and Ai?" she asked.

Uncle Waazier took a step forward, and she took a step back. He wouldn't get anywhere closer to her if she could help it. He extended one arm, holding the cup of water to show it to her. "I only wish to give you some water. You were in quite a state when I brought you here."

Myra eyed it, as she was thirsty. But wouldn't trust anything that came from him. "Put it on the table."

He did as she asked, and as he did, Myra murmured under her breath and hoped the spirit who helped before was still present in the house and would hear her. Uncle Waazier furrowed his brows, and the point of his beard quivered. "What are you doing?"

He was just a frightened man. A man frightened of what he didn't understand. But sometimes people who were frightened could be the most dangerous.

But at least it gave Myra the upper hand, even if only for the moment. "Answer my questions, and maybe I'll answer yours. What do you want from me, and where are Finley and Ai?"

Waazier glared at her and scowled. "If you'd read my letters, you would know what I want."

A slight chill filled the air, and Myra shivered. It worked. The spirit had heard her. She let this knowledge fill her with confidence. "You kicked me out of my own home and sent me away. You want nothing to do with me, nor I you. Of course I didn't read your letters. Now, what do you want?"

Myra let dark shadows circle around her hands and arms. They weren't meant to do anything but frighten and intimidate him, but that would do for now. His eyes grew wide at the sight, and goosebumps appeared on his arms.

"Your necklace."

She instinctively covered the pendant with one hand. It warmed at her touch. "No."

What would he possibly want with her mother's necklace? He hated anything to do with her mother's heritage.

The room grew colder, and a breeze wafted Myra's hair around. By now, Waazier's hands trembled at his side but took a step forward anyway. "Stop this magic now, and give it to me."

Myra let shadows fill the attic and backed away farther from her uncle, pushing various pieces of furniture to block his way. She heard him stumble about in the dark, and the spirit she'd summoned hovered in front of her. The spirit was only a pale mist—a gray and misty shadow without a form—but at least it was there to protect and help Myra.

Waazier's eyes grew wide. He might not have been able to see the spirit without Myra's assistance, but from the goosebumps appearing on his arms, Myra knew he sensed it's presence. His pointed beard trembled. "It can't do anything to me."

Myra raised a brow and lifted a chair leg. She grasped it in both hands, prepared to use it if necessary. "Can't it?"

A wind in the room swirled around, lifting discarded pieces of furniture with sharp wooden edges and rusted metal into the air, and Waazier now he visibly shook all the way to the point of his thin beard. Every piece hovering before them turned and pointed toward him and in an instant went after him.

Waazier cried out and ran to the door. He went out and slammed it shut as they all hit the door. "You can't stay in there forever!" he yelled, but then the sound of his stomps down the stairs faded away.

Myra's chest heaved with each breath, and she tried to calm herself. At least he was gone. For now. She lowered the chair leg, set it on the ground, and looked around the room until she saw the faint image of the spirit hovering nearby.

"Thank you," Myra said. "But I'm sure he'll be back."

She walked toward the spirit, and little by little, it gathered itself together to take the shape of a person. A woman in a long gown with soft hair swept on top of her head. Myra gasped and covered her mouth with her hands.

"Mama?"

The face Myra thought she'd never see again looked at her with warm eyes and a gentle smile. "My darling girl."

Myra choked out a sob and, without thinking, reached out to embrace her mother, only to remember she couldn't hug a spirit. "I… I'm sorry. I failed you. You never made it to Stula's arms."

Mama offered a sad smile. "No. But you didn't fail me. It was a large task for someone so young. Come, sit. I'll tell you everything." She gestured to the cup of water on the table. "It's not poisoned, I promise. I watched him pour the water."

Myra did as she was told and sat on the ground, and Mama's spirit sat next to her. The water tasted wonderful, and she drank the whole cup in only a few gulps.

"When I died and you helped my spirit pass on, you did a wonderful job, and it would have succeeded if Waazier hadn't interrupted you."

Myra's heart sank at the memory of that awful night. No one else in their home knew the rite to help Mama's spirit pass on, so Myra had performed it in secret. But Waazier caught her, and that was when he accused her of killing Mama and then sold her off. It was the worst moment of her life.

"So you've been existing here all this time?"

"Not exactly. I was stuck in an in-between world. If you'd stayed, you might have been able to sense me with your necklace."

Myra touched the red pendant and looked at it. "I didn't know it had magic."

"Indeed, it does. But we're getting ahead of ourselves. I wasn't able to stay in our world or move onto the next, at least until this past winter solstice."

Myra's jaw dropped. "The rite I performed. It worked?"

Mama waved her hand back and forth. "You were out of practice. But it was enough to bring me back to this world, and over time, I was able to gather myself together to take on this form."

Tears now formed in Myra's eyes, and they trickled down her cheeks. "I'm so sorry, Mama. If I knew it was you, I would have helped you. I didn't mean for you to be stuck like that."

Mama reached out to Myra to wipe away her tears, but her transparent hand only passed through Myra's body like air. Myra shivered. "Don't be sorry, because now I am able to help you. You see, over the past few months, I've been able to watch Waazier and what he's been up to."

Myra took in a few deep breaths to try to calm herself. "What does he want with the necklace? I don't understand. He's never cared about our magic before, other than wanting it out of the house."

"Your uncle has been working with someone named Amelia and helping her to escape from a mirror."

The world stopped, and Myra's breath escaped her. Waazier. It had been Waazier wanting to help Amelia this whole time? "Wh-What?"

"She seems to be some sort of powerful sorceress who has promised your uncle more power and riches than this estate can give him. He's always been a power-hungry man, so it doesn't surprise me he wanted to team up with her. You know this woman?"

Myra nodded. "She was my former mistress. Waazier must have found out I used to work for her somehow." She then filled Mama in on the events of the past several months with the poisoning of King Brennan and Myra's involvement, all the way through the pageant and how Myra got there to be speaking with her.

Mama listened to Myra's story, only asking a few questions periodically. They sat side by side as Mama pondered all she'd been told, and if it hadn't been for the fact that Mama was transparent, Myra would have felt like they were on one of their picnics when she was a child. Sharing every detail without feeling the need to hold back anything lifted a weight off her shoulders.

"The necklace, the mirrors, and the stone table are all connected," Mama finally said. She gestured to the necklace and for Myra to turn it over so the symbol showed. "This is an ancient symbol. Many think it was created by one of Stula's priests, but it wasn't. It was made by Stula herself."

Myra blinked a few times and tried to gather her bearings. "What? I've been wearing something of Stula's this whole time?"

Mama nodded. "I wanted to tell you about it, but then it was too late. It's been handed down to each woman in our family. The artifacts Stula made are rare, but if you see this symbol, it was made by her."

"Which is why I felt a connection to the mirror inside it, and Malle's spirit is so strong by the table, and my necklace glows when I'm near it."

"Exactly. Does Amelia know about the table?"

"I don't think so. But it's possible since she traveled between the two mirrors."

"I wouldn't be surprised if she did know, and I'd imagine that was one of the reasons she was interested in keeping you as her servant."

Myra rubbed her temples. All this information gave her a headache. Or perhaps that was the aftereffect of all the alcohol she'd had prior to her capture.

"And it wasn't your friends, Finley and Ai, who helped Amelia escape."

At least there was one piece of good news. While Myra believed them when they told her they hadn't helped Amelia escape, she was glad to know her trust wasn't misplaced. "Who was it then?"

"Charis."

All it would have taken was a breeze, and Myra would have been knocked over there in her seat. "Excuse me?"

Mama nodded. "Or at least Waazier suspects it was. I heard she left the palace once the ball was over. She'd intercepted one of Waazier's letters to you and was intrigued by what she read and presented herself as someone to help. She must have already known Prince Alvis wasn't going to choose her for his bride and wanted another avenue for power. Waazier knew Finley and Ai didn't want to cooperate with him, so when Charis came into the picture, he was glad to have her on his side. She stole someone's flute and would use it to put the guards to sleep. But she went against the plan. The mirror and Amelia were supposed to stay together and be taken away to the ship while Nell was being kidnapped. But she was already gone. When Waazier returned with you yesterday and reported all that transpired to the woman he's been working with, she was furious."

"What woman?"

Mama shrugged. "I'm not sure. I've never seen her face, only heard her voice. It could be another mirror they're communicating through."

Myra pulled her legs up and wrapped her arms around her knees. There were far more players in this game than she'd anticipated, and it was difficult to keep them all straight and determine which pieces fit together. There were still so many unanswered questions. Especially who this mysterious woman was and who attempted to kidnap Nell.

"So what now?" Myra asked.

"For now, I would say the most important things would be to get you and the necklace as far away from Waazier as possible and back with your prince. It's clear Waazier and whoever he's working with want the necklace, and that you're hopelessly in love with Alvis."

Myra rested her chin on her knees. "The first thing, yes. The second... Alvis doesn't love me. He just stood there and didn't say anything or let me explain. It would never work anyway. It was a fantasy."

"And who says fantasies can't come true?" Mama nudged her with her shoulder. While they might not have been able to touch, Myra still found comfort in the shiver that ran through her from the spirit. "Alvis should have stood up for you and spoken up. You're absolutely right. But it was an unusual situation, and he did come after you. It wouldn't hurt to hear him out and let him do the same for you. It seems as though he made you happy, and that's all I ever wanted for you."

Myra wanted her to be right but couldn't let herself believe it. Going back to Alvis would only open her up again to be hurt and to imagine something more than what they had. She wasn't sure if she could handle more disappointment in that area.

"But if it's truly not what you want, then we can just be sure you're away from here and Waazier. It's your choice."

Myra swallowed the lump in her throat. Mama was right in that regard—she needed to get out of there, and she should go back to the Golden Palace to warn them about the connection between the necklace, mirrors, and stone table as well as everything else she'd learned. Maybe even capture Waazier or find Finley and Ai. Those last things were a lofty aspiration, but she had to try. Then she could go on her way.

"All right. We can do that."

"Then we better get started."

Chapter Twenty-Eight

ALVIS

THE SCENE FELT ALL TOO FAMILIAR AS ALVIS HELD OUT A SUN TORCH and descended the stairs to the Golden Palace dungeon. Only a few months ago, he'd been making the same journey in Farren Castle to visit Cal. This time, he didn't have to go in secret, and instead of Myra being there to assist, she was a potential prisoner. He couldn't decide if he hoped she was in one of the cells or not.

A guard led Alvis through the dungeon to the back where Finley, the pirate queen, was held captive. She sat on the bench, feet stretched out on the bench, crossed at the ankles, arms folded across her torso as though she were taking a leisurely nap instead of imprisoned in a royal dungeon. Her long blond hair fell in front of her face, making it difficult to tell if she was truly asleep or not.

The guard pounded a club against the metal bars, and Finley only glanced up at him with a bored look. "Wake up. The prince wants to talk to you."

Finley rolled her shoulders. "You don't have to make such a ruckus about it."

"She's been a pain in my ass ever since she arrived," the guard said and looked at Alvis over his shoulder.

Alvis waved his hand. "It's fine. I'd like to speak to her in private please."

The guard's mouth tightened into a thin line, but he nodded and bowed. "Very well, your highness. Call if you need me."

Alvis was fairly certain he wouldn't, for if the pirate wanted to kill him, she would have done so weeks ago. Deities knew she'd had ample opportunity. He set his torch on the holder against the wall and approached the cell once the guard left.

Finley pushed her hair back and leaned against the wall. "They took my hat."

Alvis sighed. "I'm sure you'll survive."

"It's my favorite, and the feather came from a phoenix. Do you know how difficult that is to come by?"

It was incredibly rare to have a phoenix feather, and he hated to admit that he couldn't help but be impressed. But what else would he expect from a pirate queen? He'd heard about her of course, but images of her were rare, and he didn't know what she'd looked like. Even so, he felt foolish for not realizing who she and Ai were until now. Finley had dozens, if not hundreds, of ships under her command. Her adventures weren't as well-known inland, but when Alvis visited the coast and the surrounding islands, tales of her exploits were whispered about in hushed and reverent tones.

"If you cooperate, I'll do what I can to ensure you receive it back in good condition."

"*Pristine* condition."

He could see what the guard meant.

"Fine. Pristine condition." He crossed his arms in front of his chest. "Where's Myra?"

She raised a single mocking brow at him. "*Now* you decide to care about her? Where was this concern at the ball when she was run out by your guests at the mere mention of her heritage? Or are you just wanting to know so you can persecute her too?"

A spark lit inside Alvis, but he kept his face neutral. The only sign of anger or annoyance was a slight whitening of his knuckles. She wanted to make him upset. But she was right and was a good friend to Myra for coming to her defense so quickly. "I know I should have spoken up for her," he said in a low voice. "I tried to go after her—"

"But it was too late," Finley snapped and pushed herself up from against the wall, her back as straight as one of her ship's masts and blue eyes as intense as the ocean waves. "Your silence was all she needed to know."

He knew she was right and couldn't help but admire her loyalty to Myra. That was what Myra deserved, someone who stood up for her no matter what and not the coward he was. He'd been so shocked at what happened during the ball and was still reeling from Nell almost being kidnapped. By the time he'd realized what was going on, Myra was already out the door. He'd been able to hold off the guards from chasing after her at least for a little while. But the look of hurt and betrayal in her eyes when he called after her that night haunted him.

"I know," he said. "I've been searching for her so I could get to her before our soldiers did. Cadeyrn, Aytigin, Eira, and I have gone all through the capital in search of her. Nell and I took our horses and went down the river, but there was no sign of her anywhere."

Mother was furious at the outcome of the ball and insisted he pick another bride, but Alvis wouldn't hear of it. Flying on Aytigin's back the last few days was one of the most terrifying things he'd ever done, and he soon opted for searching on land. Nell insisted on joining him, and he let her, despite the protestations from her governess about the dangers of her being kidnapped again. But the best place for Nell, he felt, was at his side where he could keep an eye on her. Besides, he owed her several outings now and knew she needed to get out of the palace occasionally.

There hadn't been any sign of Myra though. He went around to every tailer he could find and showed them the shoe Myra left behind on the palace steps in hopes he would find their maker and then find out if they'd seen Myra. But none of them recognized it as their work as much as they wanted to. Along the river, there hadn't been any ships or boats with people recognizing Myra's description or someone who had the other shoe.

From the reports Eira, Cadeyrn, and Aytigin gave from their searches along the coast, they had the same unfortunate luck.

A twinkle appeared in Finley's eyes, and she smiled and leaned back against the wall again. "I suppose you weren't looking in the right places. But I don't know where Myra is. We were separated while attacked, and she was taken away by someone else. I don't think she's here."

Alvis clenched his jaw. Who else would have taken her? "Damn it all to Stula's realm."

"Ai might know though," Finley added. "I…passed out…when they took me. Ai might have seen more."

So there was at least a sliver of hope. He swallowed the lump in his throat and nodded. "And Amelia?"

Finley scoffed. "I don't know where she is, and I don't care. We didn't help her escape."

"They say you're related to her, and I'm sure someone in your position would find her power and connections valuable, so pardon me for not believing you."

Finley looked up at him through her long locks, the playful and mischievous young woman gone, and in her place, something dark rolled behind those blue eyes. "I don't need Amelia's power or connections or anything else from her or her family. In case you didn't know, I do fine without them."

"So you have nothing to do with the mirror."

She raised her chin and clenched her jaw. "As I said, and as I told the guards, we didn't help Amelia escape."

Alvis matched her glare. She didn't directly answer his question, but he knew if he pushed her now, she'd lock up and not tell him anything else. He should push her. Threaten her with his fire magic or find a guard to get more information out of her about Amelia. But if he did that, there wasn't any way he would have Ai's trust, and then he wouldn't be able to find out where Myra was.

Right now, getting his fiancée back and showing her she could trust him was more important.

"Very well. Where's Ai?"

Finley only shrugged. "They won't tell me."

He should have figured. Putting the two of them near one another was only asking for trouble.

"I'll go search for her myself then."

Alvis grabbed the torch from its holder and went down the hallways. He should have had a guard escort him, but this was something he needed to do on his own and didn't want any more risk of someone overhearing his conversations.

The corridors were dark as not many people filled the cells. King Brennan in Cresin didn't use his dungeon, so when Cal had been held captive there, the space hadn't been well taken care of. While Alvis's family didn't go to the extreme of never using theirs like their ally, the cells that were occupied were few and far between. With each step, Alvis grew more impatient, wanting to find Ai so he could more quickly find Myra.

"Ai?" His voice echoed around the corners and he memorized the paths he took in case he needed to seek her out later.

"Prince Alvis?" Ai's gentle voice eventually called back.

Alvis went toward the sound to find Ai in a lone cell. No other prisoners were held nearby, and a small light shone from a window overhead. She sat on her bench cross-legged, as if in mediation.

She smiled when she saw him. "I didn't expect to have you as a visitor."

"I didn't expect you to be a pirate."

"I did tell you not to choose me as your bride."

Alvis chuckled. "That you did." He put the torch in its holder and stood in front of the barred door, his shoulders and body more relaxed than they'd been when he was with Finley. "Your family said you were traveling when we asked about you before the pageant started."

"I was traveling." Ai turned to face him and placed her hands in her lap. "How can I help you, your highness?"

As curious as he was to dig deeper into her history and what led her to work with Finley, there were other matters at hand. "Do you know where Myra is?"

Ai tilted her head to one side and took in a deep breath before answering. "I have my suspicions, but I can't say I know for sure. What do you want with her?"

"Honestly?"

"Always."

Alvis looked at the ground and then back up at her. "To apologize. Help her escape if she's in trouble. Am I a fool to hope she may take me back?"

Ai only kept the same warm smile she always wore. "All people in love are fools, I think. But in the best of ways."

Alvis leaned against the bars. He was exhausted and had barely slept the last few days from worry about Myra. All he wanted was for her to be all right. "Is it real? What this is between me and her? As an expert on the subject."

Now that everything was out in the open, he might as well take advantage of the skills of one dedicated to Diar.

"The bond between you and Myra is strong. I've seen it in a few others."

Alvis straightened himself, and something in his chest jumped. He should have known more about Diar, but until now, he never thought he needed the 'deity's help. "You talk about this bond you can see, but I've never understood that. Is it one you can manipulate? Does it tell the future? Are we fated to be with certain people? And does it look a certain way for each person?"

"I don't always understand it either. Love isn't something you can define by what you read in books."

Which was part of the problem. Those sorts of things Alvis was good at. If there was a question, he went to his books and found the answer. The end. This? There was no straightforward answer.

Ai stood and went into the center of the cell, the small light from outside making a halo around her raven-black hair. The light turned pink from the glow of Ai's tattoo on her back, and between her hands, a radiant image of two people with a line connecting them appeared. The line pulsed like a heartbeat and turned red, but toward one end, it frayed as though it were an old rope.

"This is you and Myra. You see this line? It's the love between the two of you. When a connection is formed, this line is usually is thin and blue. As the relationship grows and changes, it gets either thicker as the relationship gets stronger or it gets thinner. Sometimes it breaks," Ai explained. "Your line has turned red, showing it's not only friendship but love, and it has grown thicker faster than I've seen it with many others. Already, you have a strong and powerful bond." She pointed to the bit of it that frayed. "But it has been compromised. Because it is strong, it was not broken as it may have been with other people, but without proper repair, it could be."

The image was both a comfort and a discouragement. He'd created that compromise in their relationship and hated himself for it. Ai wiped away the image, and the glow around her turned back to its usual pale light from the window.

"Ai, where do you think she is? Who took Myra?"

For the first time, Alvis saw her face harden as she thought. "Tell me where Finley is."

There was a bond between Ai and Finley too, Alvis was sure of it. He didn't think it was romantic, but who knew? What he did know was that Ai and Finley were likely willing to fight for one another with the same vigor as he did for Myra.

"Tell me where Myra is first, and then I'll tell you where Finley is."

It was stupid and irresponsible. He was certain they had something to do with the disappearance of Amelia and the mirror, but at this point, he was willing to risk it. From what he could tell, they were secretive about Myra because they didn't know if they could trust him, and they were loyal to their friend. He had to respect that.

Ai gave him a single nod. "Waazier took her. Finley and Myra were both passed out, and Waazier appeared. He convinced the soldiers to give her to him. I don't know where he took her, but I'd check her father's estate first."

Waazier. He'd said such terrible things about Myra and seemed to want nothing to do with her. Why would he take her? And he would need to have words with these soldiers. But it was a place to start.

"Thank you. And Finley isn't far." He pointed down the hall. "You'll go down that way, take a right, then two lefts, and one more right. I don't know how you'll get to her or how it'll help you, as I can't justify setting you free. But she's here. And she's well."

The relief on Ai's face was evident, and she relaxed her shoulders in a heavy sigh. "Good. That's all I need. Thank you."

Alvis nodded to her and took the torch off the holder to take his leave.

"Alvis."

He turned to see Ai standing at the barred door. "Yes?"

"Myra didn't do it. She didn't help with the mirror, I promise you."

Alvis smiled. He knew this, but it was still good to hear. "I know. Thank you."

He hurried through the halls to the entrance but stopped at Finley's cell first. "Ai is here, and she's all right." He pointed in the direction he came and told Finley the directions to get to her. The pirate queen only stared at him with furrowed brows, but a shimmer of hope was in her eyes. "And I'll get you your hat. But I need to get my fiancée first."

WHEN ALVIS CAME UPSTAIRS, NELL WAS WAITING FOR HIM. SHE PACED back and forth in front of the door and almost jumped out of her skin when Alvis returned. She looked at him with wide eyes and rushed to his side. She pulled on his tunic. "Well? What's happening? Where is she?"

"We need to get the horses."

He'd never seen Nell smile brighter.

Chapter Twenty-Nine

MYRA

MYRA GRASPED THE DOOR HANDLE AND JIGGLED IT AROUND, BUT IT wouldn't budge. She tried to feel for any magic that could have kept the door locked, but it didn't find any. He must have used the normal way with a simple lock and key. It was amazing how even in some cases, magic didn't help at all.

At least not her type of magic. If Finley were there, she might be able to erode the lock with water to open the door like she had when Myra was locked in her room before the ball. But that was not the case.

"I would go get the keys myself, but Waazier would sense me even if he can't see me. I'll get Odalis and see if we can retrieve it," Mama offered.

Myra's heart jumped in her chest. The last she'd seen her was when Uncle Waazier threw Myra out and pushed Odalis to the side. "Odalis is all right? And she can see you?"

"She's learned a few things these last couple of months. I may be able to recruit some other assistance as well."

With that, Mama passed through the door, leaving Myra alone. She paced about the attic as she waited. What was she going to do if and when she saw Alvis again? She would need to tell them all she knew and then be done with it. She just hoped she had the strength enough to do so.

There was a soft jingle at the door, and Myra rushed back to it. It unlocked, and before her stood Odalis, looking as healthy as ever. Relieved, Myra embraced the woman. "I'm so glad you're all right."

"And you as well, my lady. We were worried about you. The goings-on around here since you've been gone, you wouldn't believe."

"You'd be surprised," Myra said dryly. "Now, where's my uncle?"

"Drinking in the study. He's in there almost as often as your father was."

Myra grimaced. "Has Father not returned yet?"

Odalis's shoulders slumped, and she gave Myra a sad smile. "No, my lady. We've barely heard a word since he left."

The news wasn't encouraging, but at least he was one last person to worry about as Myra made her escape. If she left the manor today, she might never need to come back. She knew she shouldn't worry about what would happen to him and what Waazier might do with him to get his way after how he essentially abandoned her, but Myra couldn't help but wonder if she should come back someday.

Not now. That was a problem for another time.

"If he stays in the study, I should be able to get to my room and gather supplies and the grimoire," Myra said as she started her way down the staircase. It was old and winding, and each of her steps creaked as they went down. She tiptoed as best as she could, but there was no way to stop the noise completely.

"Where's Mama?" Myra asked over her shoulder to Odalis, who followed. She tried to keep her voice down.

"Gathering some help. She's not the only spirit lurking around here."

Myra smiled to herself. Well, wasn't that interesting?

"Well, hopefully I can keep quiet, and if I don't, they'll keep Waazier distracted."

They made their way through the halls of the manor until they reached Myra's room. A place she didn't think she'd be seeing again so soon. Not much had moved since she was so unceremoniously thrown out, but it was apparent Odalis tided things up for her. Which, thankfully, made it easy to find one of her satchels.

As much as Myra knew she should head directly to the front door and run away as fast as her legs could carry her, this was her only chance to gather some of Mama's things—including the grimoire—which she hadn't had the chance to bring with her in the past. As much as Myra hated to admit it, even though her magic seemed to bring trouble wherever she went, it was a part of her life. A part of her she didn't want to let go of or ignore any longer.

If there was anything she'd learned in the few days on *The Mystic* with Finley and Ai, it was that it didn't matter what others thought. The two of them played by their own rules and didn't care about the opinions of others. They were their best when they were able to be who they truly were, even if it was unusual.

Why couldn't it be the same for Myra?

This time, she was going to embrace her heritage and magic in her own way on her own terms. To do that, she wanted whatever she could carry from Mama's old trunk.

Myra grabbed a satchel and knelt before Mama's trunk as she opened the lid. The familiar scents of candles and spices filled her nostrils, and Myra dug around. Small boxes tied in twine with ingredients, candles, cloths, and spices. But…where was the grimoire? All of this was useless without it. Myra would have to go from memory and whatever other books she could find, but she didn't trust either of those options. Myra's already tired heart sank. Uncle Waazier must have disposed of it.

"Looking for this?" Odalis stood at her side and held out *The Book of Shadows.*

Myra gasped. "You still have it?"

"I couldn't bear to let your uncle's hands get on it," Odalis explained. "It's been in your family almost as long as that necklace."

Myra hugged the woman again and held the book against her chest. "You are worth more than diamonds, Odalis."

"Now, now, my lady. No need for such a fuss. I served your mother's family for years before she married your father. It's all in a day's work. Now go. No time to dawdle."

Right. There would be time for thank-yous later. Myra hoped.

When everything was packed away as much as possible, Myra hurried back out into the rest of the house. It was tempting to just leave, but she had to take care of Waazier first and say good-bye to Mama.

But it turned out Myra wouldn't have to search for Uncle Waazier long. He turned a corner and appeared before Myra; any trace of the fear he'd had in the attic was gone. "Didn't think you'd get out that easily, did you?"

Only days ago, the same voice sent fear shooting through Myra, but now she found she wasn't afraid of him anymore. That little girl who didn't know how to defend herself was gone, and her uncle had revealed who he truly was.

A frightened and slimy man. A snake, but one she could easily scare away. Nothing more.

"I know what you've been doing. With Amelia and the mirror and Charis." Myra told him. "And I won't let you get away with it. I'll lead the palace guards right to your door."

They walked toward one another until they were nose to nose. Myra might have had to look up at him, but she wouldn't let him intimidate her the way he did in the past.

"You have no idea who I've been working with and what they could do to you."

Myra raised a brow. "I have an idea, and I'm not afraid of them."

Maybe a small part of her was, and with good reason. But she would cross that bridge when she came to it. The challenge of her uncle was enough for now.

"And I won't let you or anyone else have this necklace."

Waazier lifted his arm to strike her, but Myra summoned her magic and nullified his before he could get to her, keeping his strength at a normal level, and she stopped him with her arm.

"This dark magic of yours, killing the magic of others, must be ceased. When I thought your kind couldn't get any worse," he snarled.

"You're one to talk," Myra shot back and twisted his arm around. She wasn't very strong, but it was enough to get him distracted.

The air grew cold, and Myra could see her breath in white puffs before her lips as spirits filled the hall. Ever since Odalis told her there were other spirits in the house and Mama was gathering them, Myra had been searching and summoning her magic to bring them to her. The more power she had on her side against Waazier, the better.

Waazier shuddered, and his face grew pale. He struggled beneath Myra's grasp until he broke free. Which was fine, as Mama was at her side along with all the other spirits who'd been haunting the house. The faces of people she must have been descended from or who used to live here before she did. People from the village of Taka who felt a connection to the manor. They all floated around her. A small army of spirits at her command.

He looked around, sensing that something was near, but without Myra's help, he couldn't see them. He shivered uncontrollably. "What evil did you bring here?"

Myra smiled. "Your worst nightmare." She gave a single nod to the spirits. "Go."

They all rushed toward him, pushing him up and down the hall, his feet flying off the floor. He screamed as the spirits dragged him through the manor and back up to the attic. Myra followed behind.

"What are you planning?" Mama asked in her ear.

"Just to scare him a bit," Myra answered.

They came up to the attic, and Mama pushed open the attic window, the old and fragile shutters falling apart, and pieces of wood floated to the ground far below. The spirits held him up and out the window. He flailed about and shrieked. "Bring me back! Bring me back!"

Myra channeled some of Finley's captain swagger and approached the window, placing one foot on the sill and leaning her arm on it. "Who have you been working for?"

He squirmed again and shook his head. "She'll kill me."

So it was a she. Interesting. Myra nodded to the spirits who held him, and they released their grip just enough so he sank a bit.

He cried out again. "Her mother! It's Amelia's mother, Mariah. She arranged all of it. Please, please, let me back in."

The spirits raised him back up.

Myra wagged a single finger back and forth. "Not so fast. What does she want with the necklace?"

Waazier grasped at the invisible hands holding him, but he only passed through them like air. "I...I don't know..."

They lowered him again.

"It's connected to the mirror and the curse on Luana's Castle! That's all I know, I swear! She won't tell me anything else."

It wasn't as much information as she wanted, but it was something. Myra stepped off the windowsill and dug into her pocket. Out of it, she pulled a handful of dark, sparkling dust, and she gently blew on it so it landed on Waazier. His eyes grew heavy, and he fell asleep in the spirits' arms.

They carried him back in and brought him downstairs into the sitting room. It was a sleeping dust Mama kept but rarely used. It wasn't anything as strong or powerful as the potion Amelia made Myra create for King Brennan or the curse her mother put on Finley. This would only last a few hours but kept him in a deep enough sleep so she could get away.

The spirits set him down on a chair, and Myra set to work on tying him up. She wasn't completely sure what she would do with him next, as there wasn't any way she'd be able to take him with her to the palace. But hopefully, she could report what she knew and royal soldiers would come arrest him.

"It appears as though you were able to rescue yourself."

Myra's heart stopped at the voice. No. It couldn't be. She wouldn't dare hope.

Against her better judgment, Myra turned toward the sound of the voice. Alvis stood in the doorway, a sword at the ready and Nell at his side.

"Myra! You're all right!" Nell squealed and ran to Myra, almost knocking her over with a hug.

Myra gulped and hugged Nell back, but she was unable to take her eyes away from Alvis. "You...you're here. But...but why? How?"

"I've been searching for you ever since the night of the ball. Ai told me that it was your uncle who took you away. I came as soon as I could." Alvis lowered his sword and walked into the room.

"You have?"

From his pocket, Alvis pulled out a slipper. "Well, you forgot your shoe. I figured you would need it."

Myra couldn't help but laugh. That damned shoe.

"I would search to the ends of the world for you if I needed to. You're my fiancée and the love of my life."

Myra's bottom lip quivered. He couldn't be saying these things. It was impossible. It gave her too much hope. "You would? But…there's so much you don't know. All those things my uncle said—"

Alvis now stood directly in front of her, and Nell moved to the side, a smile as wide as the ocean plastered on her face. "It doesn't matter what he said. I know you, and I trust you. I'm sorry I didn't come to your defense at the ball. I was in shock, which is no excuse, but know that if you could find it in your heart to forgive me, I will stand by your side for as long as you'll have me and never let what others say get in the way of that ever again."

Little by little, the bricks Myra had put around her heart broke apart as Alvis spoke. His golden eyes were full of regret, but there was still a glimmer of hope, and it was enough to make her melt.

Mama's spirit at her side nudged her forward. "He's handsome," she whispered.

For once, Myra was glad Alvis couldn't see or hear the spirits. All the others leaned forward and listened in. It was probably the most excitement they'd witnessed in years.

"I meant to tell you everything, I promise."

Alvis held a single finger against her lips. "It doesn't matter. You have nothing to explain. I knew you had a history that may not be the easiest to bear. I know who you are and know I can trust you. But can you trust me?"

That was the question, wasn't it? The worst of it was that silly and hopeful side of her wanted to believe him. Did believe him. It wasn't sensible. It didn't make sense. But Myra wrapped her arms around his neck, pulled him down, and kissed him.

Chapter Thirty

MYRA

Myra walked out of her father's manor, one arm wrapped around Alvis and the other around Nell. Overhead, Aytigin soared across the sky with Eira and Cadeyrn on his back, a glittering trail of stardust in their wake.

Alvis shaded his eyes with his hand and called to them. "What are you doing here?"

Aytigin's wings flapped as he lowered them to the ground, making a hot wind that blew their clothes about as though they were in a desert storm. "When we figured out where you and Nell went, we weren't about to let you go on your own," Cadeyrn explained once they got to the ground. "I can't believe you didn't tell us."

Alvis squeezed Myra closer to him, his grip tight around her waist. She could feel his warm golden eyes on her. "I didn't want to wait."

Myra squeezed him back and then looked over her shoulder toward the house. "Although, it is helpful that you're here because we have one more person we need to bring with us, and I don't think we should take him on the horses," she added.

. . .

WHILE EIRA AND CADEYRN TOOK THE SLEEPING WAAZIER TO THE Golden Palace by air, Myra, Alvis, and Nell went back on their horses, racing through the desert. Nell whooped and hollered in delight as they traveled, and Myra couldn't erase the smile off her face. A warmth that overpowered her magic swept through her as the knowledge of her new reality set in. This was her family. A servant girl, a prince, and a sorceress's daughter somehow made an odd little family together, and Myra couldn't be more delighted. It filled a hole she never realized had been empty.

It took hours, and during their short breaks to rest, Myra and Alvis were able to update each other on what happened and what they learned while apart. By the time they arrived at the palace, the three of them were tired and dirty from the desert sand but exhilarated. The first thing they did was head to the dungeon hand in hand, not willing to let the other person go.

"I have one thing I need to get first," Alvis said when they reached the guard.

Myra furrowed her brow. "Whatever would we need to stop for?"

He went to the guard and asked him something Myra couldn't hear. The guard nodded and led them to a storage room. He moved to fetch his key, but when he went to unlock it, he found that the door was already open.

"That's odd. I swore I'd locked this earlier."

Myra and Alvis exchanged looks. "What were you wanting to get?"

"I promised Finley I would get her hat back."

Naturally. That would be the one request Finley would have while imprisoned. They all stepped inside and looked around through the light from a sun lantern. But there was no hat.

Alvis swore. "She's going to be furious."

Myra pursed her lips and raised her brows at Alvis. "No, she already has it."

They ran out of the storage room and toward Finley's cell, but Myra already knew what they would find there.

Or not find, rather.

The cell was still locked, but no one was inside. The guard let them in, and all they found was a single note left on the bench. Myra walked over and picked it up.

Tell Myra we'll come back for her.

"Are you sure you want to do this?" Alvis asked. "We can go back if you want."

It was days later, and they sat on their horses back in front of Myra's childhood home. Waazier was under top security in the palace dungeon. Alvis's mother and father were in shock to hear of Alvis and Myra's engagement. Then Eira, Cadeyrn, and Aytigin returned to the Paravian mountains. Before they left, Myra promised they would come visit so she could finish what she started with putting Malle's spirit at ease, and they could find out more about what her necklace did with the mirrors and stone table. But there were things they needed to deal with in Oxare first, one being to ease the kingdom into the idea of a daughter of Stula being their next queen of course. But there were matters at home Myra wanted to attend to.

"I'm sure," Myra answered.

They slid off their horses and approached the front door. She took in a deep breath and pulled the rope to ring the bell like she had so many weeks ago. But now, instead of old traveling clothes she was embarrassed of and begging for any scraps of kindness she could find, Myra came home in her Golden Palace finery with her head held high.

Within a few minutes, Odalis opened the door and curtsied. Her mannerisms were proper and respectful, but her smile went from ear to ear, and the sparkle in her eye showed how delighted she was they were there. "Your highnesses, we weren't expecting you."

"My apologies for dropping by so unexpectedly," Myra said. "Did you receive our gift?"

Odalis blushed. "I did. It is far too much."

"It is the least we could do for all you've done for me and my family."

Myra's first request as an official member of the royal family was to
send Odalis a handsome sum of reward money along with a
shimmering bracelet. Which Myra was pleased to see was around
Odalis's wrist.

"Your father is home," Odalis told them as they walked inside. "He
arrived a few days ago."

This was news to Myra, but she also hadn't been keeping track of
his travels. She hadn't come for him. "I see. I wanted to see Mama. May
I go to her first?"

"Of course. Right this way."

Odalis led them to the yard where Mama's grave stood beneath the
tree. Mama's spirit sat on top of the stone and looked up into the
branches. She smiled at the sight of Myra and Alvis and floated over to
them.

"You came home. I was hoping you would."

Myra held Mama's transparent hands in hers. "I could never leave
you. Not forever," Myra told her. "I'd like you to meet my
fiancé...properly."

"I would love that."

Myra released one hand and held on to Alvis's. She spread her
magic to him, and his eyes widened at the sight of Mama's spirit. "I'm
so happy to meet you."

"I'm pleased to meet you as well," Mama said. "I can hardly believe
my daughter is to be a queen. But I can see you make her very happy."

"And she makes me unbelievably happy. You have an amazing
daughter."

Mama smiled, pleased with herself. "I know."

"Are the others ready?"

Mama nodded and went off to go get the other spirits. When she
returned, they all hovered around the courtyard, and Myra and Alvis sat
on a bench side by side. He held her hand as she spoke with each one,
and those who wished let her say the rites to let them pass into Stula's
arms. Tears ran down Myra's face for many of them, happy to let them
finally have their peace, but knowing that with each, she came closer to
what she was sure would be the final ending.

Mama leaving forever.

Alvis was silent the whole time, only speaking to be sure Myra was all right and offering any assistance. But he watched and greeted each spirit and remained a peaceful comfort as Myra helped them. Finally, he was able to witness the most sacred of all her powers.

"Myra?" Papa walked out into the courtyard, a bewildered look on his face. He blinked a few times at the sight of Alvis and bowed. "Your highness, I didn't realize…"

"No need to apologize," Alvis told him. "We came unannounced."

Papa stepped toward them with hesitant steps. "I'd heard you were engaged, but…I wasn't sure if it was just a rumor…"

"We were going to come see you next," Myra said and shifted in her seat. She wasn't ready to face him. She didn't know what to say.

Mama floated over by them and stared at her husband. He shivered and looked around but was unable to see her. "Will you let him see me?" Mama asked.

Myra was taken aback by the request. Their marriage had been a political one, not of love, and always had tension between the two of them. She gulped. "Papa, Mama's spirit is here. She would like to see you." She held out her free hand to him. "Would you like to see her too?"

Papa's jaw dropped, but eventually he nodded and took Myra's extended hand. He shivered again with Myra's magic spreading to him, and he gaped when he finally could see Mama's spirit. "I…can't believe it. You're here."

Mama smiled softly. "Hello, Genn. I'm glad you returned home in time."

"You've been here all this time?" he asked.

"More or less."

The truth of it was far more complicated than that, but it wasn't worth going into. Not now. It was all in the past, and Mama seemed at peace with everything.

"I…I'm sorry," Papa stammered out. "I know I've failed you. Both of you."

Mama patted his hand as best she could. "I forgive you. It has been a long time since then, but there is time to make things right again. I know you can."

A small smile came to Papa's lips. Something Myra wasn't sure she'd ever seen before, and a tiny piece of her softened toward him. He turned to Myra. "I'm sorry."

Myra nodded. "I know."

"Can you ever forgive me?"

Myra was silent for a long time, and Alvis squeezed her hand. Whatever she said, she knew Alvis would support her, and it gave her courage. "I want to, but I don't know if I can. Not yet. Maybe someday."

There was too much hurt still. How he let her be sold off, abandoned, hurt, and the way he shunned her and her magic—it was the opposite of what a good father would do. But she knew he had his own pains and struggles. Ones at this point he might not be able to control anymore, and he should have her compassion. But she wasn't ready to forgive him. Not yet.

"But I promise I'll still come home from time to time. Help you with the estate. We can put things back to how they were. Together."

Papa breathed a sigh of relief. It seemed like enough for him for the time being. She didn't think either of them were ready for a true father-daughter relationship quite yet.

Mama looked back and forth between her daughter and her husband, a soft and sad look in her eyes. "Myra, I'm ready."

Myra's lip trembled, and she bit back tears. "Are you sure?"

Mama nodded. "I've made amends and have seen the amazing woman you've become. It's time for me to go to Stula now. I'm ready."

"Would you like to see?" Myra asked Papa. It seemed like the right thing to do.

"If I may."

Myra and Alvis rose from the bench, and the three of them stood in front of Mama's gravestone. Myra took in a deep breath, knowing she would never truly be ready for this moment but had to be anyway. She closed her eyes and said those sacred words she now knew as though it was her own name.

When she opened her eyes, Mama's spirit glowed a bright lavender and rose higher and higher into the sky. Mama's eyes were closed and a peaceful smile on her face. As Myra finished the rite, Mama's spirit slowly vanished, and lavender shimmers floated down on them, covering Myra's tears.

But she smiled.

She knew that at last, Mama was free. She looked at Alvis and smiled through her tears. Deep in her heart, Myra knew she was free too.

The End

Epilogue

AMELIA

AMELIA FLOATED IN THE DARK WATER AND FELT THE GREEN-AND-BLUE scales across her naked body soak it all in. It wasn't an ocean or a lake, but the swamp still nourished her body and soul, and she soaked it in like a wilting flower. For too long, she'd been trapped in the mirror in a desert land, unable to get to the water. There was a flowing stream in the mirror, and the Attendants had made sure she was properly hydrated. But they didn't understand the need to be connected to a body of water like this.

But what did you expect from sun worshippers?

She splayed her arms out wide and moved them up and down, making waves that looked like a dark angel's' wings around her. Whatever creatures lurked in the water swam around her and avoided touching her, like they knew she was a formidable being that belonged there as much as they did. It was dark in the swamp, even if thin streams of sun tried to break through the tree branches, and everything was fuzzy around the edges of her vision. Ever since she'd given birth a few days ago, it was as though Amelia had been walking through a fog. Only when she was in the water did she have any sort of peace or clarity. The moment she'd recovered enough to get out of bed on her own, Amelia stripped off her sleeping gown and engulfed herself in the swamp.

Maybe she could stay here forever. Let the water and the plants and the creatures take over, and Colma would nourish her body. The water would be her domain, and she'd control it all. The swamp witch, people would call her in hushed and fearful tones. Children would avoid the swamp lands, and adults would come to her when they were the most desperate and in need of some sort of curse or potion, their hands trembling when they remembered how this witch used to be a powerful queen. A shadow of a smile played on her lips, the first real one she'd had in months.

"He won't stop crying!" the shrill voice of Charis rang through the air.

Amelia turned her head to see the young woman stand on the edge of the swamp. The hem of her fine pink gown was soaked and stained with mud, and her arms trembled in the crisp early spring air. Everything the noblewoman had with her was entirely impractical for their surroundings.

"And your mother wants you!" Charis added, then turned on her heel and stomped back to the cottage.

Amelia only turned her head to face toward the sky again. The baby was always crying, and Mother always wanted to see her. This was nothing new, and they would be dealt with when she was ready.

She was ready about twenty minutes later and dragged herself out of the water, bits of the plant life and algae still clinging to her skin. She took the thick robe she'd discarded onto a nearby rock, shrugged it on, and made her way up to the cottage. It was built onto a tree off the shore of the swamp where the land was a little more stable with wooden ladders and planks and vines to lead to the door, which creaked and wobbled beneath Amelia's feet as she wiped the swamp water off her while she climbed the steps. Not quite a castle, but there was a mysterious and foreboding sense that came from it. It would do for now.

The baby indeed was crying, and after Amelia sat in front of the fire, Charis passed him to Amelia. She scrunched her face and turned away from Amelia. "You smell horrendous."

All the young woman did was whine and complain ever since they'd arrived at the swamp, and Amelia was ready to toss her out. The baby didn't seem to mind, for once Amelia pulled aside her robe to reveal one of her milk-swollen breasts, he latched onto it like a leech, and the crying stopped. This was one of the worst parts of the whole business of having a child, other than her body being completely ruined. At least with Nell she had a servant to feed her.

"Make yourself useful and get us some tea," Amelia ordered Charis. "I'm tired of your complaining. Unless you wish to go home in disgrace?"

Amelia's sharp words quieted Charis, and with a huff, she went to the cupboards to gather the tea.

Across from Amelia sat Mariah. An elegant older woman with pure white hair piled on top of her head in a soft bun, sharp cheekbones, and eyes blue as the sea.

Mother.

"It's about time you came out of that water," Mother said, looking down her pointed nose at Amelia. "I was getting a headache from all that crying. After all I did to free you, the least you could do was take care of your own child. What's his name again?"

"I haven't decided yet," Amelia answered and averted her gaze to the fire. "I'l name him when I know what to do with him. And the least you could have done was to get me my other child along with my servant. The job was not complete without them, so I will come and go as I please. But at the first sign of trouble, you let Nell go, *Mother*."

Mariah rubbed the space between her eyes as though she were getting a headache. Her voice took a strained tone, to which Amelia only rolled her eyes. Mother was famous for her "headaches."

"My dear, there are several things that could have happened with Nell, including just leaving her with me when you became queen as we originally planned. Do not blame that on me."

Amelia shifted her position so the baby was propped on a pillow and she could face the other two women. "Never fear, Mother. There are many other things I can blame you for. But luckily for the two of you, I've been thinking of a plan of how to fix the mess you've both made."

Charis brought a tray with steaming but chipped teacups to the chairs. "I thought you didn't know what to do with the child yet."

"I didn't say anything about that, and I'll deal with it when the time comes. Myra knows her necklace has powers and will be going to the Paravian mountains to assist Eira in time. I have no doubt Alvis and Nell will join her, and I'll have all of them in one place." She gazed out the window to the swamp as though she could see through the thick vines and trees all the way into the rest of Eral Forest. "But there are others we need to worry about. People who won't let us near Eira or any of the others by miles if they can help it."

Charis sat on a stool and took a teacup, her back straight and head held high as though she were still in the Golden Palace among the royals. "And who is that?"

Amelia smiled. The second true one in one day. Her mood must be taking a turn for the better. "Rose and her grandmother, of course. Kutlaous's minister."

Thank you for reading! Did you enjoy? Please add your review because nothing helps an author more and encourages readers to take a chance on a book than a review.

And don't miss more of the The Cursed Queen series coming soon, and find more from E. E. Hornburg at www.emilyhornburg.com

Until then, discover SECOND STAR TO THE LEFT, by City Owl Author, Megan Van Dyke. Turn the page for a sneak peek!

You can also sign up for the City Owl Press newsletter to receive notice of all book releases!

Sneak Peek of Second Star to the Left

BY MEGAN VAN DYKE

Nothing attracted attention like free booze. The Lazy Mule wasn't usually this popular, or so the locals said, but the promise of free drinks lured every shopkeeper and down-on-their-luck sailor into the dirty, ramshackle building near the docks. Tropical air, thick with humidity and the promise of rain, filled the bar as tightly as the patrons crammed into every nook and cranny.

Tink pulled her braid over one shoulder, careful not to dislodge the sections covering her pointed ears. She rubbed the loose ends between her fingertips, feigning nervousness as she glanced over her shoulder.

Men and women alike clamored toward the far table where a large, blond man regaled the crowd with tales of his crew's success. He was attractive, with bulging muscles, towering height, and a chiseled jaw. But if he made one more crude joke about plundering something, Tink was going to toss her drink at him. *Stupid pirate*. Soon enough he'd stumble and fall, or the rotting table would finally give way. She grinned. That alone would be worth the cost of the trip.

But the blustering first mate of the *Jolly Roger* wasn't her target. No, to get what she needed, only the captain would do. Tink licked her lips as her gaze caught on the equally tall but leaner man with one shining black boot propped on the seat of a nearby chair. He shouted colorful additions to the first mate's tale and called for another round of drinks for all his "friends."

The poor ale Tink sipped turned sour on her tongue before she forced it down. The captain's arrogance knew no end. He traveled from one pirate-friendly port to the next so he and his crew could rave of their accomplishments. At least it made them easy to track.

Tonight, they bragged about their theft of the Heart of Fire, a stunning ruby set in gold. A half-grin pulled at her lips. What would they say when she stole it from them?

Captain Hook, so named for the distinctive metal weapon that replaced one hand, raised a pint in the air. Dark ale splashed over the side. Mugs clinked, rising with cheers from the crowd who joined in the toast.

Finally, *finally*, the captain glanced her way.

Her heart gave an involuntary leap as sinful lips twitched on a strong face. Or perhaps it was his coal-dark eyes that twisted her up inside. He raised his mug, taking a long swig, but his attention never left her.

Perfect.

One look and she'd hooked Hook. A small laugh burst from her lips that she covered by biting her bottom lip in feigned embarrassment.

Before he lowered his drink, Tink twisted around back to her mug warming on the bar. Warm ale and filthy pirates. Every girl's dream night.

She snorted. *Sure.*

Her stomach turned as she rubbed the mug between her palms. This wouldn't be her life. Not anymore, not after tonight.

A woman squealed as a drunkard yanked her onto his lap, nearly sending them both tumbling to the ale-soaked floor. How did she ever enjoy these horrid human bars? She and her cousin Lily used to slip through the pixie doors—the circles of trees, stones, mushrooms, or whatever the elders of old selected—for a little fun in the human world all the time. They'd drink, dance, flirt with whichever handsome human caught their eye, then sneak back home before the elders were ever the wiser. They'd done everything together for as long as she could remember. The elders frowned on such elicit exploits. But really, only allowing them out to trade and gather goods not available in their homeland was, well, boring.

Her chest grew tight. *Had Lily made it home? Was she okay?* The bracelet around her wrist with its broken gem weighed her down. Tink had committed an unforgivable sin—selling her pixie dust—to save Lily from that wretched Captain Blackbeard and his crew. A nastier man never drew breath. *Filthy pirate bastard.* That act got her banned from her homeland, Sylvanna Vale, rendering her unable to pass through the magical doorways. Pretending to be human and hiding her wings was a pain. *By Durin's beard, binding them hurts!* Without the cloak around her shoulders, someone would notice where she'd lashed them to her back, and that…well, best they didn't.

"Hey there, lovely lady." A man brushed against her at the bar, smelling of sweat and sour ale—or something even fouler.

"Hello." *And please go away,* she added silently, barely giving the man half a glance. If he had any wits, he'd leave.

"You here with anyone?"

Somehow his breath was worse than the stench clinging to him. Hanks of greasy hair lay against dirty skin. When was the last time he bathed? Humans were disgusting in general, but this one was something extra.

Tink glanced back at the pirates and stiffened. The captain was gone. *Shit. Where did he—*

The intruder slid in front of her. "I'll put the wind in yer sails if ya raise my mast."

Tink gaped. He did *not* just say that to her.

A burning flush rose from her chest to the tips of her ears. Her lips thinned. She needed to ditch this slob and quick. If she lost her chance to get the Heart of Fire because of this fool, she'd… Her nails dug into her palm. She didn't even know, but something horrible.

His filthy hand latched onto her arm. "Come on." Grime-crusted nails dug into her skin. "I can pay ya."

With one quick move, Tink *accidentally* knocked her drink over. Ale splashed across the man, some of it splattering her as well.

"You bitch!" He stumbled back. The man behind him barked in outrage.

Tink slid off her barstool, aiming to flee, but the man grabbed her arm again. She wrenched it back, her other hand sliding under her cloak, searching for her hidden dagger.

"I'll—" The man paled as a hand closed over his forearm. Clean, black cloth and fine stitching caught her eye.

"You'll leave the lady alone," the velvet voice rumbled just behind her.

Unexpected heat raced up her stiff spine. Captain Hook pushed the man away and wedged himself between them.

"You...you're..." the man stammered before turning and shoving his way through the crowd in haste.

"Good riddance." Hook faced her, glancing over the splatter of ale on the billowing tan shirt tucked into her tight breeches. "You all right, love?"

"I can take care of myself."

His eyes widened.

Shit. She was supposed to seduce him, not brush him off. "But..." She licked her lips before glancing away, then back. "I really appreciate the help."

He tipped an invisible hat, the motion as natural as if he rarely went around without one. "Always happy to help a lady in distress."

"How very gallant of you." It took everything she had to keep the sarcasm out of her voice.

"Can I buy you another drink..." He cocked his head, waiting for her name.

"Tinker Bell." *Oh, Beryl's wings.* She hadn't planned to give him her real one. She grinned through her error and slid closer. "And I do believe you already ordered another round for everyone."

His fingertips, with nails painted a midnight black, grazed the edge of her shoulder before he pulled back. The touch, so brief and fleeting, sent a thrill down to her toes. It shouldn't have. He was a pirate—a notorious one. Worse, her target. But if he was interested, it made her job so much easier. Stealing the ruby was a test, and she couldn't fail, not if she wanted the merfolk's queen, Titania, to trust her. She needed her trust before the queen would even discuss a trade for the black pearl —the only object known to fix anything broken, even her bracelet.

"Tinker Bell." He took his time with her name, and the way he drew out the words melted her more than any drink.

"Just Tink is fine," she added, suddenly warm.

"Aye. Not that swill, Tink." He gestured to the nearby drinks. "The barkeep has a few more pleasurable options."

"Well…" Tink ran her hand down his sleeve. "I think I might enjoy that."

Don't stop now. Keep reading with your copy of SECOND STAR TO THE LEFT, by City Owl Author, Megan Van Dyke.

And find more from E. E. Hornburg at www.emilyhornburg.com

A Guide to the Deities

LUANA, GODDESS OF THE MOON
Other influences: stars, darkness, winter, ice, night
Color: blue
Common Symbols: moon in various stages, stars, snowflakes
High Temple Location: Farren Castle in Cresin
Appearance: slender woman with long dark hair and pale skin

RAY, GOD OF THE SUN
Other influences: clouds, light, summer, fire, day
Color: yellow
Common Symbols: sun, fire, sand, cloud, phoenix, dragon
High Temple Location: Cyre Palace—the Golden Palace—in Oxare
Appearance: large, muscular man with golden skin and flaming hair

KUTLAOUS, GOD OF NATURE
Other influences: forest, jungle, agriculture, animals, plants
Color: green
Common Symbols: vine, stag, horns, leaves, flowers, animals
High Temple Location: Eral Forest
Appearance: human man with horns on his head and hooves for feet, green skin with vines wrapped around his body

AROS, GOD OF WAR
Other influences: hunting, fitness, athletes
Color: red
Common Symbols: sword, arrow, snake, lion
High Temple Location: Khadi Desert

Appearance: tall, almost giant man with white skin, red eyes, and shaved head

Colma, god of water
Other influences: water creatures, other liquids, drinks
Color: blue or green
Common Symbols: waves, fish, pitcher, ship, mermaid tail
High Temple Location: Dravian Islands
Appearance: lanky yet muscular man with translucent skin, long blue hair, often wearing blue robes

Stula, goddess of death
Other influences: sickness, disability, change, maturity
Color: purple
Common Symbols: skull, bones, rose, clock, raven
High Temple Location: Underworld
Appearance: woman with dark skin, purple hair, and black robes

Yla, deity of birth
Other influences: fertility, childhood
Color: pink
Common Symbols: footprints, lotus flower, baby animals, egg
High Temple Location: Oxare Coast
Appearance: no one knows their "true" appearance, as they come as they are needed. A middle-aged woman to be a midwife; a young man preparing for fatherhood; a pregnant woman; a grandparent, etc. The commonalities are brown hair and a tattoo of the lotus flower.

Diar, deity of love
Other influences: beauty, desire, charity
Color: red or pink
Common Symbols: rose, heart, ribbons intertwined or tied together, doves
High Temple Location: Belovian Islands
Appearance: a nonbinary being containing anatomy of both male and female, long and flowing pink hair and light-brown skin

EFARAE, GODDESS OF INSPIRATION
Other influences: the arts, keepers of the deities' tales
Color: Lavender
Common Symbols: music notes, a quill, paint brush, owl, scroll
High Temple Location: Kingdom of Marali
Appearance: petite woman with blond hair, purple eyes, and often wearing glasses

GALLIS, GODDESS OF RESTORATION
Other influences: healing, health, fitness, building
Color: gold
Common Symbols: a chalice, building tools, bandages, tonic bottles, hands
High Temple Location: Kingdom of Imare
Appearance: a round and plump yet strong woman with brown hair and golden robes

Don't miss more of the The Cursed Queens series coming soon, and find more from E. E. Hornburg at www.emilyhornburg.com

Until then, discover SECOND STAR TO THE LEFT, by City Owl Author, Megan Van Dyke!

Tinker Bell, banished from her homeland for doing the unthinkable, selling the hottest drug in Neverland—pixie dust—wants absolution.

Determined to find a way home, Tink doesn't hesitate to follow the one lead she has, even if that means seducing a filthy pirate to steal precious gems out from under his…hook.

Captain Hook believes he's found a real treasure in Tink. That is, until he recovers from her pixie dust laced kiss with a curse that turns the seas against him. With his ship and reputation at the mercy of raging storms, he tracks down the little minx and demands she remove the curse. Too bad she can't.

However, the mermaid queen has a solution to both of their problems, if Tink and Hook will work together to retrieve a magical item for her.

As they venture to the mysterious Shrouded Isles to find the priceless treasure, their shared nemesis closes in. However, his wrath is nothing compared to the realization that achieving their goal may mean losing something they never expected to find—each other.

All reviews are **welcome** and **appreciated**. Please consider leaving one on your favorite social media and book buying sites.

For books in the world of romance and speculative fiction that embody Innovation, Creativity, and Affordability, check out City Owl Press at www.cityowlpress.com.

Acknowledgments

Writing a second book is a journey. I had so many ups, downs, struggles, and highs. I'm so thankful for every single person who was with me along the way.

First, I want to thank God for guiding me through all of this.

Thank you to my editor Tee Tate, who is always there with an encouraging word, ideas, advice, and challenges me while still building me up and making me a better writer. You've been amazing through it all and I can't wait to continue making amazing books with you!

Tina, Yelena, and the rest of the City Owl team who have been cheering me on, answering my questions, and giving me all the encouragement to keep going, thank you.

All the other authors with City Owl, I still can't believe I get to be part of such an amazing and talented group. You all are my inspiration!

The talented team at MiblArt, once again you nailed the cover of this book and I'm in awe at your skills and talent.

Rachael of Cartographybird who designed the map, this was incredible! You've truly made this world come to life!

To Paris, Ginny, Kim, Piera, Trina, and all the people who let me talk books and plot and share the latest new with my book and help me dig through plot holes, I don't know what I'd do without you!

Julie, Jen, Jo, Emily, Kristen, Erin, Lauri, and Sarah, you all are the greatest and most supportive friends in the world. You've been there since day one and have never stopped encouraging me.

Dale, thank you for being there through all the stress and worries and doubts, along with the excitement. I know you've been there too and am so grateful to have someone who understands the way you do.

Mom, Dad, Natalie, Tim, Elsie, Patrick, and my whole family, I don't know where I'd be without you all. Thank you for all of your love and support through everything.

About the Author

E. E. HORNBURG is a Chicago South-sider, consumer of nachos, dog mom, aunt to the greatest niece ever, and owner of far too many mugs and travel cups which hold her coffee. When not creating or devouring books you can find her pretending she can rap along with the *Hamilton* cast and plotting how she can get to Disney World (again). *The Night's Chosen* is the first in the *Cursed Queens* series and her debut novel.

You can follow along and get free stories by signing up for her newsletter at

www.emilyhornburg.com

 twitter.com/eehornburg

 instagram.com/eehornburg

 facebook.com/EmilyEHornburg

About the Publisher

City Owl Press is a cutting edge indie publishing company, bringing the world of romance and speculative fiction to discerning readers.

Escape Your World. Get Lost in Ours!

www.cityowlpress.com

facebook.com/CityOwlPress
twitter.com/cityowlpress
instagram.com/cityowlbooks
pinterest.com/cityowlpress
tiktok.com/@cityowlpress

www.ingramcontent.com/pod-product-compliance
Lightning Source LLC
Chambersburg PA
CBHW060608030726
47498CB00005B/1592